A BLACKGUARD'S REDEMPTION

By

Ta`Mara Hanscom

REATA
PUBLISHING

Sioux City, Iowa

Cast of Characters

Joshua Hansen – married to Mona (Spencer) Hansen

Noah Hansen – brother of Joshua Hansen – was married to * Carrie (Miller) Hansen
Carrie passed away March, 1981

Ty Hansen – Carrie's son by Dr. Schneider Rauwolf a/k/a Roy Schneider, raised by Noah Hansen

Jake Hansen – Noah's son with wife, Carrie

Guiseppi Caselli – Married to Rosa (Rosa Matilde Rochelle) Caselli

Petrice Caselli – Eldest Caselli son, married to Ellie (Elaine Netherton) Caselli
               Michael Petrice Caselli – son of Petrice & Ellie Caselli
               Gabriella Elaine Caselli – daughter of Petrice & Ellie Caselli

Vincenzo Caselli – Second Caselli son, married to Kate (Katlin Martin) Caselli
               Alyssa Katlin Caselli – daughter of Vincenzo & Kate Caselli
               Angelo James Caselli – son of Vincenzo & Kate Caselli

Marquette Caselli – Youngest Caselli son, married to Tara (D`Annenci) Caselli

Tillie (Matilde Rosa Caselli) Martin – Only Caselli daughter – Nicknamed "Angel" by her brothers, married to Alex James Martin III

Angelo Caselli – brother of Guiseppi Caselli – passed away 1964

James Martin, Jr. – married to Frances (Dale) Martin

Sam Martin – Eldest Martin son – married to Becky-Lynn (Tucker) Martin

Katlin Martin – Only Martin daughter - married to Vincenzo Caselli

Alex James Martin III – Youngest Martin son - married to Tillie (Caselli) Martin
               Alex James Martin IV – son of Alex & Tillie Martin
               Laura Rose Martin – daughter of Alex & Tillie Martin

Burt Engleson – married to Diane Engleson

Rev. Andy Engleson – son of Burt & Diane Engleson – Pastor at Christ the King Church

Ginger (Engleson) Maxwell– daughter of Burt & Diane Engleson and life-long friend of Tillie (Caselli) Martin. She is married to Bobby Maxwell and they live in Las Vegas, Nevada.

Mario Ponerello a/k/a **Jack Nelson** – married to Della (Miller) Nelson – Carrie Hansen's mother

> *Mario is the arch nemesis of Marquette Caselli. Marquette has sought after Mario since The Great Palermo Diamond Heist of 1968*

Antonio Ponerello – Eldest son of Mario Ponerello a/k/a Ben Simmons

Charise Nelson – daughter of Mario Ponerello & Della Nelson

Salvatore Ponerello – brother of Mario Ponerello. Presumed dead.

Dr. Schneider Rauwolf a/k/a Roy Schneider – biological father of Ty Hansen

Reata—Ranch near Centerville, SD – Vincenzo Caselli inherited Reata from Uncle Angelo, the brother of his father, Guiseppi. Vincenzo and his family live there, and there are many events throughout the year that take place on Reata. Also, Uncle Angelo and his beloved wife, Penny, rest there.

To my beloved friend, Ronette, who read through more than a million words and thousands of pages of rough drafts. She was a loyal and true friend who encouraged me, laughed with me (and at me!), and inspired me.

Just as this book was going to print, Ronette went Home to Jesus. I rejoice for her in the Lord, but I will miss her each time I write about the Casellis.

— Ta`Mara

LOVE NEVER FAILS.
BUT WHERE THERE ARE PROPHECIES,
THEY WILL CEASE; WHERE THERE ARE TONGUES,
THEY WILL BE STILLED; WHERE THERE IS
KNOWLEDGE, IT WILL PASS AWAY.
FOR WE KNOW IN PART AND WE PROPHECY IN PART,
BUT WHEN PERFECTION COMES, THE
IMPERFECT DISAPPEARS...

I CORINTHIANS 13:8-10, NIV

Foreword

Tara dropped her focus away from Tillie and pretended to study the photo in her hands. She floundered with what was the truth, and what had actually come to be. She wanted Tillie to know, and wanted it desperately. *But of what use would the information be? Noah is happy with another, who has just given birth to his son, and Angel has vowed her life away to Alex...a blackguard in disguise... Marquette was right all along....*

Tara slowly began to shake her head as she decided to lie. "He is not the same man, Angel."

January, 1981

PART I

TRANSGRESSION

Chapter 1

June 1986
Rapid City, South Dakota

Maggie May West was sixty-one years old and still wearing her hair in the puffy beehive style she'd pinned around her head since 1963. Her jet-black hair was sprinkled with streaks of silver swirled within the old-fashioned hairdo, and her old black eyes had begun to line with age. *Still*, she thought, *me and Estelle look pretty darn good for two old black women, running a tough business on our own, without husbands.*

Maggie was cleaning off her bar when she saw Noah's pickup park out front. He jumped out and trotted through the door. *That's weird.* She frowned as she watched him. Normally, his regular stride was slow and purposeful, as it had been for many years now, but not today.

Noah's sandy-colored hair had started to gray slightly at his temples, and his young eyes were lined with weather and grief. He had grown a terrible beard after losing his wife, Carrie, five years before, and it made him look older than his thirty-four years.

But there was a lightness in Noah's step today, and a certain sparkle in his blue eyes that had been absent for too many years. Maggie's heart skipped a beat when she saw the renewed expression. *Something's happened*, she thought as she watched her oldest friend settle himself on a stool before the bar and gaze fondly at the old portrait that had hung on the wall for the last eleven years. Maggie's sister, Estelle, was lovingly dusting it today, always so dedicated to taking care of her most-prized possession.

"Hello, Noah," Estelle greeted him with a smile. "I'm keeping her pretty for you. She'll be so surprised."

"Thanks Stellie," Noah replied, and he smiled at Maggie. "What's your special today, Maggie May?"

He'd asked that question a thousand times over the last twenty years, but somehow today it was *different*. His tone, his eyes, the spring in his step....

Estelle noticed it too, and she slowly walked to where Noah had seated himself and stood next to him.

"Cheeseburgers," Maggie answered quietly. She narrowed her eyes and stared him down as she asked, "And what's gotten into you?"

Noah laughed and gave the counter a loud slap, making Estelle jump with a startle. He looked at the portrait hanging in Maggie's bar, and then he glanced from one lady to the other. "You're never gonna believe it," he said with a wink. *That* was something they hadn't seen in at least a decade.

Estelle narrowed her stare and studied Noah's expression. She watched his eyes sparkle and dance with the delight of youth, and her heart began to pound. *He's finally found her!*

"Ha!" Maggie mocked a laugh. "Let me guess," she said as she looked him over. His eyes had always been a dead giveaway, and they almost danced now in a way they hadn't in years. They still held the sadness and grief that had been there since Carrie's passing, but today his eyes danced as Maggie had only seen in his expression one time before. And all at once Maggie knew! She struggled to swallow the soft ball that had gotten into her throat.

"You've seen Angel," Estelle whispered as she watched the joy sparkle from his expression.

Noah laughed out loud again, nodded his head, and took a deep breath before he answered. "*Almost*, ladies. I saw her picture when I was in Sioux Falls."

Estelle gasped and covered her open mouth with her hand. She had prayed for Angel to return for so long, and now it was finally coming true.

"Where did you see that, Noah?" Maggie asked seriously. The hair on the back of her neck prickled, and she reached below the counter for her favorite whiskey. Noah had been terribly depressed and lonely since Carrie's death. *Perhaps he hasn't seen anything at all. Perhaps he's only imagined it. There's just no way.* Even though Maggie attempted to deny the revelation, she'd known for many years that it was only a matter of time before he found out.

Maggie poured herself a shot and quickly belted it down. She remembered all too well the young lady who'd called herself "Angel." She was a beautiful girl Noah met in the spring of 1975, the artist who'd painted the cherished portrait entitled *Obedience* — the very one hanging in Maggie's bar. A yellowed snap shot was still carefully tucked in the corner of the frame of the portrait. It was a photograph taken by Estelle of Noah and Angel standing before the bar. In the photo, Noah was giving her the most tender of kisses upon her beautiful cheek.

Noah had spent an entire weekend with the young lady, and then she'd returned to her home, wherever that was. She'd promised to come back and marry Noah, but the arrangement never materialized. Noah went on a search for her that consumed the next eighteen months of his life. He drove hundreds of miles, searching small towns throughout South Dakota for the girl he was supposed to marry. He even built a monstrous house, expecting to find her and bring her back. Tragically, he never located Angel and eventually married a young woman by the name of Carrie. What had happened to Noah, however, after that single weekend with Angel had never stopped amazing Maggie and Estelle. Noah hadn't had a drink since that time and had completely changed his life. He went back to school and built a successful business developing and selling property.

Maggie took another shot, then let out her breath with the confession, "Listen, Noah, I've known for the last five years —"

Noah and Estelle gasped at the same time.

"I know, I know." Maggie rolled her eyes.

"But how —" Noah began.

"At Carrie's funeral," she replied. "Marquette Caselli was that guy who came around in '75 looking for Ty's father…Remember that?"

Noah nodded. "You thought he was a fed or something."

"Thought he was gonna take down the whole town and you with 'em, so I lied my butt off for you," Maggie continued. "Anyway —"

"But you kept it to yourself?" Estelle accused with a scowl.

Maggie frowned at her younger sister. "What good was it gonna do anybody? Gimme a break." She looked at Noah and pointed her index finger at him.

"She's married to your best buddy, and you were all screwed up about losing Carrie. I just didn't think it was the smartest thing in the world to tell you."

Estelle gasped softly again, made a "tsk" noise between her teeth, and shook her finger at Maggie. "You shoulda told us, Maggie May."

Maggie rolled her eyes again and shook her head.

"I guess I should have known." Noah thoughtfully scratched his head and said, "I knew I saw one of her sketches in her father's new restaurant in Sioux Falls, and it was even signed 'Angel.' I've thought forever that Mr. Caselli sure looked like Angel, but then, there were things that were different. Like she told me that she wanted to be an art teacher, and Alex's wife studied Russian history and comparative literature."

Maggie wrinkled up her nose. "What's *that?*"

"Beats me," Noah answered with a shake of his head, "But I had to go over to Sioux Falls and meet with Alex and when I walked into his office, and there was the painting...." He pointed to the portrait at Maggie's bar. "I asked him where he had gotten it, and he told me Tillie had painted it and then showed me her photograph." Noah shook his head. "I nearly passed out."

"That's her name?" Estelle's old voice tried to croak out. "Tillie?"

Noah nodded. "Her family's nickname for her is 'Angel.' "

Maggie swallowed hard and looked woefully at the whiskey bottle in front of her. She wanted another shot, but two was her limit. She reluctantly capped it and put it back in its place under the counter.

"They bought a house here," Noah blurted out.

"What?" Maggie whispered in astonishment, and Estelle could only gasp again.

Noah replied, "I know they were in town a couple of days ago and bought a house up in Carriage Hills. They're *moving here*, ladies."

"Well," Maggie began in her shocked whisper, "have you talked to her?"

Noah shook his head, "I've completely avoided her." He bit his lip and sighed. "I wanna see her again so bad, just to ask her why she didn't come back."

"Well, you *deserve* an explanation," Estelle encouraged with a frown.

Maggie swallowed and looked into Noah's eyes. "Have you told Alex?" Noah shook his head and looked away from Maggie as she asked, "Have you told Josh?"

"No," Noah shook his head again. "I'm not telling him about this, and hopefully I can keep it from Mona. They'll just get worried and think I'm flippin' out or something —"

"Well, maybe you are," Maggie interrupted.

"No, I'm not, Maggie," Noah insisted. "Besides, I've got a few questions for her. Like why didn't she at least call me and have the decency to let me know she was gonna dump me for a Harvard Law graduate."

"Yeah," Estelle snorted and nodded in agreement. "He *deserves* an explanation, Maggie. Look how long we've wondered what happened to her."

"And don't be telling Mona on me when you see her for your Bible study," Noah instructed as he shook his finger at Estelle. "Promise?"

Estelle nodded.

Maggie slowly shook her head and swallowed. "Noah, I don't know if it's such a good idea. Something happened in here eleven years ago." She hesitated and shook her head again. "I don't know. *Something really strange.*" She looked into Noah's eyes with a sigh. "I just don't want to see you get hurt again. It was really hard for you. Don't you remember?"

Noah rolled his eyes, obviously dismissing Maggie's warning, and he shook his head. "I'm *totally* over all that, Maggie. Don't worry."

Maggie wanted to agree with him, but a strange weight suddenly pressed upon her heart. If she believed in God, she would have gotten on her knees at that moment and prayed.

*****

Guiseppi Caselli was nearly seventy years old, and the only hair he had left was the white fringe outlining the center of his skull. His black eyes still sparkled with life, but the tremendous secret he'd carried within himself had taken its toll over the years. Especially now. His wrinkled hand lovingly touched the brush strokes of the old painting, and he slowly shook his head. Of all the mistakes he'd made in his lifetime, *that* one was the most difficult to live with.

"What are you doing down here, Guiseppi?" Rosa gently questioned in Italian.

Guiseppi turned his head to see his lovely Rosa watching him from the doorway of their daughter's old photo developing lab in the basement of their home. Together, they'd hidden the portraits when their Angel married Alex in 1977, nearly nine years ago.

Rosa's lovely old eyes shone with tears as she slowly walked to where her husband crouched beside the paintings. Her hair was a magnificent silver, and she wore it piled atop her pretty head. There was not a creature on this earth who glowed with beauty like Rosa Caselli, and Guiseppi had dearly loved her for more than the last fifty years.

Rosa comfortingly put her hand upon her husband's shoulder.

"How she must have loved him," Guiseppi whispered in Italian, as they always spoke in their first language when they were alone. He looked at the portraits of Noah Hansen they'd stashed in their basement all those years ago and reminisced, "Not before or since have we seen work such as this come from her hands."

Rosa swallowed and agreed as she looked at the paintings their daughter had done eleven years ago. "Even her new *Obedience* does not compare."

Guiseppi reached for Rosa's hand and whispered, "Alex's father called me this morning." He hesitated and took a deep breath. "It seems Alex is toying with the idea of running for office."

"Oh, no!" Rosa slowly shook her head.

Guiseppi frowned and continued, "It is as if he cannot find enough reasons to be away from Angel and the babies —"

"He loves her," Rosa interrupted. "He is just very ambitious."

"His ambition will be his undoing," Guiseppi grumbled. "Especially now."

Rosa looked into her husband's eyes and studied the expression she'd loved for so many years. "Should we tell them?" she whispered.

"No." Guiseppi shook his head. "We will let God deal with it from here, my dearest Rosa, as I should have in the beginning."

"Will she ever forgive us?" Rosa began to cry.

"I pray so," Guiseppi said as he gently caressed Rosa's back. "And I pray for it every day."

"Angel is a good girl," Rosa reminded. "And she loves her husband."

"And God," Guiseppi added.

Rosa agreed. "She will be faithful to her vows." She forced a smile and looked into Guiseppi's eyes. "It is probably nothing and the two of us — old fools that we have turned into — are making mountains out of little bitty molehills."

Guiseppi forced a smile in return and gave Rosa's hand a tender squeeze. "But we will pray."

"As we always have," Rosa said. She had prayed for Noah for twenty-six years, and she wouldn't soon be stopping.

*****

The twins were playing on their swing set today beneath the magnificent old oak tree Alex had feared would never have any leaves. Its sprawling branches were laden with greenery, covering the backyard and the entire west side of the house.

It was Tillie Martin's twenty-ninth birthday. She had taken her easel outside and set it up on the back patio so she could watch her children play. After years of squelching her tremendous creative desires, she had finally given in and started to paint and sketch again, forgetting the reason she'd forsaken it for so long. Why had she done that? She couldn't remember anymore, but it was as if she couldn't paint and sketch enough now. She had repainted her husband's very favorite portrait, *Obedience*, and gave it to him for his birthday.

The portrait was a beautiful representation of Guiseppi's most cherished photograph, one he'd taken on the day they left Italy in 1956. In the photograph, Rosa's hand rested beneath Delia's chin as she watched her family pack their few bags into a relative's car. Rosa had told Tillie of the day many times. She related that, shortly after Guiseppi snapped the photo, she tied Delia to the back of the D'Annenci's buggy. The horse was left in their care, as arrangements could not be made to bring the animal with them to America. It was a very dramatic photo, and Guiseppi had loved it for years. He even enlarged the photo and had it framed and hung in the entryway of their home in Sioux Falls. Tillie had named the portrait *Obedience* because that is how she saw her mother's actions in leaving her beloved possession behind in order to follow her husband.

In 1975 Tillie painted two of the portraits. She sold one of them to the old black bartender in Rapid City, South Dakota. The other she gave to Alex for his office at home, even though he'd begged her for years to allow him to hang it in his office downtown. Tillie had laughed and refused, saying it was an immature piece of art. Last year, when she could no longer fight the urge within her, she started the same painting over again and created a masterpiece beyond belief. She gave the new portrait to Alex for his birthday.

Tillie glanced from her new painting and into the backyard where her five-and-a-half-year-old twins were laughing on the swings. They had gotten one of each, a boy and a girl, and Tillie thanked God every time she looked at them. Their birth had been traumatic, leaving Tillie's womb horribly scarred from placenta abruption and the resultant cesarean section. Even surgery couldn't correct the problem, and Tillie was forced to accept the fact that there wouldn't be any more babies.

She looked back at her painting and frowned. It needed something. For years she'd been intrigued by the old English Tudor in their neighborhood, visible from the Martin's backyard. It had winding flower gardens and a glorious pond, and she attempted to paint it into her scene. The portrait was nearly half complete, but it still needed something...*but what?*

Tillie sighed and looked back at her playing children. *Twenty-nine today. The time has gone so fast.* She looked back at the portrait and smiled. "*That's* what it needs. Ma'ma and Delia," and she changed the color on her brush.

Alex came home early that day to surprise Tillie for her birthday. He hesitated at the edge of the patio just to watch her for a moment. It was so seldom he actually saw her standing still. She had drawn her curly, black hair up into somewhat of a bun on top of her head, exposing the delicate shape of her neck and face. A gentle breeze came up, blowing a few strands of loose curls into her eyes. She quickly brushed them away, and attempted to refocus on the portrait at hand.

Alex smiled and slowly started for where she stood, paused just behind her, and gave her a very soft kiss on the back of her neck. "Happy birthday, Honey."

Tillie startled slightly and turned around. Alex was smiling and holding a bouquet of white roses and a white package tied with a pink ribbon. At the age of thirty-six, Alex Martin was an astoundingly handsome man. He stood six and a half feet tall, with broad shoulders and a small waist. His expensive, tailor-made suits perfectly complemented his form. His hair was black, and so were his eyes.

Alex graduated magna cum laude from Harvard Law. He had practiced law for the past eleven years with his father and his brother and held an all-wins record no one had been able to touch. He was extremely well-known in the state of South Dakota as a concise interpreter of the law, and no one in his right mind wanted to oppose Alex Martin. His dark eyes smiled down at her, and he gave her a soft kiss on the lips.

"What are you doing home so early?" she asked with a smile.

Alex laughed and teased, "Heard it was your birthday. The big twenty-nine today."

Tillie groaned and pretended to grimace at his comment, but excitedly took the roses from his arms. "My favorite. Thanks, Alex." She put her nose into the blossoms, and inhaled.

"And this," Alex said as he handed her the box.

"Alex, thank you." She smiled into his eyes.

"Daddy!" A.J. noticed his father was home and dashed to greet him. His sister, Laura, struggled from her swing and was on his heels. Alex knelt down and gathered his children into his arms.

"How are my little treasures today?" he asked, holding them at the same time.

"Fine," they said in unison, and Laura giggled.

"It's Mommy's birthday today," A.J. said excitedly. "Are you gonna tell her now?"

Tillie couldn't hide her surprise, and she looked from her little son to her husband. "What doesn't Mommy know?" Laura giggled and covered her mouth, looked at the ground, and then shyly turned her little body away. Tillie laughed at the little girl's actions and asked, "What's goin' on?"

"Daddy has a surprise for you," A.J. said, and Alex pretended to gasp.

A.J. giggled and covered his mouth in the same way his sister had.

"Should we tell her?" Alex whispered to his children, and they both nodded. "Well, you better tell her then," Alex whispered as he looked into Tillie's curious eyes. " 'Cause I think Mommy's about ready to burst over there."

The two little twins looked at their mother and said at the same time, "*The Sound of Music!*" Laura clapped her hands together and excitedly gave her father a kiss on his cheek. "Daddy's taking you to the beach!"

Tillie's eyes opened wide, and she smiled. *The Sound of Music* was her favorite story, and she and Alex had attended the play on their first date. She looked curiously at her husband and smiled. "The beach?"

"We get to stay at the farm," A.J. added. "Uncle Vinzo is gonna let me ride a horsey."

Tillie laughed and shook her head, "What?"

Alex smiled at his wife as he got to his feet and put his hands on her waist. "We haven't been away together since before the babies were born, and I was thinking maybe you might be interested in a hot couple of days with me somewhere romantic."

Tillie laughed. "And you must have already asked Kate and Vincenzo?"

Alex nodded and glanced at his two children who were already scrambling back to their swing set. "And they actually kept the secret for the past week and a half. *Amazing.*" He looked back into Tillie's eyes and smiled. "I made arrangements for us to stay in Clearwater Beach, Florida, for a couple of days and see the play while we're there. It'll be a formal occasion, so maybe you can bring that great black dress you wore to Dad's 85th birthday party."

"When do we go?" Tillie asked.

"Tonight."

Tillie laughed out loud and threw her arms around him, roses and all, and squealed softly with delight.

"You still have to open up your present," Alex reminded as he held her in his arms and inhaled the soft, wonderful scent of her perfume.

Tillie laughed again. "Okay." She set the flowers on the nearby table and fumbled with the tissue and ribbon. Inside the package was a felt box, and she knew immediately it was jewelry. She hesitated as she looked into Alex's eyes. "Alex, you shouldn't have." She lifted the lid and gasped. *A diamond choker with matching earrings.* "Oh, my goodness!" She drew in a soft breath, looking from the box into Alex's eyes. "You *really* shouldn't have."

"But won't they look great with your black dress?"

Tillie had to agree, but she felt the strangest sensation in the pit of her stomach. Alex always appeared with diamonds when he had something to tell her. She swallowed away her fear and smiled into his eyes. "They're beautiful. Thank you, Alex."

"Here we are!"

Tillie and Alex both looked around to see her brother Vincenzo and his wife, Kate, Alex's sister, walking into the backyard with their two children, Alyssa and Angelo. Alyssa was fourteen, tall and slender like her mother, and she adored her little cousins, A.J. and Laura. Angelo was thirteen and very tall for his age — even taller than his father now — and had inherited the broad Martin shoulders. He followed Alyssa, who was on her way to the swing set.

Tillie smiled at Vincenzo and Kate. "They just told me."

"We're here to pick up the kiddos," Kate said. She gave Tillie a kiss on her cheek. "Happy birthday." She made a funny face and teased, "Twenty-nine. Ooo, so scary."

"Not too scary," Tillie chuckled as she looked at her sweet sister-in-law. Tillie could not remember a time when Kate hadn't been there with them. Kate and Vincenzo's romance had blossomed before Tillie was even born. Tillie had many wonderful memories of stories told on Kate's lap and of walking between Kate and Vincenzo on warm summer evenings. There had been trips to the DQ and french fries at the Barrel, weekends at their ranch near Centerville, South Dakota, to visit the baby pigs, and buggy rides behind Ol' Platinum into the apple orchard.

Vincenzo put his arms around his younger sister and gave her a kiss upon each cheek. "Happy birthday, Angel."

Tillie returned his embrace and looked into his eyes. Vincenzo was forty-five years old and had just started to gray. Soft streaks of silver wound their way in and out of his thick, wavy black hair. His many years of ranching and farming had weathered his handsome face, but his black eyes still sparkled from his happy life. He had been married to Alex's sister, Kate, since the summer of 1962, and they lived out their dreams on a ranch Vincenzo had named "Reata," after the ranch in his favorite movie, *Giant.*

"Let's get some stuff together for the kids so you guys can get going," Kate smiled.

7

"Okay," Tillie agreed. She sighed and looked at her babies who were playing on the swing set with their cousins. "I've never left them overnight before. Even when I had my surgery, I was home that afternoon."

"It'll be okay," Kate promised as she put her hand on Tillie's shoulder. "But I know how you're feeling."

"I remember the first time we left Alyssa and Angelo." Vincenzo raised one of his black eyebrows. "We *both* cried. Remember?"

Tillie nodded at the memory. Vincenzo and Kate had wanted to go away for their twentieth wedding anniversary when Alyssa was ten years old and Angelo was nine. They had never been away from their children except for short dates in the evening.

"It was okay, though," Vincenzo assured as he smiled into his wife's eyes. "Once we got away together, it was wonderful."

"And the kids had a great time with Sam and Becky-Lynn," Kate added.

"Sometimes our little ones need an adventure," Vincenzo suggested as he looked at his children, who were now growing into teenagers. "I will promise you, my Angel, your babies will have the time of their lives while they stay with us. Remember all of the fun you had on Reata when you were small?"

Tillie remembered. Those were some of the best days of her life.

"Come on," Kate gently took Tillie's hand into her own and coaxed her toward the patio door. "I know your flight leaves in about three hours, so let's get some things together for the kids."

Tillie collected her roses and went with Kate into the house, leaving Vincenzo and Alex alone on the patio.

"Let us sit for a moment," Vincenzo suggested as he strolled to the patio furniture and took a seat.

As Alex took a seat across from Vincenzo, he got a peculiar feeling...*I wonder if Dad said anything to them about the election?*

Vincenzo took out his pipe, dipped it into the pouch in his shirt pocket, and lit the bowl with a wooden match. He took a deep draw, slowly let out the smoke, and looked into Alex's eyes. "Your father is not very happy with you, my friend," he said in the soft accent Alex had gotten familiar with over the years. When the Casellis first came to America, they could barely speak English. Now, nearly thirty years later, it was almost soothing to listen to their accented diction.

Alex sighed. "He completely misunderstood the situation."

Vincenzo took another long draw from the pipe. "How so?"

Alex took a deep breath. *Why can't they keep their noses out of my business?* "It was only the one meeting. I haven't committed either way."

"Have you told Angel?"

Alex shook his head. "Not yet, but I plan to ask her about it while we're in Florida. If she's not comfortable with it, I won't do it."

Vincenzo smiled and nodded at Alex. "I understand you, Alex, and I respect you. You know I feel a man must work." He sighed nervously and looked into Alex's eyes as he continued, "And I would not even bring it up, but in prayer my heart was prompted to speak with you about this. I feel somewhat *uneasy* about your move to Rapid City."

Alex frowned. "If anything, there will be far less for me to do when I get there. My biggest client lives there for one thing, so I won't be going out of town as much as I do now. It's a good move for my family life."

"And how are things with Noah Hansen these days?"

"Very well," Alex answered, allowing himself an easy smile, thankful to be off the hot seat. "He's started to see a very nice lady."

Vincenzo raised his eyebrows with interest. "I thought he was through with women."

"Well, it's Melinda."

"His assistant?"

Alex nodded and continued, "They've gone to church together for about ten years, and she's worked for him for about that long. I think they'll get along well."

"Hmm," Vincenzo mused with a thoughtful expression...*She is a bit on the nasty side for someone as gentle as Noah.* "I guess I never saw Miss Melinda to be his type."

"Well, she really seems to like him," Alex said with a smile. "Besides, don't you think Noah's been alone long enough?"

Vincenzo shrugged. "He took a severe jilting when he was left at the altar in 1975, and then another dreadful blow when his beautiful Carrie died. It will take a very special lady to change his mind." *And I do not think she can possibly be Miss Melinda....*

****

Guiseppi put the last of the six cannoli into his mouth and washed it down with the strong coffee Burt had given him. They sat together in the back office at *Angelo's II*, contemplating a way to get Guiseppi's secret out into the open in a safe manner.

Guiseppi watched Burt finish off his own cannoli and was suddenly struck with the image of Guiseppi's brother, Angelo. Angelo would have been about Burt's age had he lived. In many ways, Burt had replaced Angelo, especially in the matter of confidences.

Burt set down his empty coffee mug and raised one brow. "You need to leave this matter alone, Guiseppi, as you and Rosa have agreed. Why do you keep going back to this?"

Guiseppi frowned. *Too much like Angelo...always telling me what to do.* "Because I am concerned, my friend. Certainly she will find him —"

"And then what? What, *exactly*, are you afraid of, Guiseppi?"

Guiseppi sighed and shook his head. "I do not know."

*****

A few hours later, Alex and Tillie glided through the skies on their way to Clearwater Beach, Florida. Tillie had cried when the twins said good-bye, and her brother joined in with her. Even after all of these years in America, Alex was still amazed at the Casellis' passionate Italian spirit and the way they supported their siblings through traumatic events. Vincenzo comforted and reassured her that everything would be fine.

Alex put his arm around Tillie and looked down into her pretty eyes as they flew into the darker side of the horizon. "We haven't been away together since our trip to Mexico in 1980," he reminisced.

Tillie remembered how sick she'd gotten when they returned and learned later she was pregnant. She smiled at the old memory and shook her head. "Remember how sick I got?"

"I was so worried. I thought you'd picked up that bug Becky-Lynn caught when they went."

"Me too," Tillie agreed.

Alex's expression suddenly looked very concerned, and he actually frowned into Tillie's eyes.

She noticed the sudden change in his demeanor. "What?"

"I still feel so bad about what happened when the kids were born," he answered.

"Oh, Alex," Tillie scoffed with a smile and shook her head. "Everyone else has gotten over it."

"Not my father," Alex corrected.

"Oh," she giggled under her breath. "He's getting *so* old. Don't you remember your Granddad? He was the *same* way."

"Tillie," Alex said seriously, "there's something I need to tell you."

Tillie nearly panicked. *The diamonds!* A very familiar sick feeling began in her stomach.

Alex looked into her eyes and began, "I'm going to have a lot more time when we get to Rapid City, you know, with Noah being closer, and I've trained an associate to handle his Sioux Falls business now." He hesitated and took a breath as he looked into her startled expression. "Jackson Williams, on behalf of the Conservative Party, has asked me to run for the attorney general's office. There was an article in the *Argus* a couple of months ago. Did you see it?"

Tillie shook her head, amazed at the piece of information. Alex's love for politics seemed to develop *after* they were married, as he had never mentioned it to her before. She knew he wanted to become a United States senator some day, like her brother Petrice, but she hoped he'd wait for the kids to get a little older.

"I'm flattered by the offer," Alex continued, "and I can still get my name on the ballot."

Tillie felt her mouth fall open in surprise. There was so much she wanted to say but couldn't even begin to find the words.

"Of course," Alex went on, "if you're not comfortable with it, I won't even consider it."

Tillie sat in silence as she looked back into the dark eyes of the man she loved so intensely, wondering how long he'd been thinking about this. The attorney general's office would probably require them to move to the state's capitol of Pierre, South Dakota, and they hadn't even relocated to Rapid City yet. She swallowed. "Would we have to live in Pierre?"

Alex shook his head. "No. We can stay in Rapid City, and I could go to Pierre whenever the need arises. Pierre is only a couple of hours by car and just a few minutes by charter."

Tillie took a deep breath and slowly let out the air, remembering the last time he'd attempted the pursuit of a political career.

"Honey," Alex said as he took her hand into his own and kissed the top of it. "I promise, it won't be like it was the last time. I won't get so caught up in things that I forget about you and the kids. I'm really sorry about all of that."

Tillie slowly began to nod her head as she smiled into her husband's eyes. "Okay, let's give it a try."

Alex pulled her a little closer to his body and gave her a soft kiss on her lips. "I promise, I *won't* do that to you again."

*****

Elaine Caselli snuggled under the warm quilt beside her husband, Petrice, as they sat together on their deck in Cape Vincent, New York, overlooking Lake Superior. Petrice had been elected as a junior senator nearly ten years before and then won reelection in 1982. Now he was a senior senator, and currently held the position of Chairman of the Senate Committee on Intelligence. He was a popular speaker and quite well-known throughout the country. He had just shared his plan to endorse Alex Martin for South Dakota attorney general.

"Do you really think it's such a good idea?" Elaine questioned. "He gets so carried away. I don't know about this, Patty."

"Oh, Ellie, he is older and wiser. Remember, Alex is thirty-six now. He will not leave Angel again. He knows better how to handle himself."

"He seems extremely driven to me," Elaine insisted. "He's not like you at all. And what if he gets so completely caught up in the politics of it? He's got a wife and family to think of, and we've seen a lot of marriages suffer because of this job —"

"It will be all right," Petrice interrupted with a smile. "He has given me his word, and as a man of honor, I am inclined to believe him. We have nothing to fear from this, my Ellie."

Elaine remained quiet, but the intense feeling of dread weighted down her heart. Alex was *different* from the Casellis, and no matter how they wished to make him one of their own, he just never would be.

*****

It was nearly one o'clock in the morning on Como Lake in the province of Lombardia, Italia, and Tara Caselli couldn't sleep. *How much longer can I hide this secret from my Marquette?* In nearly twenty years of marriage, the two of them had shared every single detail, every hour of every day. There was only one small omission, and Tara had promised his parents she would never speak of it with Marquette. Her heart pounded as she remembered the conspiracy to help his sister, Angel, get to Rapid City eleven years ago; her head ached with regret.

She crept from their bed, leaving her sleeping husband snoring softly on his pillow. She gathered her robe from the chair near the terrace and left their room, hurried through the dark house, down the marble steps to the veranda below. In her bare feet she sprinted to the railing overlooking the lake and breathed a sigh of relief. She took several deep breaths, attempting to calm herself, and turned her warm and perspiring face into the soft Italian wind.

"God, please forgive me," she whispered as she dropped to her knees by the marble railing and bowed her head. "I should not have agreed to keep this secret from my husband, and now You are sending her back...sending us *all* back." Tara took another deep breath and looked into the dark heavens above her. "What will you have me do, Lord?" Suddenly overcome by shuddering sobs, she bowed her head again and wept, "Father, *please* have mercy on us all."

Chapter 2

"Just stay out of their way, my Antonio," Mario instructed his son. "This is like any other prolonged visit. They have all seen you, including Marquette, and no one is the wiser —"

"But Caselli will be spending more than just a few days here and there," Antonio whispered. "My biggest concern is that it will attract Sal's attention. I have already seen far too many newspaper articles about the famous Senator's sister moving to town. Sal's black heart is hell-bent on revenge —"

"Please do not panic, my son. He is still living in Jacksonville under an assumed name. He does not know that we are here, and he will never come back this way to look for us."

Antonio took a deep breath and slowly let it out. "I suppose you are right...as always, Papa."

"Now calm down, my dear son," Mario said with a pretended chuckle. "How are things going otherwise?"

"Very well. Everything else seems safe and in order."

"Good. Your sister is roasting capon for tonight, and she has asked me to invite you. She has a very funny story about that neighbor's dog trying to get to her beautiful Sasha."

Antonio allowed a small laugh. The antics of his sister's neighbor's dog attempting to breed with Charise's lovely golden retriever, Sasha, were becoming a common topic.

"I will be there for certain," Antonio promised. "Have a good day, Papa."

Melinda's body was pressed close to the wall nearest the doorway of Ben Simmon's office. He was talking in that foreign language again, but this time she'd clearly heard him say "Papa." When she heard him hang up the telephone, she stepped into the doorway and narrowed her eyes.

"I know you're up to something, Simmons."

Ben smiled politely. "Well hello, Miss Melinda. Do you need me to find you something to do?"

"Who's Papa?" she stormed.

Ben pursed his lips together with an amused smile. "If you had done a better job of eavesdropping, you would already know."

Melinda's growl was interrupted by a hand on her shoulder.

"Hi, Melinda." It was Harv Meyers.

Harv was Noah's personnel manager. He stood barely five and half feet tall, and was stout from stem to stern. He had serious brown eyes and a balding head. His round spectacles rested on the end of his nose. His suits were obviously expensive, but the tails of his pressed white shirt were never tucked into his trousers. Contrary to his appearance, Harv performed his duties flawlessly, and maintained his professionalism in the most stressful of situations. And even though Melinda tore into him for nonexistent errors whenever she had the chance, Harv had started to see something lovely in her black eyes.

Melinda rolled her eyes and huffed at Harv, "What do you want?"

"Newkirk's charged us for the same load of lumber twice," Harv informed her. "And they'll only deal with you. Here's the file." He handed her a manila folder.

"Oh brother," she sighed and shook her head.

"Hey, Melinda," Harv took off his spectacles and smiled into her eyes, "ya wanna go to dinner at the Alex Johnson tonight?"

Melinda's face looked as if she was about ready to explode at the invitation, and Ben had to tightly clamp his jaw closed in order to keep his guffaw from escaping.

"No, thank you," she managed as she turned on her heal and stomped away.

"Too bad," Harv sighed with regret. He cast a glance at Ben and raised his brows. "I think I could make her very happy."

Ben laughed out loud. "If you believe that Miss Melinda can ever be happy, then, my friend, you are the best of men. And perhaps you were not aware, but she is dating Noah."

Harv's mouth fell open in surprise. "But she doesn't seem like his type."

Ben shrugged. He didn't think so either.

*****

Mona and Estelle were in one of the back booths at Maggie May's going over their weekly Bible study. Estelle had been strangely quiet throughout their time together, and Mona was beginning to wonder if there was something wrong. Estelle was only fifty-six years old, but her short-term memory had started to slide years ago — the same deteriorating symptoms her mother had experienced, except at a slower rate.

"It seems like you got somethin' on your mind, Darlin'," Mona drawled in her wonderful Southern accent.

Estelle shook her head, but she could not look at Mona. How she wanted to share Noah's secret, but she had promised.

She glanced at Maggie who was drying glasses at the bar. Maggie bit her lip and shook her head, hoping Estelle wouldn't spill the beans.

Estelle sighed and began flipping pages in her Bible. "Let's just read about Jesus today," she said, turning to the book of John.

Mona nodded reluctantly and turned her attention back to her Bible.

*****

Alex parked his new black Mercedes in Vincenzo's driveway, noticing several rental cars parked there as well. He recognized his family members' cars and smiled at Tillie. Now that they were back from Florida, they had driven to Reata to pick up their children. However, Vincenzo's designated parking area was filled with cars. Obviously there was some kind of a get-together in progress.

"I think they've planned a little something for us," he said.

Tillie saw the giant group of people by the fire pit where Georgie and old Doria cooked up their famous hot meat sandwiches.

"Did you know anything about this?" she asked.

"No. I thought maybe *you* did."

Tillie shook her head and looked at her husband. "I didn't have a clue."

Their three very romantic days in Florida had been spent attending the beloved play, walking along the warm beach at Clearwater, and talking for hours about their new house and their new life in Rapid City. It was a wonderfully sentimental trip, reminding Tillie of their earlier days of marriage.

"I had a great time." Alex smiled into her eyes.

"Me too."

They got out of the car and began to walk up to the main house, where a huge party was already in progress.

Petrice saw them first and waved as he yelled, "There they are!"

Elaine was next to her husband. As she looked up to see the two approaching, she smiled and shook her head with a soft laugh. "I just can't believe it, Petrice."

"What, Ellie?"

"Your sister. She looks the same as she did when I met her eleven years ago. How does she do that?"

Petrice laughed and shook his head as he watched his younger sister approach them. There had always been something about Tillie, practically from the time she was born. She had an energy and sparkle about her everyone noticed — even now — just walking along beside her husband. She had a certain spring in her step and a humor in her expression that her family had loved for years. While she'd matured from a teenage girl to a young lady and now into a woman, she was still the unwearied and happy spirit who'd entertained their hearts since her childhood.

A.J. and Laura yelled as they ran to their parents. Alex scooped up his little boy, and Tillie picked up Laura.

"We didn't even *miss* you!" Laura smiled into her mother's eyes.

"You didn't!" Tillie pretended to gasp. "Well, we missed *you!*"

Laura giggled and whispered into her mother's ear, "Uncle Vinzo told me to say that."

Tillie laughed and kissed her daughter on the cheek. "Did you have fun?"

"We had *so* much fun." Laura smiled wistfully. "Peggy had puppies two days ago. They're this big." She stretched out her thumb and forefinger to show Tillie how big the puppies were, and then she squinted her eyes together. "And they can't open their eyes yet, and they *squeak* all of the time —"

"Tell her about the pigs," A.J. interrupted from where he was still being held in his father's arms.

"Oh, the baby piggies," Laura went on, rolling her eyes. "They *stink!*" Alex and Tillie laughed at their children. "Uncle Vinzo made them leave their mommy —"

"Because they're big enough now," A.J. finished.

"And I rode Angelo's horsey all by myself," Laura said excitedly.

"You *weren't* all by yourself," A.J. disagreed, rolling his little black eyes the same way his sister had, making his parents laugh again. "Angelo had to hold onto the bridle."

"I was on the horsey *all by myself*," Laura insisted, frowning terribly at her brother.

"Surprise! Surprise!" Guiseppi's voice called out, and Tillie and Alex saw him trotting up to where they had been stopped by their children.

"Hi, Papa," Tillie greeted her father.

Guiseppi kissed her cheek and offered his hand to Alex. Alex smiled and shook Guiseppi's hand, and then A.J. asked to be put down. Alex set the little boy on the ground, and he ran off to rejoin his cousins. His sister followed.

"We have planned a little party for the four of you," Guiseppi cheerfully announced. "You know, something for going away."

"Thanks, Papa." As Tillie looked into her father's eyes, she noticed something unfamiliar in his expression. She softly frowned through her smile and asked, "Is something wrong, Papa?"

Guiseppi shook his head and laughed. "Heavens no! Why would you ask such a thing?" Tillie shrugged with a smile and shook her head. "Come along!" Guiseppi took her hand into his own and coaxed them to follow him. "We are starving, and the food is nearly ready." They went with him to join the rest of their family and friends gathered at several picnic tables beneath the largest stand of trees in Vincenzo's yard.

James and Frances Martin, who were the parents of Sam, Kate, and Alex, were there, and they had included Becky-Lynn's mother, who'd been living with Sam and Becky-Lynn for several months now due to her bad health. Becky-Lynn was married to Alex's older brother, Sam. Sam and Becky-Lynn had graduated from Harvard together in 1963.

Burt and Diane Engleson were there as well, along with their son, Andy, who was still the church pastor at Christ the King in Sioux Falls. He'd been Alex's best friend during most of their childhood and was the one who'd performed Alex and Tillie's wedding. His younger sister, Ginger, had been Tillie's best friend from the time they were born.

All of these families had lived on the same block in Sioux Falls since 1956. While the children had all grown and gone, their parents still remained in the same homes where they'd raised their children and watched America change over the last thirty years.

"Ginger!" Tillie suddenly exclaimed when she saw her red-headed friend's face in the familiar crowd.

Ginger squealed and put her arms around Tillie. "We flew in last night. Your parents thought it might be a great surprise."

"*It is!*" Tillie laughed as she held her dearest friend. Ginger and her husband, Bobby, had moved to Las Vegas, Nevada, in the fall of 1980. She and Tillie had corresponded by letter and telephone but had not seen each other since.

"It's *so* good to see you," Ginger said, getting tears of joy in her blue eyes. "And I can't believe how big the twins are now." She laughed through her tears and looked at Tillie. "And I can't believe how skinny you still are!"

Tillie laughed. "Well, you don't look so bad yourself. And when are you guys gonna start having babies?"

Ginger's blue eyes shone with excitement. "December 1st. I'm due on December 1st."

"That was *my* due date," Tillie exclaimed. She gave her another hug and looked down at Ginger's flat stomach. "But you're not showing at all."

"Tillie," Ginger replied with one raised eyebrow. "I only have *one* baby in there. Didn't get lucky enough to have two at a time."

Tillie's brothers and their wives joined them. They congratulated Ginger and shook Bobby's hand.

"And you have not changed one bit!" Marquette exclaimed as he gave Ginger a hug and looked her over. "You are still the same little girl who used to come over and pester me about my ponytail."

Ginger laughed and looked from Marquette's black ponytail to the handsome expression in his eyes. "And you haven't changed much either. When are you gonna cut that thing off?"

Marquette had grown his elegant ponytail in 1956 and had only cut it off once — when he was drafted and sent to Vietnam in 1965. When he returned, he immediately grew it back and had kept it ever since. Marquette was also the tallest of the three brothers, having reached a slender height of six feet. His brothers were the size of their father and their sister, which was barely five feet six inches. Marquette had bragged of how he was the tallest of his family — that is, until Petrice married Ellie, who towered over her tiny Italian husband and was nearly as tall as Marquette.

Marquette laughed, "Perhaps when I am fifty."

"The oldest hippie in South Dakota," Guiseppi grumbled from nearby. "I cannot believe your dear wife puts up with it."

"She insists I keep it," Marquette informed him with a smile.

Petrice drew Ginger into his arms and gave her a hug. "Everyone has stayed so young and look at me."

Ginger smiled into his eyes. His face hadn't aged nearly as much as his black hair had grayed. There was not one strand of black amongst the wavy gray hair upon Petrice's head, and it made him look older than his forty-six years. His brothers had not grayed at all, except for Vincenzo's few wisps of silver. "I saw you on TV last week," she said with a smile. "Great speech. You give it to 'em, Senator."

"I intend to," Petrice assured with mischief in his black eyes.

Georgie and Doria announced the meat was finished and called Rosa and Guiseppi over to help. Their famous sandwiches were soon prepared, and everyone was enjoying a delightful feast beneath the trees. They visited about all of the times over the past thirty years they'd gathered in the same spot and reflected on how the family had grown.

Vincenzo's children were the oldest, just approaching their teen years, and Petrice's son and daughter were not far behind: Michael had turned ten that past May, and Gabriella was nine. Michael and Angelo were great friends, and talked of nothing else but joining the military when they were old enough, while Alyssa and Gabriella were beginning the wistful dreams of the day when they would be married and have babies of their own to take care of. They had followed and doted on the twins for the past several years. However, the twins had recently found some independence and were not willing to be the *babies* anymore. After all, A.J. had won the coveted position of catcher on his T-ball team, and Laura was becoming a painter like her mommy. They would start school in the fall and could hardly be considered *little kids* anymore, as A.J. had so eloquently put it to his older cousins.

"Perhaps you *should* suffer yourself some dignity in your older age," Vincenzo observed to his brother Marquette as they ate their sandwiches.

The three of them had collected together in a small group to discuss politics and the uncertainties of being in their mid-forties. And, at least with respect to their age, they did not have to make the journey alone. They'd been born so close together, which kept them all at the same stage of life, even though the three of them had chosen different directions.

"What are you talking about?" Marquette questioned with a soft frown. They were speaking in Italian, as they always did when they were alone.

"That hair of yours," Vincenzo clarified. "Why do you insist upon keeping it?"

Marquette looked proudly at his brother and answered, "My Tara says it gives me style and grace."

Petrice laughed out loud. "It makes you look dishonest."

Marquette frowned at Petrice and replied, "That is not what Remington said to me during our last little get-together."

16

Petrice laughed again. "You misunderstood the Secretary —"

"Doubtfully," Marquette interrupted. "I rarely misunderstand *anything*."

Vincenzo smiled curiously at both of them and slowly shook his head. "You two. You speak of these public figures as if they were your closest friends. What business do you have with the Secretary of Defense?"

Marquette raised both of his eyebrows as he leaned closer to Vincenzo and whispered, "Tara and I have been doing some investigating for the Secretary."

"Unbelievable." Vincenzo chuckled.

Guiseppi saw his sons gathered together and gave Rosa a soft nudge. They'd seated themselves in the grass for a brief time of quiet. "Look at the three of them," he chortled. "What do you suppose they are discussing?"

Rosa followed his gaze to their three sons, laughed, and shook her head. "Our Lord only knows. Perhaps they are worrying about their age again."

Guiseppi nodded, and then his eyes caught sight of his daughter, holding the hand of her husband and looking into his eyes. "They seem very happy together these days."

It was then that Tara took a seat with them, and they smiled at their only Italian daughter-in-law. Petrice and Vincenzo had taken American brides, but Marquette had held out for the one true love of his life, and that was Tara D'Annenci. They'd been friends from the time of their birth in the same valley in *Italia,* and were tragically separated during their fifteenth year when the Casellis moved to America. Tara's family was killed in a train crash in Rome, just a few days later, and it was assumed she'd died along with them. However, twelve years later, Marquette unraveled the greatest mystery of his lifetime and found her, alive and well and living with her aunt and uncle in Chicago.

Old "friends" from *Italia,* Luigi Andreotti and his father, had conspired to hide the truth from Marquette so that Luigi might have Tara as his bride. They also hid Marquette's location from Tara, but the Lord Himself saw to it that their plans be foiled. Marquette and Tara married less than two weeks after he found her, and Tara had become an extra-special member of the Caselli family. Guiseppi and Rosa spoke the same regional dialect with Tara, as if they were with one of their own children, and they shared secrets with Tara they would never dream of telling their other daughters-in-law.

Her round, black eyes reflected fatigue today and maybe even a little sorrow when she sighed with a faint smile and took a seat close to Rosa. Rosa put a tender arm over Tara's shoulders, kissed her cheek, and said in their old language, "You do not look well, today, Tara. Whatever is troubling you?"

"You know," Tara whispered as she bowed her head and looked into the grass in front of them. "I do not wish to keep this from my Marquette any longer."

"It will only upset him to no end," Guiseppi gently reminded.

Tara nodded and took a deep breath. "Have you spoken with Angel about this?"

Guiseppi and Rosa both shook their heads and Guiseppi answered, "Tara, it could be they no longer even think of the incident, and I have decided to allow the Father to handle it from here."

"But she will eventually meet up with him," Tara argued. "I do not know how it can be helped."

Rosa offered Tara a soft smile. "Papa and I are going to Rapid City for that first week, just to help them settle in a bit."

"And should something happen," Guiseppi added, "we will be there to help her through it."

Tara looked at the two dearest people she'd ever known and whispered, "I lied to Angel about this."

"We know," Guiseppi acknowledged. "But she will understand."

Tara took a soft breath and asked, "When is the move to take place?"

"The second week in August," Rosa answered.

"Marquette and I will go to Tehran that week," Tara whispered as she glanced in Tillie's direction. "And we will not be able to get out until early November. We will be in Tehran roughly two and a half months."

"Why must you be away for such a long time?" Rosa questioned with a concerned expression.

"And in such a horribly uncertain place?" Guiseppi added with a frown.

"Marquette's Arabic is very precise, and we blend easier than most Americans," Tara answered. She faintly smiled. "If you could see us in our garb, you would think we were born and raised in the Middle East." She sighed as she glanced at her husband. "The intelligence Marquette will be able to gather for the United States is extremely valuable." She looked back at Rosa and Guiseppi. "You must pray for us."

Later on, Petrice gathered everyone together around the tables beneath the trees, proclaiming he had an announcement of grand proportions. When everyone had assembled and were ready to listen to the very famous Senior Senator Caselli from the great state of New York, he began his announcement.

"As you know," Petrice said in the soft accent America had fallen in love with when he first ran for the junior Senator's seat in 1976, "I have just a little bit of clout when it comes to endorsing certain candidates." He paused to let his family laugh, and then he looked at Alex as he took a breath. "And I have decided to endorse a certain candidate for the office of attorney general in South Dakota. Please know I have given this much forethought and prayer, and it is my desire that Alex Martin's name be added to the ballot before November of this year."

While everyone cheered and clapped, giving Alex congratulations and a few "way to go's," Alex's father, James, frowned harshly at his son.

Marquette shot an angry glare at his brother, Petrice, but Petrice only looked away. As Marquette took a step toward him, he felt the insistent hand of his other brother upon his arm.

"Let it go, Marquette," Vincenzo demanded under his breath. "We should not deal with our brother in front of all of these relatives."

"He should be thrashed on the spot for this!" Marquette angrily whispered.

Vincenzo had to agree, and he replied, "I cannot believe he would tempt Alex into sin in such a way. What has gotten into him?"

"He has obviously been a politician for far too long," Marquette retorted. "Everyone here knows Alex cannot handle a little limelight. He will surely lose his mind, and Angel will lose her husband."

"So what shall we do?" Vincenzo asked with a frown. "We cannot very well reverse the course now."

Marquette shook his head. "And I am bound for Iran in just a few months. I cannot be here to keep him in line —"

"Which would be disastrous anyway," Vincenzo interrupted. Marquette looked curiously at his brother, and Vincenzo explained, "It is your temper, Marquette. You allow it to run away with you, the same way Alex allows his passion for his work to run away with him."

Marquette sighed and rolled his eyes. *When will the rest of them see what is crystal clear? Alex is nothing but a blackguard in disguise.*

James Martin was dear to all of the Casellis. Not only had he been their immigration attorney, but he had met their ship in New York Harbor thirty years ago and helped them find their way to South Dakota on the trains that crossed America. James was quite advanced in years compared to the Casellis, having recently celebrated his eighty-seventh birthday. His father had lived to be one hundred years old and dutifully practiced law until the day he died. The Martins did *not* believe in retirement, and James had vowed to practice law until the day *he* died.

He sidled up close to Tillie, put one of his hands on her shoulder, and whispered into her ear, "Did you know about this?"

Tillie smiled into James' concerned expression. "Don't worry, James. We've already talked about it, and he's promised he won't let it get so out of hand like he did before."

"But this is a public office," James argued. "And you're in the middle of a relocation."

"It's gonna be okay." Tillie took her father-in-law's wrinkled hand into her own to give it a gentle pat. "He's different now, James. You'll see."

Tillie's soft smile and devoted demeanor softened James' heart, and he allowed himself a small smile. He slowly nodded his head and sighed, "Well, okay then, as long as it's okay with you."

Tillie smiled. "It's *totally* okay with me, James. He's bringing Shondra to the Rapid City office, and she'll be able to help him out a lot." Shondra Payne had worked for their law firm since 1968, the year Alex went to Harvard. She had been a lawyer for twenty-five years and was also the law firm's administrative manager. She was almost fifty years old and had never married. She said she'd chosen a career instead of a family, as she did not desire to shortchange either one.

"Be happy for your son," Tillie whispered with a smile as she looked at Alex who was speaking with his brother. His incredible reputation alone would win him the election, and Petrice's endorsement would create a disastrous landslide for whoever tried to oppose him. Tillie looked back at her old father-in-law, gave his hand a tender squeeze, and stood on her toes to softly kiss his cheek. "He loves us, James, and he won't make the same mistake he made before." She laughed quietly as she smiled into James' eyes. "He's smarter than that."

Later on that night, an extremely agitated Marquette stormed around his and Tara's room at his parents' house. He wore nothing but a pair of pajama pants and was *still* sweating profusely. He threw his arms in the air and whispered his angry frustrations to his wife.

"This is such *nonsense!*" he raged under his breath. "The *only* reason the blackguard would choose a political career *now* is because he is moving away from the constraints of his father and brother!"

"Marquette!" Tara whispered as she watched her husband from the bed. "Keep your voice down! What if Ma`ma and Papa hear you?"

"Let them hear me!" Marquette growled. "Papa *knew better* than to give her into this *ridiculous* marriage in the first place!"

"Do not speak so disrespectfully of Papa!" Tara whispered. "And Alex has behaved like a perfect husband for the better part of six years now. Can you not forgive him?"

"For being absent at the birth of his children?" Marquette asked with astonishment. "While my sister lay dying trying to give us those babies? No, Tara, I *cannot!*"

"Marquette," Tara said as calmly as she could, "you have carried this bitterness toward Alex long enough. They have been married nine years now, and it is time for you to come to your senses about it and accept that they will be *staying* married. Angel loves him, and it is time you submit with good grace and make the best of it."

Marquette abruptly stopped his pacing, frowned at his wife, and pointed his index finger at her. "And *that*, my Tara, is what has me nearly dead! The fact that she *must* remain married to a man with so much ambition tears at my heart!" He clutched at his chest and grimaced as if he were in pain.

After sitting quietly for a moment, Tara patted the place in the bed beside her and gently coaxed, "Come now, Marquette. Come to bed and relax. We have such a difficult journey ahead of us this summer, and you should not be wasting your energies on hating Alex."

"I cannot help it," Marquette growled. He took a deep breath and shook his head. "It is hotter than Hades in this house. I am going outside to sit for a moment. I will come to bed later."

Tara watched her husband storm out of their bedroom. She heard his soft footsteps head down the hallway and then the stairs, and soon she heard the patio door below open and close. She sighed and shook her head. *Poor Marquette. He has tried for years to lay aside his differences with Alex, but, if anything, it is worse. Hopefully Alex will be able to control himself this time.*

*****

He could still imagine what she would look like as she swept down the winding staircase and into the formal entryway to greet their guests. She would be wearing her favorite color — the wonderful softness of pastel pink — and her hair would glide along on her beautiful, dark shoulders. Her black eyes would sparkle as she smiled at him. Just as she reached the bottom step, he would take her hand and she would look lovingly into his eyes. "I love you," he'd whisper. She'd smile again and tenderly kiss his lips, because there would be no one else in the world she'd rather be with…*or at least that's what she'd said.*

Noah sighed and tried to shake himself back into reality and the job at hand. He was on a ladder as he repaired the light fixture in the elegant entryway of Angel's Place. It was so easy to lose himself in the memories while he was there. He looked around for a moment, recalling the reason he'd built the house in the first place.

It was the summer of 1976, and he had made some money selling houses in Rapid City. His father had left him the land, which was situated behind the fish hatchery on Rimrock Highway. He chose the hill at the top of the meadow so the window of her studio would face west, giving her a view of the Black Hills while she painted.

It was a very old-fashioned, two-story Victorian home with a brick front and a sweeping, wrap-around porch. Wooden shutters were hung on paned windows, and a hand-carved oak door with beveled glass greeted the guests at the front door.

Upon entering the home, a large kitchen and a formal dining room were on one side of the entrance hall. The dining room had a built-in hutch, complete with glass doors and inside illumination. A dainty parlor and a great room were on the other side of the large entrance hall. The first floor is also where Angel's studio was located. It was a nice-sized room, and Noah had found the perfect glass for the windows. They reached from floor to ceiling, so she could see the Hills she loved while she worked on her paintings.

An open and winding staircase led the way upstairs, where there was a master bedroom, complete with bathroom and walk-in closet. There was a small, adjacent nursery so the baby wouldn't be too far away.

There were five more oversized bedrooms upstairs and two more bathrooms to accommodate all of the children they would have had together.

Of course, now Angel couldn't have any more children.

The floors were hardwood except for the bedrooms, and each piece of woodwork trimming the doorways and floors had been cut and finished by hand. Noah's hands. He hung the lights, the shutters, and the front door, leaving no detail untouched and sparing not an ounce of perfection in his finished work. It was the *perfect* place to bring home a new bride and start a family, but that hadn't happened. Noah wound up leasing the place to a little old lady named Vivian Olson, whom Alex affectionately called 'Cruella de Vil.' She had operated a bed and breakfast out of the place for the past ten years. He had always hoped she would buy it so he could forget about all it meant to him. However, Viv had repeatedly refused the purchase. Every June and then again in November, the old gal had him up there doing spring and fall maintenance. He could have sent a crew up to do the work, but he wanted to see for himself that Viv took care of his place. He was sure whatever work needed to be done was done in a manner worthy of keeping with Angel's memory.

"Do you just about have that light fixed, Hansen?" Viv barked from the bottom of his ladder.

"Just about," Noah answered with a smile as he glanced down at the blue-haired old woman who seemed to love to torture him while he was there.

"Well, that's good news," she barked again. "We're having a wedding reception here this weekend, and we're gonna need that light."

"It won't be much longer, Viv."

The bar was empty that morning, and Estelle had lovingly spread the saved snapshots out on the counter, while Maggie watched her from the kitchen. The snapshots were of Angel's Place during its construction period, and Noah had given them the photos so they could watch its progress. First there had been the hole, then the foundation and framing, walls, floors, woodwork. Eventually, Angel's Place was finished.

Maggie sighed and shook her head. Now that Estelle knew Angel was coming back, she had started to look at the photos and talk about how Noah would have to kick Vivian out and move Angel in.

Maggie walked to where Estelle looked at the ten-year-old photos and stood quietly beside her sister. "Whatcha doin', Baby?" she asked.

"Oh, just looking at Noah's pictures," Estelle answered wistfully. "I'll bet he's anxious to get her back."

Maggie swallowed hard and put her hand on Estelle's shoulder, "Angel went and married that other guy. Remember? Alex?"

Estelle looked horrified and started to shake her head. "What are you taking about, Maggie?"

Maggie took a deep breath and reached for that morning's paper. She carefully laid it down over the photos so Estelle could see the front page. There was a picture of Alex Martin and his beautiful wife, along with the famous Senator Caselli. The caption read: CASELLI ENDORSES MARTIN FOR ATTORNEY GENERAL.

"What is she doing with *him?*" Estelle gasped in a whisper.

"She married him, Baby. Come on now, you remember this."

Estelle let out a heavy sigh and reluctantly nodded her head. "Poor Noah. What's he gonna do, Maggie?"

"Probably something really stupid," Maggie grumbled.

*****

At their kitchen table, Joshua and Mona Hansen, Noah's brother and sister-in-law, shared the morning paper before Joshua left for the church he'd pastored for nearly thirty years.

"Gee, she's familiar," Mona drawled as she studied the photo on the front page of the *Rapid City Journal*.

Joshua squinted for a better look and slowly nodded his head. "She must have been around with Alex sometime."

"I don't remember ever meeting her," Mona commented.

Joshua slowly shook his head and looked at the photo. "Me neither."

"Pretty gal," Mona said. "Boy, that Alex looks so tall standing next to her and her brother. He must be at least a foot taller."

"He's a big guy. He's even bigger than Noah."

"Says here they're relocating to Rapid City," Mona said as she skimmed the article. "Bet that'll make Noah happy."

*****

The same photo and article were run on the front page of the *Sioux Falls Argus Leader*, and James Martin stewed while he read it in his office in Sioux Falls. He took off his glasses, sighed, and got out of his chair. He shuffled down the hall and into Alex's office, where he found his son absorbed in a code book. James stood in the doorway for a long moment, but Alex was so deep into his work that he didn't notice his father patiently waiting. James abruptly cleared his throat to get Alex's attention, and Alex lifted his head and smiled.

"Hi, Dad," he greeted, and then he noticed the newspaper James was carrying.

"Hi, Alex," James said with a serious frown. "Nice article. Nice picture."

"Thanks," Alex replied.

James sighed and shook his head as he stepped into Alex's office and took a seat in one of the chairs in front of Alex's desk. "You know I don't like this," he grumbled. "And why didn't you talk to me about it before you jumped in like that?"

"Dad, this is something I've always wanted, and I've got the opportunity now, so I'm taking it. Tillie and I have discussed this, and she's fine with it."

James raised an eyebrow. "I saw her birthday present. It looks like you *bribed* her into it."

"Dad," Alex began as he tried to smile at his cranky father. *Granddad acted much the same way when he reached this age.* "I didn't bribe my wife. We talked about it."

"You made promises you don't intend to keep, and then slipped her about ten thousand dollars' worth of diamonds."

"I have every intention of keeping my promises to Tillie," Alex insisted. "Why do you have to hammer down so much guilt on me over this?"

James took a deep breath. "Because, Alex, I thought that moving you out to Rapid City might slow you down a little. You've got a wife and young children. They need your time and attention right now."

"I give them plenty of time and attention. Shondra's an expert manager. I just don't see what you're so worried about."

"I worry about you losing control," James answered. "You have a real problem with losing yourself to the work. You're just like your Uncle Mac, and I worry that you'll make the same mistakes he made."

"Oh, brother." Alex rolled his eyes and frowned at his father. "You know, sometimes I think you wish I'd screw up so that you could sit back and say 'I told you so,' but it's not gonna happen. I *won't* make the same mistakes that Uncle Mac made, because I'm a completely different man than he is."

James nodded and took a deep breath as he got out of his chair. "I probably never told you enough that *I love you and I'm proud of you*. I'm sorry about that. You're a fine man, Alex, and there's nothing wrong with the way you practice law. I'd just like to see you spend some more time with Tillie and the kids. That's all."

Alex nodded. "Thanks, Dad. I appreciate that. And don't worry, Tillie and the kids are the most important things in my life."

Chapter 3

Mid-August, 1986
Rapid City, South Dakota

Alex and Tillie's new home was located in a subdivision of Rapid City known as Carriage Hills. It was nestled within fragrant pines, and a bubbling creek rolled through their backyard. Just above their pines was a view of the Black Hills, and dry, mountain air blew their fragrance into the open windows.

The first level of the home had a large kitchen, a formal living room for entertaining, a hidden family room, and a beautiful sunroom encased in three sides of glass. It opened onto a cement patio with a view of the creek. A winding staircase took them upstairs, where there were five bedrooms with bathrooms. At the very end of the hall was another smaller sunroom and a master suite for Alex and Tillie.

A.J. and Laura each got their own room, which they were very excited about as they had shared a room since their birth. Two rooms were planned for guest bedrooms, because Tillie hoped her family would visit often. Alex took the smallest bedroom for his office at home, and Tillie took the tiny sunroom at the end of the hall for her studio. From there she could see above the trees and to the Black Hills in the distance. The view brought back a memory she thought was long forgotten.

Parts of the memory were truly wonderful. Mt. Rushmore had been majestic, and the blue waters of the Pactola Reservoir beneath a clear, Black Hills' sky had overwhelmed her. Spearfish Canyon had been beautiful, with its mixture of pine and hardwood trees just leafing out in the early spring heat. The waterfalls were captivating, and the wonderful story about the brave, Indian warrior...she always stopped the memory there.

Tillie shook her thoughts away. She glanced below and saw that Papa and her children had found their way to the creek in the backyard. Guiseppi was showing them the finer points of baiting a hook and casting, hoping to turn the two little ones into great fishers. Tillie smiled as she watched them. Laura was *not* going to touch that worm, but she was willing to hold the pole once it was baited. A.J., on the other hand, was more than excited about getting his hands on the slippery little pieces of bait and piercing them through on the hook.

"Time for a break," Rosa announced, and Tillie turned to see her ma`ma with two icy glasses of tea.

"Oh, thanks, Ma`ma," Tillie said, reaching for a glass. She took a long gulp and said, "That hits the spot."

The movers had unloaded each box with care, exactly where Tillie had instructed, and she and Rosa diligently went through each of them, transforming the empty house into a home.

"Whew!" Rosa sighed and sank her petite body into one of the white wicker chairs that had been unloaded into Tillie's new studio. She looked around at the furniture, "Is this new?"

Tillie shrugged. "Sorta. I couldn't resist. Me and the kids were at this garage sale right before we left Sioux Falls. I actually spray painted it a couple of days before the movers came." She laughed and shook her head. "Alex thought for sure I was going crazy. He didn't think it would be dry before we had to load it up."

Rosa smiled. "It looks perfect in here."

"Thanks, Ma`ma." She closed her eyes and took a deep breath of the pine aroma floating through the open window. "I *love* that smell. It's so different from the air in Sioux Falls."

"Indeed it is. All that we smell are the crops and the dirt." Rosa inhaled deeply. What a wonderful, fresh smell, and no air conditioning. Rosa lived by the air conditioning vents this time of the year in Sioux Falls, and yet the air was dry and cool in Rapid City. "Where is Alex this day?"

"The office. He and Shondra have several things to get in order, and he had to make a few phone calls." Tillie noticed the pensive look between her mother's brows. "What is it, Ma`ma?"

"I…" Rosa hesitated and looked away from Tillie. She let her gaze drift to the distant hills, took a soft breath, and managed to say, "I have something I wish to ask you."

"Okay."

"My Angel," and Rosa gulped. She looked into her daughter's eyes and bit her lip. "Do you ever think of *him* anymore?"

Tillie frowned with confusion. "Who, Ma`ma?"

"Noah," Rosa whispered, as if saying his name aloud would summon him into their very presence.

"Noah? Noah Hansen? Alex's friend?"

Rosa nearly fell from her chair. *Yes, that would be the very Noah I am speaking of.* She took a deep breath. "*Your* Noah."

"*My* Noah?!" Tillie exclaimed. "You mean that *jerk* who almost wrecked my life when I was out here in 1975?!"

Rosa nodded and took a careful sip of her tea.

"Boy!" Tillie went on, rolling her eyes as she shook her head, "Why on earth would you bring *that* up?!"

Rosa shrugged her tiny shoulders. "I suppose I am getting old —"

"Sixty-six does not constitute old age." Tillie shook her head again and waved her hand in the air. "Thank God He didn't let me get caught up with *that* guy. My life would have been over before it even began."

Rosa faintly smiled at her daughter's comical antics. Even though Tillie had been born and raised in America, there were those precious and wonderful moments when she would react with such Italian enthusiasm that it filled Rosa's heart with delight.

"But," Rosa persisted, "what if you were to see him again, you know, now that you are living in Rapid City?"

"Oh, Ma`ma," Tillie sighed, rolling her black eyes again and shaking her head. "He's dead by now. I told you, he was a terrible drinker. There's no way he's even around anymore." She raised one of her dark eyebrows, "Besides, do you really think a guy like that would even move in the same circles with Alex and me? He was a *loser!*"

Rosa took another careful sip of the tea.

"Ma`ma," Tillie continued with a soft laugh, "Alex made all that ugly stuff go away." She knelt beside her mother, put a gentle hand upon Rosa's knee, and smiled. "I know I scared you and Papa so bad that year and I'm still really sorry for what I did, but *please* don't worry anymore."

Rosa smiled into Tillie's eyes. *Well, at least she does not think of him.*

*****

Melinda watched Noah nervously pace his dingy little office on the other side of town. He had forgotten to close the door, and she saw him going back and forth behind his desk. Melinda refused to have her own private office. She preferred having the ability to keep her eyes on the entire office at once. And even though Noah had offered her an office several times, she'd always declined. Her central location amidst the employees was where she wanted to stay, earning her the nickname, "Queen Bee."

What's he up to? She got up and went inside to talk to him. "Everything okay?" she asked.

Just the sound of her voice made him jump, and he stared at her for a moment. *Where'd she come from?* He swallowed to find his voice. "Everything's fine. Why?"

Melinda shrugged. "You've been pacing for a while now. Something up?"

Noah felt his face blush hot beneath his beard. *Is there something up? Is there ever!* He shook his head and seated himself at his desk.

Melinda gave him a confused frown. "Mom and Dad are having a barbecue tonight. Do you and the boys want to come over? You look like you should relax a little."

"Sure," he found himself answering, and then wished he hadn't. This "dating" thing, or whatever it was, that he had gotten into with Melinda was getting way out of hand. She used to be as mean as could be. But over the last several months she'd shown Noah and his children warmth and kindness. They saw each other nearly every evening after work, and she had even started to show up at the baseball practices Noah coached for his boys.

Ty and Jake *loved* Miss Melinda because she supplied them with enough blue Kool-Aid to satisfy a small army, chocolate chip cookies from Albertson's deli, and strawberry Jello with whipped cream and sprinkles.

The receptionist buzzed him at that moment. "Alex Martin on Line Three."

"I need to take this call," Noah said with a dismissive expression. "I'll see ya later."

Melinda nodded with a frown and left his office, closing the door behind her.

"Alex?" Noah happily greeted.

"Hey, Noah," Alex's voice came through from the other end, and Noah could tell by his tone that he was smiling.

"How did the move go?" Noah casually inquired, but in the back of his mind he wondered if Angel had made it to Rapid City after all or, if by some fluke, she'd stayed behind in Sioux Falls.

"Great," Alex answered. "Tillie's parents came along, and they're giving her a hand with the kids and things."

So, she came with him after all. After all these years, Angel is in the same town with me. "So, what can I do for you, Alex?"

"Well," Alex began, and Noah heard the shuffle of papers in the background. "I'm trying to set up a meeting with Scott McDarren. He's in town for a few days and would like to meet with you about that warehouse project over on St. Joe. I think you need to get this guy to sign on the dotted line, Noah. He's having a hard time making a decision."

26

"I've got the next couple of days open, except for a building inspection at one o'clock on Thursday," Noah answered. "Other than that, you can pick just about any time you want."

"Okay. I'll have Shondra take care of it as soon as possible and let you know what we're gonna do."

"Oh, by the way," Noah added, "have you thought about a church yet?"

"No. We really haven't had the time. Doesn't your brother still pastor that church over on South Canyon?"

I don't believe it! He's playing right into my hand! "Yes, yes he does. Sunday school begins at nine-thirty and service is at ten forty-five."

"We'll give it a try then," Alex smiled into the phone. "And Shondra will call you with the meeting time when it's scheduled."

They said their good-byes and ended the call. Noah swallowed hard and let out the breath he hadn't realized he was holding. *What am I thinking?*

*****

Ty and Jake were with their Auntie Mona in her garden that afternoon. They helped her harvest the vegetables and listened to her tell one wonderful story after another. She had spent many a day in the very same place with Noah when he was their age, and so it was fitting that his sons do the same. They gathered apples from the small orchard as well, washed everything, and prepared it for Mona's canning process.

"School starts in two weeks," Mona said in her heavy Southern accent. "You guys excited?"

"I am," Ty admitted with a smile, and Mona saw his mother's expression shine from his eyes. His strawberry-blond hair shimmered in the late summer sun, and his smile was the same as Carrie's.

"Not me," Jake replied with his demeanor instantly changing from sweet to indignant at just the mention of school.

"Why not, Jake?" Ty smiled at his little brother. "You'll *love* it."

"Will not," Jake muttered. "I wanna stay at home with Vera and Auntie Mona all day long." Vera Smith was Noah's housekeeper.

"Well," Mona said as she smiled at her nephews and took a deep breath, "do you wanna hear a story about that?" They nodded because Auntie Mona had the best stories. She was from a large family in Atlanta, Georgia, and they had done all kinds of funny things that Mona liked to talk about.

"You know my brother, the one we call Dancie Darlin'?" Mona began, and they nodded, so she continued. "Well he never liked to go to school either and was always finding ways to get out of it. Why, I remember once he crawled up on top of the school bus that used to come and pick us up, and he laid down real flat up there so nobody could see him. He just figured he'd get himself a ride into a town on the top of the bus and crawl down when nobody was looking. Well, I suppose that old school bus got a good half mile down the road when Old Man Fletcher saw a steer in the road and slammed on the brakes. Poor little Dancie Darlin' went flying into the side of Mr. Tucker's chicken coop..." The boys began to giggle, and Mona paused to smile at them. "Now, boys, it's a true story."

"What happened to Dancie Darlin'?" Ty laughed.

"Why, he broke both his legs and arms," Mona answered, sending her nephews into laughing hysterics.

"Did he get out of school?" Jake asked eagerly.

"Not really." Mona frowned as she looked at the little rebel. *You're just like your dad,* she thought. "Mamma brought him his homework every day."

"What a drag!" Ty laughed hard and gave his little brother a soft slap on the back. "I bet Auntie Mona brings you your homework if you wind up in the hospital, Jake."

Jake disgustedly shook his head, and Mona chuckled. "Yes, I would, Jake my darlin', so you stay in school and be a good boy."

Jake gave his Auntie a small smile and begrudgingly nodded his head. "Yes, Auntie Mona." He looked so much like his father at that moment, it almost startled Mona. His sandy-colored hair was always messy, just like Noah's, and his blue eyes sparkled and danced when he smiled.

Just then they heard Noah's pickup out front, and Mona got to her feet. "Here's your dad. Let's go and see what he's been up to."

When Mona and the boys rounded the corner of the house, Mona almost didn't recognize the man getting out of Noah's pickup. She froze in her tracks. The Noah who'd left his sons in her care that morning had a terrible, bushy beard. The Noah returning this afternoon was clean shaven, and looked at least ten years younger.

"Dad!" Ty shouted excitedly. He laughed and rushed to his father. "Where's your beard?"

"You look *great*, Daddy!" Jake exclaimed.

Noah hugged and kissed both of his little boys and smiled.

As she watched him, Mona noticed something different in his expression — something she recalled seeing before, but she couldn't exactly remember when.

"Thanks, guys," Noah said to his boys. "What have you been up to all day?"

"Gardening," Ty answered with a smile.

"And stories," Jake laughed.

Noah nodded. "Auntie Mona's stories are the best."

"Hey, Noah." Mona smiled into his eyes, noticing *again* that eerily familiar sparkle. "Why did you get rid of your beard?"

Noah laughed nervously. "I was checking on that warehouse site over on St. Joe today and decided to stop in at Fudds for a haircut. One thing led to another, and pretty soon I just had him shave the thing off. It gets so hot in the summertime anyway."

"Summer's nearly over." Mona raised one eyebrow questioningly.

"So." Noah shrugged.

Mona nodded, unable to take her eyes off of Noah's unusual expression. He looked handsome without the beard, but there was something hiding behind Noah's dancing blue eyes today. "I've got some lemonade out on the back step," she offered. "Do ya got a minute?"

She noticed him hesitate. His reaction fit well with the several times this past spring and summer he'd refused her invitations. It was almost as if he had started to avoid her and Joshua. Of course, there was also the matter of the delight in his eyes. Whatever had happened in Noah's life was giving him incredible joy, and yet he was unwilling to share it with his brother and Mona.

Noah noticed Mona's perceptive stare. Of course he had to accept the invitation. She'd start to suspect something if he didn't.

"Sure, I got a few minutes," he answered.

Mona turned and led the way to her backyard, while Ty and Jake raced ahead and into the apple orchard. Noah seated himself at the picnic table, and Mona poured them each a tall glass of lemonade. She sat directly across from him.

Noah smiled into her green eyes. "Thanks, Mona, this hits the spot. It was really warm in town today."

Mona sipped her lemonade as she looked back into Noah's expression. He turned his eyes away and took a long drink.

She wants something...it's like she already knows, he thought.

"You've certainly been in a good mood lately," she began with a smile.

"Business has been really good lately."

"How's Melinda?"

"We're going over to her folks' tonight for a barbecue," he answered quickly.

Mona caught the look in his eyes when he avoided her question, and she repeated, "How's Melinda?"

*Oh, dear...wrong answer...*He wanted to grab his little boys and run for the truck, but he answered as casually as he could, "She's great, Mona."

Mona frowned. "How long you gonna play with that girl, Noah?"

"I thought you *liked* my ruthless assistant."

Mona raised one eyebrow. "Do *you?*"

Noah's eyes opened with faked surprise. "Do *I* like her?" He shrugged. "I like Melinda. She's okay."

"What's goin' on, Noah?" she demanded in the tone she'd used on him when he was little and had been caught in the middle of disobedience.

"Nothin'," he answered as he tried to maintain a calm composure and eye contact with Mona.

"You've been acting strange all summer now," Mona quietly accused. "I think you're keeping somethin' from me and Josh. Is Melinda pregnant or somethin'?"

Noah's jaw dropped. "Good grief, Mona! Of course not!"

Mona sat up very straight on the wooden bench beneath her, her eyes searching Noah up and down, "Well *somethin's* going on. You certainly look different, especially without your beard. And you sound different too."

"Oh, Mona," Noah pretended to scoff with a laugh. "You don't have anything on me."

"Come on, Noah, what's goin' on?"

Noah shook his head and took a deep breath. "Listen, Mona, I'm thirty-four years old. If I want to keep a secret, I think I should be entitled."

"Well, well," Mona smiled and let out her breath. "Sorry I bothered you. I won't mention it again."

Noah sighed and rolled his eyes. He wanted to tell her, but she might not understand. He knew she'd mention it again; she just said that to get him to tell on himself. It was an old trick she'd used on him as a child. It had worked then, and it was going to work today. He looked away from Mona and at his boys playing in the orchard. He scratched his head and turned his eyes back to Mona. "I found Angel," he breathed.

"You what?" Mona gasped in a whisper.

"I found my Angel."

"Where is she?" Mona whispered. Her surprised mouth hung open and her eyes were wide and round.

"She was in Sioux Falls — I found out when I went to see Alex last spring."

"Did you talk to her?" Mona questioned, still unable to bring her voice above a whisper.

Noah shook his head and reached for Mona's hand. His dancing eyes were suddenly filled with the familiar grief again. "Mona, she's *married* to Alex."

Mona thought her heart might stop. She took a tight hold of Noah's hand and gasped, "Alex? Didn't they just move here?" Noah nodded and Mona gasped softly again. "Noah, what will you do?" But in Noah's expression she saw there was yet another secret behind his eyes and she groaned. "Noah, what have you *done?*"

Noah sighed and gave Mona one of his lopsided grins. "Alex was looking for a church. He asked me if my brother still pastored the same church. I said yes."

"You what?!" Mona shot off the bench like someone had set her on fire. She looked down into Noah's eyes. "Does Alex know about this? I mean, about you and Angel?"

Noah just sat very still and looked into his sister-in-law's blazing eyes.

"Oh for Pete's sake, Noah!" Mona said in a tone he didn't recognize. He couldn't tell if she was angry or frightened or a little of both. "*That's* why you shaved off your beard. What do you think you're doing?! The two of you were just kids when all that happened. She'll *never* remember you!"

"She *will*," Noah argued with confidence.

"And then what?! Do you think you're gonna go ridin' off into the sunset on a Harley you ain't started in years?! You must be outa your mind, Noah! You gotta tell Alex and your brother!"

"No!" Noah said, and he slapped the table. "No way, Mona, and you're not telling either —"

"Oh, yes I am," Mona scowled.

"No," Noah persisted. "Besides, nothin's gonna happen anyway. I just want to see her again. Don't you want to see her, Mona? Aren't you the least little bit curious?"

"Of course I'm curious," Mona spat out. "But I remember what this did to you eleven years ago. It almost killed you when she didn't come back. You missed that girl, Noah. You built that house for her. You're playing with fire."

Noah knew, somewhere inside of himself, that Mona was right. He just couldn't seem to help it. He had no thought-out plan, he just wanted so desperately to see her again…to see if he *felt* anything.

Chapter 4

On Saturday the Hotel Alex Johnson in downtown Rapid City accommodated the South Dakota Conservative Party's organizers, contributors, and supporters. The keynote speakers were none other than Senior Senator Petrice Caselli and his brother-in-law, Alex Martin III. By now Alex Martin was well on his way to becoming the next attorney general for the State of South Dakota, after burying his opponent in the polls. This appearance with Senator Caselli would only tip the scales even further in his favor.

Noah watched on his television set at home as the famous Senator Caselli gave one of his magnificent speeches and then introduced the ever-popular Alex Martin. While the crowd cheered and applauded, waiting for Alex to present himself, the camera followed Petrice off of the stage to where his wife and children waited with Alex...and *Alex's* wife and children. Noah watched the camera close in on Angel just long enough to capture the soft kiss Alex gave her lips right before he sprang to the stage and into the spotlight. She smiled tenderly into his eyes, and Noah felt a pain within himself he never imagined possible. Tears burned the backs of his eyes, but he couldn't turn away from the scene before him. There she stood, dressed in her favorite color, soft pink, and he remembered how beautiful she was the morning he picked her up from the hotel. She had worn a pink sweatshirt that day, and her long, soft curls were in a ponytail behind her shapely face. He closed his eyes and lost himself in the memory of one of her kisses, the scent on her hair, and the softness of her hands.

He slowly opened his eyes to see that Alex's smiling face had replaced hers on the screen before him, and he slowly shook his head. He'd *never* gotten over that woman, no matter how many times he had tried to convince himself that he had. Carrie had been a wonderful wife and mother; had she lived, she would have certainly erased Angel's memory forever. But Carrie had been gone for a long time, and the painful recollection of his short time with Angel had resurfaced even before he had realized she was married to Alex. There was so much unfinished business with Angel and so many unanswered questions.

With a heavy sigh, Noah turned off the television and got to his feet. He tried to shake off the old memories, but the heaviness in his heart made him ache. God's Spirit pressed upon him the treachery of what he had set up to happen tomorrow at church. *I shouldn't have set Alex up like that. If I honestly, truly loved her — and I do — I'd stop this nonsense. She probably had very good reasons for doing what she did all those years ago.*

But, like he had a thousand times in the past few months, Noah shook his head and forced away his righteous thoughts. He would go through with his plan, ask her his questions, and then leave her alone. *It's not going to bother her anyway. After the look she just gave Alex, it's pretty obvious she loves him. Probably always has.*

Who knows why she had her little "fling" with a sleazy biker. She went back to Alex, and now I just want to know why.

*****

Petrice gathered his family together that Sunday morning, along with his parents, and took them to the airport. They'd be stopping over in Sioux Falls, and then the Senator would continue on to New York. That left Alex and Tillie and their children alone. Alex suggested they try out a church, and Tillie agreed.

"My friend, Noah," Alex said as he drove Tillie's black Mercedes wagon north on Sheridan Lake Road. He stopped at the light on West Main and turned left at Camp Rapid as he finished, "His brother has been the pastor at this church for something like thirty years."

Tillie frowned with confusion as Alex's words touched off the memory of a forgotten conversation...*I have disappointed my brother since I was a little kid...You see, he's a preacher....*

"Noah's brother?" she asked. Old recollections and discarded memories began to blur before her. She slowly shook her head and looked out her window as Alex turned onto South Canyon Road. *There's NO WAY it could be the same Noah*, she thought. She remembered having a conversation with Tara shortly after the babies were born when she briefly suspected it was Noah who'd become friends with Alex. Noah had driven Alex to the hospital the night the twins were born. Her entire family, including Tara, met Noah and had been very taken with the man — especially Tillie's brother, Marquette. Tillie asked Tara if it was the same Noah she'd been acquainted with in 1975, and Tara had said it was not. Tillie hadn't thought of him again until just a few days ago, *when Ma`ma brought him up.*

Tillie shook her head again, willing away the suspicion. *Certainly Ma`ma would have said something, for they all knew what Noah looked like from the photographs I brought back.*

Her parents and Tara were the only ones Tillie had trusted with the secret, and she made them all promise to *never* tell her brothers or their wives.

Alex smiled as he pulled into the parking lot of a huge brick church and parked the car. "You'll really like Noah. He's a real down-to-earth guy." He glanced into the backseat at his children and said, "And you're really going to like his boys."

"Boys?" Laura wrinkled up her nose. "*Yuck.*"

Alex laughed at his little girl and touched the tip of her nose with his index finger. "I hope you'll *always* feel that way."

Tillie laughed, and they all got out of the car together. They paused after they'd closed their doors and hesitantly looked at one another.

"I'm scared," A.J. admitted in his very serious, little man voice. He reached for his father's hand.

"Me too," Laura whispered, reaching for Tillie's hand as they stared at the big, unfamiliar church before them.

Tillie took a deep breath and whispered, "This is weird." She looked up at the foreboding building before them and realized that she had never gone to church anywhere else but Christ the King.

"It's going to be okay," Alex assured them. He reached for Tillie's free hand and coaxed them all toward the building.

"I miss Nonna," Laura whispered, and Tillie was afraid the little girl might cry.

"I want Grandpa," A.J. said as he trudged dutifully along beside his father. He was going to be a little man about the whole thing, but he had misgivings as well.

"They had to get back," Tillie reminded them. "But they'll be out for a visit on your birthday."

Alex led them through the door, where they were engulfed into a vestibule of visiting people. They all held tightly to one another's hands as they entered. They were immediately approached by an elderly couple.

"Good morning," the tall, gray-haired gentleman said with a smile. "I'm Merle Nixon, and this is my wife, Doris." They offered their hands in greeting, first to Alex and Tillie and then to their small children.

"Noah told us to expect you," Mrs. Nixon said with a friendly expression. "You must be the Martins?"

"Yes," Alex answered.

"I saw you on television yesterday," Mrs. Nixon winked at Tillie. "You look lovely in pink."

"Thank you," Tillie replied with a gracious smile.

"We've got Sunday school upstairs for the little ones," Mr. Nixon said as he put his hand on Alex's shoulder. "Maybe you should take them up and get them acquainted with some of the other children. It'll make 'em feel more comfortable."

A.J. and Laura bristled at the suggestion. They reclaimed their tight grips on their parents' hands and frowned at the older gentlemen.

"They're a little shy," Tillie excused. "Maybe they should just stay with us for the first couple of times."

Mrs. Nixon nodded her head in agreement and smiled at Tillie, "And *you*, young lady, are really an answer to prayer."

Tillie smiled politely but looked confused. "How so?"

"Oh, my goodness," Mrs. Nixon began with a laugh. "We have a Russian missionary coming to visit us in October, and we've been praying for an interpreter."

"Really?" Tillie smiled. "How did you know I speak Russian?"

"Noah told us," Mrs. Nixon informed. "In fact, our missions coordinator can hardly *wait* to meet you." She pointed across the lobby and at a closed door. "She's in there. I told her I'd send you her way if you had the time."

Tillie was surprised at how forward Mrs. Nixon seemed to be. "If I have time, I'll stop in and see her," she agreed.

Alex could tell they were going to have a difficult time getting away from Mrs. Nixon, so he delicately took a few steps toward the lobby. "Well, it was nice visiting with you both. Maybe we'll see you after church."

"Yes, I hope so!" Mrs. Nixon exclaimed.

Thankfully another family entered the church, and Mr. and Mrs. Nixon swooped upon them with the same enthusiasm they'd shown the Martins.

"Wow," Alex whispered into Tillie's ear, "I didn't think we'd ever get away from her!"

Tillie giggled and shook her head. "Me neither, and I'm definitely going to have to brush up on my Russian."

A very tall lady with a colorful flag began to march through the lobby, followed by several children about the same age as A.J. and Laura. The children were clapping their hands and singing a song the Martins recognized from their church back home.

"They must be going to Sunday school," Laura whispered to her brother as she looked curiously into the little crowd of children.

A.J. only frowned. He wasn't about to go anywhere without his father today, and he tightened his grip around Alex's big hand.

Alex crouched low and looked into the sweet faces of his children. "Come on, guys. I'll go up with you for a few minutes, and Mommy can go talk to this lady about Russia. If the class is totally lame, I'll get you out of there."

A.J. smiled at his father's choice of words and put his hand on one of Alex's broad shoulders. "Daddy, they're *different*."

"Of course they're different," Alex agreed with a smile. "But you can't just stop going to Sunday school because we moved."

"And besides," Laura interrupted with a frown for her brother, "I *like* Sunday school and I want to go." She looked tauntingly at A.J. and whispered, "*Are you chicken?*"

"Young lady," Alex scolded under his breath, "don't talk to your brother like that."

"I'm not a chicken," A.J. retorted, and he gave Laura a shove with his shoulder.

"All right, that's enough," Alex demanded in his "father" voice, wondering if the two would get into it right there in the lobby of the church.

Tillie nearly laughed. It was as if her precious twins were about to come to blows over the Sunday school issue. She bent over and whispered, "Go with Daddy for a few minutes. It'll be fun to meet some new kids."

Laura nodded and took a step away from them, hoping her angry brother would follow. "Come on, A.J.," she coaxed.

Alex stood up and gently took a hand of each child. He looked into Tillie's pretty eyes and asked, "Will you be okay?"

Tillie nodded and answered as she smiled into the eyes of her babies, "You two be good."

"Yes, Mommy," they said in unison, and it made them both giggle.

Alex led them away, catching up to the small group following the colorful flag. They fell in line and marched up some steps. Tillie smiled and shook her head, looking toward the door where she hoped to find the missions coordinator.

She headed slowly in that direction thinking, *all these years I've known how to speak Russian and have never used it once. Maybe that's why God moved us to Rapid City.*

As Noah came into the lobby, he saw her heading in the direction of the missions coordinator's office. He stopped to stand still and just watch her for a moment. He was only a few short steps away from Angel! Her hair was down today, perhaps a little shorter in length than she used to wear it, her soft curls resting upon her slender shoulders. She was wearing a white, gauze summer dress that fit her feminine body perfectly, setting off the beautiful darkness of her soft skin. She walked with the same elegant gait he'd watched her move with eleven years ago. She gracefully strolled toward the door, reached for the knob with one of the delicate, pretty hands he remembered, and found it locked. She turned around and softly frowned with obvious confusion, and that's when her black eyes found him. They were just a few yards apart, and she stared intently into his eyes. Her mouth dropped open with a soft gasp, her expression beyond surprise.

Noah took the few steps to close the gap between them. He extended his hand as if in greeting, and she hesitantly did the same, placing her hand into his. As he looked into her eyes he noticed she still carried with her the same soft fragrance she had back then.

"Angel? Is it you?"

Tillie's mouth hung open as she looked into the eyes of the man who'd crushed her spirit when she was only seventeen years old. His eyes were lined with age and weather now, and his soft, sandy hair had grayed slightly at the temples. His skin was tan, probably from working outside so much, and his chest and his arms were fleshed out with the muscles of his hard labor. Even though his appearance had changed remarkably, the expression in his beautiful eyes had not. She would have recognized Noah anywhere.

"Noah," she whispered.

"Hi, Angel," he said, fighting the urge to take her into his arms and tell her all was forgiven — that he still loved her and everything was going to be just fine now.

Tillie's expression went quickly from surprise to *intense* anger. She yanked her hand from his and took a step backward.

"What are *you* doing here?" she whispered with a scowl.

Noah was surprised. *Is she mad?* "Listen," he said, managing the most friendly expression and tone he could, "I'm just as surprised as you are."

Tillie shook her head and frowned at Noah, "Please *don't* tell me you're Alex's friend."

Noah smiled and began to nod his head. "I guess I always suspected he'd married you, but I was really surprised when —" He stopped. He'd nearly told on himself. He finished with, "I was really surprised to see you here."

Tillie was surprised at the anger so easily pouring out of her heart, and she barked, "Do you have any idea what you did to me?"

Now it was Noah's turn to look confused. He shook his head. "What are you talking about? I'm the one that got left at the altar, while you went home and hooked up with a Harvard suit. Guess I wasn't good enough for you."

"Oh, brother," Tillie rolled her eyes and fought the urge to slap his face. "You're nothing better than a blackguard, and I have no idea what Alex ever saw in you."

"A blackguard?" Noah frowned. "*You're* the one who didn't keep your promise. The least you could have done was call and tell me you were dumping me."

"Oh, man," Tillie said with a shake of her head. "I *did* keep my promise, and I came to Maggie's that night —" She swallowed hard to fight her tears, surprised at how much the old, forgotten memory still hurt.

"Then why didn't *I* see you there?" Noah frowned and sarcastically added, "Maggie doesn't have a very big place."

"Because you were too busy with whoever was crawling all over you that night," Tillie retorted. She narrowed her eyes, stomped one foot, and aggressively leaned toward him. "I thought maybe her tongue was stuck in your throat!"

Noah took a reflexive step backward. This wasn't the sentimental trip down memory lane he'd fantasized about. He stood in silent amazement, shaking his head and trying to find his voice. He'd always wanted to know what had happened and, now that he did, was horrified to realize it had been just a misunderstanding. He'd remembered that night vividly for the last eleven years. Carrie had come into Maggie's so terribly drunk, and Roy was trying to get her to come home. That kiss had been Carrie's transaction entirely. He'd had nothing to do with it.

"Angel, that wasn't what it looked like —"

"Oh, bull," Tillie retorted. "And if you call me 'Angel' one more time, I'll slap your face."

"Well, that's the name you gave me," Noah frowned. "And you *did* misunderstand the situation. How could you even *think* I'd do something like that to you? You should have at least had the decency to ask me about it."

"I was a child and you *knew* it! I was scared and hurt. Do you have any idea what it felt like to see you with someone else?" She paused only for a moment to collect her composure, and then she continued, "You can't imagine the *hell* I went through when I came back. That was the *worst* year of my life."

"Oh, come on," Noah said as he rolled his eyes. "You got over me the minute you left town. I know you took up with Alex *immediately* because all he talked about was his *dearest friend*, but I was so *miserable* I didn't even put two and two together."

Tillie shook her head. "You think you know *everything* —" She stopped suddenly and looked into his eyes. "Was it *you* that brought Alex to the hospital that night?" Noah nodded his head in an affirmative answer. Tillie was horrified, and she belligerently pressed, "Did you know *then?*"

Noah shook his head. "I told you, I didn't have any idea."

Tillie took a breath and tried to relax her frown. She didn't recall ever being this angry in her life, except for maybe the time Patty canceled his trip to her graduation.

"Tillie, I'm sorry for whatever pain I've caused you, but please believe me. There just wasn't anybody else after you came along." He forced himself to smile. "You changed my life, you know."

Tillie swallowed hard as she frowned into his sincere, beautiful eyes, wondering why God had allowed such a strange twist of events. She slowly began to nod her head and offered, "Let's just forget about it."

"Sure. No problem…are you gonna tell Alex?"

"Heavens no! He thinks you walk on water. I'm not going to throw some monkey wrench into *that* —"

"I see you've already met Noah," Alex's happy voice boomed out of nowhere, and they both looked into his direction. He smiled as he strode toward them, offering his hand in greeting to Noah.

Tillie forced her angry frown away, took a breath, and pretended like everything was fine. Thankfully she'd had years of practice smiling on cue when she made appearances with her famous brother.

"I almost didn't recognize you, Noah," Alex said with a smile, and he looked at Tillie. "He used to have this *terrible* beard." He returned his gaze back to Noah and asked, "When did you get rid of it?"

"Oh, just a couple of days ago." Noah rubbed his chin. "I was just sick of it."

"See," Alex said, as he looked from Noah to Tillie and then back to Noah, "I *really do* have a wife." He looked at Tillie. "Noah used to tease me about not *really* having a wife because he never had the opportunity to meet you."

Noah forced himself to smile and nod his head.

"Oh, hey," Alex said excitedly, "isn't that Melinda?"

Noah and Tillie both turned their eyes in the direction that Alex was looking to see a very pretty lady walking toward them. She looked about Noah's age with straight, raven-black hair and round, brown eyes.

Noah forced himself to wave her over, *because I gotta make it look good in front of Angel…or Tillie…or whatever.* Melinda smiled sweetly into Noah's eyes as she looked from Alex to Tillie.

"Of course you know Alex," Noah began the awkward introduction, and Melinda and Alex politely nodded at one another. Noah took a breath and said, "This is Alex's wife, Tillie Martin. Tillie, this is Melinda Smalley."

"How do you do?" Tillie smiled politely as she extended her hand toward Melinda, who gave it a gentle shake.

"Fine, thanks," Melinda replied.

"Melinda works for me," Noah informed.

Alex laughed and gave Noah a sly wink. "I heard you guys were becoming something of an item."

Melinda giggled and shyly looked at her feet. At that moment, Tillie felt the strangest thing happen inside of her heart. She didn't think she was feeling jealousy, but she wasn't exactly thrilled at the situation either. She softly snorted and shook her head...*always was the ladies' man.*

"Hey, our class is starting," Melinda said as she gave Noah another sweet glance and took him by the hand. She looked at Tillie and Alex. "We gotta go. See you later." And then, without any kind of resistance from Noah, Melinda led him away from where the Martins stood.

Alex chuckled. "She's got him wrapped around her finger."

Joshua watched Noah's fidgeting from the pulpit that day. He saw him shifting his position and turning his eyes somewhere else, making Melinda increasingly uncomfortable. Joshua wanted to stop church right then and there, pull Noah from the pew by the ear, and drag him outside to find out what on earth was going on.

When the sermon ended and Joshua had given the benediction, he noticed the new couple seated just a few rows in front of Noah and Melinda. Joshua suddenly realized *that* was where Noah's eyes had been for the majority of the sermon. After just a couple of seconds, Joshua recognized Alex, and then he glanced at the attractive woman holding his hand. *Must be his wife,* Joshua thought.

Joshua hurried into the parking lot. He caught up to Noah and Melinda as they helped the boys into the pickup. "Hey, Noah," Joshua called as he trotted toward Noah's truck.

Noah looked up and saw Joshua stopping just short of the truck. He left Melinda with the boys and strolled toward his brother, wondering if Mona had spilled the beans. The meeting with Angel this morning had been bad enough, and he certainly didn't want to rehash everything with Joshua. Especially *not* in front of Melinda.

"What do you need, Josh?" Noah asked with a fake smile.

Joshua's brown eyes frowned, and he lowered his voice so Melinda would not hear him. "I saw Alex Martin and his wife in church this morning." He hesitated as he looked into Noah's eyes, which were unusually sorrowful today, and asked, "Did I misunderstand something, or were you looking at his wife?"

"I wasn't," Noah said with a slow shake of his head, turning his eyes away from Joshua.

"You were too," Joshua accused in an insistent whisper. "I'm not blind, Noah. She's beautiful, but that's just not like you to be so lewd."

Noah shook his head and frowned. "Did you actually *see* me looking at her, Josh, or did somebody *say* this to you?"

"Noah," Joshua scowled, "I'm the preacher. I see *everything* from where I stand."

"Josh," Noah began. He took a deep breath and closed his eyes for a moment, trying to find the words for an explanation. Obviously, Mona had *not* told him. He opened his eyes and looked at his brother's expression. He certainly wasn't going to tell on himself, but he had to tell Joshua something, because he was bound to figure it out sooner or later.

"Do you remember Angel?" Noah whispered. Joshua nodded and so Noah continued, "She's married to Alex."

"Alex's wife is Angel?" Joshua gasped in a whisper.

Noah nodded and added, "They moved here about a week ago."

Joshua put his hand on Noah's shoulder and gave it a hard grip. "Are you okay, Noah?"

Noah slowly shook his head, feeling some relief at having told his brother.

"Man, I *thought* she looked familiar," Joshua whispered. He shook his head and looked into Noah's eyes with concern. "Hadn't you ever met her before?"

Noah shook his head. "Today was the first time I've spoken with her since she ditched me."

"Did she have an explanation for that?"

"Yep. It was all a big misunderstanding. Apparently she walked in on a situation involving Carrie and thought I'd gotten another girlfriend or something. I don't know. I'm just sick about it, Josh."

"Does Alex know?" Joshua asked.

"Nope."

"Did she know that you and Alex were friends?"

Noah shook his head. "She says she didn't have a clue."

Joshua wrapped his arms around Noah and whispered, "I'm so sorry for you, Noah. I can't imagine how hard this must be."

Noah had to fight to keep his composure. He wanted to just lay his head against Joshua's shoulder and bawl like he had when he was a little kid. Instead, he "sucked it up like a man" and gave Joshua a sad smile. "I gotta get rid of Melinda —" He rolled his eyes. " I mean, I gotta get Melinda home so I can feed the boys some lunch."

"Do you guys wanna come over and be with me and Mona today?"

"No, I just wanna be with my kids and do some thinking."

"Well, if you need anybody to talk to," Joshua offered, "you know I'm always here for you."

Noah nodded and started to back away. "Thanks, Josh."

Joshua watched Noah walk back to his truck where Melinda and the boys waited, and he sadly shook his head. Of all the crummy things that had happened to Noah over the years, having to see his Angel with another man had to have been the worst yet. And even though he was a minister of God's Word, Joshua found himself wondering how the Lord could possibly work *this* out for good.

*****

Later that afternoon, Tillie Martin brought her sketch pad and a pencil out onto her stone patio facing the creek. She positioned herself so she could watch A.J. and Laura attempt to teach their father how to bait a hook and fish. He was so tall and they were so small. It warmed her heart just watching them interact. A.J. held up a worm for his sister's inspection, and she simply nodded, indicating it was okay to bait her hook. A.J. expertly placed it onto the sharp hook at the end of her line, just as his grandfather had taught him. Laura and Alex both grimaced, and Tillie laughed and began to sketch the three of them.

While she sketched, her mind began to wander. Tara had *deliberately* lied to her the day she had asked about Noah, *but why?* This horrible surprise could have been avoided had she just been truthful with Tillie when asked about the man. Tillie shook her head. All the warning signs had been there for years. For instance, Marquette's fascination with Noah and their commonality of service in Vietnam. Tillie had ignored it because of what Tara had told her. And she couldn't even call Tara and let her have it because she was running around in the Middle East somewhere.

Tillie sighed and continued to sketch. *And Papa and Ma`ma kept it from me too. No wonder Ma`ma brought it up out of the clear blue the other day. No wonder. Why in the world did they all keep this from me? Do they believe my heart to be so fickle I couldn't handle it?*

Tillie looked up from her sketch and watched Alex with their children for a moment. She smiled and shook her head. She and Alex shared a special bond *no one* could possibly ever interfere with. Even *if* Noah was telling the truth, and Tillie suspected he was *not*, it wouldn't matter. God had chosen Alex for Tillie's lifelong partner. They had vowed to love one another forever. There was no going back now; and, even if she could, she wouldn't.

Chapter 5

Noah's housekeeper and part time nanny, Vera, came over early so Noah could get several things out of the way at work. He had to check on a building site, finish several equipment orders, and meet with an inspector before noon. The rest of his day would be taken up with the boys. They had to register for school, which would begin after the Labor Day weekend.

After he'd checked on the site and met with the inspector, Noah hurried over to his office to get the equipment orders together. Of course Melinda was already there, waiting with her plastic smile behind her desk. She had expertly organized his day for him so it would go smoothly.

"Good morning," she said with a smile. She noticed his downcast expression and wondered what had happened. She noticed, too, how quiet and uncomfortable he was at church the day before, though she hadn't been able to figure out why.

"Hi, Melinda," Noah said with a tired smile, and he reached for his messages. "Anybody important call?"

"Mr. Martin. He needs you to call him right away." Noah briefly acknowledged her answer as he looked through the rest of his messages. Melinda frowned. "What's wrong, Noah?"

Noah shrugged and shook his head. "Oh, nothing really. Just got a lot on my mind."

"Did that inspector give you a hard time?"

Noah forced himself to smile. "Don't they always?"

Melinda agreed with a nod. "Those equipment orders are on your desk. Oh, and Jake just called."

Noah's mood seemed to lighten a little, and he looked curiously at Melinda. "What's the little guy want?"

"He wants to know if he still has to register for school this afternoon."

Noah half-smiled. "He's been trying to figure out a way to get out of it for months now. Anything else?"

"No," Melinda answered.

"I'm gonna finish those orders, and then I'll probably be with the boys for the rest of the day," Noah said as he slowly walked toward his office. Out of the corner of his eye he noticed Harv sidling up to Melinda's desk. He took a deep breath and prayed, *Please, Lord, maybe Harv can take her off my hands…he's such a great guy.*

"Good morning, Miss Melinda," Harv greeted her.

Harv's formal greeting made Melinda clench her teeth. Ben Simmons was the one who'd insisted on the "Miss Melinda" title, and she *hated* it.

Melinda sighed disgustedly. "What do you want, Harv?"

Harv put on his best smile and took a deep breath. "Listen, I know you're dating Noah, but I was wondering if you'd —"

"No way, Harv. And *don't* ask me again."

"But I understand you, Miss Melinda," Harv pleaded. "I understand your ambitions and your needs —"

"If you understood those things you wouldn't be standing there begging me for a date," she scowled.

Harv took a breath and was about to speak when Melinda snapped her fingers and shook her index finger under his nose.

"Just shut up, Harv," she commanded. "Get out of my hair. I've got work to do."

Harv smiled and backed away. He raised his eyebrow and whispered, "Someday you'll change your mind."

Noah dialed Alex's office. *It's strange not having to dial long distance now,* he thought.

"Martin, Martin & Dale," Lori's friendly voice answered. She'd faithfully been in that position since Noah could remember.

"It's Noah," he said with a smile. "Is Alex around?"

"Hi, Noah. Hold on a second."

Noah waited for just a moment, and Alex picked up. "Hi, Noah. Thanks for calling me back."

"What's going on?" Noah asked as he slowly thumbed through the rest of his messages.

"I'm thinking about going over to Pierre today, and I was wondering if you or Melinda had heard from McDarren. Shondra and I don't have anything, and he won't answer our messages."

Noah shook his head, "The Joker's hard to nail down. He hasn't called us." "The Joker" was Noah's nickname for Scott McDarren, who was probably the wealthiest man in America. McDarren was eccentric and was always backing out on deals. "What's going on in Pierre?"

"Cattle dispute," Alex answered. "Tillie's brother called us this morning. It's for one of his old classmates, but I told him I had to see if you and McDarren had any irons in the fire before I could leave."

Noah shook his head and double checked the messages Melinda had given him. "I haven't heard a thing from that guy, and I'm just about ready to dump him. I'm sick and tired of the way he does business. Besides, we don't *need* the work."

"Just hang in there, Noah," Alex encouraged. "We'll get something hammered out with the guy." He took a breath and said, "I gotta go. I've got about a million things to look up before I try to tackle this cattle dispute."

"Well good luck," Noah said with a quiet sigh, and that's when Alex heard the strange tone in Noah's voice.

"Everything okay, Noah?"

"Fine. Why?"

"You sound a little down today."

"I'm great, Alex," Noah said, trying to make himself sound happy. "I've just got a bunch of stuff to get done this morning, and I have to register my kids for school this afternoon."

"Us, too. Tillie was talking to me about that before I left this morning."

Noah frowned curiously. "What school are they going into?"

"Pinedale. How 'bout yours?"

Noah coughed. "The same." Good grief. He was going to have to face her again today at registration. Hopefully she wouldn't be as hostile as she had been the day before. That had been about too much for his heart to take.

"Well, have a good day, Noah."

"You too," Noah said, and they hung up.

Noah sighed, shook his head, and rubbed his chin. This thing with Angel was quickly turning into a nightmare *and I'm the one who set the whole thing into motion.* He rolled his eyes and shook his head. *It's bad enough having to hear Alex talk about her, let alone having to face her and pretend...and I know she didn't believe me yesterday.*

A soft knock on his office door drew Noah away from his thoughts. He looked up and was surprised to see Mona letting herself in. She gave him a small smile, closed the door, and took a seat in one of the old chairs in front of his desk.

"Hi, Mona."

"Hi, Noah. Do ya got a minute?"

"Got lotsa minutes for you, Mona." Noah tried to smile at his sister-in-law, but she saw the sadness behind his eyes this morning.

"I saw her yesterday," she whispered. "She's lovely, Noah."

"You sound surprised."

"I guess I didn't expect — what I mean —" Mona swallowed and searched for words. "I guess — I thought —"

"It was all in my head?" Noah finished.

Mona nodded.

Noah shook his head and sighed. "Mona, I'm in *big* trouble."

"Josh told me about why she didn't come back. I'm just sick about it, Noah, but you should tell Josh what you did to her husband. You know, just so he knows in case this thing goes to pieces on you."

"What do you mean?" Noah frowned. "She *hates* me Mona." He swallowed hard and shook his head "My Angel, that I have *loved* and searched for, *hates* me. I thought she was gonna kill me right there in the church." He shook his head again as he remembered the angry flash in her black eyes. "I thought maybe it was going to be different, like..." he shrugged, "friendlier. I thought she'd at least be *happy* to see me after all these years." He looked hopefully into Mona's eyes. "After all that we shared, how could she still be so angry with me?"

Mona shook her head and looked at her brother-in-law. He had written his own rules since he was a little boy, and they had all backfired on him this time. He had always done what he wanted, felt what he wanted, and if it was what someone else wanted, he just changed things so that it would work for him. Now he was really in a fix.

"And now that you've seen her," Mona asked, "what are you feeling?"

Noah's frown relaxed into a small smile as he looked into Mona's eyes. "Part of it makes me want to smile, Mona. Knowing that she *did* come back after all just about thrills me to death."

Mona swallowed and whispered, "And what about Melinda?"

Noah sighed heavily, got out of his chair, and walked across the small office to the window where he whispered, "I really don't know why I got into this thing with Melinda. She's not even nice to me, and I've never really liked her...neither does anybody else around here, except for poor ol' Harv." He turned around and looked at Mona. "I want out. I don't wanna make another mistake and get married again just because I'm lonely."

Mona stood suddenly. Her face twisted into an angry frown as she snapped, "I thought you *loved* Carrie."

"I did, but that was a mistake and you know it."

"Does that make Ty and Jake mistakes too?" Mona retorted. She tried to swallow away some of her tears as she said, "What happened with Carrie was *amazing*."

"You know what, Mona?" Noah was suddenly angry and tired of protecting Carrie and the mysterious circumstances surrounding her death. "There's a lot you don't know about that situation —"

"I know that she *loved* you," Mona interrupted. "And she gave you two beautiful sons who think the world of you."

Noah swore, his voice thundering through the office. In his life, he had *never* raised his voice to Mona, nor had he ever taken the Lord's name in vain, and it made Mona take a hesitant step back. "Carrie died in Custer State Park," he shouted. He scowled and pointed his finger at her, "Did you know *that?*"

Mona shook her head and swallowed. Noah had never told them.

"Do you have any idea *why* she was in Custer State Park?" Noah yelled, and Mona shook her head again. "Well neither do I, Mona, but she'd been going down there twice a month for about six months and never *mentioned* one of the trips to me. Every time she called you to sit with Ty and told you she was running errands, she was going to Custer. And that's not even the half of it. She cashed out a quarter of a million dollars in stock about six months before her death and who knows what she did with the money, because I never saw it again, and I never had the chance to ask her about it!" Noah caught his breath, swallowed, and stared at Mona, regretting what he'd just done. He had never intended to tell anyone about Carrie's mysterious death. Even Alex did not know.

Mona looked at the floor for a minute and then she stepped closer to Noah and looked into his eyes. She scowled and abruptly slapped his face. "Don't you *ever* take the Lord's name in vain again. You're the one that's deceived your best friend and made a mess for yourself."

"Mona, I know what I'm doing."

"I've heard *that* before," Mona snapped. She turned on her heal and left the office, slamming the door loudly behind her.

From her desk, Melinda, along with the entire office staff, heard the angry shouting, though none of them could make out any of the words. They all looked the other way when Mona tearfully stomped out.

Melinda got to her feet and looked at Mona with concern as she passed by her desk. "Are you okay, Mona?" *What in the world happened in there?* She thought. *It's not at all like Noah to shout.*

Mona sadly shook her head and kept walking until she reached the door and left the office without responding to Melinda.

Melinda quickly walked to Noah's office and reached for the knob to let herself in, but he had locked it. She frowned curiously and made her way back to her own desk. *This is getting really weird....*

*****

After Tillie had fed her children lunch, she sent them upstairs to shower and change their dirty clothes. They had played in the muddiest part of the shallow creek all morning and were filthy from head to toe.

"And you need to hurry," she instructed as they meandered up the stairs. "We have to register for school in about two hours."

Laura happily announced, "I'm gonna wear my new blue dress with the matching shoes."

But A.J. sighed as he drug himself along behind her. "I don't wanna go. We don't have any friends here."

"Come on, A.J.," Laura encouraged her brother with a smile as she reached for his hand. "I'll give you one of my real silver dimes that Grandpa gave me if you go."

A.J.'s little black eyes seemed to light up at the offer. "Really?"

Laura's curly head bobbed yes. "And we'll be able to make lots of friends once they all find out that our dad is gonna be the general."

Tillie covered her mouth and tried not laugh at the precious conversation happening between her two children. *The general? That's funny.* She heard them chatting all the way up the stairs, until they were in the hallway and she couldn't hear them anymore. She sighed with a frown and reached for the telephone.

On the counter in Guiseppi and Rosa's kitchen, the phone was ringing and ringing, while the two of them stood beside it and looked at each other with terrified expressions.

"Do you suppose it is her?" Guiseppi whispered.

Rosa took a nervous breath. "Let the machine answer it, Guiseppi. I still do not know what we will say."

"So you think she has discovered him already?"

Rosa shrugged and bit her lower lip. "I do not know. We should not have allowed this secret to go so far."

Rosa was interrupted when the answering machine picked up and they heard their daughter's voice begin to speak. "Hi, Papa. Hi, Ma`ma. I know you're probably there, so I'll just let you know that I know." Tillie paused and sighed into the phone as she continued, "He's still the blackguard he always was. He tried to come up with some lame excuse for what he did. Says I misunderstood the situation. It was all I could do not to scratch his eyes out. No wonder Ma`ma wanted to talk about him the other day. Why didn't you just tell me, Ma`ma?" She paused again and went on, "Well, I gotta go. I have to take the kids to school for registration. I love you guys. Bye." The line went dead, and Rosa and Guiseppi looked at each other.

Guiseppi rubbed his bald head. "Well, she does not sound *too* terribly upset."

Rosa sighed and shook her head. "Of course not, Guiseppi, she is trying to get us to call her back. And that happened a whole lot quicker than I thought it would."

"Noah was *never* a blackguard," Guiseppi defended.

Rosa shook her head and reached for Guiseppi's hand. "At least now they know and we do not have to hide it from them any longer."

After his horrible confrontation with Mona, Noah waited until he was sure that most of the staff had left for lunch. He wasn't in the mood to talk to anybody, and he certainly wasn't up for another one of Melinda's invitations for dinner or a barbecue or whatever else she had up her sleeve.

He cracked open his office door and peeked out. Melinda's desk was empty, along with most of the other desks in the outer office. He hurried out, dropped the equipment orders on Melinda's desk, and left the building with a sigh of relief.

Vera had already fed the boys by the time he arrived home, and they were waiting anxiously for their father to take them over to the school.

"I heard you called me this morning," Noah said to Jake as he waited patiently for his boys to get up into his pickup.

44

"I heard you didn't call me back," Jake muttered as he strapped his seat belt on without a look at his father.

Noah swallowed his laugh and slid into the pickup beside Ty. He leaned close to his oldest son's ear and whispered with a smile, "Stuck in the middle again."

"Yep," Ty grinned. "But I *like* to sit by you, Dad."

"Me too," Noah agreed.

Jake just rolled his eyes and stared out the windshield.

Noah started the truck and put it into gear. *Well, here goes nothing. Hopefully she won't rip me apart. 'Course, whatever's left over belongs to Mona, who's gonna be more than willing to finish the job.* Noah grimaced. *I didn't know I could make women this mad.*

*****

Burt put a plate of stromboli down in front of Guiseppi. "Try this and see what you think…." He paused to snicker. "Doria doesn't know, but I managed to steal the recipe from his book."

"That was devilish of you, my friend," Guiseppi muttered as he put a forkful into his mouth. He raised his eyebrows as he tasted the delicious concoction. "Wonderful!"

Burt nodded and took a seat at the familiar table he often shared with Guiseppi in the back office of Angelo's II. "So she knows. Big deal. That changes nothing."

"Except that she knows I have lied to her," Guiseppi argued through a mouthful of stromboli. "Has Ginger ever caught you in a lie?"

Burt shook his head.

Guiseppi stuffed another forkful into his mouth. "And I know that Alex is out of town this day."

Burt raised his eyebrows. "Already?"

Guiseppi nodded. "My Petrice took his plane to Rapid City this morning so they could go to Pierre together for one of his old classmates."

"Yikes," Burt whispered.

"I am deeply grieved about this thing that I have done," Guiseppi moaned. "I just cannot see how things may be fixed."

Pinedale Elementary lay situated on Chicago Street behind the church on South Canyon Road. Tillie found it easily with the map the Welcome Wagon lady had given her. The school was a small, one-story brick building set into the safe confines of old, swaying pine trees. Tillie smiled when she saw it. Perhaps she'd have to do a sketch.

Children and parents bustled in and out of the school. Some little ones cried and clung to their mothers. Tillie had each of her children by the hand as they walked toward the building.

"Just think," she encouraged, "I had to start my first day of school all by myself, but you guys will have your best buddy right there with you."

"Come on, Mommy," A.J. said seriously, "What about Miss Ginger?"

"Well, she was really sad about leaving her mommy that day and so we had kind of a little fight."

"Me and A.J. *never* fight," Laura proclaimed, and A.J. nodded in agreement.

Tillie looked at her children with surprise and nearly laughed.

"A.J.! A.J.!" A little voice called out from somewhere, and Tillie's little boy turned his head to look for whoever was calling his name.

A sandy-haired, blue-eyed boy dashed up, breathing heavily with excitement, and threw his arms around A.J. "Boy, am I glad to see you here!" he exclaimed.

"Me too!" A.J. said. He smiled and looked up at his mother. "Mommy, he's from Sunday school. This is Jake." Tillie remembered A.J. coming home from church the day before and telling her all about Jake from Sunday school class. Jake wanted to be a pitcher, like his older brother, which made A.J. very happy, because he was a catcher and thought maybe they could play sometimes.

"Well, hello, Jake." Tillie smiled into the little boy's dancing blue eyes and her heart sank. *Noah's child. He looks just like you.*

When Noah saw her looking at his son, he felt the strangest pain in his heart. She would have been Jake's mother if everything had worked out. She was still the most beautiful woman in the world, and he had known a lot of women. Her pretty curls were back in a ponytail today, and she was wearing a pale yellow, sleeveless dress that showed off the dark skin on her shoulders. Noah wondered if Alex knew just how perfect his life was and if he truly appreciated it the way Noah would have.

"Hi, Tillie," he greeted politely.

Tillie looked from Jake to Noah and got that "well it figures" look on her face. She didn't frown, but she didn't smile when she said, "Let me guess. Mrs. Castleman's room, number 104?"

Noah smiled faintly.

"Great," Tillie muttered as she led her children to the building. Jake sidled up next to A.J. and walked along with him.

"So these are the twins," Noah said. *Might as well strike up some conversation, seeing as how they'll be sharing the same kindergarten class.*

"I'm Laura," she said as she smiled into Noah's eyes. He couldn't believe the resemblance to her mother. Black, curly hair all over her head and the most beautiful sparkling eyes.

"Nice to meet you, Laura," Noah said as they walked along. "This is my other son, Ty."

"I'm in fourth grade," Ty said with a proud smile. Tillie couldn't help but notice his wonderfully red hair, and she smiled back at him.

"Mommy's friend, Miss Ginger, has red hair like you," Laura said with a smile.

Noah remembered the red-headed friend that was with Tillie when he asked her out on their first date. He mentally slapped himself then. He forced away the reminiscent thoughts and walked along in silence until they reached the doorway of the school.

"Well, I gotta go to Miss Sheldon's class," Ty said. "Do you wanna walk down there with me?"

Noah acknowledged his son's request and said, "Come on, Jake, let's take your brother over to his class and then we can catch up to A.J."

"No," Jake protested and shook his head. "I wanna go with A.J." The little boy paused and looked at Tillie. "Daddy, A.J.'s got a mommy, and she can watch me until you're done with Ty."

Tillie's heart broke for the child. She knew his mother had long passed away and that he had been raised by the wretched blackguard walking along with them. "It's okay," she offered, without even a glance at Noah. "You can catch up to us when you're finished with Ty."

"Okay, thanks," Noah said, and he and Ty started down to the opposite end of the hall, while Tillie took her children and Jake to Mrs. Castleman's room.

Tillie double-checked the registration list to be sure that Mrs. Castleman had all of the necessary numbers and birth dates that went along with registration. There was a mistake on Jake's birthday, and Tillie noticed it right away.

"Are you certain of this?" Mrs. Castleman asked.

"I'm positive of the date," Tillie answered dryly. "I remember the day as clear as a bell." Carrie was very overdue, and Jake's birth had been exactly two weeks after Christmas. *Funny, I've known practically everything about this man and his children, except that he was the blackguard who broke my heart in 1975.*

"Okay then," a very friendly Mrs. Castleman acknowledged. She jotted down the note and cleared her voice. She looked at the parents who were still close to their children. "Ladies and gentlemen," the sweet teacher said loudly, "could I please have your attention. I would like to have just fifteen or twenty minutes alone with my new class and am asking that all parents please wait outside."

Tillie nearly gulped. *Leave them alone?* That part wasn't supposed to happen until next week. While the other parents obediently shuffled toward the classroom door, Tillie's feet stood frozen near where A.J. and Laura visited with Jake.

"I put your name on your desk," Mrs. Castleman said. "If you do not know how to spell your name yet, I will help you find it."

"I can spell my name," Laura beamed. She turned from the little group and began checking the big tags on the top of the desks.

Jake made a "tsk" noise, shook his head, and rolled his eyes. "That's a cinch," he said. "I can spell 'dad' and 'dog' and 'truck' and me and Ty's names too." He started for the desks, with A.J. beside him.

"Wow," A.J. said as he walked beside his new buddy. "You can spell lots of stuff."

Tillie had to swallow away her tears as she watched her little ones search for their names and visit with some of the other children.

"Mrs. Martin," Mrs. Castleman said as she gently placed her hand on Tillie's shoulder. "Please wait outside. It's good for the class to get just a little preview of what school will be like when you're not here."

Tillie submitted with reluctance to the teacher's wishes and made her way to the empty hallway. She paused by the glass door…*as long as they can't see me, it shouldn't hurt anything.*

She positioned herself in such a way that the class couldn't see her but she could watch A.J. and Laura. They smiled and peeked into their empty desks, touching the letters on the name tags, and talking quietly with each other. They had been seated side by side, and they looked so little in those desks that it made Tillie lose most of her emotional control. Tears accidentally slipped from her eyes.

Noah had finished with Ty and was slowly making his way down the hall toward Mrs. Castleman's room. As he got closer, he saw Tillie watching through the glass in the door and had to smile. He had done the same thing when it was time for Ty's kindergarten registration.

Tillie heard the footsteps of boots behind her and turned to see Noah approaching. He saw her tears and offered his handkerchief when he was close enough.

"Thanks," she whispered as she took his handkerchief, turned away from him, and dabbed her tears while she continued to watch her babies.

"I cried on Ty's first day," Noah whispered. He peeked over her head and into the room. He found Jake's little face and smiled. "Jake didn't want to come today."

"Neither did A.J.," Tillie whispered. She caught the faintest scent of Old Spice on the handkerchief, suddenly realizing he was way too close to her. She moved a few feet into the hall and allowed him enough room to watch through the glass in the classroom door.

Noah eagerly moved into the space she'd vacated and watched his son for a moment. Tillie saw him swallow very hard and shake his head. "I can't believe he's already starting school," he whispered. "He sure doesn't seem old enough."

Tillie was surprised at the tenderness in Noah's eyes and the sweetness in his tone as he watched his son. He certainly wasn't acting like a blackguard. Wouldn't a blackguard have sent the housekeeper over with the kids so he could have some "quality time" with his girlfriend?

Noah smiled as he looked into the room and whispered, "Jake was so excited to meet A.J. yesterday." He looked at Tillie. "A.J. must love baseball as much as Jake does."

Tillie nodded her head. A.J. was obsessed with baseball.

Noah turned his eyes back into the classroom and sighed. "He just looks so little."

Tillie only nodded in answer. She turned away from him and began to make her way down the hall and through the doors that took her outside. She fought the intense urge within her to sprint from the building and away from him. That would be too obvious, and she couldn't bring herself to hurt his feelings. He looked terrible today the way it was, and even when he smiled, his eyes held the dreadful expression of grief and sorrow.

What's happened to him over the years? The man I knew eleven years ago had the world by the tail and was in love with his life. Of course, he lost his wife, but that was years ago, and would that really bother a blackguard? You'd think he'd be relieved to get rid of her and carry on with his blackguardly life, which probably consists mostly of chasing women and coercing them into compromising their honor. Thank you, God, he didn't get that far with me.

Once outside, Tillie found a bench close to the door so she could watch for her children when they were done. She sat down with a heavy sigh and looked at the handkerchief in her hands. *Humph. A blackguard with a handkerchief? That's weird. This whole thing is weird.*

She found it unbelievable that this was the same Noah her brothers had touted for all of these years. They had absolutely loved and adored this man from the moment they met him in the hospital the night he'd driven Alex back to Sioux Falls in the middle of a snowstorm. Vincenzo often mentioned the "dreadful jilting" Noah had taken in 1975, but Tillie *never* put two and two together, *because Tara had lied*...and Tillie, for her own opinion, was always under the impression *she* had been the one who was "*jilted.*" *What would Vincenzo say if he found out it was his very own little sister who'd done the jilting?*

Marquette had talked about Noah's service in Vietnam many times, which was suddenly very unusual seeing how Marquette just *didn't* talk about Vietnam with anyone else but Ginger's brother, Andy. It was known in the family that Marquette made stopovers in Rapid City whenever he traveled in a westerly direction, just to say "hi" to Noah and the boys. The rest of the Caselli family, including Tillie, noticed the unusual bond that had developed between Marquette and Noah. *How did I miss that?*

Petrice was really too busy in Washington to have struck up any kind of a relationship with Noah, and that was a relief. At least she had one brother that hadn't been duped by the blackguard in disguise.

Noah denied knowing anything about her until yesterday morning at church, but Tillie suspected he was lying to her. How could he have *not* known? She sighed and shook her head...*I didn't know...maybe I just didn't want to know.*

As she glanced at the doorway of the school, she saw Noah was coming toward her, looking fairly uncomfortable. Her heart softened slightly. He had raised two little boys on his own for the last five and a half years. That was worth *something,* and maybe she should just forgive him and get on with the rest of her life. She had Alex now anyway, and whatever had happened between the two of them eleven years ago just didn't matter anymore.

Noah took a seat on the opposite end of the bench and asked, "Is it okay if I sit here?"

Tillie handed him his handkerchief and offered him a faint smile. "I guess I won't bite."

Noah nodded with his own faint smile. "That's good, because I really thought you might."

Tillie *almost* laughed, but she fought away the feeling to keep her guard completely intact. She looked into his sad blue eyes. "Listen, I need to ask you for a favor."

"Anything," he answered, surprised at her words.

Tillie sighed and swallowed hard as she looked at him. *Hopefully I can trust the old blackguard.* "I never told my brothers about you and me, and I don't want them to know."

"Why not?"

Tillie shrugged and looked away. "It's something I'd rather they didn't know." She paused as she thought about her next words. "I'm just not sure they'd understand. You must know by now that my family does things just a little differently than the rest of the world." She nervously cleared her throat and brought her eyes back to Noah's.

"And we should've gotten your father's permission before we went off together," Noah stated simply.

Tillie nodded. "And I know that you and Marquette are fairly close, and there's some stuff there between him and Alex you probably don't know about. It's just better that he not know about you...and me."

Noah slowly nodded. Whatever she requested of him, he would agree to. "I won't tell them," he promised. He took a soft breath, "And may I ask a favor of you?"

"Sure."

"I need you to believe me," Noah said with a quiet earnestness that surprised Tillie. "I need you to know that I didn't do what you think I did back then."

Tillie bit her lower lip. She took a deep breath and looked away from him. If she allowed herself to believe that, then she would also have to accept that her suffering that year had been all for naught. That she was actually the one at fault for ending the relationship.

"And blame myself?" she whispered as she looked into the distant Hills, feeling a strange, nostalgic pain.

"No, don't blame anybody. It was just a stupid twist of events."

Tillie brought her eyes back to Noah's and wished she didn't have to deal with this.

"Please," Noah whispered. "It's been so hard for me —"

"But you took a wife, *and* you had babies."

Noah nodded. "But it was still hard. There's a lot of things I haven't told your brothers, or even Alex for that matter, and so you probably don't know *everything* about me." He smiled. "I'm not the blackguard you think I am, and after all these years with your brothers, I *know* exactly what a blackguard is."

Tillie smiled, surprised to hear him use the term, and she began to nod. "Okay," she agreed, feeling a weight slip from her shoulders. She hadn't even realized it was there until she felt it leave her. She smiled at him again, and the doors to the school began to flow with children looking for their parents.

Tillie got to her feet, as did Noah, and he looked at her one last time. "Thanks, Tillie," he said with a gentle smile. "I really appreciate that."

Tillie nodded with a soft smile and went to find her children.

Chapter 6

"The Senator has been in town twice now, and I am afraid."

"Afraid of what, my son?" Mario frowned.

Antonio pressed his lips together and gazed out the window of his stepmother's room.

"Papa, it's in the paper every other day. He is afraid that Sal will notice how often the Casellis are visiting," Charise whispered. She looked into her mother's sleeping face and placed a soft kiss upon her forehead. She turned from her mother and tried to smile at her brother and father. "It's only a matter of time before he comes up with a way to get close to the Casellis...and there's something else —"

"No, Charise —" Antonio tried to stop his sister's words.

"Noah invited Angel and her family to church," Charise continued. "Angel is well aware of Noah now."

Mario groaned. "How unlucky we have been."

"And who knows what they have spoken about." Antonio took a deep breath and shook his head. "Should they ever speak of the night she left him, it is quite possible the two of them could put the pieces together."

"Perhaps not, my son. Their grief in the matter is substantial. They may just leave the matter alone."

Charise sighed. "I sure wish we didn't have to gamble like this."

*****

Noah awakened to the sound of quiet giggles, and he forced himself to open his eyes. To his surprise, he was still in the chair in his office at home, holding the framed photo in his hands and dressed in what he'd worn yesterday. Jake and their housekeeper, Vera, were in the doorway, and it was Jake's giggle he'd heard.

Noah took a deep breath, slid the old photo into its place in his top left-hand drawer, and stood up to greet them.

"Did you sleep there?" Vera asked with a curious expression.

"I think so." Noah smiled and reached for Jake, who had come around to the other side of the desk. He picked up the little boy, and Jake put his arms around his father's neck.

"Good morning, Daddy." He gave his father a hug and looked into his eyes. "You could have slept with me."

"Good morning, Jake," Noah grinned. He looked at Vera and asked, "What time is it?"

"It's about seven o'clock."

Noah grimaced. That was late for him. He was usually up before six.

"I gotta get goin'," he said. He looked hopefully at his housekeeper. "You didn't start any coffee, did you?"

Vera smiled. "Sure did."

"You're the best, Vera."

"I know," she answered as she turned toward the door and led them into the kitchen. She thought it was strange that Noah had spent the night in that chair with what looked like an old photo, but she pretended not to notice.

"Let's have Pop-Tarts," Jake happily suggested as he and his father walked into the kitchen.

"How 'bout some eggs," Noah offered.

Jake stuck out his tongue and pretended to gag. "Yuck. Eggs are gross."

Noah laughed. "Eggs will make you big and strong. We'll scramble 'em up and put some bacon in 'em."

"Blah," Jake replied with a frown. "If I can't have Pop-Tarts, I'll just have some cereal."

"Suit yourself," Noah said. He set Jake down and reached beneath the stove for a pan. "But I gotta have some eggs."

Vera poured a cup of coffee and offered, "Why don't you let me make you some breakfast while you shower."

Noah smiled curiously at Vera. "Are you sure?" Vera nodded. "Thanks," Noah said with a sigh, and he gave Jake's head a pat. "But don't let him have Pop-Tarts. The sugar makes him crazy."

"Then why do we even have them?" Jake frowned.

"I have no idea how those things got into the house," Noah answered. He looked mischievously at his little boy and asked, "Have you been doing the grocery shopping, Jake?"

"No," Jake scoffed, trying not to smile. "I don't know *where* they came from."

Noah just smiled and hurried to the shower, while Jake went to wake up his brother and Vera started Noah's breakfast.

When Vera could hear Jake and Ty's voices down the hall and Noah's shower running, she stole into Noah's office for a look at the photograph. She knew she shouldn't. After all, it was Noah's private business. If he had wanted her to see the photo, he would have shown it to her. *But I'm older and wiser,* she justified, *nearly sixty-five now. It'll be okay to have just a peek at whatever kept Noah in the chair all night long. He's looked so terrible for the last couple of days. Maybe that photo will shed some light on things.*

She pulled open the top left-hand drawer and gazed in at the photo. She recognized the younger version of Noah right away. *But who's that girl? She's familiar.*

Vera bent over for a better look and gasped. *Senator Caselli's sister!*

*****

Melinda watched Noah as he came in shortly after eight o'clock that morning. He looked even worse than he had yesterday. He walked up to her desk, tiredly smiled, and reached for his messages.

"Good morning, Melinda," he said with a heavy sigh. "Anybody important call?"

Melinda smiled. "The Joker called just a few minutes ago. Wants you to call him back."

"Hey, good," Noah said as he turned and walked to his office.

Melinda sighed and shook her head. *Why is he avoiding me? And what's wrong with him?*

Noah closed his office door and breathed a sigh of relief. Finally, some time by himself where he could think some more. He slumped into the chair behind his desk and looked out the windows. From his little office downtown, he could see the First Federal Bank building at the corner of St. Joe and West Boulevard. That's where Alex's office was now. He wondered if Alex was in yet this morning and then shook his head. He couldn't tell Alex. He wanted to because he had shared everything else with Alex over the last eleven years, but this information would only make Alex uncomfortable. After all, Alex knew all about the house Noah had built for the mysterious disappearing girl in his past. They'd spoken of her several times over the years.

Noah thought some more about his terrible argument with Mona. He hadn't realized he was still upset with Carrie about all of those things until they came boiling out at Mona. And it certainly wasn't Mona's fault, but she really pushed him. Why did she always expect him to be so *perfect? And it's not like I asked for this situation.*

He reached for the phone and dialed McDarren's number in Texas, surprised to find the Joker actually in his office. After speaking with him for a few moments, Noah learned he'd be in Rapid City next Tuesday and was interested in looking at a couple of sites for his grocery warehouse. Noah promised to get back to him as soon as he talked with Alex, and then they hung up. Noah dialed Alex's number, feeling just the tiniest bit of excitement at having possibly hit a breakthrough with the Joker. At least *something* was going right this week.

"This is Noah," he said when Lori answered the phone at Alex's office.

"Hi, Noah," Lori replied with a smile. "Are you looking for Alex?"

"Yep," Noah answered.

"Well, you'll have to settle for Shondra today. Hold on."

Before Noah could respond or ask a question, Lori had transferred him to Shondra.

"Shondra Payne."

"Hey, Shondra, Lori transferred me to you, but I need to talk to Alex."

"He's still in Pierre," Shondra said as she reached for her calendar. "Can I help you?"

Noah shook his head. *I finally get ahold of McDarren and I can't talk to Alex? Great.* He took a breath. "I thought he was coming back last night."

"He should be back on Thursday morning," Shondra explained. "He's arguing before the Supreme Court tomorrow."

Noah nearly fell out of his chair. *So, he's already left Angel home alone with the kids to get famous. Figures.* He shook his head as he remembered the last time Alex had pursued his political career. He cleared his throat. "Listen, Shondra, I just talked to the Joker, and he'll be in town next Tuesday. Can Alex be available that day?"

"Let me see," she replied, and Noah heard the shuffle of papers in the background. "Yes. He's got the whole day open."

"Well glory be," Noah muttered, and he heard Shondra laugh.

"Do you want me to pencil you in for the entire day?" she asked.

"Yep. Don't let him put anything in on Tuesday, and if he calls from Pierre, tell him to get a hold of me right away."

"I will," Shondra promised, and they hung up.

Noah leaned back in his chair and closed his eyes. Sleeping in that chair all night long had left him really tired. He sighed and thought of Angel at home, *alone*, in her house across town. *What's she wearing today? What's she doing? Is she thinking of me?*

He imagined her in a lovely, pink summer dress, showing off the lovely contour of her legs and the delicate shape of her waist and hips. Maybe her hair was down today and she was painting a beautiful portrait of her children or reading them a story. Whatever she was doing, she was probably smiling, and that thought made Noah smile. His imagination carried him further into the dream, like he was actually there with her, holding one of her pretty hands and leading her along the path they'd followed at Canyon Lake…but someone kept saying his name, over and over again….

"Noah."

He slowly opened his eyes, exerting extreme effort to focus in on whoever was standing in the doorway of his office. "What?" he said as he finally began to make out Melinda's familiar face…*did I fall asleep?*

"You've got a building inspection in about a half hour," Melinda informed with a curious expression. When he hadn't answered her soft knock, she let herself in and found him sleeping soundly in his chair with a smile on his face. His behavior had become strange on Sunday and was getting more abnormal as the days went by.

Noah took a deep breath and sat up straight in his chair. He appeared to be just a little disoriented as he chuckled and looked at Melinda. "Was I sleeping?"

Melinda frowned. "What's wrong, Noah?"

Noah felt his own forehead crease into a frown…*boy, I hate it when she makes that face at me…like she's the boss or something.* He slowly shook his head. "I'm not sure. I don't think anything is *wrong*. Why?"

"For starters," Melinda began as she raised one eyebrow, "I've never seen you sleep behind your desk before."

"Well," Noah scoffed with a spontaneous smile and looked away from Melinda. "I'm getting older. Maybe I just need a few more winks at night."

Melinda didn't smile at his attempted humor. She sighed. "Are you and the boys still going to help me clear out my garden this weekend?"

"Sure."

Melinda's face held the most peculiar expression as she began to back out of Noah's office. "Well, you'd better get going if you're gonna make that inspection. And Viv Olson called. She needs to change out a screen at Angel's Place. Do you want me to send somebody up?"

"No, I'll take care of it myself."

Melinda nodded and left him alone. She went back to her desk and took her seat. Right before Noah had awakened, he'd whispered, "Angel."

Unlike in Noah's beautiful dream, Tillie Martin was knee deep in the shallow creek, along with her two disobedient little children. Instead of a graceful summer dress, she wore cut-off jeans and a t-shirt, and was completely covered in mud. Her hair wasn't exactly flowing. It had been tied on top of her head with an old rag in an effort to keep it out of her eyes while she did laundry and attempted to unpack a few more boxes.   A.J. had gotten the bright idea to drive his Big Wheel straight into the creek, and now it was stuck. Tillie had only been in the laundry room for a couple of minutes, so when Laura came for help, she was really surprised they'd managed something so dreadful in such a short period of time.

"I can't believe you did this," Tillie scolded while she pulled on the handle bars of the Big Wheel. She yanked on it as hard as she could and finally managed to pull it from the bottom of the creek. "Whatever possessed you to drive your bike into the creek?"

"The devil, Mommy," A.J. ashamedly answered.

His comment caught Tillie off guard, and she clenched her lips together in an effort to fight off the laughter.

"It's a really fast hill," Laura casually observed as she watched her mother pull the bike from the shallow water and set it safely on the bank.

Tillie looked at her two children and raised both of her eyebrows. "You mean you drove this thing down the hill and into the creek?" Her two little ones nodded, and Tillie shook her head. "You could have *killed* yourselves. Let's get this thing up into the backyard and hose it off. And the two of you are grounded off of it for a whole week."

"Come on, Mommy," A.J. began to plead. "I promise never to do it again."

"Good," Tillie said. "Now push this dirty thing for me because I'm muddy enough."

A.J. obediently began to push the plastic bike up the hill as he begged, "Please, Mommy, don't ground us off the bike."

"You'll be lucky if you ever play with it again," Tillie threatened with a frown. "Don't beg me anymore."

It was quiet until they got the Big Wheel into the backyard, where Tillie sprayed it off with the garden hose. Then she undressed her children, washed the mud off of them as best she could, and finally gave herself a good drenching as well.

"Now, let's get into the shower," she said with a heavy sigh. "Man! I'm not gonna get *anything* done today." She shooed them into the house and up the steps, while she took their muddy clothes directly to the laundry room, where she got rid of her own clothes and found an old robe to put on. She started upstairs to her own shower but paused to listen in the hallway to make sure her little ones were doing as they were told. Sure enough, she heard their showers running, and she went into her own room. She laughed as she passed by the mirror on the dresser. She looked awful. The phone rang, so Tillie changed direction, heading for the nightstand beside her bed. "Hello."

"It is me, Angel," Rosa's timid voice came through on the other line.

"Ma'ma," Tillie breathed with a smile. "Did you get my message?"

"I did, Angel," Rosa sheepishly admitted. "And I am so sorry for your surprise. We just did not know what to do."

"It's sorta okay," Tillie answered. "But it's awkward, and I don't want my brothers to know about this. Okay?"

"Okay, Angel," Rosa said, and she took a nervous breath. "How did it go?"

"Fine. You know, it was uncomfortable, but he seems like a nice guy, I guess. Maybe he's not the jerk that I've hated all these years."

"Maybe not," Rosa hesitantly agreed. "Did you tell Alex?"

"No. Can you imagine how awful that would make him feel? I can't do that to Alex." Tillie was quiet for a long moment, and then she swallowed and asked, "Why didn't you tell me, Ma'ma?"

"Oh, Angel," and it sounded as if Rosa may have been crying, "I cannot say."

"Why can't you say?"

"I do not know what to say about that."

Tillie felt a wall between herself and her mother. Was there more to this story that Rosa was keeping to herself?

"Well, I guess it doesn't matter anyway," Tillie replied.

"No, it really does not," Rosa agreed. "It was just a strange coincidence."

"I suppose. I mean, who'da thunk it?"

"Yes, my Angel. Who would have ever guessed?"

*****

Maggie watched Noah get out of his pickup and walk through the glass entry doors and up to the bar. He winked at her as he took a seat on one of the stools, gazing wistfully at the portrait hanging on the wall. He sighed and smiled at Maggie.

"Turkey clubs," she said. When Noah nodded, she scribbled it down on her pad and put his order on the wheel behind her. "How's things?" she asked as she reached below the bar for a bottle of Coke, uncapped it, and set it before him. She noticed he wasn't as happy as he had been the last time he was in.

"Oh, fair," Noah answered as he took hold of the Coke, taking a long gulp. He set the bottle down and looked into Maggie's eyes. "I talked to her. Twice."

"Really," Maggie said with an interested glint in her expression. "What did she have to say for herself?"

Noah smiled and shook his head. "It was all a big misunderstanding, Maggie. She saw Carrie kissing me, thought I had changed my mind, and ran away."

"No kiddin'?"

Noah nodded. "But she really came back, Maggie. She really loved me."

Maggie slowly nodded as she looked into Noah's face and saw the faintest sparkle behind his blue eyes. "So what happens next?"

"Don't know," Noah answered. He took a deep breath and let it out, "I guess I have to learn to just live with it."

Maggie's frown deepened. "Learn to live with it? Can you do that?"

"I can do anything, Maggie. If I just put my mind to it, this thing won't even bother me anymore. It's just a decision. Listen, Maggie, Melinda really likes me and the boys, and I think maybe, if she and I get along okay, we should just go ahead and get married."

"Oh, brother," Maggie moaned and rolled her eyes. "Are you nuts? That woman is as mean as a badger in a burlap bag. She don't like you and she never has. She's only been nice to you for the last few months so she can get your money."

"No," Noah said with a laugh. "Come on, Maggie. It worked for me before, you know, with Carrie."

"Oh, yeah, that's right," Maggie dryly admitted. "Go off and get married so you can get over Angel again." She shook her head and muttered, "That's rich."

"Come on, Maggie. Melinda's a nice lady, and the boys really like her. You just need to get to know her."

"Humph!" Maggie raised one eyebrow and quietly accused, "I think you're tryin' to make Angel jealous."

"I wouldn't do that," Noah scoffed and shook his head.

"Humph." And Maggie walked away to wait on another customer.

Chapter 7

Jake sat in the middle this time, holding a bundle of freshly cut white daisies, and Ty was on the other side, with a box of Auntie Mona's favorite tea. Noah was quiet as he drove along the gravel road, nearing the home of his "favorite" sister-in-law. They hadn't spoken since their argument on Monday, and he knew he owed her an apology.

"So, why does Auntie Mona get all this stuff?" Jake asked as they pulled into the driveway.

"Because I was mean to Auntie Mona. Now I've gotta go and say I'm sorry."

Ty was flabbergasted. "Wow...how could you be *mean* to Auntie Mona?"

Noah sighed and shook his head. "I don't know what came over me, but I've gotta make it better 'cause she's such a great lady."

"I hope she didn't tell Uncle Josh on you," Jake said with a mischievous sparkle in his eyes. "He might take you down and whip your butt."

Noah laughed nervously. "Uncle Josh hasn't whipped anybody's butt in a long time."

"Did he ever whip your butt?" Ty asked curiously. "You know, when you were little?"

Noah laughed again. "Not nearly enough. I wasn't good like you guys. I was *really* naughty."

They all got out of the truck and walked up to the porch. Mona must have seen them pull in, because the old screen door opened and she stepped out onto the porch.

Jake was the first one up the steps. He smiled into her eyes and handed her the daisies. "Hi, Auntie Mona. Daddy's *really* sorry."

Ty came up behind him and presented her with the box of tea and smiled. "And he thinks you're a really great lady."

Mona smiled at her nephews, gave them each a hug and a kiss, and said, "Why don't you check the cookie jar? I wanna talk to your daddy."

Ty and Jake nodded and left their dad alone at the bottom of the steps.

Noah looked up into Mona's very sad eyes, and after a long moment he said, "Mona, I'm so sorry. Please forgive me."

"Why didn't you tell us about Carrie?" she whispered.

Noah came up the steps and reached for Mona's hand. "Can we sit down? Just for a minute?"

Mona nodded, and he led her to the porch swing. It was quiet for a long time again, and finally Noah took a deep breath and explained, "I guess I didn't want to believe that there could have ever been a problem between me and Carrie. Everything had just gone along so well." He shook his head and looked at the beautiful hills in the distance. "You know, me and Carrie *never* fought after Ty was born. She changed so much." He looked into Mona's tearing eyes and said, "I couldn't really accept the possibility that there may have been someone else on the side, and so I just never told you guys about it."

"Noah," Mona said as a tear rolled out of her eye, "Carrie wasn't a mistake."

"I know. And Ty and Jake are blessings. I didn't mean it that way. I was just being a big jerk when I said that — you know, trying to justify why I should dump Melinda."

Mona nodded with a faint smile. "You're totally forgiven. And I didn't even mention it to Joshua. If you wanna tell him, that's your business, but it's been so long ago now that you should probably just leave it in the past."

Noah nodded and gave her a hug. "I love you, Mona. You're the best."

"I love you, too, Noah." She looked at him curiously and asked, "Have you seen Angel since Sunday?"

"Yes, but, please, don't ever call her that. She goes by the name Tillie. Just her family calls her Angel. Even Alex calls her Tillie."

"Gotcha," Mona said with a nod, and then she gently asked, "How's all that goin'?"

Noah shrugged with a smile, and that's when Mona noticed that his downcast expression from Monday was gone. His eyes were almost dancing this afternoon, and it made her heart pound.

"Where did you see her?" she cautiously inquired, hoping he hadn't been going over to her house or something crazy like that.

"School," Noah answered. "Her kids are in the same class with Jake. I guess I would have seen her sooner or later. I didn't need to set it up at the church like that."

Mona took a breath and slowly let it out. She searched Noah's eyes for something to reassure her that he wasn't falling for this girl again.

Noah quietly laughed and shook his head. "I'm in *big* trouble, Mona. I even told Maggie at lunch this afternoon that I'm thinking of marrying Melinda." He saw the startle in Mona's eyes, so he tried to explain. "Because it worked so good with Carrie." He shook his head and sighed. "I don't know."

"Well, how much do you really *like* Melinda?" Mona asked. "She's never been a very *nice* person. She's always been kind of a nightmare for you, and she hates your foreman."

Noah chuckled. "Maggie thinks she's after my money."

"Maybe she is."

"Well, she's not *Angel*," Noah went on. "But she really likes me and the boys, and that's gotta count for something."

Mona slowly shook her head. "Please don't do that again, Noah. Don't marry because you're lonely or you're feeling like you have to do something drastic to get your mind off of what's really happening. And, like you said, she's not Angel, and it would be wrong to try and make her Angel. Know what I'm sayin'?"

Noah sighed. He knew *exactly* what she was saying.

*****

On Thursday morning, when Alex returned from Pierre, the Martins headed for the southern Black Hills and their extended weekend at the Blue Bell Lodge in Custer State Park. They planned to stay at the small resort until Saturday and then travel up to Mt. Rushmore to visit the memorial before coming home.

Before settling into the lodge, Alex and Tillie decided to take their children hiking along the banks of French Creek. They had lunch at the main house and then went for a leisurely pony ride. By the time they returned, it was getting on toward supper time, and the twins were cranky. Alex and Tillie took them back to the main house of the resort, where they ordered dinner.

Their wonderful little children bickered and argued during the whole meal, and by the time they returned to their cabin, Tillie was ready to put them to bed. While Alex helped them into their pajamas, Tillie pulled out her secret weapon: *On the Banks of Plum Creek*. In only a matter of minutes, the two crabby little people were sleeping soundly in their covers and their parents crept out of their room.

Tillie sighed with relief as she and Alex went into their own room. "Man, they were *terrible* at dinner," she commented with a tired smile and a shake of her head.

"They were just exhausted," Alex said as he reached inside their suitcase. "I got you something while I was in Pierre." He handed her the small felt box. "It's something I should have gotten you a long time ago."

"What is it?"

"Open it up."

Tillie lifted the lid on the tiny box to reveal an incredible ring. The center stone was a magnificent diamond, with two large citrine stones on either side of it. Tillie recognized the citrine as their children's birthstone.

"It's a mother's ring," Alex said. He took the ring out of its box and put it on Tillie's right hand.

"Wow," Tillie smiled as she admired the new ring on her hand. "You have really got some taste."

"Well, I married you, didn't I?" Alex replied with a smile.

Tillie looked into his handsome dark eyes. "Thank you. That was so thoughtful."

Alex took her in his arms and passionately kissed her. "I really missed you," he whispered.

"Me too," and she lost herself in the safety of his arms and the reassurance of his whisper. Hopefully he wouldn't have to go away again.

*****

Bright and early Saturday morning, Noah loaded up his little boys and drove them over to Miss Melinda's house in the Robbinsdale subdivision. Ty and Jake loved to visit Miss Melinda because she had a big, fun, black Labrador named Merry and a huge yard the three of them could run through.

Merry had lots of rubber squeak toys, and the big dog kept the boys busy for hours as they tried to catch her and take away the toys. Merry was quick and clever. She would lay down very close to the toy Ty or Jake wanted and try to entice the boys into coming closer to her. When they were just about upon her, she'd quickly pick up the toy in her mouth and the chase would begin. The big dog's antics made the boys laugh hysterically, and they chased her through the yard, forever trying to take the toy but never being able to catch up with her.

"Thought they were supposed to help us," Noah said with a smile as he watched his boys run behind the dog, who had yet another toy. It was nearly lunchtime and he and Melinda had cleared a significant portion of the garden alone.

Melinda laughed and looked at the three of them as they ran through her backyard. "It's okay. Merry loves to run, and it's good for her." She smiled into Noah's eyes and said, "And you seem to be feeling better today."

Noah looked at her with confused smile. "What?"

Melinda shrugged. "You seemed a little out of sorts this week." She hesitated for a moment and added, "I know you got into it with Mona."

Noah nodded. "I talked to her on Wednesday. It's okay now."

"I can see that." She took a deep breath and began to remove her gardening gloves. "It's time for a break. Why don't you sit down on the deck, and I'll get us some lunch. I made some sandwiches this morning and I'll bring 'em out."

"Sounds good to me," Noah replied as he removed his gloves and followed Melinda toward the house.

The boys saw them heading away from the garden and instantly scrambled in behind them. Merry brought up the rear.

"Miss Melinda," Jake breathed heavily, taking a gentle hold of her hand.

"Yes, Jake?" Melinda smiled down at him and caught the briefest reflection of his father.

"Do you have blue Kool-Aid today?"

Melinda laughed and nodded. "You know I do."

Jake squealed with delight.

Melinda brought out sandwiches, chips, and apples and they enjoyed their lunch behind the shade of the house. Merry danced around the table, hoping to be thrown a scrap, but Melinda told the boys not to feed her from the table.

"I thought we'd order pizza and watch a movie over at our place tonight," Noah said as they ate.

Melinda was surprised. Normally their "dates" lasted only a few hours, and he had just committed his entire day to her. The overture was unusual but delightful at the same time. She hadn't been over to his place yet. She hid her excited surprise with a simple nod of her head and a bite into her sandwich.

"What movie did you get?" Ty asked curiously. There was one particular movie he wanted, and he wondered if his father had remembered.

"Some John Wayne movies," Noah answered casually. He smiled at Ty and said, "And I bought *Robinhood.*"

"Yes!" Ty exclaimed. "Thanks, Dad."

After lunch, the boys played another round with Merry, while Noah and Melinda finished with her garden. It was nearly six o'clock before they picked up their pizza and headed over to Noah's house. As Noah showed her around, Melinda was surprised at how neat and orderly the home was kept. She knew Noah had lived there alone for a long time, and she complimented him on his great housekeeping.

Noah blushed. "Well, Vera *really* takes care of the place. Me and the boys are slobs." He pulled a card table out from behind the couch and began to set it up so they could eat their pizza while they watched the movie. "Oh, I left that movie in my office," Noah said as he unsnapped the legs of the table and locked them into place.

"I can get it," Melinda offered as she glanced around. "Which way to the office?"

"The doorway off of the kitchen," Noah answered. He set the pizza on the table, while the boys seated themselves on the couch and waited for the fun to begin.

Melinda hurried into the kitchen, through the door, into Noah's office. The westerly sun hung low on the horizon, and its glow filtered into the small room. She smiled as she realized his desk at home was as messy as his desk at work. She took a deep breath, and Noah's scent filled her nose. Old Spice and soap.

She gingerly looked through the papers on the top of his desk and found the video. But out of the corner of her eye she noticed that his top, left-hand drawer had been left open. Lying in full view was the photograph. Curious about it, she stepped a little closer and let her focus fall to the photo. *A younger version of Noah and a girl...who's that?* Carrie had been lighter in coloring and had strawberry-blond hair, so it wasn't his wife. Melinda squinted and bent over the photo for a better look. Her heart began to pound. *It can't be! Tillie Martin!? When was this taken?* She noticed Noah's ponytail. *Sometime before I met him, and I've known him for almost ten years. This has to be even before he married Carrie.*

"Did you find it?" Noah called from the living room, startling Melinda back to the duty at hand.

"Yes," she quickly answered. She stepped away from the photograph and tried to compose herself. *What a surprise.* She had no idea Noah and Tillie were ever together. *Is that how Alex met her? Did the dashing and wealthy Alex Martin steal Noah Hansen's girlfriend? That hardly seems likely. They get along far too well to have had a situation like that in their past. Alex probably doesn't know! How in the world did Noah ever connect up with a rich kid like Senator Caselli's sister in the first place? Why didn't they stay together? Well, she's probably just a rich, spoiled brat who set her sights on a Harvard Law graduate instead of a rough working man.*

Melinda shook her head, took a deep breath, and went back to the living room with the video. She didn't know whether to hide her discovery or to just ask Noah about it. She couldn't very well say anything in front of the boys, so it would have to wait. She hid her shock, smiled and handed Noah the video. She took a seat close to the boys on the couch. Noah had already gotten plates and napkins for them, and they were ready to start.

"Let Melinda go first," Noah said sweetly, while he loaded the video into the VCR.

Ty and Jake giggled and looked at Melinda. She smiled at them and forced herself to take a slice of pizza. Then they helped themselves. Noah sat down next to her and got himself some pizza, and the movie began.

Melinda ate her pizza in stone silence, thankful for the comical cartoon entertaining the boys and their father. The events of the past week slowly began to make sense. It started with church last Sunday and the horrible expression in Noah's eyes. She recalled he'd been visiting with Tillie Martin earlier that morning, near the missions coordinator's office, and it appeared they were having quite a discussion. *Tillie actually looked angry at one point,* Melinda remembered. Noah acted strangely during the entire sermon, and Joshua appeared to comfort him shortly after the service ended. The next day, he and Mona had that loud argument. *No wonder Noah has had such a rotten week. He isn't over her yet.*

Melinda felt like someone had knocked the wind out of her. However, she just sat there, pretending to enjoy the pizza and the movie.

What am I gonna do? My plans are about finished now. If Noah hasn't gotten over her after all these years, he probably isn't going to. But then, he was happy with Carrie, so he must have been able to forget about Tillie for a little while. Of course, Melinda justified, *Tillie was probably out of the picture at that time —* and then a big bell went off in Melinda's head. *I have to find a way to get Tillie out of the picture again, but how? Alex and Noah are practically connected at the hip.*

Even I noticed the discomfort Noah went through when he first saw the woman, but did anyone else, besides Josh and Mona? Did Alex notice? What would happen if Alex were to realize that Noah had a thing for his wife? Alex is an extremely competitive man. He would probably never allow Noah and Tillie to see one another again, and that would be just for starters.

I need a plan. I can't very well just go over to Alex's office and tell him what I know. That would alienate Noah. No. Noah will have to tell on himself, and judging from the way he behaved on Sunday, it probably won't take very long for Alex to catch on. He's a smart enough guy. All I need to do is to get Noah and Tillie together a couple of times, and all will reveal itself in short course.

61

A horrible scheme began in Melinda's heart, and she squelched the warnings of the Holy Spirit. Darkness quickly found its way into her mind, and she made an evil decision.

Poor Noah. He and Alex have shared such a wonderful friendship for so many years. On the other hand, it really can't be helped. Tillie will be too much of a distraction for Noah, and things are going along so well between Noah and me.

Noah will be a little uncomfortable at first. However, when he doesn't have to worry about seeing Tillie anymore, his life can begin again, with me, and I'll make him forget he ever knew Tillie Caselli.

*****

Melinda could hardly wait to get to church the next day. She had been up all night long, calling in favors and putting together a plan to expose Noah's feelings for Tillie Martin. As she watched the Martin family walk in, her perfect plan went into motion. Noah was already distracted by an older parishioner, and he visited him just inside the lobby.

She hurried into the lobby to say good morning to Alex and Tillie and their children. "Hi," she smiled sweetly into their eyes, bending over to greet their children. "I guess I didn't get to meet your kids last week."

"I'm Laura."

"I'm A.J."

"Well, I'm Melinda," she introduced with a smile, shaking both of their little hands.

She stood up and looked at Alex. "Do you know about the meeting with McDarren on Tuesday?"

Alex frowned curiously. "Didn't Shondra get a hold of you?"

"Oh, yes," Melinda smiled and nodded. "But I came across some notes she doesn't have, and I wasn't able to get a hold of her before she left on Friday."

"Okay," Alex replied. "Well, we can go over them on Tuesday morning, before he shows up."

"I'm going to walk the kids up to Sunday school." Tillie smiled at Melinda. "I'll be right back."

"Okay, Honey," Alex said.

Tillie left with A.J. and Laura, and Melinda and Alex were alone. *So far so good.*

Alex couldn't resist asking about the additional notes on McDarren's project. He just hadn't wanted to talk business in front of Tillie. "So what's up with the Joker?" he asked as he and Melinda stepped away from the crowd of people.

"Oh, my goodness," Melinda excitedly began. She had to swallow to keep her heart from racing as he took her bait. She knew Alex couldn't resist talking about new projects, and she began to delicately feed him information. "Of course, we all know he wants to build a warehouse over on the south side," she went on, mysteriously raising one eyebrow, "but did you know he wants to put in a grocery store over on the corner of Chicago and Deadwood Avenues?"

"No," Alex replied, and his jaw nearly dropped to the floor.

Melinda almost laughed. She had him hooked now and would be able to keep him busy for the next few minutes while her devilish plan unfolded.

While Alex was engrossed with Melinda in the corner, Noah tried his best to get away from the parishioner who'd engaged him in a conversation about the *old days* and how they used to build things *back then.* Of course, Noah was polite and stayed where he'd been caught, quietly listening to every word the old-timer had to say.

When Tillie returned, the mayhem began. A news camera, led by a reporter, burst through the doorway of the church, meeting Tillie in the lobby. She attempted to avoid him, stepping off to the side, but the reporter backed her against a wall. A bright light came on, and a microphone was shoved into her face.

Melinda observed what was happening, but she kept her cool and continued to talk to Alex, who just happened to have his back to the situation. He had no idea about what was taking place behind him. Out of the corner of her eye, Melinda saw that Noah had noticed the commotion and was now on his way across the lobby. *This is gonna be perfect.*

"Ms. Caselli," the aggressive reporter began, "sorry to bother you at church, but I thought maybe I could ask you a few questions about what Marquette and the Secretary of Defense are up to."

Tillie despised this sort of thing. Nevertheless, she had two extremely famous brothers and a husband who was running for attorney general. Sometimes it managed to bring the rookies out of the woodwork. Everyone in Sioux Falls was used to who she was, and these situations seldom occurred. When they did, she had become very good at getting out of them.

Her first inclination was to take the man's microphone and thump him on the head with it. However, if the camera was rolling, that probably wouldn't be the *best* publicity she could give Alex. She politely smiled at the reporter, shook her head, and tried to walk off in Alex's direction.

"Come on," the reporter said, and he grabbed her arm. That surprised Tillie, and she thought about slapping his face.

By now, Alex had heard the commotion behind him and turned just in time to see Noah charging across the lobby. Noah jerked the reporter's shoulder with one hand. With his other, he roughly removed the grip of the reporter from Tillie's arm, allowing her to escape more gracefully. Alex raced to her side, and she shook her head with an angry frown. He appeared to fold her protectively into his arms.

But it took only about three seconds for Tillie to slip from Alex's arms and reach the cord hanging from the back of the camera. In one fluid swoop, Tillie managed to drag the cord around the feet of the haughty reporter, and down he went. Before he hit the floor, Tillie quickly stepped back into Alex's arms and pretended to frown with curiosity.

Perhaps no one saw that, she told herself. *Well, Alex saw it, but he won't care.*

The people visiting in the lobby were suddenly still as they watched the unusual scene before them. They had never had a celebrity in their midst before, and they were more than just a little curious.

Melinda surveyed her handiwork, quite pleased with how everything had transpired. From her angle, it appeared as if *Noah* had dropped the reporter. He had behaved like a gallant knight as he rushed to the side of the woman he loved and rescued her from that fiendish media shyster. Hopefully Alex had noticed.

Noah saw clearly what Tillie had done and almost laughed. However, he growled angrily at the reporter he still had by the shoulder, "Get outa here. Unless you've come to pray, you need to be leaving."

The reporter was clearly embarrassed, but he smiled at Noah as he picked himself up from the floor and left the church. His mission was complete, and he certainly hadn't come to pray.

"I *hate* that so much," Tillie complained as Alex hurried her into the corner near Melinda.

Alex squelched a laugh as he muttered into her ear, "I can't believe you did that."

"Are you okay, Mrs. Martin?" Melinda asked with concern.

"Oh, I'm fine," Tillie scoffed with an angry frown. "But every now and then some rookie gets a wild hair, and I have to be polite."

Alex laughed nervously as he held her tightly against him. "But she'd rather rip 'em apart I think."

Tillie relaxed with a soft smile and rolled her eyes. "As if *I'm* gonna know what Marquette's up to!"

"Everything okay?" Noah was there now, after having ushered that *mean old* reporter out of the church.

"It's fine," Alex smiled thankfully at Noah. "Thanks, Noah."

"What a nightmare," Noah shook his head. "I can't even believe that happened. I've been going to this church for thirty years, and nobody's *ever* done a thing like that."

Melinda was suddenly very confused. *Didn't Alex notice that? How could he not? Didn't he see the soft blush on Noah's cheeks as he looked at Tillie? That idiot actually thanked Noah.* Melinda looked at Tillie and inwardly sighed. *If she's not willing to be a victim, that's gonna make things a little more difficult for me.*

"What's going on over here?" Joshua said, and his voice drew Melinda out of her thoughts as she realized that he and Mona had joined their little group in the corner.

"I'm sorry," Tillie apologized as she smiled at Joshua and Mona. "It doesn't happen very often — actually, hardly ever."

"It's okay," Joshua said, offering her his hand. "I don't think we've ever met. I'm Joshua Hansen."

"Nice to meet you," Tillie replied as she smiled into his friendly brown eyes.

"And this is my wife, Mona," Joshua introduced, and Mona offered Tillie her hand.

"It's nice to meet you," Mona greeted with a smile.

"You too." Tillie smiled in return.

"So what did the guy want anyway?" Joshua asked.

"Oh." Tillie rolled her eyes and shook her head. "He wanted to ask me about my brother. Marquette Caselli is my brother."

"The guy with the ponytail?" Mona asked.

Tillie laughed and nodded her head. "And just think, he probably could have had a *great* interview with the future attorney general."

"But I'm sure I'm not as cute in front of the camera," Alex said with a dry smile, and everyone laughed.

No one else seemed to notice, but Melinda did. Noah gazed endearingly at Tillie the whole time they visited. *Now, if I could just somehow get Alex to see that!*

Chapter 8

When Alex arrived at the office on Tuesday, Shondra was edgy and stressed. She followed him into his Uncle MacKenzie's old office and closed the door. "Melinda's really intense today," she murmured as she waited for him to set his briefcase on the desk. She handed him a small stack of papers and said, "She faxed this over for you to look at this morning."

"She told me about these notes on Sunday." He noticed Shondra's pensive frown. "What's the problem, Shondra?"

She pursed her lips together and shook her head. "I don't know. Melinda just acted awfully strange this morning."

"Strange *how?* Are we still set to go with the Joker?"

Shondra bit her lip with contemplation and answered, "Everything is still on with him...but...she just seemed...." She paused and looked at Alex. "I don't know, Alex. I don't think it's such a good idea to date your boss, but I guess that's none of my business."

Alex frowned. He couldn't very well *agree* with Shondra. After all, he had been the one who told Noah to go for it. "Well, they seemed to be fine at church. She was happy. Noah seemed okay."

Shondra smiled faintly and took a breath. That was her subtle way of telling Alex she heartily disagreed, and she changed the subject. "We received the Supreme Court's decision this morning."

"Already?" Alex's eyes brightened as he looked at Shondra with anticipation. "How'd we do?"

"Complete reversal."

Alex nodded his head in a prideful way. "Naturally."

"And Jon McFadden from *KDLT* called," she went on. "They're one of the local news stations, and he was wondering if you could do a quick interview?"

"I wonder if he's the punk who harassed my wife at church on Sunday," Alex said with a frown.

Shondra shook her head. "The first thing out of his mouth was that neither he nor his station was involved with that. That particular crew was from another station. Apparently, someone called them on Saturday night and tipped them off about Tillie. *KDLT* refused to do the piece — and they don't know who picked it up."

"That's strange. Who would have done something like that? We don't know anybody in town yet, except for Noah and Melinda."

Shondra shook her head. "Well, Noah would have *never* done something like that, but maybe somebody recognized her the week before and decided that a little excitement in the church would be fun."

Alex responded with a chortle, "Yeah, it would have been fun if Tillie would have torn him apart. She was *really* mad."

"Remember the time she *accidentally* tripped Chase Jacobsen from *CBS*?" Shondra said with a smirk.

Alex laughed as he remembered the comical scene. "This guy also *accidentally* tripped…but I got her away from him before she could kill him. If he only knew how close he came."

Shondra nodded, and her pensive frown returned. She slowly turned and said over her shoulder, "Well, I'll get you that decision and McFadden's number. You can decide whether or not you want to call him."

Alex acknowledged Shondra's departing instructions, sensing her strange demeanor. He shook his head and sat down behind his desk to begin his day.

*****

Melinda slammed down her phone with an ugly scowl and glared at Ben. "*Now* what do you want?" She regretted her words and tone immediately…*if I'm going to pull this off, I'd better be nice.*

Ben swallowed and took an instinctive step back. Melinda had come into the office in the foulest of moods, and everyone was avoiding her. Unfortunately, Ben had to do business with her before he could begin his day. He forced a smile.

"Good morning, Miss Melinda. I need to confirm those equipment orders for the St. Pat site and a lumber order for the job on Rimrock. What do you know of my supply situation?"

Melinda took a deep breath and slowly let it out. She seemed to have calmed down slightly when she answered, "Your equipment should be in place, Mr. Simmons." She smiled cattily. "Just let me know if something doesn't show up."

Ben shuddered. *That was nice of you, Miss Melinda…too nice.* He took another step back. "Okay, then." He nodded with a hesitant smile. "I will let you know."

Harv approached with a thick file, smiling at Ben and then at Melinda. "Hi guys. Am I interrupting?"

"No." Melinda smiled, standing from her chair.

"Oh, good." Harv set the file on her desk. "Here's that file you asked for, Miss Melinda…." He hesitated and leaned closer to Melinda, "Do you want to try lunch today?"

Behind Melinda's artificial smile, she ground her teeth. "No thank you, Harv. I have to go to the dentist today." She quickly turned and walked away.

Harv sighed with obvious regret, and Ben let out the breath he was holding. He put a hand on Harv's shoulder. "I have known brave men, Harv, but you must be the bravest of all, for I would never risk her temper the way you do."

Harv raised his eyebrows. "Perhaps my courage will win her heart."

Ben forced himself to smile and nod, and then he walked away.

*****

The halls at Pinedale Elementary were empty and quiet as Tillie hid behind the door of A.J. and Laura's classroom. *Just one more peek*, she promised herself, *and then I'll go.* They were so sweet and so little, sitting in their desks like angels, hanging on every word Mrs. Castleman said. Tillie took a soft breath and felt a tear escape from her eye. *This is crazy! They're not old enough to go to school! Are they?*

"Hey," someone whispered behind her. "Let me have a look."

Tillie recognized Noah's whisper and gave him room to have a peek at his son. She couldn't help but smile at him when they had eye contact, but she returned her focus back to the classroom.

"Look at how cute he is," Noah whispered with a smile.

Tillie looked at Jake and saw the strong resemblance between father and son. "He looks like you," she whispered and then wished she hadn't. The situation was suddenly *too comfortable,* and that was the *last* thing that needed to happen — especially after his gallantry on Sunday.

Tillie stepped away from Noah, and he followed her. They began walking down the hall together in an awkward silence until Tillie finally decided to speak. "I thought you guys had a meeting with the Joker this morning."

Noah smiled. "We do, but I told Alex I had to take the boys to school first, then I'm going over to his office."

As they stepped into the empty school yard, Tillie said, "Well, have a good day," and started to walk away in the opposite direction.

"Oh, I'm parked over there too," Noah said with a curious smile. "Is it okay if I just walk over there with you?"

No, it's not okay, Tillie thought, but she answered, "Sure."

Noah took up his place beside her again, and they continued the awkward silence.

"Well, there's no reporter here today," he observed. *How can I get her to talk to me? Just a few words won't hurt. It's been so many years, and I've missed her so much.*

Tillie shook her head with a smile, accidentally looking into his wonderful eyes. He looked better today than he had last week, and she sweetly added, "Thanks, Noah. I really hate reporters."

Noah smiled and blushed. She had said his name, and it was all he could do to keep from doing handsprings the rest of the way to his pickup.

"My car's over here," Tillie said, starting in the direction of her black Mercedes wagon. Over her shoulder, she casually added, "Tell Melinda I said hi."

Noah only nodded and smiled. He obviously hadn't heard a word she'd said. He continued walking beside her until they arrived at her car, then pulled open her door.

"Thanks," she frowned...*this attentiveness is inappropriate.*

"No problem," he nervously replied as he realized what he had done and started to back away. "See you later."

Tillie nodded, looked away from him and closed the door.

Noah watched her pull away from the curb and smiled wistfully. Angel was finally back in his life. As long as he could have these few, precious moments with her, that would be enough...for now.

By the time he floated into Alex's office, the news station had set up for its interview with Alex and his future deputy, Robert. Shondra saw Noah arrive and noticed his blissful expression. He was definitely in a better mood than Melinda, and she walked over to give him the McDarren file. "Here ya go," she said as she handed him the file with a sly wink. "I know you won't read it, but Alex told me to give it to you as soon as you got here. They should be done in a minute."

"Oh, thanks, Shondra," he said with a smile. He glanced at the lights and cameras set up inside of the conference room. "What's all this for?"

"Alex reversed the circuit's decision. He and Robert are giving an interview for tonight's news."

"That'll be good PR for the campaign."

Shondra affirmed with a nod. "By the way, where were you this morning? Melinda's really been intense about this meeting with McDarren, and she couldn't get a hold of you."

"Oh, I took the kids to school," Noah answered in a dreamy, almost melancholy tone as he remembered his encounter with Tillie. He sighed with obvious delight, and Shondra saw the enchantment in his eyes.

The intensity of his cheery mood was contagious, and she smiled. "That must be *some* school."

Noah smiled. "It's Jake's first day of kindergarten, and he was so excited to see A.J. this morning."

"Did Alex's kids get into the same class with Jake?"

"Yep." Noah's cheeks suddenly showed a faint blush. "Tillie dropped them off this morning."

"Hmmm." Shondra chuckled and shook her head. *Poor Noah's really got it bad. Well, he's certainly not the first man to have had a little crush on Alex's wife.* "Come on, Noah. Let me get you a cup of coffee and you can wait in Alex's office."

"Okay," he agreed as he followed her down the hall.

*****

Mona's mouth hung open as she listened to Maggie May and Estelle confess their knowledge of Angel's identity. She'd come down to the bar for her usual Tuesday Bible study with Estelle, only to find the two guilt-ridden women waiting to unload their secrets. Maggie had known that Angel was married to Alex Martin since Carrie's funeral, and yet she'd stayed silent on the matter. Furthermore, the sisters were convinced that Noah was going to do something really stupid if Mona and Josh didn't intervene.

Maggie refilled Mona's coffee cup and gave her a slice of her favorite blueberry pie. "Have a couple bites…you'll feel better, Mona."

"But why?" Mona whispered as she looked back and forth at the two of them.

Maggie sighed. "Because Noah was so screwed up after Carrie died. I just didn't think it was a good idea." She took a deep breath. "And then, pretty soon, the years started piling up and I just didn't think it was important anymore —"

"She never dreamed they'd move to Rapid City," Estelle whispered through teary eyes. She reached for Mona's hand. "Please forgive us, Mona. We should have told *you* at least."

Mona shrugged. "Of course."

"At any rate," Maggie continued, "we're coming to you now. Noah's been yackin' about marrying that Melinda woman, and we don't think it's a good idea."

Mona nodded. "I know. He said something like that to me a couple of days ago."

"She's an *awful* woman," Estelle whispered, glancing from side to side as if she might hear them.

Mona nodded again. "I know."

"But you and Josh will do something before it goes that far?" Maggie asked with a frown.

Mona swallowed. "We'll have to pray about this a lot."

Maggie rolled her eyes and walked away.

*****

At home without her children — for the first time in nearly six years — Tillie felt strangely alone. As she unpacked boxes and put things away, she kept having the strangest compulsion to check on the kids. She laughed at herself and tried to focus on the duty before her.

The movers had left a number of boxes in Tillie's studio upstairs. The first box she opened revealed several old textbooks from college and she wondered why she had kept them. *They could just as well be taken to the trash.* She started to slide the box aside when the tattered, little red cloth-covered book caught her eye. She hadn't looked at that since that day in January 1981.

She reached inside and pulled out the small book. She sat down and laid it delicately in her lap. Her heart began to pound as she wondered if it was still in there — not sure why she even cared. She held her breath and opened the book to reveal the old black-and-white photo, placed between the pages so many years ago.

"Oh," she breathed in a whisper as she took the photo into her hand and lifted it out for a better look. He really had been a handsome man. No wonder she'd been so crazy for him. Tillie let her eyes fall to the words of the poem that the photo had been placed beside, remembering that stormy day just outside of Spearfish, South Dakota, in April 1975.

He had kissed her, just beside Bridal Veil Falls, after telling her the romantic tale of a how a brave warrior saved his beautiful bride. It started to thunder, and they jumped on his Harley and sped out of the canyon in search of shelter, finding the old cowboy bar near the exit. They barely made it out of the rain. She could almost hear the sound of his voice as he sang the words: *And 'twas there that Annie Laurie gave me her promise true, gave me her promise true, which ne'er forgot will be.*

"*Annie Laurie,*" Tillie whispered, and tears suddenly rolled down her cheeks as she looked back at the handsome man seated next to her beside Roubaix Lake. He had his arm around her, and her head was resting on his chest as she looked up into his eyes. A thousand memories she had squelched for the last eleven years were suddenly at the surface, and she could almost feel the warmth of his embrace and hear the sound of his soft laughter.

Tillie slowly shook her head, *of course he's telling the truth. How could I possibly believe otherwise? He loved me...but I was too young for such a commitment.*

"I'm really sorry I screwed things up for us," she whispered as she lovingly touched the old photograph. "But I can't do anything about it now." She swallowed hard and looked at his image again and shook her head. "And you're gonna have to stay away from me."

*****

Martin Campaign Headquarters was set up at the First Federal Bank building, in downtown Rapid City, one floor up from where Alex's office was located. Shondra was his campaign manager, and she had become extremely busy, to say the least. On top of managing Alex's campaign, she also managed his office staff and oversaw the Hansen Development files. Once Alex won the election — and everyone knew that he would — she would be in charge of the transfer of files from the previous attorney general.

"I think we should keep an office here just for Robert," she suggested as she scribbled down notes in Alex's office. "That will make it a lot easier for him when the files are transferred."

Alex agreed. "And what about staff for him? Does he have his own assistant or what?"

"He's got a secretary in Pierre, but he claims he doesn't need any additional staff here in Rapid City. His secretary will be staying in Pierre, even when he travels."

"Well," Alex said with a thoughtful frown, "just make sure we have someone handy whenever he's here."

Shondra nodded and took a deep breath. "And McFadden called from *KDLT*. He's wondering about doing an exclusive piece on you and Tillie and the kids this weekend. What do you think?"

Alex shrugged. "He was decent when he was here on Tuesday, but we'll have to ask Tillie about it first."

Shondra nodded and looked at Alex with a smile. "As your campaign manager, I highly recommend the piece. Tillie's really good in front of the camera when it's a nice reporter, and you guys haven't done that since your announcement in June. Maybe I can talk her into it."

"Go ahead and give it a try."

"He's also interested in whatever is going on with McDarren. The Joker's really a big shot in these parts. Do you think Noah would say anything on camera?"

Alex's dark eyes became curious. "Well, it would be nice if he would, but he might not like that. Why don't you give him a call and see what he says."

Shondra made some notes and added, "You guys are going to have to drop the *Joker* bit if we're going to talk about this in front of a camera."

Alex laughed. "Make sure you mention that to Noah."

*****

Shondra made a special trip over to the Martins' house on Thursday morning, because she knew Tillie would be home alone and they could visit without interruption. Tillie was surprised to see the very professional Shondra Payne show up at her front door, but also excited to see a familiar face. She impulsively hugged Shondra and then showed her through the house.

"It looks wonderful in here, Tillie," Shondra complimented. "As always, you're an impeccable decorator."

"Thanks," Tillie sweetly accepted as they took seats in the large sun room on the main floor. "It's finally starting to come together. It was so big and empty before. How 'bout some coffee?"

"No thanks," Shondra answered with a smile. "I drink too much the way it is."

"Okay, then, to what do I owe this lovely surprise?"

"Well," Shondra began as she looked into Tillie's sparkling black eyes. Tillie's sweet expression always made Shondra feel like smiling. No wonder men were so taken with her. Even now, dressed in just a pair of jeans and a t-shirt, Tillie Martin was the most captivating individual Shondra had ever been with. She had a special grace about her that was reflected in her open smile and even in the smallest of her gestures. "I'm Alex's campaign manager, and you know I set up press releases and interviews, so I was wondering if you'd agree to do a short, family interview this weekend."

Tillie slowly began to nod her head. "Sure, but absolutely no questions about Marquette and Petrice. Make sure you tell them that."

"Of course," Shondra agreed. That was easier than she thought it would be. "And also, could you wear something casual in pink?"

Tillie giggled. "Why?"

"Because it's your best color."

"Well, it's my favorite, you know."

"I know," Shondra acknowledged with a smile. "There will also be a tiny segment on the Joker —" Shondra stopped herself and laughed with a shake of her head. "—I mean McDarren, so they'll have to do just a little blurb with Noah and Alex together, maybe pull in Melinda for a minute because she's done so much work on that project. Is it okay if they just do the whole thing here? The producer has promised me it won't take more than a couple of hours out of your Saturday."

Tillie tried to hide her frown with one of her open smiles. "Sure." *Great. Noah and his girlfriend — together at my house. What a delightful twist.*

Shondra instantly sensed the sudden change in Tillie's demeanor. She leaned closer to Tillie and rested her hand on her knee. "Are you sure that's okay? Because if it's not, we can move it over to Alex's office."

"It's fine," Tillie promised.

*****

Melinda was delighted with the opportunity; she wouldn't have to wait until Sunday for her next plan of action. Noah's boys stayed behind with Joshua and Mona.

"I really like Tillie Martin," Melinda said as she and Noah drove over to the Martins' home that Saturday morning. "She seems like a sweet girl."

Noah just nodded, pretending to watch the road as he drove along. He was already uncomfortable enough the way it was, and he silently prayed for Melinda to talk about something else.

"I imagine she doesn't know anybody in town yet," she prattled on. "Maybe I should call her or something."

"She's pretty shy," Noah murmured as he watched the road. *That's the last thing Angel's gonna want.*

Melinda softly cackled, "She doesn't seem shy to me. We should all do something together. Go out to eat or something fun."

Noah slowly shook his head and frowned. "Alex is too busy, and I don't think they have time for stuff like that." *I'm not about to start double-dating with Angel and Alex. That's weird.*

Melinda sighed. "Well, what are you going to say about the McDarren project?"

"As little as possible," Noah answered. *Man she really talks a lot.* "I just wanna get in there, get this over with, and get out."

Noah turned onto the winding road where Alex and Tillie lived. Their driveway was filled with vehicles, and he had to park on the side of the road. As they walked up to the house, Melinda shyly reached for Noah's hand and smiled into his eyes when he looked at her. He forced himself to smile back, and took her hand.

Alex met them on the front porch and showed them in with a smile. He was dressed in nice Levi's, a white Ralph Lauren polo shirt, and, of course, his Gucci leather loafers. Noah just had to say something.

"I've never seen you in anything other than a suit and tie," he remarked with a lopsided grin.

"Is that good or bad?" Alex asked with a smile.

Noah laughed with a shrug as they followed Alex through the formal living room and into the sunroom, where lights and cameras were set up everywhere.

There was an overpowering scent of cinnamon in the air, and Noah wondered where that was coming from. It made him instantly hungry, and he glanced around for boxes of rolls or donuts. He couldn't see anything, but *something* was making the house smell like a bakery.

Alex's children sat on the bottom steps of the winding staircase. Their little mouths hung open in wonder as they watched people racing around, checking the lights and sound, and positioning everything just so.

"The producer says the lighting is better in here," Alex said. "But it's going to be just a few minutes before they get started."

"Where's Tillie?" Melinda asked.

"She's in the kitchen," Alex answered, and he gave them a faint smile. "She's been up since about four o'clock this morning. This kind of thing makes her a little nervous, so she made some sweet rolls. Enough to feed an army. Do you guys want one?"

"I do," Melinda said with a smile. "Which way to the kitchen?"

"Through the sunroom and straight back," Alex instructed.

Melinda left them alone together and found her way into the kitchen. Tillie was just pulling a cookie sheet out of the oven, filled with freshly baked cinnamon rolls.

How cute, Melinda thought, as she looked at Tillie, noticing her pretty, pink denim dress and matching sandals. *Even her toenail polish matches.*

"Hi, Mrs. Martin," Melinda said with a friendly smile.

Tillie nearly dropped the cookie sheet when she saw Melinda in her kitchen. She steadied her hands and placed the cookie sheet on top of the stove. She closed the oven door and forced herself to return Melinda's smile.

"Please, call me Tillie."

"Sure," Melinda said as she came closer and inhaled the delicious scent of the cinnamon rolls. "We could smell these practically in the front yard."

"Would you like one?" Tillie offered, praying the interviewer could just appear now and whisk Melinda away for some questions.

"Yes, please," Melinda answered.

Tillie put one of the warm rolls on a plate and handed it to Melinda. "There's coffee too. Can I get you a cup?"

Melinda raised an eyebrow and cocked her head. "Goodness, but aren't we domestic."

Tillie smiled nervously and filled a Styrofoam cup.

"Thanks," Melinda said.

From the other side of the sunroom, Shondra saw the discomfort on Tillie's face as Melinda attempted to make small talk. *That's odd. Tillie gets along with everybody.*

Shondra made sure everything was moving along with the camera people, and then she went to the kitchen to see what in the world was happening. Tillie couldn't hide the look of relief in her eyes when Shondra walked in and she impulsively stepped closer to the older woman.

"How's everything going out there?" Tillie asked as she plastered a charming smile on her face.

"Great," Shondra answered. "I think they're just about ready to start." She paused and looked at Melinda. "They'll probably want to do a lighting check on you." She pretended to admire Melinda's black satin blouse. It was a little more formal than what she had told Melinda to wear, but perhaps, with the right lighting, they could soften it up a bit. "Over there," Shondra said, pointing in the direction of a man standing near a bright light with a small box in his hands. "His name is Henry. Please ask him if he's ready for you yet."

"Sure," Melinda answered with a smile, and she looked at Tillie. "Thanks for the roll."

"You bet," Tillie replied, forcing another smile.

Melinda set down her cup and hurried off. Tillie sighed and looked at Shondra. Shondra frowned into Tillie's eyes and put her hand on her shoulder. "Everything okay?"

"I just want to be done with this," Tillie groaned.

Shondra studied Tillie's strange expression. "I know she's kinda pushy; I've been working with her for years. But I've gotta admit she's been super intense lately. She probably shouldn't have started to date her boss."

Tillie seemed to swallow as she looked away from Shondra, found Melinda, and quietly inquired, "How long have they been dating?"

"Since about March," Shondra answered, sensing the strange discomfort in Tillie's demeanor. She took a breath and asked, "Tillie, are you *sure* everything's okay? If you're not feeling good or something's not right, maybe we should reschedule this thing for next week."

"No." Tillie shook her head and brought her eyes back to Shondra. She smiled one of her wonderful smiles and said, "Let's just get it over with."

"Okay," Shondra hesitantly agreed. "I'll go and see if they're ready. We'll do you and Alex and the kids first."

Tillie nodded, and Shondra left her in the kitchen. She went directly to where Alex and Noah were with the twins, listening to them talk about their pony rides at the Blue Bell.

"Hey, Alex," she said as she crouched down beside where he sat, "you'd better give Tillie a little pep talk. She's a nervous wreck about something."

Alex frowned and looked at Shondra. "She was just fine about a minute ago."

"Well, she's not anymore. I think we'd better get this thing over with as quickly as possible. Henry's checking the lighting on Melinda, and he'll do Noah next." She smiled at Noah and said, "Hi, Noah. Sorry I didn't come over sooner."

"That's okay," he answered in his friendly way.

"You look perfect," she said with a smile, pleased to see him dressed in his usual comfortable attire: a clean, tan work shirt, sturdy jeans, and cowboy boots.

"Thank you, Shondra."

Shondra smiled at the twins, who were dressed in simple play clothes. "And nobody is as cute as the two of you." They giggled in response, and Shondra touched each of their noses with her index fingers.

"Okay," she sighed, stood up, and looked at Alex. "You talk to your wife, and I'll see if I can get this show on the road."

Alex acknowledged Shondra's instructions and went to find his wife.

"Hi, Honey," Alex said sweetly as he came into the kitchen.

Tillie was beside the stove, looking more than just a little nervous.

He smiled and gently took her into his arms, holding her close and carefully running his fingers through the soft curls resting on her back. "You okay?"

Tillie nodded.

"Shondra thought maybe you were getting nervous about this."

"Maybe a little," she admitted as she looked up into his dark eyes.

"We're ready in here," they heard Shondra call from the sunroom.

"Let's just get it over with." Tillie smiled. "I guess I *am* a little jumpy today."

"You probably got up too early," Alex said as he took her by the hand and led her to the love seat near the stairs, which the producer had picked for their interview, and they sat down.

"That looks great," said Jon McFadden, who stood in front of them. He smiled down at Tillie. "Mrs. Martin, you look wonderful."

"Thank you," Tillie politely received his compliment, looking away bashfully. She saw her children on the steps close by, and they waved and smiled at their nervous mommy.

"Now don't be shy," McFadden said with a friendly smile and a shake of his head. "That's *not* the Tillie Caselli Martin all of us reporters know and *fear*."

Tillie chuckled, and Alex laughed at McFadden's attempt to make her more comfortable.

"That was immature," Melinda wryly commented, and both Shondra and Noah looked at her with surprise. The three of them were standing away from the cameras for the moment, but had a clear shot of what was being taped.

"She's just a little nervous," Shondra kindly defended, trying not to frown at Melinda.

"What for?" Melinda scoffed. "This is her turf. She even got to edit the questions."

"Melinda!" Noah whispered with a frown, attempting to quiet her. What had gotten into her all of a sudden? *Hopefully nobody else can hear her.*

McFadden squatted before Alex and Tillie and whispered, "I promise, no questions about the senator or Marquette. This is strictly about Alex and the attorney general's office."

"Thanks," Tillie acknowledged with a smile.

"No problem. Now, are you guys ready to go?"

"Ready as we'll ever be," Alex answered, beginning to feel a little nervous himself.

"Okay," McFadden said as he stood up and backed toward the hard, wooden chair where he would be sitting. "Let's get rolling."

There was a strange hush over the huge group of people, except for A.J. and Laura's soft giggles. McFadden smiled at them and pointed his index finger in their direction. "Okay, you two," he said with a smile.

In just a matter of ten or fifteen minutes, the interview was over and McFadden had released Alex and Tillie from their positions. They had both done extremely well, and McFadden was pleased. He hurriedly moved in on the kids, who were beginning to fidget around on the steps. When he told them to sit still, they politely did so and answered his questions in the sweetest way. Their interview was probably all of about three minutes long, and McFadden let them skip over to where their mommy waited. She had deliberately steered clear of where Noah, Melinda, and Shondra stood and took a place near the doors of the sunroom.

"Are we off our grounding yet, Mommy?" A.J. asked with a smile as he looked up into his mother's eyes.

"I think so," Tillie answered as she mentally counted off a week's worth of days.

"Can we go play with the bike?" Laura asked curiously.

"I suppose," Tillie quietly allowed. "But if you take it into the creek, it's gone until next spring."

"Okay," they agreed in unison, and hurried outside.

McFadden smiled. That was perfect. He called to Tillie. "Mrs. Martin," he said as he waved her over to a small screen. "Can I show this?"

She peered at the screen while he replayed the conversation she'd just had with her children. She smiled with surprise and looked at McFadden. "I didn't know you were doing that."

"That's what makes it so great," McFadden said. "I hate using only scripted material. May I use this piece?"

"Sure," Tillie agreed with a smile.

"Good," McFadden said, and then he looked for Noah. "Okay, Hansen. You ready to go?"

"Ready as I'll ever be," Noah said as he came toward McFadden, trying his best not to have eye contact with Tillie. She was obviously uncomfortable, and he felt terrible that she had to go through this. *Maybe I should just tell Alex the whole, gory truth and find myself another lawyer. Keeping this secret from him just isn't worth the torture Angel seems to suffer every time I'm around.*

"Now this is what we'll talk about," McFadden said as he led Noah to the two chairs directly across from the love seat. Alex was already sitting in one of them, and McFadden indicated that Noah should take the other seat. "We'll spend some time on how you got started in the developing business, and I'll ask questions that lead Alex into our conversation concerning his part in that. Then we're gonna bring in Ms. Smalley, and she's gonna talk in a little more detail about the McDarren Project — specifically what it will do for our community." As he spoke, someone led Melinda to the love seat, where she sat down and waited patiently.

Shondra stepped close to Tillie and put her arm around her as they watched the interviews begin. "You did great," she said. "Feeling better now?"

"A little." Tillie smiled nervously at Shondra and then looking at Alex. "But he's a lot more comfortable with this sort of thing than I am."

Shondra agreed. "Noah's sure doing a lot better than I thought he would."

Tillie allowed herself to finally look at him. She watched his blue eyes dance as he answered McFadden's questions, obviously comfortable talking about his business and what he loved to do. He carefully explained his youthful mistakes and that he had re-entered school when he was nearly twenty-four years old. His father had left him property, and he had used it as collateral for a line of credit with the bank. He and Alex took turns explaining the comical financial situations that occurred when Noah first started the business, and both of them laughed heartily as they remembered. As Tillie watched, it became starkly obvious that he'd taken all of the advice she'd given him more than eleven years ago and had done *exactly* what he'd promised he would do.

The interview progressed from there, and soon Melinda was answering questions in front of the camera. She finished up with her own ideas and theology with regard to what the McDarren Project would mean for Rapid City, South Dakota.

As soon as Tillie could see that the interview was completed, she quickly moved toward the doors of the sunroom and smiled at Shondra. "Tell Alex I had to check on the kids. I'll be right back."

Shondra nodded and watched a very anxious Tillie hurry out of the house. *What's going on with that girl today?*

Just a few moments later, Melinda walked up to Shondra with a curious expression. "Where did Tillie go?"

"To check the kids."

Melinda went through the sunroom doors and into the backyard, and suddenly the whole thing started to click for Shondra. *Melinda must know about Noah's little crush!* Shondra sighed and rolled her eyes. *Melinda's jealous. Well, who wouldn't be?*

Shondra went over to where Alex and Noah were still seated. Now that the cameras were off, they were hamming it up, referring to McDarren as the Joker, and bragging about how they would trick him into several other projects. Their joking antics got quite a few hardy laughs out of the crew around them, which only encouraged them to continue. She smiled and shook her head, bending close enough to Alex's ear so that he could hear her whisper without being overhead by Noah. "Tillie's in the backyard, and Melinda just followed her out there." Alex slowly began to frown, and Shondra continued, "She really seems to be after Tillie today. Maybe you should go back there."

Alex pretended a professional expression and smiled at Shondra. "Thanks. I'll get right to it." Shondra stepped away, and Alex stood up. "Come on, Noah, you haven't seen the backyard yet."

Noah got to his feet, and he and Alex went to the backyard. A.J. was pushing his little sister around on the Big Wheel, and Melinda had Tillie cornered under a tree. Tillie was being polite, but Alex saw the irritation in her eyes when she looked at him. Noah saw it too, and he suddenly wished he hadn't started dating Melinda. *What's her fascination with Angel anyway?*

"Hey, you guys," Alex said, as they quickly walked to where the two women were making small talk.

"Hi," Melinda smiled sweetly at Noah. She took his hand into her own when he was close enough and shot Tillie a haughty look. "Tillie and I were just talking about where a great place to eat would be."

Alex put his arm around Tillie and gave her a gentle hug. "You did great in there."

"Thanks." She smiled faintly and forced herself to greet Noah. "Hi, Noah. Sorry, I didn't get a chance to come over earlier."

"That's okay." Noah smiled into her eyes and looked away. Melinda caught the faint blush on his cheeks, but it didn't appear that Alex noticed. *What's with that guy anyway? Is he asleep or what? Can't he see this going on right under his nose?!*

"Hey, I got an idea," Melinda suddenly suggested. "Why don't we all go up to The Sluice for an early dinner?"

"Oh, they don't want to go to The Sluice," Noah scoffed, and he deliberately looked at Tillie with a near frantic expression in his eyes. "It's just a little dump up near Spearfish Canyon where they *play old cowboy music* all day long." He immediately averted his eyes toward Alex and hoped he hadn't been caught. Somehow he had to send her the message. They definitely didn't want to go up there together. That's where they had spent their last date.

"Oh, it's not a dump," Melinda laughed quietly. *Hmmm...seems to have historical significance. Now we have to go.*

"Tillie loves old cowboy music," Alex chimed in excitedly.

"But I don't know anyone that could babysit," Tillie interrupted with a smile. "And it's hard for my little ones to sit still in a restaurant." She had caught Noah's message. Going back to that little, romantic restaurant with him and Melinda was the last thing she wanted to do.

Melinda was beside herself with delight. The two of them were so uncomfortable they were almost squirming, but Alex didn't even seem to notice.

"I know a couple of girls from church," Melinda quickly offered. "They come from really nice families and could use some extra cash on the weekends. We could call them for you." What Melinda didn't say was that she had already secured two babysitters, just in case. However, she had no idea that mentioning The Sluice would make Noah and Tillie so incredibly uncomfortable. This was going better than she had even hoped.

"It might be kinda fun," Alex said as he smiled and looked at Tillie. "What do you think, Honey?"

Tillie struggled with being polite or just flat out rude and refusing to go. Melinda was obnoxious, and Tillie suddenly hated her. She had never been put in such a horrible situation in her life. She looked into her handsome husband's dark eyes and could see that he really wanted to go. He liked Noah and wanted to spend time away from work with him. Certainly she could grit her teeth and get through it, if only for the sake of her husband. Who knows, maybe she would somehow be blessed with the stomach flu before they got there.

"I can't," Noah suddenly blurted. "I just remembered I promised to take the boys to *The Flight of the Navigator* tonight." He smiled at Melinda and sweetly asked, "Remember?"

"No," Melinda shook her head in adamant disagreement. *Baloney! There were no movie plans!* "I don't remember that. I thought *we* were going out tonight."

Noah shrugged and smiled at Melinda. "Well, you are coming with us, aren't you?"

"Well, sure," Melinda said, forcing herself to smile. That plan had been sailing along perfectly until Noah shot it down.

"And we really need to be going," Noah said. He extended his hand toward Alex and said, "Great interview." He looked at Tillie and added, "Great rolls. See you guys tomorrow at church." He quickly turned and led Melinda out of the backyard.

"See ya, Noah." Alex smiled with confusion as he and Tillie watched them walk around the side of the house. When he was sure they were out of ear shot, he said, "Wow. Melinda's really gotten weird."

Tillie sighed heavily, leaning against her tall husband and looking up into his eyes. "She's really intense."

Alex agreed. "I can't imagine what Noah ever saw in her —" He suddenly paused and laughed. "Oh, yeah. I'm the one that set that up."

"You what?" Tillie questioned with a smile.

"She was always giving him the eye, and I thought maybe Noah was lonely — so I told him to ask her out."

"Oh, brother," Tillie groaned and playfully slapped her husband's shoulder. "She certainly won't let him be lonely."

"Hopefully he won't die from exhaustion," Alex kidded, but in the back of his mind he had another thought...*poor Noah.*

Chapter 9
October, 1986

"There she is," Noah whispered to himself. Angel was alone on a bench just outside the little brick school. She wore a pretty, soft pink, sleeveless sun dress. The delicate curve of her exposed collar bone caught the rays of the sunshine, while a gentle wind blew the soft curls around her beautiful face and over her dark shoulders. The schoolyard was empty, and he took a seat very close beside her. She didn't try to get away this time, but instead smiled into his eyes and lovingly touched his face with one of her pretty hands. He smiled as he reached for her hand, kissed it tenderly, and touched her lips with his own. "Angel," he whispered, feeling the warmth and softness of her cheek against his own, "I love you —"

"Dad!" Someone was shaking Noah out of the wonderful dream, and he tried to open his eyes. "Dad!"

"What?" Noah forced himself to focus on his smiling son. He frowned into Ty's eyes and asked groggily, "Who are you?"

"It's me, Dad," Ty laughed. "You fell asleep in front of the game. Come on, it's time to pick up Miss Melinda. Did you forget?"

"Oh," Noah groaned and closed his eyes, trying to will back the dream. "Why do we have to pick up Miss Melinda?"

"Dad!" Ty laughed hard, and somewhere in the background, Noah heard Jake's giggles. "Remember, the Russian missionary is at church tonight? A.J.'s mom is gonna interpret."

"Oh, yeah." Noah sighed and rubbed his eyes. It was all coming back to him now. He had stretched out on the couch for just a few minutes in front of a football game. He must have fallen asleep immediately, because he couldn't remember anything but his dream about Angel.

"Who's Angel?" Jake asked with a silly giggle.

"What? What are you talking about?"

"You said," Jake began, and then he giggled and flopped himself into the couch beside Noah. "Angel, I *love* you." Jake laughed so hard he slapped his knee and kicked his little legs.

"I don't know," Noah grumbled with embarrassment. *Good grief, am I talking about her in my sleep?*

"What were you dreaming about, Dad?" Ty smiled.

"I don't remember," Noah grumbled again. He rubbed his face and looked at the hysterical little boy next to him. Jake's giggle was uncontrollable by now, and Noah couldn't resist just one little tickle into Jake's ribs. He smiled and reached for the small boy's middle with his index finger and gave him a gentle tickle.

"No, Daddy!" Jake giggled as he tried to cover his middle with his hands.

"Well, then, don't tease me!" Noah laughed and stood up from the couch. "Come on, you guys. Let's go get Miss Melinda and take her to church."

Every day Tillie tried to make it to the school before Noah arrived. Then she'd leave her children in the classroom and hurry away before he had a chance to speak with her. Sometimes their eyes would meet for the briefest of moments, and she would see the disappointment in his expression. But what else could she do? He really didn't seem willing to set any kind of limit on himself when they were alone, and she was terrified of what other risks he might take.

Sunday mornings in church, on the other hand, were quite the opposite. He would steer himself and Melinda clear of the Martins, or even go so far as to park Melinda in a pew and then get up and leave her there if he wanted to visit with Alex. His behavior with Tillie was polite and appropriate, and he only said things like, "Good morning, Tillie," and, "How are you today?"

Of course, Noah's behavior became increasingly frustrating for Melinda, and she plotted and schemed all kinds of ways to somehow get the four of them together. With the perfect little Tillie Martin still hanging around in the church, it would be impossible to get Noah's attention. Especially now with that stupid Russian missionary that was getting ready to make his visit. It was all that everyone talked about — Tillie Martin this and Tillie Martin that — until Melinda thought she would probably scream. On top of all that, Tillie's famous family would be arriving in Rapid City in little less than a month, which would be their twins' sixth birthday and Election Day for Alex. The church talked about *that* constantly as well. Tillie Martin's popularity blossomed around her, and she didn't have to do one thing to earn it. The woman had to merely walk into a room and she was its beacon of light. Melinda *hated* her.

Melinda had tried several times to arrange a "double date" with her and Noah and Tillie and Alex. Each time someone thwarted the plan. It was amazing how Noah was able to pull other social engagements out of his hat when he normally just hung out with his boys. All of a sudden Noah and Melinda attended functions together sponsored by such organizations as The Home Builders' Association of the Black Hills, The Cattlemen's Club, and The Rapid City Realtors Association.

Alex was extremely busy with public speaking engagements here and there, and didn't have time to go along with Melinda's plans. She had even tried to contact him herself to set things up, because she knew she couldn't get anywhere with Tillie. Tillie proved to be as good at stonewalling as Noah. She came up with all kinds of excuses why they couldn't go out together.

Alex tried to bring Tillie and their children with him whenever he could, but this time their schedules collided. Tillie was already committed to interpret for the Russian missionary, and Alex was scheduled to meet with his future deputy, Robert, in Pierre. Tillie was excited about the opportunity, but a little disheartened that Alex wouldn't be able to attend. After all, this was the very first time she'd be speaking Russian in public. However, Alex's meeting couldn't be rescheduled.

It was a Wednesday evening, and heavy rain was falling in Rapid City. The Soviet National, Dmitri Romanov, along with his wife, Marta, of German ancestry, and their five-year-old daughter, Heidi, stood quietly on the platform before the church. Tillie was with them. She waited with a polite smile as they spoke and then perfectly interpreted their message to the congregation.

Dmitri was actually a member of the Socialist Party, and, therefore, was allowed to move freely in and out of his country. In secret, he spread the message of Jesus; however, it was becoming increasingly difficult and dangerous. He expressed concern that his government would learn what he was doing and have him imprisoned.

Noah watched only Tillie as she spoke and gracefully gestured with her pretty, dark hands, occasionally looking out into the congregation with her sparkling black eyes. She was wearing a flattering dark green knit dress, not at all like the light, summer sundress she had worn in his dream, but it fit her petite figure perfectly. Her hair was up this evening to show off the soft curve of her neck and the shimmering diamonds dangling from her earlobes. He smiled as he imagined what it would be like to catch one of her hands into his own, kiss it delicately, and lead her out of that place.

Melinda noticed the soft blush upon his cheeks, *again,* and she sighed. *Why can't things like this happen when Alex is around?*

Noah's boys had teased him unmercifully almost all the way to church about what he had said in his dream. Melinda suspected that *Angel* might be a nickname he'd given to Tillie. Her thoughts progressed from there, until suddenly she was hit with yet another suspicion — *Angel's Place? Did he build that monstrosity out on Rimrock for her? Well, of course he did! Does she know about it?* Obviously, Alex knew about it because he was always the one updating the leases for Vivian Olson, but did Alex realize that the house was intended for his wife?

The interpreting went along extremely well. The Romanovs would tell Tillie what they had accomplished in the U.S.S.R., and she would translate for them. Occasionally, a member of the congregation would have a question, and then Tillie would ask the Romanovs the question in Russian. Near the end of message, Tillie's face suddenly looked surprised. She smiled and quickly asked Mr. Romanov a question in Russian. He nodded and smiled, and repeated what he had said. Tillie's eyes became huge and round. She nodded in hesitant agreement and searched the congregation for Joshua. "Pastor Hansen?"

Joshua stood by his place in the pew. "Yes, Mrs. Martin."

Tillie nervously cleared her throat. "Mr. Romanov wishes to become a member of this church body."

Joshua smiled politely. "Of course. I think I've heard enough of his testimony to ask the Elder Board to consider his request."

Tillie took a deep breath. "And then his family would like asylum in the United States. It is their wish to defect."

The congregation collectively gasped, and Joshua's mouth fell open. He quickly approached the platform to reach for Mr. Romanov's hand. "Tell him that I will do what I can," he instructed Tillie with a smile.

Tillie nodded and passed the message on to Mr. Romanov and his family. Mrs. Romanov smiled and bent over to whisper in her little daughter's ear.

Mona went to the platform to shake the Romanovs' hands, and the congregation erupted in applause.

"Well, I'll be," Joshua laughed. "That's the first time that's ever happened."

From her place beside Noah, Melinda rolled her eyes and fumed.

The congregation was dismissed to the church basement for coffee and desserts. From across the room, Noah watched Tillie speak with Walt Livingston and felt himself being pulled in her direction. Alex wasn't there, and Melinda had gone off somewhere. *Who knows where, but at least she's gone.* He slowly walked to where they were visiting. When Tillie turned her head to see who was coming, he smiled at her.

"Hi, Tillie."

"Hi, Noah." She smiled in return, noticing the faint blush upon his cheeks.

"Hi, Hansen," Mr. Livingston said as he extended his hand in friendly greeting toward Noah. Noah accepted it and nodded at Mr. Livingston. "Saw you on TV last month. When will the McDarren Project begin?"

Noah politely smiled at Mr. Livingston, but in reality he was trying to think of a way to get rid of the old lawyer so he could talk to Tillie alone, just for a minute. He promised himself he wouldn't say anything stupid, like 'I love you,' for instance.

"McDarren's stalling," Noah replied as he tried to frown professionally, like he'd seen Alex do when he was withholding information from the other side.

"I heard he was sort of eccentric," Mr. Livingston commented. "But I'm sure Alex will work it all out." He looked at Tillie. "I gotta get going, but I'll see you about eight-thirty over at Alex's office?"

Tillie confirmed, "I'll make sure the Romanovs know what's going on. I can pick them up after I drop my kids off at school."

"Sounds great. Thanks, Tillie." He smiled at Noah and said, "Good to see you, Hansen."

"You too," Noah replied. *Thank You, God...I promise to be good.*

Mr. Livingston walked away, and Noah sighed and looked at Tillie. "So what was that all about?"

"He's going to help with the Romanovs' papers. We'll have to file most of them through the Sioux Falls offices, so he wants to have a conference call with Alex's father in the morning."

"And you'll be the interpreter?"

Tillie nodded.

"How are the polls looking?" he asked, unable to think of anything else to say.

"Good. Alex is ahead."

"Where is he tonight?"

"He's meeting with Robert in Pierre," Tillie answered. "Didn't he tell you?"

Noah slowly smiled and answered, "Yeah, but I guess I forgot."

Tillie took a deep breath and looked all around. "I wonder where my kids are. I really need to be getting them to bed." She gave Noah a nervous smile and started to back away.

Noah's eyes, as always, gave him away, and he accidentally reached for one of her hands. "Please, don't go yet," he blurted. She was still so wonderful, and it was all he could do not to take her into his arms and tell her that he loved her and that he'd wait until eternity if he had to just to be with her.

"Noah," Tillie whispered as she took her hand out of his and prayed no one had seen that. "I *have* to."

Noah looked embarrassed as he realized what he had done. He swallowed and quietly apologized, "I'm sorry."

Tillie only nodded in return. She turned away from him to hide the tears dropping from her eyes and hurried from the room.

Joshua and Mona watched the scene from the other side of the room and wondered if anyone else had noticed. The animation on Noah's face every time he looked into Tillie's eyes was becoming increasingly obvious; it seemed that he wasn't even *trying* to hide it anymore.

"I think he loves her," Joshua whispered to his wife as he took a sip from his Styrofoam cup.

Mona slowly nodded her head and whispered in return, "She's a really sweet lady."

"But she's *not his* anymore."

"It might wear off. Maybe it's just some leftover infatuation," Mona suggested. She took a deep breath and continued, "After they've been here for a little bit longer and he gets used to seein' her again, he'll probably be okay."

Joshua wanted to agree. "Maybe. I'm so thankful that Alex wasn't here tonight."

Mona sighed and shook her head. "Joshua, maybe you oughta have a talk with Noah."

*****

Joshua didn't go into his office at the church the next morning but drove directly to Noah's office downtown. It was still early, and Joshua knew Noah would check in there first before he visited any building sites.

"Is your boss around?" he asked Melinda with a smile.

"He's in his office," Melinda answered with her fake smile.

"Does he have any time for his brother?"

"Go on in, Pastor. I'm sure he'll make time for you."

"Thanks, Melinda," Joshua replied with a smile.

To Joshua's surprise, Noah was reclining in his chair, feet up on the desk, staring into space. His eyes lazily focused on Joshua and he smiled. "Well, hello, Josh. I was just getting ready to leave."

Joshua raised one eyebrow and took a seat in one of the chairs in front of Noah's desk. "What's up, Noah?" He nervously bit his lip as he thought about exactly how to start the conversation.

"Nothin' much. I'm going over to work on the St. Pat site today. How 'bout you?"

"I came to talk to my little brother," Joshua began with a frown, " 'cause I think he's got a little bit of a problem."

Noah's smile immediately faded. He rolled his eyes and sighed, "Brother, that ain't even the half of it."

Joshua nodded. "Listen, Mona tells me that you're thinking of marrying Melinda. Is that true?"

Noah shrugged. "The boys really like her."

"Oh, really." Joshua lowered his voice to a whisper. "What do *you* think of her?"

Noah shrugged again. "She's okay. She doesn't want to have any kids or anything. Wants to always work full time. Build a big house."

Joshua's eyes narrowed into an incredulous frown. "Have you guys been talking about this?"

"A little. We're goin' to the mall this weekend to look at rings."

"What?"

Noah frowned and shook his head. "Well, she's all over Angel constantly, trying to get the four of us together. I thought maybe it would make her a little more secure. Maybe get her to back off."

Joshua's jaw fell open, but he managed to close his mouth and quietly protest, "You can't marry Melinda."

"Why not?" Noah asked. He raised one eyebrow and smiled. "She really likes me, Josh. I can tell."

Joshua shook his head. "I saw you last night."

"Saw me what, Josh?"

"I saw you with Angel…" Joshua stopped himself and shook his head, "I mean, *Tillie*. I don't know if anyone else noticed or not."

"Saw me what?" Noah frowned.

"You know. The way that you look at her. Don't you have any control or what?"

Noah sniffed and looked away. "I thought I handled myself pretty good."

"You reached for her hand, Noah."

A soft smile slipped from Noah's lips. "That was an accident. It won't happen again."

"You need to stay away from that woman," Joshua warned. "I think you're coveting her. That's beyond being in love, Noah. That's sin."

"I know," Noah answered without argument. "And I think if I marry Melinda it will help me a lot."

"Oh, man." Joshua shook his head and frowned. "We're back to that. Listen to me, Noah. Don't expect me to perform the ceremony."

"Well," Noah said matter-of-factly, "I'm tired of being alone."

"I'm trying to understand, but you gotta pray about this, Noah, because only God knows why this has happened."

Noah pretended to agree with Joshua, but out of the corner of his eye, he watched the clock on the wall. He'd get to see her again when he picked up Jake...

*****

Now that her home was finally put together, Tillie used the few hours she had in the mornings to paint and sketch. She had already sketched several images of the brick schoolhouse, but the view from her studio upstairs had been calling her for weeks now. It was Friday morning, and the rain was still drenching the Black Hills. Tillie's canvas was covered with beautiful hues of purples, blues, and grays as she painted the distant hills upon it. *Alex will love this*, she thought, hoping to have it finished before he returned home tomorrow.

The landscape came out of her quickly. She was amazed at the ease with which the image appeared before her — and surprised at the memories waking up within her. They took her back to a time when painting was all that mattered. She sighed and shook her head as she continued to paint. She had planned on becoming an art teacher. *Remember that? Why didn't I do that? What were my reasons behind that incredibly stupid decision, and why did my parents allow it to happen? Painting was all I ever wanted, from the time Vincenzo and Kate gave me my first easel and a set of paints, until....*

Tillie swallowed hard and tried to shake off the old memory. As she painted the image of the beloved hills, however, she couldn't help but drift back in time and remember. *He was the reason. My last portraits and sketches were of him....*

After what she thought to be his betrayal, she'd effectively squelched the desire to ever paint again. When she could no longer ignore it, she gave in to God's request and painted *Obedience* for Alex. It was the same painting the bartender had purchased from her in 1975. She wondered if it still hung there and if Noah remembered.

"Who cares anyway," she muttered to herself. "I was just a stupid kid, and I did a stupid thing." She let out a heavy sigh as she continued to paint and whispered, "I don't know why You had to remind me of this, Lord. I repented. I was truly sorry for what I had done. Why do I have to go through this again?"

Tillie's phone rang, startling her from her thoughts. She set down her brush, wiped off her hands, and reached for the extension that hung on the wall of her studio. "Hello."

"Angel?"

"Oh, hi, Ma'ma," Tillie sighed as she took a seat in a wicker chair.

"Angel, you do not sound well. Is everything alright?"

"Fine," Tillie answered. "What's up, Ma'ma?"

"You have not called in so very long. I thought I should check on you...and things."

Tillie frowned and shook her head. She tried not to sound angry when she answered, "You mean with Noah?"

"Yes."

"Well, you know, Ma'ma," Tillie began as she sighed into the phone, "this whole nightmare could have been avoided if you would have only told me about him."

Rosa swallowed hard. "So, things have gone badly?"

"I don't want to talk about it," Tillie said abruptly, and then she changed the subject. "James and Frances are staying here when they come for the election. Are you and Papa going to stay here too? I have two guest rooms."

"Yes," Rosa answered hesitantly, sensing the tension in Tillie's voice. "And I have already heard from Marquette and Tara. They had to pull out of Tehran early."

"Is everything okay?"

"No, my Angel, but praise the Lord they got out with their lives."

"When will they be here?" Tillie asked. *I'm gonna just let Tara have it for her part in this mess.*

"Patty is bringing all of us next Saturday, that way we can be there for the party you have planned for the twins on Sunday."

"I'll have to make sure we have enough rooms out at the Howard Johnson."

"My Angel," Rosa tenderly prodded, "please talk to me. What has happened?"

"Nothing has happened, Ma'ma," Tillie responded sharply. "And nothing *will* happen. It's just *very hard* for me right now."

"Does he make it hard?"

"Yes, Ma'ma!" Tillie retorted. "If you really want to know, he makes it *very hard* for me. He can't stay away from me, and his wacky girlfriend is constantly bothering Alex and me to go out with them because *she's* noticed it too! I am so thankful that Alex wasn't in church on Wednesday! He made an absolute spectacle of himself, and I could hardly get through my interpretation." Tillie took an angry breath and stormed on, "How many years did I refuse to paint and sketch because of *him* and what I *thought* he had done to me? How many, Ma'ma? And now, I'm face to face with the reality that *I* was the one who screwed it up. *Me*, Ma'ma! And he's lost somewhere in the past and can't fight his way out. Do you have any idea how *guilty* I feel?" Tillie's ranting suddenly caught on a soft sob that began in the back of her throat, slowly worked itself out, and brought tears to her eyes. In her life, she had never raised her voice to her mother, but she couldn't stop crying long enough to apologize.

"Oh, my Angel," Rosa cried softly along with her. "I am so sorry, but I will be there in just a few short days."

"I'm sorry, Ma'ma," Tillie finally managed to whisper. "I love you, and I'm truly sorry for all that stuff I pulled. I had no idea the consequences would follow me this far."

"Please do not blame yourself," Rosa quietly pleaded. "We can work through this, like we did before. We will pray."

"I didn't have to see him *every day* before," Tillie cried.

"*Every day*, Angel? I thought you only saw him at church."

"His little boy is in the same kindergarten class with A.J. and Laura," Tillie cried. "He's A.J.'s new best friend. Every day I have to try to get away from him at the school. He's there in the morning, and he's there in the afternoon when I pick them up."

"Oh, my," Rosa breathed.

"And here's another good one," Tillie said as she sniffed away some tears and continued, "Alex invited him to the birthday party because, you know, Ma'ma, it would be weird if he didn't. Noah's been friends with Vincenzo and Marquette for years. He can hardly say no to the invitation." Tillie sniffed again. "This is so ridiculous, Ma`ma!"

Rosa swallowed hard and asked, "When will Alex be home?"

"Saturday. He calls me every night, and he talks to the kids. Ma`ma, I love Alex so much. This guy shouldn't even bother me anymore."

"It will be okay," Rosa assured. "You know, my Angel, you have just moved away from home for the first time in your life, and you are probably more upset with that than you would like to admit." She took a deep breath and tried to continue on as convincingly as she could. "Listen to me, my little one. You just need to spend some time with your husband and your family. We will all be there next week. Just wait until you hear all of the exciting news from Marquette and Tara. They have had such an adventure, and Vincenzo has purchased a new sleigh for when you visit at Thanksgiving. Patty and Ellie are so excited to visit Rapid City, and I know he's got quite a speech planned for Election Day." Rosa took a soft breath and attempted to smile. "Do not worry yourself about this birthday party, my Angel. We will all be there, and you will be safe with us. I am quite certain Marquette and Vincenzo will keep him so busy that he will hardly have the time to make another scene."

As Tillie listened to her mother's calming voice, she began to pull herself together. "Okay, Ma`ma." Feeling that wonderful comfort that only Ma`ma could give, she sniffed away her tears and slowly nodded her head. "Thanks. I'll be okay now."

"Of course you will." Rosa pretended to laugh quietly into the phone. "And Noah will be okay too. Do not feel guilty for what happened. It was not your fault. Perhaps Noah just needs a little more time. Perhaps the shock of seeing you again has not yet faded, but God will be quick to mend things for the two of you. Remember,. Angel, God knows what He is doing."

Tillie sighed with relief. No one could comfort her like Ma`ma. Everything would be okay. It just had to be.

*****

When Alex arrived home the next morning, he was met at the door by a very excited wife. She threw herself into his arms and hung onto him as tightly as she could. He laughed and kissed her as he looked into her eyes. "I'm really glad to see you, too. Where are the kids?"

"In the backyard," she answered. "It started raining on Wednesday and didn't clear up until last night. They just had to get outside for a little while."

"Are they getting excited about their party?" Alex asked as he peeked out the kitchen window and saw his little children in the backyard.

"They can hardly wait," Tillie said with a smile. "All they can talk about is their cousins coming."

Alex took one of Tillie's hands gently into his own and led her to their loveseat by the steps. "Dad called me yesterday."

"He did?" Tillie asked, nestling close to Alex. "What was he up to?"

"Oh, you know," Alex began with a smile, shaking his head. "Had to give me a little grief about the election and not being there for you on Wednesday."

"Oh, man," Tillie laughed and rolled her eyes. "Alex, it was *really fun*. Well, at first I was really surprised, but then we got everything together with your dad and —" She hesitated and looked at him, "You know, I told you all of this when you called on Wednesday and Thursday."

Alex nodded and his dark eyes shone. "But you didn't tell me about the part where you sounded so wonderful interpreting for the Romanovs. Dad was really impressed."

"Well," Tillie scoffed and bashfully turned her head away. "That wasn't anything. Just finally using a few of the marbles God gave me."

Alex laughed as he gently reached for her chin and slowly turned her face toward his. He looked into her smiling eyes and softly kissed her lips. "Do you have any idea how special you are?"

Tillie put her arms around his neck and held him close. "Do you have any idea how much I love you?"

As Alex held his pretty wife in his arms, he caught the soft scent of her perfume and felt the warmth of her body against his own. "I love you too," he whispered.

Tillie sighed with contentment as she remembered her mother's words from the day before: *It will be okay.*

Chapter 10

Petrice Caselli landed his Learjet safely at the Rapid City Regional Airport on the first Saturday of November, 1986. Everyone had managed to squeeze onto the small jet: Guiseppi and Rosa, all of their sons and their wives, their children, James and Frances Martin, and Sam and Becky-Lynn. Tillie and Alex and their children waited excitedly in the terminal. When they saw Petrice's plane begin to circle and finally land, the twins jumped up and down, clapping their hands.

Naturally, there was the usual small gaggle of reporters that tended to follow Petrice and Marquette wherever they went, and it made Tillie laugh as they assembled on the tarmac.

The door on the jet opened and the steps were lowered by Vincenzo and Marquette. A reporter attempted to ask Marquette a question, who frowned terribly and waved him away. That surprised Tillie. He was usually more than willing to entertain them with his charm and drama. Tara was just behind him, and Tillie noticed her anxious expression. She wondered if it was due to their trip to Iran or if it was because Ma`ma had told her about the unfolding events in Rapid City with Noah.

Petrice was the last one out of the jet, and he stopped to visit with a man in a uniform while airport employees unloaded their luggage and everyone collected their things. Petrice also waved away the reporters. He frowned and shook his head while he and his brothers herded the rest of the family toward the terminal and up the steps. Finally they entered the airport where Tillie and Alex and their children waited.

Rosa went to her daughter, embraced her tightly, and whispered, "Oh, my Angel, we are here at last. How are things going?"

"Better," Tillie whispered.

"I have talked to dear Tara," Rosa whispered. "She is so very sorry. Please do not be angry. She has had a devil of a time on their latest adventure."

"I'm not angry, Ma`ma."

Guiseppi collected both of the twins in his arms, kissed their little cheeks, and held them as tightly as he could. They had their arms around his neck and giggled at their grandfather's passionate gestures.

"Have you caught some fish yet?" Guiseppi asked excitedly.

"None," A.J. frowned, scratching his chin just like his grandfather. "All of the fish in that creek are *very* clever."

Guiseppi laughed at his grandchildren.

Alex stepped away from Tillie to greet his own family, and Tara took the opportunity to approach Tillie. She looked into her eyes, and the expression on Tara's face softened Tillie's heart. Tara put her arms around Tillie and sighed with relief when Tillie returned her embrace.

"Angel, I am sorrier than you can ever know," she whispered as she held her close. "Ma`ma told me how terrible things have been."

"Why didn't you tell me?" Tillie whispered.

"I cannot say at this time, but perhaps we can find a quiet moment together this day."

Tillie could only nod as Marquette was suddenly there, taking her into his arms. He held her close. "We are so happy to finally be here," he said. "Our trials have been significant these past weeks."

"What happened, Marq?" Tillie asked as she looked into his worried face.

"Oh, it was dreadful!" Marquette rolled his eyes and shook his head. "We have got the Ayatollah's son-in-law after us —"

"We barely made it out with our lives," Tara interrupted. "Pray that we do not have to go back again."

"We will *not* go back again, my love," Marquette said as he looked from Tara to Tillie. "They are not at all hospitable to women in that country."

Petrice and Vincenzo interrupted at that moment, with their wives in tow, and greeted their sister with embraces and kisses.

"Just wait until you see our new sleigh!" Vincenzo exclaimed with a smile. "Oh, little one, it is *so* wonderful! Pray for snow so that we may take it for a ride at Thanksgiving."

"I will," Tillie promised with a laugh.

James saw the expression of excitement and anticipation in Alex's eyes, and his heart began to soften. "I hear you're ahead in the polls," he said with a frown.

"Dad, I'm *burying* the other guy."

James allowed a small smile. "I guess Shondra's been doing a pretty good job keeping things in order for you?"

Alex nodded. "She's been great, Dad. We hired her an assistant, and they work really well together."

James put his hand on Alex's shoulder and looked at his son seriously. "Alex, I know I've been stubborn about this whole election, but I want you to know how proud I am of you. You really are the *best* man for the job." He put his arms around his youngest son and held him close.

Alex wanted to cry at his father's surprising, yet very welcome, overture, but he maintained his emotional self control and smiled. "Thanks, Dad. That means a lot to me."

"Just don't leave Tillie and the kids behind," James reminded, glancing over at his daughter-in-law.

Alex followed his father's gaze, smiled at his pretty wife, and promised, "I won't, Dad."

When they'd finally finished with their greetings, Alex and Tillie showed them to their vehicles. Alex had arranged for two large vans to carry their guests from the airport to the hotel. For their parents, however, Alex and Tillie would drive them to their home in their own cars. Vincenzo agreed to drive one van, and Marquette the other. Tillie told them she had rooms for all of them over at the Howard Johnson's on LaCrosse and, as soon as they were checked in, they should come straight over to her house for supper.

"Just follow these directions," she explained, handing each of her brothers a homemade map to help them find their way.

Alex helped their parents load their luggage into his and Tillie's cars, and they were all off in separate directions.

*****

"I think it's bigger than my house," James commented as Tillie and Alex showed them through their new home.

"You can really decorate," Frances complimented with a smile. "It must be that artistic spirit you have."

"Thanks, Frances." Tillie looked at Alex. "Why don't you show them to their room, and I'll take Ma`ma and Papa to their's."

Alex nodded and led his parents down the hall, while Tillie took hers in a different direction.

"I cannot believe how wonderful it looks now," Rosa commented as Tillie showed her and Guiseppi to their room. "You have put everything away perfectly, and I love the new paper in your kitchen."

"Thanks, Ma`ma." Tillie gestured toward the bathroom in Rosa and Guiseppi's guest room. "There are clean towels and washcloths in your closet, and I put some extra toothpaste and shampoo in there in case you need any."

Guiseppi raised one eyebrow and rubbed his bald head. "I do not believe I will need any shampoo on this trip." Rosa giggled at her husband, and so did Tillie. His face became very serious, and he walked to where his daughter stood, reaching for her hand. "Angel, we are so sorry for our omission. How can I ever tell you that our intentions were meant for the good of your own tender heart?"

"Papa," Tillie said with a soft smile and a shake of her head, "it's gonna be okay."

"We never wanted you to have to know," Guiseppi went on as his eyes filled with tears. "He had hurt you so desperately —"

"It's okay," Tillie gently interrupted. "Let's just put it aside for now, because he'll be here tomorrow, and I don't want my brothers to somehow find out that I'm the *hussy* who *severely jilted* him." She comically rolled her eyes and smiled at her father. "Can you imagine what kind of trouble *that* would make?"

Guiseppi agreed hesitantly. "Whatever you say, my Angel. But please know that your Ma`ma and I have not stopped praying for you."

"Well, I'm doing okay, but it wouldn't hurt to say a few prayers for Noah. He's having kind of a tough time of it."

It wasn't long before the rest of the family arrived and all twenty of them were trying to find places at the two tables Tillie had beautifully set for their supper. Her main dining room table sat only twelve, so she and Alex had set up a spare table with eight additional places, putting it at the end of the first.

Tillie's sisters-in-law helped her serve up a tender roast beef with mashed potatoes and gravy, Sicilian green beans on the side, and tiramisu for dessert.

"Oh, my favorite," Petrice sighed as he took a bite of his most treasured dessert. "Who taught you this recipe?"

"Georgie," Tillie answered with a smile.

"Oh, heavens!" Vincenzo suddenly exclaimed with a laugh. "I nearly forgot to tell you. I spoke with Georgie last week, and you will be delighted to know that he has accepted the Lord Jesus Christ as his very own Savior." Several gasps went up around the table. Georgie had worked at Angelo's since 1956, and had made it known that he was a practicing homosexual. Vincenzo laughed and continued, "And I was quite surprised to find out that he has not seen any men for a number of years."

"When did all this happen?" Marquette asked.

"Oh, let me think." Vincenzo frowned. "It was on Wednesday. He drove out to Reata, had one of my hands saddle him up on a tame mare, and then he rode out into the field to find me. He asked me all kinds of questions and then…" Vincenzo paused to smile and sigh. "We prayed together. It was a most wonderful moment."

"Praise the Lord," Sam said with a mischievous smile. "Georgie's in."

Everyone laughed and James asked, "How old is Georgie now?"

"He is fifty this year," Vincenzo answered. "Just a shade older than my brothers and I."

"Fifty is a far cry older than where we are, my brother," Marquette abruptly corrected. "For I am only at the tender age of forty-four."

Sam suddenly cleared his throat and frowned. "Fifty isn't exactly *old* —"

"Especially when you're only two years away," James interrupted. "And just wait until you turn eighty-seven. Now *there's* a number."

Guiseppi laughed and slapped his old friend on the shoulder. "But you have aged so well, my friend."

James rolled his eyes and smiled. "When we met, I was fifty-seven years old. Can you believe that this much time has passed by?"

Guiseppi quietly nodded with a wistful expression. "This Thanksgiving will mark thirty years in America." He looked all around the tables where their families sat and said, "Can you believe all of the people that have joined us, James?"

James smiled as he looked from face to face. "Let's see, Tillie was sort of there, because Rosa was pregnant, but Becky-Lynn was not. Tara was still in Italy. Elaine was just a little girl in New York, and, of course, all of these grandchildren we share were not even glimmers in their parents' eyes yet."

"Oh, but I saw a glimmer in the eyes of Vincenzo and Kate that day." Guiseppi smiled at his son and daughter-in-law. Everyone chuckled, and Vincenzo took Kate's hand into his own to give it a soft kiss.

"Oh, yes," James agreed. "I knew on that day that my *Lovely Kate* would soon leave me for another man."

Vincenzo laughed for he remembered the nickname 'Lovely Kate' he'd given his wife in 1956; he still frequently called her by that name.

"Remember the snow, Papa?" Marquette asked. Guiseppi nodded.

Kate looked at her husband. "I remember watching Vincenzo from the window above the driveway. He was trying to catch the flakes on his tongue."

"I remember Granddad and Grandma," Alex added. "They were there with me and Kate in the window."

"Oh, that's right," Kate said, smiling at Alex. "Granddad had given you a book about Chianti and the Nazis, and you were telling us all about it when the Caselli's drove up."

"I was amazed with your hair, Alex." Rosa smiled at her son-in-law. "You know, it looks blue when you stand in the light just right."

Alex was clearly embarrassed, but Tillie laughed and reached for his hand. Beneath the light of the chandelier, she saw the blue glint her mother was talking about.

"I thought, my goodness!" Rosa went on, "What makes his hair so blue!" Everyone around the table laughed.

"You know what my favorite memory is?" Frances said with a mischievous smile in her eyes. "It was after the Thanksgiving dinner. The men all tried to slink off by themselves, but these wonderful young gentlemen from Italy came back and insisted they help with the dishes." Everyone laughed and Frances continued, "Petrice said, 'Did your hands prepare this meal?' " Frances paused to laugh, and then she added, "Grandma Martin was thrilled."

"And Dad and I were so embarrassed," Sam said. "We jumped in and started helping."

"It was a wonderful adventure," Petrice said with a smile. "One I am certain we shall never forget."

While the men did the dishes (supervised by James and Guiseppi, who gave wise instruction to their young grandsons on the finer points of washing and drying) the ladies relaxed in the family room.

Tillie and Tara managed to sneak away to the studio upstairs and whispered a conversation that had been put off for far too long.

"Why didn't you tell me?" Tillie began with a frown.

"Angel, I found out only the night Noah brought Alex to the hospital."

"And then you lied to me, Tara," Tillie quietly confronted. "Were you afraid that I would leave Alex or something?"

Tara shrugged and frowned. "Perhaps. Alex had just done something so dreadful, and the babies needed their parents."

"My heart is not that fickle."

"Oh, Angel, I know that, but even while you were still in the hospital, Marquette began to make amends with Alex. I feared that, if *he* knew about Noah, things would most certainly become awkward." Tara sighed and shook her head. "And Marquette was *instantly* attracted to Noah. It has been the strangest thing. I just did not feel it wise to reveal it at that time."

Tillie agreed reluctantly. "I guess I understand. It's just plain weird, though, isn't it Tara? I mean, meeting Noah in the first place, having him become friends with my husband and two of my brothers, and then throwing me back into the picture. What is God *thinking?*"

"I do not know," Tara admitted. "But I am sure our Father has a wonderful plan."

Tillie's eyes became thoughtful. "You know, for years I have listened to Vincenzo and Marquette talk about Noah's tragic past with a young woman that," she paused and mimicked her brothers' soft accent, "*so severely jilted him*...so I know he's spoken of me, and it must not have been in a very favorable light."

"Oh, Angel, that is not true at all. When Noah speaks of that young lady, it is nothing but exultation and sincere gratitude. Your dearest brothers have embellished the stories and added names to the young lady out of their affection for Noah."

"Did you ever tell Marquette?"

"No." Tara swallowed hard and shook her head. "And it has been very difficult. The two of us have never kept anything from one another."

Tillie let out a breath. "Thank you. Please don't ever tell. I can't imagine what he would think of me."

"And will Noah be at the party tomorrow?" Tara asked.

"Humph. Along with his wacky girlfriend."

"*Wacky?*"

Tillie snorted and shook her head. "She's just a lot different than the women I'm used to spending time with. Of course, she's *really, really* smart." She rolled her eyes and continued, "She has a career, of course, and gobs of fancy clothes. She had her own individual interview on the TV, and she speaks Lakota fluently...and..." Tillie paused and sighed, "She's very pretty."

Tara frowned. "Angel, I hope you are not jealous."

"Maybe," Tillie said with a slow nod. "But I think, somehow, she knows something about Noah and me because she's always trying to throw the two of us together in awkward situations. She's called me several times, trying to arrange a time when she and Noah and Alex and I can all get together."

"Why would she do that?"

"Who knows," Tillie answered. "I feel like she's trying to make me sick of him or something, or make him sick of me. I don't know."

"Has Alex noticed anything of this?"

"No. He's been too busy, thank goodness. He doesn't have a clue. He just thinks Melinda's a little intense."

"That is her name? Melinda?"

Tillie clarified, "Noah's assistant."

"Oh yes, I remember her now…I believe we met her before we went to Iran."

"They've been dating since early spring, I guess," Tillie went on.

"Does Noah seem to like her?"

"I don't see how he can *stand* her," Tillie replied with a frown.

Tara took a deep breath and asked, "Angel, how do you feel about Noah?"

Tillie swallowed hard, surprised at the question. "I feel very *guilty*. I can't believe I was the one that did that horrible thing to him."

*****

Sunday morning dawned bright and unusually warm for the second day in November, promising to make the day wonderful for A.J. and Laura's birthday party. While most of the Casellis and Martins attended church, Tillie, Rosa, and Tara stayed back to prepare for the party. Tillie had allowed her children to invite five friends each, and everyone was to arrive shortly after church.

For the children, Tillie made her version of "piggies in the blanket," which were little smokies wrapped in a pastry and baked. Then she'd made them raspberry Jello, whipped with cream and put into individual plastic cups. Of course, they had to have something fairly nutritious, so she sliced green apples and sprinkled them with cinnamon and sugar. No soda and no punch. The little ones would have to drink milk.

For the adults, Tillie had prepared ravioli — Petrice's favorite and focaccia bread — Marquette's favorite. She'd made several pans of the ravioli earlier in the week and stored them in her freezer. She warmed them in her oven on Sunday morning, sending the delicious smells of garlic, cheese, and basil throughout the house. For dessert she'd prepared old Doria's special cannoli recipe for Vincenzo so he wouldn't feel left out.

Shortly after noon, the Casellis and the Martins returned from church. Alex, Sam, and all of their nieces and nephews went to the backyard to play ball, while Petrice, Vincenzo, and Marquette waited in the driveway for Noah. Tara, Kate, and Ellie were decorating the family room with streamers and balloons.

"She's really a little piece of work," Ellie mumbled as she taped a balloon to the ceiling. "Did you see her flashing her ugly engagement ring under everyone's nose?"

"Yuck," Kate groaned, being careful to unroll the streamers without tearing them. "I can't believe that someone like Noah would have anything to do with her."

Tara listened with wide-eyed wonder. "Did you say that Noah is engaged?"

"Yep," Kate answered with a nod. "They announced it at church this morning. I thought Marquette was gonna flip out."

Ellie giggled.

Kate noticed Tara's surprised look and she asked, "Whatsamatter?"

Tara slowly shook her head. "I am just very surprised. They have not dated very long."

"Well, I'm sure Marquette will give you all of the gruesome details," Ellie went on. "Just wait until you meet her. She's kind of a meany."

"Angel, come and help me!" Guiseppi's excited face peered into the kitchen as he beckoned his daughter to come with him.

"What is it, Papa?" Tillie asked. "I have a lot to get ready."

"Come, Angel," Guiseppi insisted with a smile. He took Tillie's hand gently into his own and led her into the living room. He didn't stop until he had reached the magical cabinet he'd found. James Martin was still there, thoughtfully scratching his head, and he looked at Tillie with relief. It was obviously a stereo system of some sort. That they knew for sure. However, the two of them had not been able to figure out how to work it. "How do you work such a thing?" Guiseppi questioned. "Would it not be wonderful to hear some music on this day?"

Tillie smiled at her papa and turned on the power switch. The house was filled with music of the station that had been used last. "This system can be played anywhere in the house," Tillie explained to a very engrossed Guiseppi. "I can turn on the speakers in just the formal living room or just in the kitchen. I can pick any room in the house or all of them."

"Incredible," Guiseppi said with a thoughtful expression as he looked over each and every control his daughter described for him.

"See, Papa," Tillie explained with a smile as she opened a compact disc and showed him the shiny disc. "I can put a CD in here."

"What is that?" Guiseppi looked over the small disc with a frown.

"It's a compact disc. Pretty soon they won't even make records anymore."

"How crazy," Guiseppi mused.

"But I do have a turntable," Tillie continued as she smiled at her father. "And look what I found at this scary old record store." She pulled an album from the cabinet and put it into her father's hands.

"Oh, my!" Guiseppi's old, black eyes lit up when he saw the familiar Dean Martin album. "This one was my favorite." He looked hopefully at Tillie and requested, "You must play this now, before any more guests arrive or we will not have the time to listen to it."

"Okay," Tillie agreed with a nod as she took the album from her father and set it on the turntable. Soon the music began to play, and Guiseppi smiled wistfully.

"Come, my Angel," he said as he took her into his arms. "You *must* remember this one." He began to sing in Italian with Dean Martin as he slowly waltzed his daughter around the living room.

"Oh, Papa," Tillie laughed at her wonderful father as she remembered the old tune she'd learned her first dance steps to.

Noah and Melinda had to park in the road and walk to the house. Ty and Jake ran up ahead, pausing politely at the place where the Caselli men stood.

"Your little buddies are all in the backyard playing ball," Marquette said excitedly. "Hurry and join them!"

Ty and Jake ran around the corner of the house and disappeared into the backyard.

Vincenzo watched Noah and Melinda slowly make their way up into the driveway, noticing they were holding hands. "He actually touches her," he whispered. "He is a braver man than I thought."

Marquette swallowed as hard as he could so as not to laugh.

Petrice shot them both an *older brother* frown. *Can they not behave for one day? And especially at their ages.*

"My friend Noah," Marquette said as he reached for Noah's hand and gave it a hearty shake. "Again, many congratulations."

"Thanks, Marq," Noah replied with a smile. He was still a little embarrassed at Melinda's sudden outburst at church. Shortly before Joshua began the sermon, she stood up and announced that she wanted everyone to know of her and Noah's engagement. Noah thought poor ol' Joshua was going to drop where he stood, but he covered with a nice smile and some "congratulations," and then delivered the sermon like a pro.

"And what a lovely lady you have chosen," Petrice said politely. He reached for Melinda's hand and delicately placed a kiss on the top of it.

Vincenzo rolled his eyes and shook his head. *Petrice has been a politician for far too long.* He looked at Marquette, who pretended to cringe. Vincenzo quickly looked away for fear he would smile. *I pray dear Noah has not seen our dreadful display.*

"Let us go inside and see if my sister has a little something to tide us over," Marquette said, starting for the house. "I am quite starved."

When they entered the kitchen through the garage door, it was empty, but the smell of something wonderful cooking was in the air, and trays of Marquette's favorite bread were just waiting for him to sample.

"What is that smell?" Noah asked.

"Angel has prepared for us her delicious ravioli," Marquette answered with a smile. "And just wait until you taste it."

Melinda caught Noah's suddenly worried expression. She gritted her teeth and raised an eyebrow. "Who's Angel?"

Noah wanted to die. *Please, Lord, take me now.*

"Our sister," Vincenzo answered, and Noah thought he might faint. "She makes ravioli for Petrice."

Noah let out his breath and waited for Melinda to react, but she said nothing. She continued to smile as if everything were perfectly normal.

"Because he spoiled her," Marquette interrupted, giving Petrice a friendly slap on the back.

"I did nothing of the sort," Petrice protested with a frown.

Melinda wanted to slug somebody. Angel's brothers had just confirmed her suspicions. *So she is the mysterious "Angel" Noah's been talking about in his sleep — and the inspiration for Angel's Place. I hate her so much. Just wait until they see the house Noah will build for me....*

Rosa came into the kitchen, laughing and shaking her head. She smiled with surprise when she saw her sons. "Hello, my children. How was church this day?"

"Wonderful, Ma`ma," Petrice answered.

"Do I hear Dean Martin?" Marquette asked.

"We do, my brother," Vincenzo agreed. "Let us see what Papa has gotten into."

"They are in the living room." Rosa laughed, and then she greeted Noah. "Well, hello, Noah. And how are you on this day?" She offered Noah her hand in greeting.

"Fine, thank you," Noah answered, politely taking Rosa's hand into his own.

"And who is this lovely lady by your side?"

"This is Melinda Smalley," Noah introduced. Melinda politely extended her hand to Rosa, and Rosa gave it a gentle shake. "Melinda, this is Mrs. Caselli," he continued, "Tillie's mother."

"How nice to meet you," Rosa graciously greeted

"And you as well," Melinda said with a smile.

"Come, Noah," Marquette waved from the entryway in the kitchen. "You must see this."

"Oh, goodness," Rosa tittered. "Angel has been showing my husband the stereo system in the living room, and I fear we will have to have one installed when we get home!"

Noah smiled and followed Marquette, Petrice, and Vincenzo into the living room where Guiseppi was still singing in Italian and waltzing his daughter around the room. She looked so beautiful at that moment — dressed in ordinary blue jeans and a soft, white sweater — that it nearly took Noah's breath away. She gracefully stepped in time to the music that played, following Guiseppi's lead and looking at him like they were the only two people on the planet.

Guiseppi smiled at Vincenzo and exclaimed, "Fetch me my Rosa! The next song is my favorite." And then he began to sing in Italian again, and Tillie laughed some more.

Vincenzo laughed at his father and obediently left to "fetch" his mother.

"What's he singing?" Noah whispered to Marquette.

"*Non Dimenticar*," he answered. "It means, *do not forget.*" He smiled and laughed quietly at his father. Dean Martin's voice had quieted for the background music solo, but Guiseppi's soft voice sang the words in Italian. Marquette whispered, "He is singing 'do not forget, my love is like a star, my darling, shining bright and clear, just because you are here.' " He smiled at Noah and said, "My father has three sons, but only one Angel."

Melinda came up beside Noah and gently placed her hand into his own, immediately drawing his attention away from the enchanting sight captivating everyone in the room.

How does she do that? Melinda thought.

Noah looked at Melinda and gave her a friendly smile. She forced a smile and complained, "It's loud in here."

Noah nodded. "But it's fun, isn't it?"

Melinda shrugged and turned her eyes back to Guiseppi and Tillie.

Vincenzo appeared with his giggling mother just as the tune was ending, and Guiseppi released Tillie and held his arms open for Rosa.

"Please, my Rosa," he said with a very dramatic bow, and his sons began to laugh. "Have at least one dance with me."

Rosa laughed all the way into his arms. As the next tune started, Guiseppi once again began singing along in his first language.

Tillie slowly backed away from her parents, turned, and suddenly saw Noah. She covered her surprise with a smile, looked from him to Melinda, and said, "Hi. How are you guys today?"

"Fine. Thanks for inviting us," Melinda answered, and Noah only nodded.

Tillie smiled nervously and said, "I gotta check on some things. I'll be right back."

Noah sighed as he watched her hurry from the room...*she won't be right back....*

"Is it not amazing!" Guiseppi exclaimed. "We had to come to America to hear great Italian music!" Everyone in the room laughed.

"Where is my Tara?" Marquette said with a smile. "She must dance with me," and he hurried out of the room.

"I thought we were coming to a birthday party," Melinda grumbled under her breath as old James Martin started to slowly waltz his wife around the living room.

Noah couldn't help but smile. "Well, they're Italian, and I've heard they really live it up."

Vincenzo coaxed a laughing Kate into the living room, while Petrice took the hand of his tall wife.

"Wow, she's even taller in person," Melinda whispered, as she watched the famous Senator waltz his wife. She frowned at Noah, "How did you get connected to this family anyway?"

Noah covered his anxiety with a strained smile and answered, "You know that. It was when I drove Alex to Sioux Falls. When Tillie had the babies."

"Oh, yes, that's right," Melinda nodded with a frown. "How appropriate that you be here for their birthday." *Since you were nearly the one who fathered them.* "I think I'll go and see if *Angel* needs any help." She removed her hand from Noah's and turned in the direction of the kitchen.

Noah shuttered. *I s'pose she's gonna give Angel the great news.*

Tillie and Becky-Lynn were looking out the kitchen window and laughing when Melinda entered. Sam and Alex had quite a game of baseball going with all of the younger party goers. The Romanovs had arrived and seemed to be having a great time with them.

"Look at Sam," Becky-Lynn said. "He's so huge compared to those little kids."

"Except for Angelo," Tillie commented. "Can you believe how tall he's gotten?"

Melinda abruptly cleared her throat to make Tillie and Becky-Lynn turn from the window. "Hi," Becky-Lynn greeted with a smile. "Have we met yet?"

"No," Melinda answered, extending her hand to Becky-Lynn.

"I'm Becky-Lynn Martin," she introduced herself and took Melinda's hand gently into her own. "Sam's my hubby."

"I'm Melinda Smalley." Giving Tillie a coy glance before she brought her eyes back to Becky-Lynn, she continued. "I'm Noah Hansen's fiancée."

"Congratulations," Becky-Lynn said in her friendly way.

Tillie attempted to hide her astounded expression with a smile. "Congratulations, Melinda."

Melinda flaunted her gaudy, giant diamond, which was set between two rubies, and breathlessly informed, "I got the ring yesterday."

"Wow," Becky-Lynn pretended to admire. "Those are some spendy stones."

"I know," Melinda sighed with a smile. Looking directly at Tillie, she added, "I guess he just loves me a lot."

Tillie's stomach suddenly felt nauseous and her hands began to shake, but she covered with a gracious smile. "So when's the big day?"

"The second Saturday in July," Melinda answered. *Gotcha!*

Alex came through the back door at just that moment and smiled at Tillie. "Hey, Dmitri is trying to tell us something. Could you help us out?"

"Sure!" Tillie smiled with relief and looked back at Melinda. "Well, congratulations again." She looked at Alex and said, "Melinda was just showing us her engagement ring."

"Oh, yeah." Alex smiled and nodded. "They announced it at church this morning." He tenderly took Tillie's hand into his own and coaxed, "Come on, Honey. Dmitri specifically asked me to get you." He comically rolled his eyes. "At least I *think* he asked for you."

Tillie nodded with a chuckle and went with her husband, thankful for the genuine excuse to get away from Melinda…*it's gonna be a long day*….

Tillie coaxed the children to come into the family room, have a bite to eat, and see the decorations her sisters-in-law had hung. The little ones, as well as their older cousins, were delighted with the "piggies" and Jello and readily sat down to eat.

Laura had taken a special liking to the Romanovs' daughter, Heidi, and made sure she got to sit by her new friend. The little Russian girl spoke even less English than her parents, but somehow the two were able to communicate.

"Goodness, but it is warm in here," Marquette commented. He gently caught a hold of his sister as she crossed from the family room into the sunroom. "Do you mind if I open the door just a little?"

"Go ahead," Tillie answered. She added over her shoulder as she hurried to the kitchen, "Just don't forget to close the screen." Marquette always forgot the screen because he spent so much time in *Italia*, where there were no screens on his home.

Out in the kitchen, Rosa and Kate set up a buffet line and instructed everyone to go through and take whatever they could hold.

"She cooks enough to feed a small country," Kate said with a smile. "So don't be shy."

"What does she have for dessert?" Vincenzo whispered into his wife's ear.

Kate laughed and whispered in return, "She made *you* cannoli."

"Oh, I *love* her," Vincenzo sighed with a smile.

After dishing up, Dmitri and Marta Romanov took seats beside James and Frances Martin and were communicating excellently. To their pleasant surprise, they all discovered they spoke French. Rosa and Guiseppi visited with Sam and Becky-Lynn at the large dining room table, and their four older grandchildren, Alyssa, Angelo, Michael and Gabriella, joined them.

Tara smiled at Marquette. "I am going to play with the little ones," she said, giving him a soft kiss upon his cheek. "You should come to the family room when you are done."

"I will," Marquette agreed, holding a filled plate of ravioli and focaccia. "It will only take me one moment to eat my food."

Tara smiled and walked away, followed by Elaine and Kate. They had all promised Tillie they would help out with the games.

Marquette looked to his brothers, who were already eating their food where they stood. "Come, my brothers," Marquette said. "Let us sit outside and enjoy this fine day." He looked at Noah and smiled. "Would you care to join us?"

Noah happily accepted Marquette's invitation, and he and Melinda followed them out of the sunroom and onto the patio, where there was enough furniture for everyone.

"Ah," Marquette said as he took a seat. "That is much better." He noticed that Melinda had followed them all outside and he politely inquired, "Would you not prefer to join the ladies?" He chuckled. "For we can be quite boring."

Marquette's brothers and Noah laughed at Marquette's humor.

"What for?" Melinda answered abruptly. "We really don't have anything in common."

Vincenzo stuffed his mouth with ravioli so he wouldn't be tempted to speak. Marquette only smiled faintly and did the same thing, while Petrice merely stared at her with his mouth hanging open. She had been saying snide things of that sort all day long.

Over the course of the day Melinda discovered that, if she wanted to get Tillie out of the picture, her *perfect* family would have to go as well. And that was going to be a tough one, because Vincenzo and Marquette were extremely fond of Noah.

Noah was so embarrassed, *again*, and wished he could either just drop dead or possibly be raptured out of the horrible situation. *What's wrong with her? Everybody's bending over backwards to get along with her.* Melinda had made contemptible comments all day long. She had even gone so far as to say that she was "going to make something of her life" when Becky-Lynn complimented the way Tillie had planned her children's party. Noah had overheard Melinda tell Frances Martin that Tillie spoiled her children. Frances said nothing, but Noah pulled Melinda aside and quietly told her to be more polite. He was friends with these people, and he wanted to stay that way.

"Is Angel's recipe not the best that you have ever had?" Petrice finally said, breaking the silence as he took a bite of his favorite dish.

"This is incredible," Noah agreed through a mouth full of food.

"For many summers, we all took turns working in Papa's *ristorante*," Marquette explained. "Only Angel learned his cook's tricks this well, and she enjoys it so much."

"I wonder why," Melinda grumbled, sincerely sick of hearing about what a *great* person *Angel* was. She finished with, "What a waste of time."

"Melinda!" Noah whispered as he attempted to give Melinda some kind of a sign with his eyes that her comment had been horribly inappropriate.

Tillie's brothers fell quiet, stopping in mid-chew to stare at Melinda. Why in the world would someone say something like that about their beautiful, caring sister? To them, Angel was perfect in every way, and they had never shared any different opinion with anyone else. *Ever.*

Melinda sensed the quiet tension and stood. "Excuse me. I have to use the powder room."

The Caselli men and Noah all stood politely and waited for Melinda to disappear inside the house before they took their seats again. Tillie's brothers didn't say anything, because they felt that they had to be polite in front of their good friend Noah. As a result, they all remained quiet. The astounding surprise of what Melinda had said about their sister had turned their laughter and fellowship into deafening silence.

"I'm sorry about that," Noah apologized as he looked around at the three brothers. "Maybe we just misunderstood."

"Oh, yes," Petrice replied. "I thought nothing of it. I am sure that we just misunderstood."

Marquette glared at his brother. *Always the diplomat.*

Vincenzo only smiled. *Poor Noah should really reconsider his decision to ruin the rest of his life with that woman.*

A woman's scream from inside the house brought all of them to their feet, and they rushed inside. Kate tore out of the family room and into the sunroom and leaped into Vincenzo's arms.

"It's a mouse!" she screamed.

Vincenzo laughed as he held his dear wife in his arms. *All of her years as a ranch wife and she still can't handle the sight of a mouse.*

"He's in the family room!" Kate went on. "We were playing *Twister* and he ran *right across my hand!*"

"Oh, my dear," Vincenzo consoled, trying his best not to laugh again, for Lovely Kate seemed to have been traumatized enough.

Alex and Sam hurried to the family room, and the older cousins collected in the doorway. Rosa and Guiseppi peeked cautiously out of the kitchen, and several little children's screams were heard. Apparently the mouse was still raising havoc with the party. From where the Caselli brothers stood, Petrice saw Elaine and Tara standing on a chair together, and they each held a small child.

"Well, who shall retrieve the little bugger?" Marquette asked as he lifted one brow and looked at Petrice. He sighed and said, "As you are aware, my brother, I cannot."

"*I* certainly cannot," Petrice informed.

"Oh, come on," Noah scoffed. "It's just a little mouse."

Marquette took a breath and nodded seriously at Noah. "Go and get it then."

"Yes," Petrice nodded in agreement. "Go and get the little beast."

"Well," Noah cleared his throat and tried to look thoughtful as several more little screams were heard from the family room. "I really should have a net or something."

"Oh, brother." Marquette rolled his eyes and let his breath out. "You are afraid as well?"

"No," Noah replied as he shook his head and frowned. "I'm not afraid of a little mouse."

Melinda came down the stairs and stood beside Noah. "What's going on?"

"There's a mouse in the family room," Kate said, nearly crying by now. Vincenzo held her tightly and tried not to laugh.

"Go in there and get it," Petrice instructed with authority, frowning insistently at Noah.

It was at that moment the crowd of children outside the doorway of the family room parted, and Tillie trotted through, carrying a squirming little mouse by the tail.

"*Oh, Angel!*" Kate screamed and jumped out of Vincenzo's arms, backing into the kitchen.

"It's okay, Kate," Tillie giggled. "Is the door still open?"

Marquette made sure the door was wide open and stepped quickly out of the way as his sister hurried to dispose of the wiggling little mouse.

As Tillie passed by Melinda, she had the urge to throw it at her, but that wouldn't have been very nice, so she gave it a gentle toss out the door instead. Marquette loudly slammed the door shut.

"You forgot to close the screen." Tillie frowned and pointed her index finger at Marquette as she scolded, "You *always* forget to close the screen."

"I am so sorry," Marquette apologized as he hung his head.

"Praise the Lord," Petrice breathed a sigh of relief. "You must be the bravest woman on the face of this earth."

Rosa and Guiseppi laughed and meandered into the family room to join their grandchildren. Melinda only rolled her eyes. *She even catches live mice with her bare hands. Unbelievable.*

Tillie let her breath out and rushed to the kitchen sink where she doused her hands with dish soap. She looked at Kate, who was visibly relieved to be rid of the unwelcome visitor, and giggled. "Are you okay?"

"Fine," Kate answered with a nod of her head. "How did you do that?"

"I got him backed into a corner," Tillie explained. "And then I just grabbed his little tail —"

"Oh…" Kate rolled her eyes and looked queasy.

"Vincenzo!" Tillie called to her brother, and then she laughed. "Get in here and help your wife!"

"I must be off," Vincenzo said with a smile. "My lovely bride awaits my tender mercies," and he hurried into the kitchen.

Tara and Ellie calmed the children and got them interested in their game again. After coaxing some of the other adults to join in, they went into the sunroom where their husbands were still visiting with Noah.

"She's fast," Ellie said as she glanced at Tillie, who was making her way back into the family room to check on the party. "Believe me, I had a bird's eye view."

"Yes, we know, my love," Petrice chided. "I saw you on the chair."

Tara laughed. "But all is well again. See." She peeked into the family room and watched Tillie set up another game for the children. "Angel has made such a nice party."

Ellie glanced at Tillie. "Where does she get all of her energy?"

"Well," Marquette said thoughtfully, "she still has her youth."

Petrice bristled as he looked at Marquette. "And we do not? I hope that you are not saying we are old."

"A little hair color would do wonders for you, my brother," Marquette said with a sly smile, and Noah laughed at the two of them.

Melinda sighed. She couldn't take one more *my brother* conversation. She followed Ellie and Tara to watch the last of the party games.

Alex came into the sunroom and walked over to Petrice with a smile. "Senator, you have a phone call."

"I did not even hear the phone ring," Petrice said. "Where can I take it?"

"Upstairs in my office," Alex answered. "Second door on the left."

"Thank you." Petrice bowed politely. "If you will excuse me for a moment."

As Petrice walked away, Alex looked at Marquette and Noah. "How's everything?"

"It's a great party, Alex," Noah answered with a smile.

"I think Tillie's just about ready to get the cake out," Alex said, "and then we can call it a day." Noah almost felt sad, but he knew it had to end sometime. "I'll go and see what she's got planned," Alex said, and he went into the family room.

Noah watched Tillie as she played with the children, and a wistful smile appeared on his face. In his life, no one had ever made him feel this way. He longed to hold her in his arms again. From there, his thoughts pulled him into a memory that was eleven years old, forgetting that Marquette was standing just next to him. Noah watched her pretty hands touching the children, showing them what to do. Her black eyes sparkled as she smiled and laughed, and her graceful body moved among them...*she's just perfect...is someone saying my name?*

"Noah," Marquette chuckled, for he had said Noah's name three times.

"What?" Noah turned and looked at Marquette with a silly grin.

Marquette laughed as he took Noah by the arm. "Come with me, my friend. You need some air." Noah followed Marquette into the backyard. Marquette was sure to close the screen door this time, and he smiled and shook his head at Noah. "I have no need for screens in *Italia*, so I always manage to forget about them when I am here." He glanced at Noah. "But let us walk down and see this creek that Angel's babies speak of."

Noah took a breath and followed Marquette.

When they were at what Marquette felt was a safe distance away, he put his arm over Noah's shoulders and laughed again. "Your eyes gave you away, my friend."

"What?"

"I saw you looking at my sister. Do not deny this."

Noah swallowed and looked at the creek...*oops.*

Marquette laughed and gave Noah's back a slap. "With our Angel, it is more than beauty. I certainly cannot blame you."

Noah took a deep breath. He couldn't look at Marquette, so he looked at the distant hills. "I'm sorry. It won't happen again."

"Oh, I am not angry," Marquette assured with a smile. "You are a fine man of honor, Noah Hansen, and I know that you would not do anything inappropriate. However, it does surprise me that you would allow your heart this smallish sort of tryst while you are engaged to another."

100

Noah shrugged and looked at Marquette. "I really don't like Melinda that much."

Marquette couldn't hide his sudden look of surprise. "Why are you *marrying* her then?"

"I'm lonely, Marq," Noah answered honestly. "I want to share my life with someone."

Marquette frowned. "You would be better off with my father's ex-gay cook than the devil you have chosen."

"Your father has a *gay* cook?"

"Yes, however, that is not the point. Noah, you must not choose someone out of loneliness. God has intended a very special woman to come your way; do not doubt it for a moment. I have prayed for you for many years, and I trust our Lord to deliver to you the delight of your life when it is time."

Noah looked curiously at Marquette. "And I suppose you don't believe that the delight of my life is gonna be Melinda?"

"How could she be? She does not dance. She does not want babies. She does not like to cook." Marquette hesitated with a sigh. "At the risk of sounding old fashioned, Noah, I cannot imagine what you would want with a woman such as that. She is spiteful and ornery and tries very hard not to smile. Whatever possessed you to take up with her in the first place?"

Noah took a breath and shrugged. "I don't know, but Angel's perfect."

Marquette nodded. "That she is, my friend, but there is only one Angel; and, as I have *sincerely regretted* for many years now, she is taken."

Noah sighed heavily and shook his head. "I just can't seem to help myself, Marq."

Marquette smiled and shook his head. "Noah, if you cannot help yourself, then you must call upon the Lord to fight this battle for you." He promised, "I will pray for you to overcome this *infatuazione* so that you do not hurt Alex or Angel...or yourself."

Noah swallowed hard. *If he only knew.*

Chapter 11

"Man, Melinda, I didn't even have a chance to let my boys know." Noah frowned. He had walked Melinda to her door and left the boys behind in the pickup so he could have a few words with her alone. She'd been rude all day, beginning with her surprise announcement in church that morning.

"Oh, come on, Noah," she replied with a smile. "The boys are excited. They can't wait for me and Merry to move in."

"And why were you so rude to everyone today?" Noah went on. "What do you have against Tillie and her sisters-in-law? They're a nice bunch of ladies, and I heard you making smart remarks *to* them and *about* them all day long."

Melinda shrugged. "The truth hurts. Who cares anyway? They're just a bunch of rich, spoiled brats, especially the precious *Angel*."

"She worked really hard to make it a nice day for everyone," Noah defended. "And you worked twice as hard trying to get into it with somebody. Why did you do that?"

"Oh, please, Noah," Melinda scoffed and rolled her eyes. "Those women don't do anything but sit at home baking cookies. They don't have any idea what it's like to have real lives."

"Becky-Lynn and Tara both work," Noah pointed out with a frown. "As for the ladies that stay home, I can tell you *that* is a very hard job. As you know, I did it myself when Carrie passed away, and I didn't just *sit at home*."

"Well, well," Melinda sighed. "Aren't we touchy tonight."

Noah let his breath out and shook his head. *This argument is getting me absolutely nowhere.* "I have some meetings in the morning, so I'll be in later."

"Okay," Melinda replied, thankful that he seemed to be winding up his sermon. "Are you and the boys coming over tomorrow night?"

"I can't. I've got conferences tomorrow night."

"Do you want me to watch the boys?" Melinda asked, sounding so normal and sincere that it almost frightened Noah.

How does she go back and forth like that? He wondered. "Mona's picking them up for me tomorrow," he answered.

"Well, okay." She reached for Noah's hand, looked into his eyes, and smiled. "Why don't you kiss me good night?"

Noah swallowed hard and looked back into Melinda's expectant expression. The truth was that he *didn't* want to kiss her. He'd never had any desire whatsoever for this woman, and kissing her was the last thing on earth he wanted to do. *But we're "engaged" now, so I s'pose I'll have to start doing that.* After a brief hesitation, he gave her a soft peck on the cheek and then started to back away, releasing her hand from his own. "I'll be in for my messages before lunch."

"Okay," Melinda replied. It hadn't been the greatest kiss in all the world, but at least it was a start.

"Good night, Melinda."

"Good night, Noah."

A very frustrated Guiseppi flung himself into the bed beside his Rosa, sighed heavily, and looked up at the ceiling. "He does not *love* Melinda."

Rosa shook her head and whispered, "Keep your voice down, Guiseppi."

"I am so angry with myself and my decisions at this moment, I could just spit nails!" he whispered with a scowl.

"Oh, Guiseppi," Rosa sighed, "but what would you have the poor man do? Stay single and alone for the rest of his life?"

"No, of course not. But *anyone* would be better than the devil he was with today." He frowned at Rosa and grumbled, "Can he not just get a dog?"

"Guiseppi!" She suppressed her snickers as much as possible. "You know what it is like to be a man. Can you imagine trying to live alone, raising two children by yourself. He desires companionship."

"A dog would do nicely. And where was his brother during this *big engagement?* I will tell you where, my dearest Rosa, he was standing at the podium, nearly ready to stroke. Poor Joshua knew nothing of the announcement, and I suspect neither did Noah's sons."

"She certainly gets after Angel," Rosa said. "She seems to know something of their past."

Guiseppi agreed. "And if that is not enough, Noah cannot seem to guard his eyes at all. The man has absolutely no self control."

"But I thought Angel was truly wonderful today. She was gracious and pretended not to even notice. She seemed completely unaffected by it all."

"What a dear girl," Guiseppi said. He took a soft breath and chortled, "I did think, but for only a moment, that she would hurl the mouse at Melinda."

Rosa giggled. "She showed remarkable restraint."

"Poor Kate," Guiseppi laughed. "I thought she might faint." Then he sighed and whispered, "Let us ask God to bring someone very special for Noah."

Rosa agreed with a nod...*I will always pray for Noah.*

*****

Tillie Martin rose early, before anyone else, started two coffee makers, and settled herself into the love seat in the sunroom. The sun wasn't up yet, and it didn't appear it would shine at all today. She left the lights off and let the darkness comfort her as the rain gently drummed the glass above her. She hadn't had a moment to herself since yesterday morning before everyone arrived, and she had to speak to the Lord.

So, Melinda and Noah are engaged. That's nice. She sighed and shook her head. *Lord, it doesn't matter that Noah would choose to take a wife, but it makes a big difference in that he's chosen someone like Melinda. Why can't he find someone wonderful? Someone who loves and adores him, instead of that clinging vine who wants nothing more than to abuse him and his good nature. Noah deserves better than that.*

"God," she whispered out loud in the darkness, "I'm trying so hard to understand. Is she even a Christian?" Tillie felt an unusual pain in her heart, but she stubbornly willed it away. *I had my chance and I blew it, ruining Noah's life in the process. His engagement to Melinda will only add to his pain.*

"She's not what he wants. They have not one thing in common." She shook her head as she felt the sensation of tears in the back of her eyes. The affection and passion for Noah she thought she'd squelched for years left a horribly dull ache in her heart. She swallowed as hard as she could and dried her tears on her sleeve. *I have no right to feel this way. What happened, happened. My reasons for leaving him behind were justified at the time.*

Tillie took a deep breath...*but I misunderstood.* Her tears began to fall again, and she held her head in her hands. *After all we shared that wonderful weekend together, how could I have possibly believed he would do something like that to me?*

Guiseppi saw his daughter's silhouette in the sunroom. He took a seat beside her and put a tender arm around her, pulling her close.

"Did I wake you up?" she whispered with surprise.

"No." Guiseppi shook his head. "The Lord sent me to you."

Tillie laid her head on his shoulder and quietly let out all of the tears she'd held back the day before.

"I know how difficult yesterday must have been for you," Guiseppi whispered.

Tillie could only nod as she rested in the comfort of her father's arms. "He doesn't love her, Papa," she whispered.

"No, of course not. But dear Noah is none of your concern anymore, and you should not have such a heavy heart about this."

"I know," she softly sobbed.

Guiseppi hesitated and cautiously whispered, "Is he tempting you?"

"Oh, heavens no, Papa. It's not like that at all. I've just always —" Tillie stopped herself.

"Always what, Angel?"

"Nothing," she shook her head.

"Tell me, Angel," Guiseppi gently demanded.

She swallowed hard and shook her head again. "You'd never understand."

"Oh, really?" Guiseppi smiled in the darkness as he held his daughter. "That is what you think? That I am so old and feeble-minded I cannot understand how my daughter has a special place in her heart for a boy named Noah. A boy who swept her off her feet in the midst of rebellion, completely changing his life in order to be with her. Do you actually think me so shallow I could not understand the compassion you must feel for him?" He sighed and went on, "Besides being a child of God, Tillie Caselli, you are also a child of mine, covered with flesh and filled with heart. You must try to understand that, as humans, we err frequently; but rest assured, God will put us back on track in due time, when He feels it is right."

"And what track is that?"

"I do not know. But what I do know is that you have a husband who loves you very much, and you should not feel one speck of guilt for that. What happened with you and Alex when you came home cannot be undone nor forgotten. And as far as dear Noah goes, God will take care of him as well. God gave Noah free will, to choose as he pleases. If he decides to marry Melinda, then his beatings will be his own responsibility."

Tillie chuckled through her tears. "She's so *mean*, Papa."

"That she is, my Angel, but Ma`ma and I are praying for both of them."

Tillie sniffed and gave her father a soft kiss upon his cheek. "Thanks, Papa. You're the best."

"Oh, Angel," Guiseppi sighed with a smile, "it blesses my old heart to still hear you say that."

"I wish we hadn't moved here," she whispered. "I wish I was still in Sioux Falls with you and Ma`ma."

"Do not fret," Guiseppi encouraged. "Your Ma'ma and I will be with you morning, noon, and night in our prayers. This thing will be sure to pass, without incident. I have no doubt of the strength of your good heart."

*****

Noah walked both of his boys into the school that morning with the umbrella, praying every step of the way for just a quick opportunity to see Angel. He wanted to tell her how much fun he had yesterday — *even though Melinda tried to wreck it* — and what a joy it was to be around her brothers for the entire day.

"Please God," Noah silently begged as he hung around the kindergarten hall, "I *promise* not to do anything stupid this time."

As if in answer to his prayer, Tillie hurried by and helped the twins pull off their rain coats, hanging them on the hooks outside the classroom. They took off their little galoshes and stood them up beneath their coats. They kissed their mother and hurried into the classroom. Tillie smiled and breathed a sigh of relief. She turned for the door and ran right into Noah.

"Oh, hi, Noah," she greeted with a surprised smile. "I didn't see you there."

"Good morning, Tillie." He smiled, and his face began to warm. "How are you today?"

"Great," Tillie answered, beginning her usual *back up and get away* maneuver.

Noah frowned. "You know, I don't understand why you're always trying to get away from me. You'd think I was a leper or something."

Tillie almost laughed at his expression but allowed only a small smile. "I'm not trying to get away from you, Noah, I'm just very busy."

"Humph." Noah frowned again. "Busy trying to get away from me. I'm sorry I make you feel so uncomfortable."

Tillie's smile faded and she swallowed hard as she tried to think of something to say. She *had* to get away from him.

"I said I was sorry," he defended. "It wasn't even my fault and you *still* hate me."

Tillie shook her head. "No, I don't hate you. Please don't say that."

"Then why can't we just say hi to each other every now and then?"

"Because, we just *shouldn't*."

"Oh, really?" Noah raised one eyebrow. "You mean, you don't *trust* me?"

"Fine." She took a deep breath. "Hi, Noah. How are you today?"

"I'm fine, thank you. How about you?"

"Great." She scowled terribly as the next words spilled out of her mouth without restraint. "And how's *dear, sweet Miss Melinda?*"

Noah raised both of his eyebrows in surprise and took a deep breath as he tried to think of something to say. He held his breath for a second, smiled, and replied with a casual tone, "Well, she's awful mean. Why?"

His remark caught Tillie off guard, and she covered her mouth in an effort to hide her smile.

Noah saw the smile in her eyes and sheepishly apologized, "Tillie, I'm sorry. I wish I could have better prepared you for that."

"It's okay. Your decisions are your own, Noah. It's none of my business."

Noah sighed and smiled into her eyes. "Me and the boys had a really great time yesterday. Thanks for inviting us."

"You're welcome."

Noah stood quiet for a moment, unable to think of anything else to say. He slowly started to back away. "See. That wasn't so bad." He glanced down at his watch and rolled his eyes. "I'm late. I gotta go. Have a good day."

"Thanks, Noah," and she watched him turn and go, disappearing down the hallway and out the door.

Senator Caselli and his brother Marquette were seated in the conference room at Martin, Martin & Dale, A.P.C.L. With sullen expressions, they watched a very agitated Tara pace back and forth before the windows.

"And when did you receive this fax, Petrice?" she demanded as she looked at the facsimile of a cover story obtained by an aid in the Secretary of Defense's office. The photo on the cover of a Lebanese magazine reflected the perfect image of her husband, wearing his fake beard and dressed in Muslim garb. The article below accused him of being an unnamed channel negotiating *arms for hostages* between Iran and the United States.

"They called me yesterday at Alex and Angel's party," Petrice explained. "I received the fax only this morning."

"This is dated for Monday, November 3," Tara stormed. "In Lebanon, it is already Monday evening and this *thing...*" she angrily tossed it onto the conference table where her husband and his brother sat, "has been in print for at least *twelve hours!*"

"On top of that minor trifle," Marquette dryly added, "I am *not* negotiating any deals. I am merely the one who is *watching* the people negotiating for the hostages."

Petrice sighed heavily and took the fax into his hands, studied it carefully, and opined, "Perhaps you will not be recognized. With the cloths upon your head and the facial hair, it is difficult even for me to see any resemblance at all."

Tara stomped her foot. "Well I, for one, am not willing to take that risk! The AP must have this by now and Marquette's identity will be compromised in a most heinous lie!" She drew in her breath sharply, stopped at the window, and pointed at Petrice. "Not to mention what implications this could have on Alex's election! Call Remington this instant and tell him to advise McDaniel's team to get out of Iran."

"But, my love," Marquette carefully attempted to persuade, "they are not even aware of our presence —"

"I do not care!" Tara interrupted with a frown. "Their lives may be in danger. You know what a radical the Ayatollah's son is!" She marched to the table and tapped her index finger on the facsimile. "They quote him over and over in this article. He is obviously entrenched with the Lebanese, and there will be *no more* deals now that he is this deeply involved!"

Petrice had to agree with his sister-in-law, and he reached for the phone. "You are right, of course, Tara. Now let us all say a prayer that everyone may be brought home safely."

Marquette sighed with regret. "And I suppose we should let Alex know."

Noah hurried into Alex's downtown offices, trying to make up for the lost time he'd taken with Tillie at the school. He was still smiling when he rushed into the lobby.

"There you are!" Shondra was at the receptionist's desk with Lori. "We've been looking for you. Where ya been?"

"Got held up over at the school," Noah said with a smile and the familiar sparkle Shondra was used to.

"I see."

"Will you take him back?" Lori asked Shondra. "My phone is ringing off the hook this morning."

106

"Sure will. Come on, Noah." Shondra sighed as she led him down the hall. "We're busy this morning. It's the day before the election you know."

"How could I forget?"

Shondra paused at Alex's door, knocked softly, and stuck her head inside. "Noah's here."

"Send him in," Noah heard Alex answer as Shondra opened the door, revealing Marquette, Tara, and Petrice, all together with Alex.

Alex reached for Noah's hand and smiled. "Hey, you're late. Are the roads bad?"

"No." Noah shook his head and smiled. "Just got held up with the kids for a few extra minutes."

"Hello, Noah." Marquette shook Noah's hand.

"Hi, Noah," Tara said with a smile.

"Good morning, Tara," Noah greeted as he looked at all of them. "What's everybody doing here?"

"Oh," Tara began as she rolled her eyes, and Noah thought he saw the smallest spark of anger in her pretty expression.

"We are just stepping out so that you and Alex and can visit," Marquette answered. "But perhaps we will see you again in a bit?"

"Sure," Noah acknowledged, and he watched the three of them leave Alex's office, closing the door behind them.

"Have a seat, Noah," Alex said as he seated himself in his own chair.

Noah took a seat in the comfortable chair in front of Alex's desk and waited for him to begin.

"Okay," Alex began with a nervous smile. "I'm a wreck, but, let's get this nightmare started. First of all, the Joker is stalling."

Noah frowned. "That guy couldn't make a decision if he tried. Tell him to get lost."

Alex laughed. "I know, he's become rather difficult, but —"

"But what," Noah retorted. "I don't *need* his business, and I certainly don't need the aggravation."

"I know," Alex agreed with a calm smile. "But he says he wants to wait until after the first of the year."

"Oh, brother." Noah rolled his eyes. "He just likes jerking us around, setting up fancy, little meetings, and flying around the countryside."

"Noah, let's just give him one more try," Alex persuaded. "It's already November, and he wants to meet in January. That will give you a couple of months to cool off."

"He's just playin' with us, Alex," Noah responded. "He likes to come in here and play big shot, thinking that we're just a couple of hicks that don't know what we're doing."

"Well, we are *not* a couple of hicks, and we certainly *do* know what we're doing. Our bank accounts reflect as much."

Noah's frown softened and he took a breath. "Whatever."

"And in the meantime, Dmitri Romanov called me just this morning with a really great idea."

Noah looked curiously at Alex, "What's that?"

"He's going to manage a pizza place. He's made a deal with a guy who owns the franchise for Little Caesars Pizza in South Dakota. This guy has already set up one in Sioux Falls, and he should have another one up and going before the end of the year. He'd like to put one on Mt. Rushmore Road, here in Rapid City, but there isn't an available spot. That's where you come in."

Noah looked interested. "So what's he got in mind?"

"There's a little undeveloped lot on the corner of Franklin and Mt. Rushmore Road," Alex answered.

"Over there next to Wilson School?" Noah's frown returned. "There's a *house* on that lot, Alex."

"Can't we buy it and get it moved?"

"I s'pose."

"How many spaces do you think you could fit in there?" Alex asked.

"Five or six. But we'd have to move the house, and I only know one guy that does that. Maybe we oughta just tear it down."

"Well, I don't know what to tell you on that," Alex said as he leaned back in his chair. "You're the developer. Dmitri's friend wants the space closest to the road, and he wants his own signage."

"Sure. I'll go over and take a look at it this afternoon and see what I can put together."

Alex smiled. "Thanks, Noah." He hesitated for a moment before he said, "And I didn't get to tell you congratulations yesterday, so, congratulations."

"Thanks, Alex."

"I must say, I was really surprised."

"Me too." Noah smiled sheepishly. "I can't even imagine what my brother's gonna say. I won't be able to talk to him until tonight."

"I thought he looked a little surprised." Alex took a breath and softly frowned. "Tillie said the date's been set for the second Saturday in July?"

"No kidding?"

"That's what Melinda told her."

Noah looked so confused at that moment that Alex began to apologize. "Noah, I'm sorry. This is really awkward. I figured you knew the date of your own wedding."

Noah smiled and shook his head as he got out of his chair. "No. I guess I must have missed that one." Alex stood and started to come around the desk.

"If you're done with me for today, I gotta get going," Noah said.

Alex put a friendly hand on Noah's shoulder. "Don't forget to meet with Shondra before you leave. She wants to prep you a little on what will be happening here tomorrow night. Election stuff."

"I'll see her next."

Alex saw the pensive expression in Noah's eyes. "Noah, what's bothering you?"

Noah swallowed hard and shook his head. "It's nothing. Just a lot of irons in the fire right now."

"Me too," Alex said with a smile.

"Good luck tomorrow, Alex," Noah said as he headed slowly for the door and opened it.

"Thanks, Noah," Alex said, and he watched Noah leave his office. "Wow." He sighed and walked over to the window to watch the falling rain. His engagement to Tillie hadn't been anything like what Melinda was putting Noah through. Melinda had even picked the date herself and didn't tell Noah. Alex shook his head in disbelief. *Poor Noah.*

Noah found Shondra in the conference room with Petrice, Marquette, and Tara going over a press schedule. He politely paused in the doorway.

"Hey, Noah." Shondra smiled and waved him inside. "I only need to talk to you for just a minute."

Noah came into the conference room, took a seat beside Marquette, and smiled at him. "What are you guys doing here this morning?"

Marquette smiled, slid the fax toward him, and asked, "Do you recognize this man?"

Noah looked curiously at the fax and slowly shook his head. "No. Why?"

Tara let out a sigh of relief. *No one has recognized him yet.*

"It is I," Marquette revealed.

Noah looked genuinely surprised. He glanced at the fax again and asked, "What's all of this scribble, and how can this be you?"

"A disguise," Marquette answered. "And that scribble is Arabic."

"We are hoping the story does not break in America before Election Day tomorrow," Petrice said. "If it does, pray that Marquette's identity is kept safe, because Alex's relation to us at this point would surely hurt him."

Noah curiously smiled. "What did you guys do?"

They all laughed, and Marquette answered, "We did *nothing* wrong, but I have been identified as someone who has."

"Come on," Shondra coaxed. "Back to the business at hand." She flipped through her legal pad of notes and stopped on a specific page. "Here's how it will go. The polls close at seven o'clock p.m., on both sides of the state, so results will be coming in from East River, one hour before West River polls close. At six o'clock, KDLT will do a short interview with Tillie and Alex, talking about exit polls, blah, blah, blah; and then we're gonna throw the Senator in there, and he'll say something profound." She paused and smiled at Petrice.

"Of course," Petrice nodded.

"And then," Shondra continued with a smile for Noah, "we're going to put Alex's best friend in front of the camera, and he's going to talk about their business again. Think you can do that?"

Noah smiled and asked, "What are we wearing this time?"

"Everyone will be quite formal, Noah," Shondra said. "Except for you. I don't want you to get any dressier than a casual sport coat. Not even a tie, unless you're not comfortable coming as the 'hard-working-man-type.' "

Noah smiled and nodded his head. "I hate to wear a tie. A sport coat will be fine."

"That's great," Shondra said. "And could you hang around for just a few hours? They'll want to take different shots during the election coverage as results come in all night long."

"I'll see what I can swing."

"Then that's all I need from you," Shondra said, giving Noah a smile. "And did Alex talk to you about Davis?"

Noah nodded. "And I'll try to get something roughed out on that this week." He got to his feet. "I'd better get going. I'm gonna have a busy day. See you guys tomorrow."

"I'll walk you to the door, Noah," Shondra offered with a casual smile as she got to her feet.

Noah thought that was strange, but he only smiled at her, stepped out of the conference room, and waited for her to come alongside of him. "What's up, Shondra?" he asked as they walked along.

Shondra sighed and smiled. "I don't know exactly how to say this to you, Noah, so I'm just gonna give it to you straight." She took a breath. "I don't want you to bring Melinda tomorrow night."

Noah looked curiously at Shondra. "Why?"

"Let's just say I wanna give Tillie a break. Things will be hectic for her tomorrow night the way it is, and I don't think she should have to be trying to outrun Melinda every time she turns around. You're not upset with me, are you?"

Noah shook his head. "No. Don't worry about it."

"Oh, and by the way, congratulations. Alex tells me that you and Melinda got engaged over the weekend."

"Thanks, Shondra."

"You're welcome. When's the big day?"

Noah half smiled and shook his head. "I guess it's all gonna happen on the second Saturday in July."

"I'll make sure I leave my calendar open," Shondra promised as she watched Noah pull the door open for himself. "See you tomorrow night, Noah."

"See ya, Shondra," Noah said, and then he left the office.

As Shondra watched him walk away, she began to frown. *Engaged...How can he up and get engaged while he's still so taken with Tillie?*

*****

That afternoon, Alex and Petrice scheduled a short press conference with Alex's future deputy. The press conference had been planned; however, Petrice was more interested in whether or not the press had gotten a hold of the Lebanese story. So far, his office in Washington hadn't heard a thing. The press would have harassed them immediately if they suspected any ties to Marquette.

The press conference went along better than expected, with only one question aimed at Senator Caselli, and it was with regard to his relationship with Alex. A reporter asked for a recap of how long they had been acquainted, and then how long his sister had been married to Alex. There were no questions about Marquette, and no one said a thing about Iran or the hostages.

"We pulled that off without a hitch," Petrice whispered to Alex when it had finally ended.

"Indeed we did," Alex confidently smiled.

"Am I looking at the new South Dakota attorney general?"

"I think so."

Petrice laughed, put his hand on Alex's shoulder, and firmly grasped it. "Come along, my brother. Papa and I are taking everyone out for dinner tonight so that Angel may rest. We have reserved several tables at Copper Creek, and my taster is ready for a delicious steak." Alex smiled and nodded, and he and Petrice left the office.

*****

"It's totally going down the tubes on me," Noah moaned as he scratched his chin and shook his head. He was visiting quietly with Joshua and Mona in their kitchen, while the boys entertained themselves in front of the television.

"You mean she went ahead and picked out a date before asking you first?" Mona frowned.

Noah nodded. "And, of course, you were there when she made the big church announcement." He looked helplessly at Joshua and Mona. "I just can't believe this."

"Well, that's what you wanted," Joshua gently reminded.

"I know, but I'm just not becoming attracted to her like I did with Carrie."

"Tell me something," Joshua said as he took a deep breath, "I never asked you about this, but I really want to know. Did you pray about marrying Carrie?"

"Yes, I did, Josh, and I felt to the tips of my toes that it was the right thing to do."

Joshua bit his lip thoughtfully. "And have you prayed about marrying Melinda?"

Noah slowly nodded his head, but said nothing.

"And what's the Lord telling you to do?" Joshua asked.

Noah shrugged, sat very still for a moment, and shook his head. "I can't even begin to imagine being married to Melinda. I don't know what I'm gonna do. If I dump her, she'll probably quit her job and sue me. I should have never asked her out in the first place."

"Well, that's not a very good reason to stay engaged," Mona piped in. "But you got lots of money. Maybe you should just pay her off."

Noah and Joshua both laughed, and Noah said, "No. I'm just going to stick it out a little bit longer and see if I warm up to her. You know, the boys really like her, and she's nice to *them*."

"But she treats *you* like dirt," Mona reminded.

*****

Martin Campaign Headquarters was a whir of excitement that began early the next morning and throughout the afternoon. The intensity grew shortly after six o'clock p.m. when the East River polls closed and results started to flood in. Alex was ahead in the exit polls all day long, but he was relieved to see that the official count put him ahead of his opponent as well.

For a few hours after school, Tillie brought the twins down to be with their father. They said a few, sweet words to the nice Jon McFadden and then were taken home for their supper. Rosa and Guiseppi were the self-designated baby-sitters for the evening, and all of the grandchildren were left with them. All of the other relatives had promised to work at the campaign headquarters, doing whatever last-minute things Shondra needed finished.

After a quick supper with her children, Tillie changed into something more formal but not too flashy. A simple, navy-blue dress, with a modest collar, long sleeves, and matching shoes. Her diamond heart pendant sparkled against the softness of her dark skin, and the matching earrings dangled from her earlobes.

Noah was with Shondra, going over instructions for his brief interview, when Tillie arrived. As always, he couldn't help but give her a loving glance.

"Oh, man," Shondra chuckled. She grabbed Noah by the arm and turned him around. "You've got it worse than anyone I've seen yet."

"What are you talking about, Shondra?"

Shondra almost laughed out loud at his pretense, but she was a professional and had seen this before. She swallowed away her laugh and whispered, "Give me a break, Noah. You've got a terrible crush on Tillie." She looked him in the eye and mischievously raised one of her brows. "You're not dark like the rest of them. *Blushing* is quite an enigma around here."

So that's how they know...the white guy with the red face. Noah raised his brow at Shondra and returned her mischievous expression. "Well, maybe I'm just an alcoholic. We get red faces you know."

Shondra did laugh out loud then, and shook her head. "Don't try to BS me, young man. I'm nearly fifty years old, and I'll BS circles around you." She gave Noah a friendly pat on his shoulder. "Now go and get some punch or something cold to drink, and try not to talk to her." Noah's eyes looked almost sad, and Shondra laughed at him again. "Well, okay," she conceded with a smile. "You can talk to her, but make sure you put a bag over your head first."

Noah laughed. "Don't worry, Shondra. I'll be on my best behavior."

Shondra frowned playfully. "A charming guy like you, on your best behavior? Now I'm *really* worried."

"Don't worry," Noah reassured. "I'll try not to act like an idiot."

Tillie and her brothers gave a wonderful interview shortly before eight o'clock. They talked about the boys' childhood in Italy and then about all of the drastic changes in America since that time. Her brothers were naturally dramatic, and they loved to speak of nothing more than Italy and the times they'd had there. They all spoke very fast, apparently trying to overpower each other with their own stories, and Tillie could hardly control her laughter. They exulted their beautiful little sister, time and time again, until Tillie was embarrassed and threatened to leave.

From the sidelines, Noah watched their banter, his heart filled with grief. It wasn't only losing Angel he regretted, but her wonderful family as well. He felt a strange connection to them, though there was no reasonable explanation for it. He wondered if Joshua would accuse him of coveting Tillie's brothers as well, because he did.

Noah was, for all practical purposes, an only child, and he'd often wondered what it would be like to have a big family. As far as he could see, a big family was a great thing. He wished he could at least give it to his boys. Good ol' Melinda didn't want to have children. He reflexively shuddered at the thought anyway. That would require more than just a quick peck on the cheek.

Shortly before midnight, Standard Mountain Time, Alex James Martin III was declared the new attorney general for the State of South Dakota, and he and Robert made their victory speeches. Their opponent made a dramatic concession and praised Alex and Robert for a well-run campaign. Alex Martin's political life was finally off the ground, and the sky was his limit.

Chapter 12

Noah held tightly to her hand as they walked along the path at *Canyon Lake.* Snowflakes caught in her black locks, and he carefully brushed some of them away with his hand. She smiled up at him, and they stopped beside the lake to look into each other's eyes. He touched her face with the palm of his hand, felt the softness and warmth of her skin, and then kissed her lips as he pulled her into his arms. "I love you, Angel," he whispered as he buried his face in her curls and caught the softest scent of her perfume.

"I love you too," she whispered....

From the kitchen, Maggie and Estelle had watched him since his arrival. He paused at the painting, like he always did, but this time he eased the old photograph out from the corner of the frame for a better look. He smiled as he gazed upon the old images, and his cheeks showed the faintest of a blush.

"What do you suppose he's thinkin' about Maggie?" Estelle whispered.

"Beats me," Maggie said with a frown.

"You're not gonna let him keep my picture, are you? 'Cause, you know, Maggie, it really belongs in here, *with us. I* took the picture, Maggie."

Maggie put a reassuring hand on her sister's shoulder. "I'll get it back from him, Baby, don't worry." She left the kitchen, walked to where Noah had seated himself at the bar, and said in a gruff tone, "What'll ya have, Noah? I got beef stew or ham and cheese."

Noah looked at Maggie with surprise. "Hi, Maggie. I guess I'll take the stew."

Maggie scribbled down his order and hung it on the wheel behind her. "You can't keep Stellie's picture," she grumbled.

Noah handed her the photograph. "Here ya go."

Maggie replaced the photograph in the corner of the portrait and walked back to Noah. "So, how's things goin'?"

"Fair," he replied with a shrug of his shoulders.

"Are you still engaged to Melinda?"

"Yep." He shook his head with a woeful expression. "That woman's gonna spend me into the poor house, Maggie."

"That's a *lot* of spending, Noah."

"She's gotta have this huge house for one thing," Noah went on. "The plans alone had to be special ordered from a place in Sacramento, and the lot she wanted to put it on is way out in Quartz Canyon. It's a spendy place to build, and getting my men and equipment out there hasn't been the easiest thing in the world. We did get the foundation done and some of the framework started, but now we have to break for

Thanksgiving in a couple of days, and she's mad about that. She thinks I should make the men work through Thanksgiving. Can you believe that, Maggie?"

"Well, you *had* to have her."

Noah sighed. "And then there's this wedding that she's planning." He rolled his eyes and moaned. "It's gonna be the *mother* of all weddings. She's ordered tulips for the flowers. Can you believe that Maggie? *Tulips?* In the middle of July? Do you have any idea what that costs? And then, of course, there's *the dress*. She's special ordered one from some place in Michigan *that I can't even pronounce*, and she's gonna make us all wear tuxes. Her parents haven't forked over a measly dime for the thing. It's all coming straight out of my pocket."

"Not to mention what the divorce is gonna cost you," Maggie added dryly.

Noah shook his head. "You know I don't believe in divorce, Maggie."

Maggie scowled and grumbled, "Why are you doing this to yourself, Noah? Are you still thinking you're gonna be able to warm up to her before the honeymoon?"

"Maybe."

"When all you can think about is another woman?"

"Well, I can't exactly get out of it now."

"Why not?" Maggie sneered. "Why would you go through with this? You can't even stand to *kiss* her. Can you imagine what your wedding night is gonna be like?"

"Listen, Maggie, the boys are really attached to her, and they need a mom."

"Humph! I don't know a lot about mothering or being with children, but Melinda sure doesn't sound like parental material to me."

"Well, what am I supposed to do, Maggie?" Noah said with a disgusted frown. "The perfect wife and mother is already taken, and there aren't a whole lot of other choices out there."

"Get a dog. Me and Stellie been thinkin' about gettin' ourselves a dog."

"And just dump Melinda?"

Maggie pursed her lips together and nodded.

"I can't do that. For one thing, she'll quit her job and sue me to kingdom come."

"You got plenty, Noah Hansen," Maggie grumbled. "Pay off the ol' battle-ax."

"I'm just gonna stick it out a little bit longer. Maybe it'll be okay." He smiled at Maggie and attempted to change the subject. "Day after tomorrow is Thanksgiving, Maggie. What are you and Stellie doing?"

"The usual. I'm gonna make Stellie a little turkey, and then we're gonna play some cards with the neighbor's grandkids. How 'bout you?"

"Me and the boys are going out to Josh and Mona's," Noah answered. "Melinda has to go and see her grandmother, so I get the whole day off."

"Yippee." Maggie feigned a smile and shook her head. She had watched Noah do some insane things over the past twenty years, but this thing with Melinda was the worst.

"This must be a mistake," Shondra murmured as she looked over Judge Daniel's order for pre-trial hearing. She and Alex were going over several files that had been transferred from Pierre, coordinating their schedules and calendars with the different dates. "I didn't schedule it this way," she continued. "Who on earth would schedule a pre-trial on the day before Thanksgiving?"

"I scheduled it," Alex said without even looking up at her.

Shondra nearly gasped and her eyes opened with amazement. "I thought you were taking Tillie and the kids to Reata for Thanksgiving?"

Alex looked at his faithful assistant. *Don't give me a hard time about this.* "I'm putting Tillie and the kids on a charter tomorrow morning, and I'll catch up to them on Thursday."

Shondra couldn't hide her horrified expression as she stared back at Alex. "You can't be *serious.* You've been away all month, and I heard you promise —"

Alex held up his hand in interruption. *"Don't* start with me, Shondra. I have a lot to get done —"

"What about Robert? Can't he take this?"

"No." Alex shook his head and looked back at the file on his desk. "He can't handle this."

"Oh, yes, he can!" Shondra snapped.

Alex sighed with a frown. "Listen, Shondra, I have to get this out of the way so we can proceed to trial in January. If I don't do it now, I'll have to do it in December, and I'd really like some time off at Christmas."

Shondra clamped her jaws together and stormed out of Alex's office, giving his door a loud slam. *This is ridiculous. He's practically lived in Pierre since the election, and now he's sending his wife and children off on their Thanksgiving vacation by themselves! Robert can handle this. He's an excellent attorney, but Alex is determined to manage the attorney general's office by himself!*

She angrily stomped to her office, slammed the door, and flung the file onto her desk. She crossed her arms tightly and took a deep breath, stepped to the window, and watched the snow fall on downtown Rapid City. *No one had better dare cross him either. He's always right. It's like being with Dr. Jeckle and Mr. Hyde. One minute he's his sweet, dear self, and the next he's as stubborn as an ox.* She shook her head. *I wonder if he even knows what he's doing. Last time he did this, it took Tillie nearly dying to get his attention. How's God going to pull him out of it this time?*

Mrs. Castleman had brought puppies for her kindergarten's show-and-tell. About a half dozen tiny black Labrador retrievers were in a blanket-lined box. They squeaked, whined, stepped on each other, and strained for a better look at the children kneeling above them.

"How old are they?" Tillie asked as she looked into the box and felt the most unusual temptation to bring one home with her. She had come to pick up the twins, and when they didn't come outside, she went in to see what was taking so long. Most of the other children were gone by now, but there were a few stragglers, including the Martin children and Jake Hansen. They hadn't been able to tear themselves away from the adorable creatures.

"Six weeks," Mrs. Castleman answered.

"Who do they belong to?" Tillie asked as she reached into the box and touched one of them.

"My brother," Mrs. Castleman answered. "He's just starting to wean them now, so they'll be ready to go home with somebody in a couple of weeks."

"Can we have one, Mommy?" Laura asked.

"Oh, I don't know," Tillie answered hesitantly. "A puppy is a big responsibility."

"Miss Melinda has a big puppy," Jake smiled excitedly. "Her name is Merry, and she's *really* fun."

Tillie smiled faintly. *Do we have to wreck this perfectly wonderful moment by mentioning that horrid woman's name?*

Melinda had backed off significantly since receiving her engagement ring, and she only *occasionally* tortured Tillie. However, the things she chose to harass Tillie with were well-selected and calculated. For instance, she asked Tillie to serve punch at the upcoming wedding. Tillie was so flabbergasted by the suggestion, she couldn't think of one thing to say and accidentally agreed to do it. Tillie prayed daily for a life-threatening illness with comatose complications, if possible, to strike her shortly before the wedding.

Tillie was suddenly aware that someone had knelt down beside her when his coat brushed up against hers. She turned her head to see Noah smiling at her, and she smiled in return. "Hi, Noah."

"Hi." He held eye contact for a moment too long before he turned his gaze into the box of puppies. Hopefully she hadn't noticed. When Jake didn't come outside after school and he saw Tillie's empty car in the parking lot, he was thrilled. Obviously, there was something going on in the school holding everyone up, and it was an opportunity to just say hi.

How he had managed to keep it a secret from Melinda, he didn't know. However, she still wasn't aware that Jake shared the same class with Tillie's children, or she would have certainly put a stop to Noah dropping him off and picking him up every day. She managed to sabotage every event at the church, clung to Noah every time they were there, and successfully steered him away from Tillie. Noah didn't get so much as a glance, so their brief encounters at the school became something he looked forward to each day. Sometimes, if Noah was careful and didn't come on too strong, Tillie would actually stop and visit with him for a few moments before she hurried away. He thought perhaps her disposition toward him had softened over the past several weeks, and that thought led his heart down a dangerous path he chose to completely disregard.

"So, who do these little guys belong to?" Noah asked.

"Mrs. Castleman," A.J. answered.

"Can we hold one," Tillie asked, looking hopefully up at Mrs. Castleman.

"Sure," Mrs. Castleman answered.

Tillie carefully lifted one of the squirming little delights from the box and tried to cradle him in her arms. As her children and Jake reached for the squeaking puppy, she was flooded with a million memories of her Uncle Angelo and Duchess, and she began to smile.

"Oh, he's so cute," she whispered as she smiled into the tiny puppy's face and gently touched his miniature ears.

"He looks like Peggy's puppies," Laura said, giggling when the puppy licked her hand. Tillie laughed and nodded.

"Who's Peggy?" Jake asked curiously, reaching over to touch the puppy's face. He was suddenly licked, and he giggled.

"Uncle Vinzo's dog," A.J. answered. "She lives in the barn."

"And he's got piggies too," Laura added. "And we're all going for a sleigh ride on Thanksgiving."

"That sounds like fun," Noah said as he watched his Angel lovingly hold the puppy in her arms, patiently sharing him with all of the little hands reaching for just a touch. *She's so different from Melinda.* The soft, sweetness of her femininity and her gentle, nurturing spirit melted Noah's heart. When he was this close to her it was almost impossible to keep himself under control.

Tillie turned her head and looked at him. She didn't want to run away so often anymore, yet she knew she should. "What are you doing for Thanksgiving?" she asked with a smile, wondering if his day would be wrecked by Melinda.

"We're going out to Josh and Mona's place," Noah answered as he lost himself in her black, sparkling eyes. He wanted nothing more than to ask her if she might just run away with him.

116

Mrs. Castleman stood quietly still and wondered if she had suddenly become invisible.

"Melinda has to go and see her grandma," Jake piped in, breaking the soft spell between them. "So we don't get to play with Merry until she gets back."

Tillie took a deep breath and looked away. *This is wrong. I have to get out of here.* She gently placed the puppy back into his box with his brothers and sisters and got to her feet. "Come on, guys," she coaxed her children. "We have to get going. I still have some packing to do."

Noah stood as well and put his hands into his pockets, so as not to be tempted to touch her. "When are you guys leaving for Reata?"

"When Alex gets home this afternoon," Tillie answered. "We thought we'd drive out this time."

"Are all of your brothers going to make it?"

Tillie nodded and began to back away from him.

"Well, tell 'em I said hi," he said with a smile.

"I will," she promised, and she looked at her children who were still peering into the box of puppies. "Come on guys. Let's go."

A.J. and Laura got to their feet and trudged past their mother to find their coats.

"Happy Thanksgiving, Tillie."

"Happy Thanksgiving, Noah," she said, allowing herself to gaze too long into his dancing blue eyes. She turned and followed her children out of the room.

Noah sighed happily and looked at Jake. "Come on, bud. We gotta go."

As Tillie pulled into the driveway, she saw Alex's car already parked in the garage. Her heart jumped with excitement. This was a great surprise, and one that she had needed for several weeks now. She was extremely lonesome for Alex, and the fear that he had leaped back into the workaholic schedule he loved tugged continually in the back of her mind. That, combined with the tender overtures of Noah plaguing her daily at the school, made her long for the distraction of her charming husband. The little vacation they'd planned on Reata couldn't have come at a more perfect time.

"Daddy's home already!" Laura squealed with delight from the backseat.

"We get to leave early!" A.J. exclaimed. "Hurry, Mommy! Park the car!"

Tillie pulled her wagon into the garage next to Alex's car and turned it off. Her little ones unbuckled themselves and raced into the house, with their mother not far behind them. When they got into the kitchen, Alex was on the telephone, and he gave them a hesitant smile. "I'll have to check the file and call you on that," he barked. "But I'm sure we've got first right of refusal on the deal." He hesitated, rolled his eyes, and suddenly frowned. "I don't know. Did you actually *read* the legal on it, or did you just punt it to your secretary?"

Tillie and her children's eyes opened wide with surprise, because they had never heard Alex speak in such a cross tone.

"Go up to your rooms," Tillie whispered with an excited smile. "Hurry, quick! See who can make it faster!"

The twins giggled as they raced each other up the stairs and down the hall.

Alex muttered a nasty curse to whoever he was speaking to and abruptly hung up. He sighed and looked at Tillie. "Hi, Honey," he said, as if everything was normal and he hadn't actually uttered the words she thought she'd heard.

"Everything okay?" she asked sweetly.

Alex shook his head and pointed to the lovely cornucopia filled with an arrangement of fall-colored flowers sitting on the countertop.

"Thanks, Alex. They're beautiful."

"You're welcome." He took her into his arms, held her close for a moment, and let out a heavy sigh.

Tillie could feel how tense and rigid his body was, and she looked up at him. "What's wrong, Alex?"

Alex seemed to hesitate. "I have a pre-trial scheduled for tomorrow. I'm not going to be able to drive us over to Reata tonight."

"But Alex, the kids and I are really looking forward to this trip."

"I know, so I'm going to put you guys on a charter tomorrow morning."

"*A charter?*" Tillie suddenly backed out of his arms and frowned.

"Tillie, I'm sorry. It really can't be helped. I'll catch up to you and the kids on Thursday morning."

Tillie thought for a moment she might cry, though she didn't know why, and she didn't want to act like a spoiled child. She swallowed as hard as she could and simply stared at him. "Can't Robert do it?"

Alex shook his head. "He can't handle it. I've been working on this file, and it will go better if I handle it myself."

Tillie had to swallow again as she remembered the same excuse about six years ago when he planned to miss a family event. Of course, she was only twenty-three at the time and had obediently nodded her head in answer. This time, however, her anger burned against her husband; and she really didn't know what to say. In nine years of marriage, they rarely disagreed, and even when they had, it had never felt this intense before.

"Can you reschedule it?" she asked.

"Honey, I just can't. I'm really sorry. If I take care of this now, I'll be able to take more time off in December."

She had heard that one, too, and she began to slowly shake her head. "Well, whatever. You do whatever you feel is best for you and your family."

"Oh, come on, Tillie." He reached for her hand. "You know this is just temporary. We're just really busy getting the files transferred."

The warmth of his hand and the tenderness in his eyes softened her heart. The terrible frown between her brows slowly began to melt away, and she said, "Okay. But you promise to catch up to us on Thursday?"

Alex nodded and smiled, relieved that the confrontation was over, and he folded her into his strong arms. "I love you, and we'll still have four great days together at Reata."

*****

Vincenzo was surprised when Tillie called him that Tuesday evening to explain that her charter would land early Wednesday morning at the airfield situated twenty-five miles south of Reata, just southeast of Vermillion. He promised to be there and didn't ask why Alex wasn't coming along. He thought perhaps it was a question better asked in person.

The tiny airfield was deserted when Vincenzo arrived the following morning. The flight had landed earlier than expected. Tillie and her children waited alone inside the dirty, dilapidated metal building, and she smiled with relief when she saw her brother's four-door pickup arrive. The snowfall had gotten heavy, whipped about by a strong, northern wind, and the small building was not heated. Needless to say, Tillie and her children were very cold.

Vincenzo left his truck running and hurried into the building to hug his niece and nephew and embrace his sister. "How long have you waited?" he asked with concern as he picked up their luggage and led them to his warm pickup.

"Not too long," Tillie answered. "We were supposed to make a stop in Pierre, but it was canceled after our flight left the ground, so they brought us directly here. Oh," she said as she quickly turned around, "we're supposed to turn off the lights and lock the door when we leave."

"I can take care of that," Vincenzo said. He tossed their luggage into the bed of his truck and pulled open the passenger doors so A.J. and Laura could climb inside. "Jump in with them."

Tillie climbed into the truck with her children and sighed with relief as the warmth soaked into her. She had gotten colder than she had realized.

Vincenzo turned off the lights in the little building and locked the doors. He came back to the truck and got in with the rest of them. "So, how was the flight?" he asked as he put the truck into gear and pulled onto Old Highway 19, taking the northerly route.

"It was fun!" Laura smiled at her uncle and giggled. "I love airplanes."

"I know you do," Vincenzo touched her nose with his gloved index finger. He looked at his nephew and asked, "And how about you, A.J.? Do you love airplanes?"

"It was okay," A.J. said with a most-serious expression. "But I wanted Daddy to come with us."

"I see." Vincenzo glanced at Tillie and casually asked, "And why is he not with us this day?"

Tillie frowned, looked away from her brother, and pretended to watch the snow fly through the wind before them. "He had a hearing today. He'll catch up to us tomorrow."

Vincenzo kept his eyes on the road. It was better to stay quiet in front of the children. He was angry at his brother-in-law for this, especially after Angel and her children had waited in an unheated building in the dead of winter. What had that man been thinking when he sent his wife and children across the state alone? Vincenzo would not have done such a thing — no matter what the emergency. Did not Alex have the sense to know that women and children should not be left to travel alone into such a rural area where unexpected things can happen?

He took a deep breath, gave Tillie a reassuring smile, and returned his eyes to the road. "We have plenty of snow for a wonderful sleigh ride."

"Today?" A.J. asked, smiling slightly at the prospect.

"This day," Vincenzo affirmed. "And your Auntie Kate has hot apple cider waiting for us when we return."

"With cinnamon candy sticks?" Laura asked with a hopeful smile.

Vincenzo smiled. "As many as you can stand." He glanced at Tillie and added, "Well, as many as your mommy will allow you to have."

Tillie smiled in return, but she didn't really want to talk at all. This whole trip away from Alex was suddenly uncomfortable, making her wish they had just stayed at home. Now she would have to face her family and *his* family. They would undoubtedly have questions concerning Alex's whereabouts if he didn't show up on Thanksgiving morning. How was she going to explain that? Because, in the very depths of her heart, she knew he wasn't coming.

Kate's kitchen smelled of freshly baked bread and hot apple cider. Vincenzo carried their luggage in for them, kissing his wife who waited just inside the entryway.

"It's so good to see you!" she exclaimed as she helped the twins off with their coats and mittens.

"Uncle Vinzo said you had some cider and candy sticks ready," Laura said with a bashful smile.

Kate laughed and gave the little girl a hug. "Alyssa's in the kitchen. She'll help you." Laura and A.J. jumped with delight and trotted off to the kitchen.

Vincenzo hung his hat on the peg by the door, laid his gloves on the radiator, and pulled off his boots. Tillie hung her coat on a hanger and kicked her shoes into the closet.

"How was the flight?" Kate asked. She tried to smile at Tillie, sensing her downcast mood.

"They were early," Vincenzo scowled. "They had to wait in an unheated building."

"We didn't make a scheduled stop." Tillie looked nervously at her brother, hoping he could hold his tongue for Kate's sake.

Vincenzo sighed, rolled his eyes, and picked up the suitcases that were in the entryway. "I will take these to the guest rooms."

Kate tried to meet Tillie's eyes. "Is everything okay, kiddo?"

Tillie shrugged and looked away from Kate. Hopefully they could just go into the kitchen and drink some cider with the kids, but, to her surprise, Kate put her arms around her and held her close.

"Is he up to his old tricks?" Kate whispered.

Tillie wanted nothing more than to just break down and scream about how angry she was with her husband and how disappointing it was for her that he hadn't come along. She forced the anger away and answered, "He says he'll be here tomorrow."

Kate's dark eyes narrowed into a scowl. "He'd better be."

No other family members were scheduled to arrive before Thursday, and Tillie took comfort in the fact that *possibly* Alex would show up before anyone else. That could save her the embarrassment of an explanation as to why he hadn't come with his family. This was a touchy subject with all of them because of his actions in the past. She was so angry with Alex that she didn't know if she could adequately defend him, as she had when she was younger.

Vincenzo hitched up his new sleigh and everyone bundled themselves. Tillie loaded her father's camera, which was more than forty years old. She smiled as she remembered the time she had loaded it before her romantic tour of the Black Hills of South Dakota on the back of a Harley Davidson. Lately, she enjoyed the memory a little more than she knew she ought. However, she only allowed herself to remember certain things, and then immediately squelched it back into the place where she had hidden it for nearly twelve years.

Two solid shires pulled a bright red sleigh to the front door of the main house. Vincenzo stood down from the driver's seat, took off his hat, and bowed gracefully. Tillie smiled at her dramatic brother and snapped her first shot. It would make a wonderful sketch.

After everyone was loaded into the sleigh, Kate covered them with warm blankets. A.J. and Laura giggled hysterically as the sleigh glided along around the ranch, into the empty orchard, and finally, out into the pasture amongst the herd. The ground was completely covered with deep, white snow shining brilliantly all around them — and with more falling by the minute.

"The Widow Engberg's sons are going to sell Papa another parcel," Angelo said as they rode along.

"The Land Baron's Ball will be held shortly before Christmas," Kate added excitedly. "We expect they'll want to close after that."

"And Papa can increase his herd again," Alyssa said.

Tillie took photos whenever Vincenzo slowed down, and once when he stopped to show them the view of the main barn from just beyond the orchard. It was a dramatic scene, and Tillie got out of the sleigh for a better shot. Against the snowy, white horizon stood the bright red barn, where two horses pranced in the cold wind in the fenced area just off to the side. What was even more wonderful was the top of the silo peeking out from behind the barn. Bare trees covered in a thick, white frosting made for a beautiful backdrop.

"Perfect," Tillie whispered with a smile. She held the camera very still and waited. One of Vincenzo's ranch hands rode along the fence line in the background. *If he could just stop for a moment*, she thought, and he did! Tillie quickly snapped the shutter and smiled at everyone who waited patiently in the sleigh for her to return.

Vincenzo gave her a hand up and announced, "And now we must return, for I see that cheeks are becoming very rosy."

"Are the horsies getting cold?" Laura asked.

Vincenzo smiled and shook his head. "Oh, no, they are *very* strong, but your little faces are not, so we must get you warm again."

Kate bundled everyone back under the blankets as Vincenzo set off for the main house. He dropped them at the door, and then he and Angelo took his wonderful sleigh back to the barn.

Supper time came and went without a call from Alex, and as it neared bedtime, Tillie started to get nervous. Why hadn't he called to let them know when his flight would arrive? She thought about giving him a call but put it off because she feared his answer. Perhaps she could pretend a bit longer.

When they were too tired to wait up any longer, Tillie tucked the twins into the old-fashioned bunk beds in the guest room next to her own.

"Did Daddy call?" Laura asked, and she yawned even bigger than A.J.

"Not yet," Tillie answered. She smiled at her daughter and tried to hide her own disappointment. "But I'm sure he'll be calling soon."

"Don't forget to tell him that I love him," Laura said quietly.

"Me too," A.J. added.

Tillie swallowed hard and nodded her head. "Okay. Good night."

Kate threw her robe angrily onto the chair beside she and Vincenzo's bed and whispered with a scowl, "Can you believe he didn't even *call them?*" She made an indignant "humph" and threw the covers back on the bed.

"I cannot," Vincenzo replied with a frown. He closed their bedroom door and sat on the end of the bed to pull off his socks. "For all he knows they are still shivering at the airfield in Vermillion."

"What gets into him anyway?" Kate went on as she got into the bed and pulled the covers over herself. "I'm just gonna *kill* him when he gets here tomorrow."

Vincenzo nodded thoughtfully...*if, in fact, he does get here tomorrow.*

*****

Tillie walked along in the snow-covered orchard by herself, enjoying the wind upon her face and the crunch of the new snow beneath her boots. Reata was uncommonly enchanting in the winter, and there were times when she wished to be more of a part of it. The best memories of her childhood had been spent on Reata, picking apples, playing with brand-new puppies, and riding along in the buggy with Kate and Vincenzo before they had children.

She heard the sudden sound of horse hooves, and she turned to see Vincenzo's favorite stallion prancing toward her. As the stallion thundered to a stop, he tossed up a cloud of snow beneath his hooves. The rider dismounted and walked toward her. Tillie smiled as she watched him approach, and then she frowned. *That's not Vincenzo....*

"Noah? What are you doing here?"

He stopped in front of her and smiled with his dancing blue eyes as he reached for one of her hands. Her heart beat within her until she was afraid he would hear it, and he tenderly pulled her into his arms.

He looked into her eyes and smiled. "Angel, I love you, and I want you back." He kissed her lips so lovingly it almost took her breath away.

Tillie awoke with a start, sat straight up in the bed, and looked all around in the darkness. She was sweating profusely, and her breath was heavy. She felt completely disoriented. *Where am I?* It took a few moments to remember that she was in one of the guest bedrooms at Reata, and she reached for the lamp beside the bed. The clock said five a.m. The ranch was undoubtedly already up and chores started. She might as well get up with them and see if Kate needed any help. She remembered her dream and shook her head in disbelief. *Where did that come from?*

"I'm a horrible person," she muttered to herself as she crawled out of bed.

She found her suitcase, pulled out a warm sweater and a pair of jeans, and hurried to the shower. She had dried her hair and was dressed in less than thirty minutes. She crept into the twins' room to make sure they were still asleep, and then went down stairs and into the kitchen.

Kate was already dressed, had started two coffee makers, and had a giant turkey waiting in the sink. "Angel," she said with a surprised smile. "Happy Thanksgiving!"

"Happy Thanksgiving," Tillie greeted.

"Well, get yourself some coffee," Kate said as she turned back to buttering toast at the counter. She took a breath and said, "Vincenzo might have to put you to work this morning. It's still snowing, and he's got a couple of strays they can't find."

"Really?" Tillie raised her brows with interest as she filled herself a mug of the hot coffee. She hadn't ridden on a horse in longer than she cared to remember, but it would certainly be fun to go for a ride with her brother.

They heard the stomp of Vincenzo's boots in the entry. He seemed to growl a little as his boots hit the floor one at a time, and soon he was in the kitchen. "Hello, Angel! Happy Thanksgiving! What awakened you at this hour?"

Tillie shrugged. "Didn't want to miss any of the fun."

"Hello, my Kate." Vincenzo gave Kate a sweet kiss upon her cheek and reached for a cup and a pot of coffee.

"Where's Angelo?" Kate asked.

"He is still in the orchard, trying to coax a stubborn steer," Vincenzo answered as he filled his cup and shook his head. "I had half a mind to shoot the thing, but Angelo said that he could fetch him." He took a sip of the hot coffee and looked at Kate. "The dim-witted creature is undoubtedly confused amongst the trees, and I think Angelo will have to lead him out by hand."

"Is he coming in for breakfast?" Kate asked as she opened her oven door and pulled out a hearty eggs-and-meat bake.

Vincenzo nodded and then looked at Tillie. "Would you care to ride with me this morning?"

"I'd love to," Tillie answered, "but I haven't ridden in years."

"It is like a bicycle," Vincenzo said as he smiled. "And I could really use an extra person this day. We are trying to finish chores so everyone may enjoy Thanksgiving with their own families."

"Sure," Tillie answered with an apprehensive smile.

Alyssa came through the basement door with a smile and a huge bag of flour. "You were right, Ma`ma. It was on the bottom shelf." She looked at Tillie. "Happy Thanksgiving, Auntie."

"Happy Thanksgiving, Alyssa. What are you doing with all of that flour?"

Alyssa laughed as she heaved the heavy sack onto the counter top. "We ran out up here. I'm just filling the canisters for Ma`ma."

"So how long have you guys been up?" Tillie asked.

"Four forty-five," Vincenzo answered as he leaned against the counter top and enjoyed his coffee.

"How can you find anything in the dark?" Tillie asked curiously.

"Floodlights," Vincenzo answered as he took another sip of his coffee. "And the barn and the yard are well lit from above."

"Well," Kate said as she reached for some plates, "let's eat real quick and you and Angel can go."

"What if my kids wake up before I get back?" Tillie asked.

"I'll watch 'em," Alyssa volunteered. "I'm staying in to help Ma`ma this morning anyway."

Tillie dressed in a warm snowsuit she borrowed from Kate, boots she borrowed from Alyssa, and heavy leather gloves Vincenzo pulled off of the closet shelf. She put a stocking cap over her head and ears, and they were ready to go.

"Tracy, fetch Scottie and my Prince. They are saddled in the holding," Vincenzo instructed a young man working in the barn. Vincenzo smiled at Tillie and put his arm around her shoulders, "This will be like the old days. Remember when you used to stay on Reata?"

Tillie smiled and nodded. *The best times of my life.*

Tracy led the saddled gelding and stallion to Tillie and Vincenzo. He handed Tillie Scottie's reins and blushed profusely.

She smiled politely and took the reins. "Thank you."

Tracy tipped his hat, handed Vincenzo Prince's reins, and hurried off. Vincenzo laughed and mounted his stallion. "He was certainly taken with you."

Tillie mounted Scottie and adjusted her feet in the stirrups as she replied, "He knows I'm married...and he was sorta young, don'tcha think?."

Vincenzo laughed again. "He is actually *older* than you, my Angel. He turned thirty this year."

"No kidding?"

Vincenzo nodded as he reined his horse around. "Ranch work keeps a man young. Now, come along, Angel, we have three strays left, and I want them all close in before the wind picks up and cuts off our visibility."

Tillie followed Vincenzo out of the yard and into the darkness of the field. He flicked on the battery operated floodlight hanging from his saddle, illuminating a small expanse before them.

"Hopefully they will not *all* be in the trees," Vincenzo said as they rode along. "However, I fear *that* is where they have gone. Animals sense the storm coming, and they always run to the orchard for shelter."

"Do you think they'll be able to get a plane in at Vermillion?"

"No. We will have to drive to Sioux Falls to fetch Alex."

"If he even shows up," Tillie angrily muttered.

"Hmmm. Is there something you are not telling me, that perhaps you were afraid to say in front of his sister?"

"No."

"Did the two of you quarrel? Is that why he is not coming?"

"No. We never quarrel, Vincenzo."

"I see. Is there a problem then, with, um..." Vincenzo took a deep breath and went on hesitantly, "Alex's dearest friend, Noah?"

"I don't think so," Tillie answered quickly. Her heart pounded at just the mention of his name. "I think they're getting along fine."

Vincenzo nodded in the darkness. Her answer had been just a bit too quick. "Has Alex noticed Noah's little crush perhaps?"

Tillie pretended to laugh, surprised to hear the words come from her brother's mouth. "What are you talking about Vincenzo?" Her face felt hot, and her hands shook inside of her gloves. *Noah promised not to tell!*

"Oh, please, my Angel, do not attempt this game with me," Vincenzo admonished. "I am a man with far more wits than average. You noticed Tracy's blush for you only moments ago, and yet you deny Noah's. His affection for you at the twins' party was fairly obvious. Were you any other woman, I would be greatly troubled."

"No, Alex *hasn't* noticed!" She angrily let her breath out and added, "And he won't."

"So, Noah is still carrying on then?"

"Melinda keeps him in line," Tillie answered, deciding to fib. "We hardly see one another. I'm sure he's over it by now."

Vincenzo laughed and shook his head. "That is funny, Angel."

"Why?" Tillie's hair on the back of her neck started to prickle.

"Well, because I spoke with Noah only a few days ago. He told me that your babies share the same classroom with his little Jake and that he sees you every day at the school."

Tillie nearly fell off her horse, and she began to shake her head as she tried to think of some kind of a defense. "Well...I..." she stammered, "I suppose we see each other, but it's just in passing. It's not like we're good friends or anything." In a very cross tone she barked, "It's *his* problem anyway, Vincenzo, *not mine*, so why are you grilling me like this?"

"Angel," Vincenzo said patiently, "do not become angry with me. I just wanted to know. It seems very strange that you make a trip without your husband on such a special holiday —"

"Listen, Vincenzo," Tillie hotly interrupted, "Alex put me and the kids on that stupid plane yesterday so that he wouldn't have to drive us here himself. He scheduled a hearing for Wednesday, claimed he'd catch up to us this morning, and hasn't called. What more can I tell you?"

"Goodness, I did not mean to upset you. Has he been away?"

"Please don't tell," Tillie murmured. "But if you must know, *yes*. He's been in Pierre since shortly after the election. He says that Robert can't handle it, but I think he's —" Tillie stopped herself, swallowed hard, and refused to speak.

"You think he's fallen back into his busy ways of before," Vincenzo finished.

"Please don't tell," Tillie repeated. "It's so hard for me to have to come up with excuses for why he's gone all of the time. I feel like such an idiot."

"Why?"

"Because he asked me first if he could do this. And I, *like the idiot I must be*, agreed to it — even supported it — when his own father was against it."

Vincenzo took a deep breath and let it out. "Well, Alex has always loved his work — that we know for sure." His voice became very thoughtful. "But it is not like you to become angry with him for it."

"I know," she replied. "I probably should have just stayed in Rapid City, but I wanted to come to Reata and see everybody. It just gets so lonesome sometimes, Vincenzo. The only people I know out there are Shondra and the Romanovs."

Vincenzo understood. Loneliness was a dangerous thing, especially for someone like Angel because of the large family she was accustomed to spending time with. And he wouldn't mention it further, but there did seem to be something strange in her tone when he mentioned Noah.

He rode along in silence as he looked into the light before them, hoping to spot a stray. His mind wandered back to Noah and a conversation they'd had a few years ago. Noah had said that *her eyes were so black you could not see the pupils,* and that her hair was *curly and soft.* Noah called her a *painter* and said that her father was a *powerful warrior who fought with the Allies in World War II....*

Vincenzo swallowed hard and suddenly looked at his little sister's dark silhouette as she rode along beside him. Why had he never thought of the possibility before? *She'd traveled to Rapid City for an art show the very year Noah had met his beloved...Angel?! He calls the girl Angel!*

Vincenzo shook his head. *No, it cannot be.* Besides the horrible little monster who had taken her to the prom, Alex was Angel's *only* date, and she *never* spoke of anyone else. Certainly, she would have shared such an experience with her brothers. They knew everything about one another.

Vincenzo shook his head again. *No, it just cannot be. Just a coincidence of similarities. Angel would not have promised herself in marriage without Papa's permission, nor would she have left the young man jilted at the altar. Angel has a perfect heart, of tenderness and compassion, and she would not hurt someone as grievously as whoever dealt Noah his mortal blow.*

Shortly after sunrise, Tillie and Vincenzo made their way back to the barn. They had collected two of the strays and learned from another hand that Angelo had collected the other. They unsaddled their horses, gave them a good rub down, and allowed them into the holding corral on the other side of the barn.

They were headed across the yard for the main house when Kate stepped out onto the porch and began to wave. "Alex is on the phone!" she yelled happily.

Vincenzo smiled at Tillie. "There. He is probably in Sioux Falls and will be on his way with his brother."

Tillie smiled with relief. They hurried across the yard, up the porch steps, and into the warm entryway. Kate handed Tillie the cordless phone.

"Alex?" Tillie breathed heavily into the phone.

"Hi, Honey, what are you doing?"

Tillie smiled as she took a breath, "I was doing some chores with Vincenzo. Are you in Sioux Falls?"

"Ah…" Alex hesitated. "No, I'm *not.*"

"Well, when will you be here?"

"Honey, I can't make it."

"What?" Tillie gasped into the phone, and Vincenzo saw her pretty brow begin to frown. Kate was still standing fairly close to the entryway. She immediately narrowed her eyes at Vincenzo and beckoned him to follow her into the kitchen.

"Our pre-trial was continued," Alex went on. "We'll finish up on Monday, so I really need to stay here and get my file together."

Tillie stood in amazed silence. *He's actually skipping out on Thanksgiving. The dinner is being hosted by his own sister, for Pete's sake. What's he thinking?*

"Honey?" Alex said. "Are you still there?"

Tillie took a breath and answered, "Yeah. I'm here. What do you want me to say?" She shook her head and tried to fight the tears that blurred her vision.

"I guess that it's okay."

Tillie sadly sighed, shook her head, and answered, "Well, it's *not*. It's *not* okay that you miss this special Thanksgiving. This marks thirty years in America for my family."

"Oh, come on, Honey," Alex coaxed. "Everything they do is special. It doesn't matter whether or not I'm there —"

"It matters to me," Tillie interrupted, and the tears fell from her eyes. "And in case you haven't noticed, we haven't seen each other in nearly four weeks, and you've spent even less time with the kids."

"Tillie, I'm really sorry. I just want to get this out of the way so we can have plenty of time off together at Christmas."

More tears fell from her eyes. "What will I tell everyone?"

"Tell them that I'm extremely busy," Alex answered, "because that's the truth."

"I don't like this." She wanted to tear him apart with about a million accusations but didn't dare in front of his sister, who was still in earshot.

"Honey," Alex said with a sigh, "I asked you about this before I ever got into it —"

"And you also *promised* me that this kind of thing wouldn't happen."

"I don't want to argue with you over the phone," Alex said, his tone becoming a little edgy. "I love you."

Tillie swallowed hard. "I love you too."

"We can talk about this when you get home," he offered.

"Whatever," Tillie mumbled into the phone and abruptly turned it off.

Kate and Vincenzo stepped out of the kitchen.

"Well?" Kate asked.

"He's not coming," Tillie said, handing the phone to Kate and bent over to pull off her boots.

"Why not?" Vincenzo asked.

Tillie set her boots by the radiator and unzipped her snowsuit. She looked at her brother and answered, "He says to tell everyone *he's extremely busy*."

Chapter 13

James Martin was so upset when he learned Alex had sent his family to Reata by themselves that he could hardly eat his Thanksgiving dinner. At the age of eighty-seven, he didn't think he should have to hold his tongue; however, he did so for Tillie's sake. She pretended that everything was fine and that she was proud of her husband and his *great new position*. She smiled and visited, like everything was *just dandy*, which made James' anger burn even more.

Only Vincenzo and Kate had seen Tillie's tears, and she had sworn them to silence. She persuaded them that to allow their families to gossip behind Alex's back would make things worse. She was confident that she and Alex would be able to work things out when they were face to face again. She didn't want any family members butting into their business.

In the best interest of their only sister, the Caselli brothers slipped away after dinner for a quiet smoke in Vincenzo's barn. Vincenzo sat on the door of an empty stall and thoughtfully puffed his pipe.

"What a horrible man," Marquette muttered as he lay on his back upon the clean straw in the empty stall. "Nearly twenty years have I been married, and never once have I sent my Tara off by herself."

"I thought you had settled your differences with Alex," Petrice stated with a frown.

Marquette sighed. "I have prayed morning, noon, and night to somehow rid myself of these ill feelings I have toward the man, but I keep coming back to a point where I cannot bear that he is with her."

Vincenzo shook his head. "What makes a man able to leave his wife *so easily?*"

"Oh, Vincenzo," Petrice said, "perhaps we are blowing the thing out of proportion."

"She said *four weeks*," Vincenzo reminded. "I heard it with my own ears. Can you imagine being away from Ellie for four weeks?"

"Tara would thrash me after only one," Marquette mused.

"My Ellie would be so disappointed," Petrice conceded.

"And Lovely Kate would have me sleeping in the barn." Vincenzo raised one eyebrow. "This is not right. Perhaps we should ask Sam or James if one of them will speak with Alex."

Petrice slowly shook his head. "Perhaps we should give the two of them some time to work it out together first. After all, our Angel is no longer a little girl."

Marquette and Vincenzo relented, and Vincenzo took another thoughtful draw from his pipe. "There is another matter I hesitate to even bring up."

"And that is?" Marquette asked.

Vincenzo took a deep breath, let it out, and looked at both of his brothers. "Noah Hansen."

"Oh," Marquette scoffed with a smile and shook his head. "That was only a harmless, little crush and is probably over with by now. Besides, Noah Hansen is more honorable a man than even the three of us. He would *never* attempt anything as disgraceful as what you imply."

"I am not implying anything," Vincenzo defended.

"Then why do you bring it up?" Petrice asked.

Vincenzo shrugged and shook his head. "I do not know. Angel and I talked about him on our ride this morning, and I caught her in a smallish sort of lie."

"She *lied* to you…" Marquette pondered.

Vincenzo affirmed, "And the lie was concerning Noah and how often she sees him. She tried to tell me that she hardly ever sees him, but, unbeknownst to Angel, I spoke with Noah a few days ago. He mentioned that he sees her every day at the school. Their children are in the same class."

"Goodness," Petrice replied, shaking his head. "Why would she lie about such a thing?"

"She became very hot when I confronted her," Vincenzo continued. "She said that it is *Noah's* problem, *not* her own."

"Hmmm…" Marquette thoughtfully scratched the top of his head.

"How strange," Petrice murmured.

"And she also says," Vincenzo added, "that Alex has *not* noticed and that he *will not* notice."

"How could he *not*," Marquette laughed, "unless he is as blind as he is dumb."

"Perhaps he is not paying attention," Petrice stated.

Marquette's laughter instantly faded. "He has *never* deserved her."

"Do not say such things, Marquette," Vincenzo admonished. He took another draw from his pipe and blew out the smoke.

"I have noticed every man that has so much as glanced at my Tara," Marquette said. "I cannot believe a husband would not notice such a thing."

"Especially when Noah was so obvious," Petrice added.

Vincenzo frowned and held the pipe between his teeth, lost in his thoughts.

"What is it, Vincenzo?" Petrice asked.

Vincenzo shook his head. "It is nothing." He hopped down from the stall's door. "Come, my brothers, we must spend time with our children and our own wives this day. And do not tell my Lovely Kate that I had this smoke in the barn, or there will surely be trouble."

Marquette and Petrice laughed as they crawled out of the straw and followed Vincenzo back into the house.

Guiseppi was so furious he could hear his heart pounding inside his head. All of the buried bitterness and anger he'd had toward Alex for the past six years boiled to the surface. He tried to hide it from the rest of the family by sitting near the fireplace, pretending to read Kate's *Crochet* magazine. He hid behind the pages and stewed about things he wanted to say to Alex…*the torture of my heart when I see the ache in my daughter's eyes! How I regret giving her into this marriage!* He sighed and clutched at his chest…*just to think, the boy I prayed for was delivered unto me, and my sinful eyes could not see the Lord's hand! I disregarded His gift….*

Guiseppi heard James Martin's familiar shuffle, and he hunched deeper behind the magazine. James took a seat in the chair next to Guiseppi, but Guiseppi chose to ignore the old man, pretending complete engrossment in the *Crochet* magazine. Two wrinkled and shaky fingers pulled the magazine down from in front of Guiseppi's face, and he looked into James' reproving expression.

James looked from the magazine and then back at Guiseppi. "New hobby?" Guiseppi nodded.

"Humph." James leaned back in his chair and grumbled, "You're mad at my son, and you're afraid to say so because everyone is running around here, pretending that it's okay for him to do this. My own Kate will not even allow me to speak with her about it."

"And what would you have me say, James?" Guiseppi snapped. "What words between the two of us will make the situation better?"

"At my age, I tend to meddle wherever I can."

"Perhaps meddling will make matters worse," Guiseppi scowled.

"My son and I have never seen eye to eye on his political interests, and I think he left his wife too much *before* he became the big attorney general."

"Well, they are both grown people now. My Angel is twenty-nine years old and knows that she must work this out, on her own, with her husband." Guiseppi looked seriously at James. "We must meddle no more. Alex must make his own decisions, James, and he will then have to learn to live with the consequences of his actions."

James nodded, deciding to say nothing more. Guiseppi was right, of course, in that Alex would have to learn from his consequences, whatever they may be. But Alex was more than just Tillie's husband — he was James' son, and James' prayer was that the consequences not have too much of a sting. After all, James loved his son as much as Guiseppi loved his daughter.

*****

So they wouldn't have to hire another charter, Petrice offered to fly his sister home to the Black Hills. Bright and early on Sunday morning, he loaded his family and Tillie and her children into his small jet. Before departing Sioux Falls, Tillie left a message on their answering machine at home, telling Alex when they would arrive.

In less than ninety minutes they'd landed at Rapid City Regional Airport. Since Alex wasn't there to greet them, Tillie *again* attempted to call her husband. After dialing their home *and* Alex's office and getting no answer, Petrice rented a car so he could take Tillie and the twins home.

"I can drive myself home," Tillie insisted through clenched teeth. Her anger burned out of control. There was no reason Alex should not have been there to at least bring them home.

"Oh, this is just fine," Petrice tried to smooth her ruffled feathers. "This way I will have the assurance that you have safely gotten home. Besides, will it not be easier if you do not have to worry about returning the rental car?"

Tillie stewed...*isn't Alex expected to be responsible for anything?*

By the time Petrice pulled into Tillie's driveway, she was furious. Petrice feared she might spontaneously combust when they found that Alex's car wasn't in the garage.

"Where is he?" she growled as they walked into the kitchen.

Petrice carried her luggage behind her. "I will take these upstairs for you." He smiled at the twins. "Come along, little cherubs. You can show me where to put your things." He started up the steps, followed by the four children, while Elaine stayed behind in the kitchen with Tillie.

Tillie frowned as she tossed her keys on the counter. "I s'pose I'd better get some lunch together. Are you and Patty gonna stay or what?"

"Patty will have to file a different flight schedule at this point, so we might as well." Elaine smiled mischievously and suggested, "How about if we just go *out* to lunch?"

Tillie began to nod her head and was about to respond when she heard the automatic garage door. Her black eyes flashed with anger and she stomped her foot. "*There he is*," she whispered with a ferocious scowl.

"Now, Angel," Elaine put a hand on Tillie's shoulder, "please be gentle."

"Oh, I'll be *gentle* all right," Tillie snapped as she reached for the knob and jerked open the garage door.

Elaine turned and trotted for the stairway, quietly calling to her husband, "Petrice, we need to go *right now*."

Alex got out of his car and smiled sheepishly as he came toward her. "Hi, Honey."

Tillie nearly flew across the garage. "Don't *Hi, Honey* me!" she shouted. With a disgusted snort she slammed the door and locked it. Then she stormed through the kitchen, up the stairs, and found everyone waiting in the hallway. "Let's go eat," she said with a vicious scowl.

"Angel!" Petrice exclaimed in a whisper. "Please try to calm yourself down!"

"No! Now let's get out of here!" With that, she took both her children by the hand and led them down the steps. Petrice and his family followed.

By the time they reached the sun room, Alex had let himself in with his own set of keys and was standing in the kitchen, looking perplexed.

"Daddy!" His children excitedly greeted. They broke away from their mother and rushed to their father. He took them into his strong arms, while they lavished love and kisses all over him.

Seeing her beloved children rush to the man who'd skipped out on their Thanksgiving vacation doubled the wrath within her. She felt her face flush hot with anger, and her eyes burned with tears of rage.

Petrice delicately placed a hand on his sister's shoulder and whispered in her ear, "Let us take the children for some lunch, so that you and Alex may visit."

"I don't want to visit with him!" she shouted, making the twins jump and look at her.

A.J. raised his black eyebrows and looked at his father, "Is Mommy mad?"

Tillie's breath came in short huffs, and she turned and stormed into the living room where no one could see her. *This is ridiculous!*

Petrice grimaced at his brother-in-law, while Elaine and their children watched with open-eyed amazement from the bottom of the stairs.

"Hello, Alex," Petrice greeted. "Can I take your children to lunch so that you may visit with your wife?"

Alex raised an eyebrow. "So, she's pretty mad?"

"Oh, boy." Petrice rolled his eyes. "Only once before have I known my sister to be this angry, and it took me many months to repair the damage."

Alex was a little winded at that point because he had never experienced such anger from Tillie. On top of that, he had pulled an all-nighter at the office and was just returning home. He'd hoped to get a nap in before his family returned. He wasn't up for this kind of a confrontation. He nodded at Petrice. "Go ahead and take the kids, and I'll see if I can get her to talk to me."

Petrice gave Alex a reassuring smile and put his hand on Alex's shoulder. "Be brave, Alex, but remember, a woman's heart is difficult to reason with. You must be understanding with her so that your prayers will not be hindered."

Alex tried to smile in return. He sighed and knelt down beside his very quiet children. "Go with Uncle Patty and Auntie Ellie so I can talk to Mommy."

Laura leaned close to her father's ear and whispered, "Is Mommy mad at you?"

"Very," Alex admitted. "But it's gonna be okay."

A.J. whispered, "You were supposed to come for turkey."

"I know. And I'm really, really sorry."

Both of his precious children smiled at their father, and A.J. was the first to say, "It's okay, Daddy."

"Yeah," Laura chimed in. "It's okay. Maybe Mommy can make you a turkey today."

Alex shook his head. "Please don't say that in front of Mommy. Now you two go and get some lunch with Uncle Patty."

Petrice collected everyone, avoiding the smoldering cauldron in the living room, and hurried them out the back door.

Alex took a deep breath and went into the living room, where he found his wife, standing with her back to him and staring out the window.

"Honey," he began.

Tillie held up her hand and snapped, "Don't Alex. You are so full of it that I don't even want to hear it."

"Please, Honey," he humbly began again. "I'm really sorry. It just couldn't be helped this time."

"Oh, baloney," Tillie muttered, without even turning around.

"Listen," Alex sighed, "please don't be mad at me. Turn around so I can see you."

"No. If you're uncomfortable, that's *not* my problem."

Alex went to where she stood and tried to reach for her hand, but she snatched it away from him. She had never done that before. She was angrier than he had guessed. "I love you," he said, wondering if at least *that* might break the ice between them.

"How did you expect us to get home today?" Tillie snapped. "And why didn't you answer your phone at the office?"

"I was at the Law Library earlier. Maybe that's when you called."

"I haven't heard from you in three days. How did you expect us to get home?"

Alex bit his lip and closed his eyes.

Tillie turned around and confronted her husband. "You *didn't* think about it, did you? *Didn't even cross your mind.*"

Alex took a deep breath, hoping for words that wouldn't come, and finally shook his head.

"Oh, man!" Tillie shook her head and shouted, "Do you have any idea how *embarrassing* it was — in front of our whole, entire family — when you didn't show up for Thanksgiving?! How many people do that, Alex?! Nobody that *I'm* related to!" She took a breath. "And to top it all off, you couldn't even find your way out to the airport to pick us up! Now Patty's gonna have to file a new flight schedule!"

Alex tried to reach for her again, but she stormed into the sunroom. He followed her and wondered what to do. Had he known she would be this angry, he would have gotten her a gift of some sort to help weaken the storm.

"Tillie, please," he pleaded as he followed her. "I love you. What can I do to make this better?"

She surprised him when she stopped abruptly and turned around. Her black eyes blazed with rage as she pointed her index finger into his chest. "You can call each and every one of our family members, *tonight*, and tell them what a horrible mistake you made and that you're very sorry for what you've done!"

"Okay," Alex agreed. "I can do that." He reached for the small index finger that punched him and was relieved when she didn't pull off his hand. He held her hand for a moment and then softly kissed the top of it. He looked into her eyes. "Tillie, I'm so sorry. I didn't have any idea that it would make you this angry."

Tillie's hostility began to melt, and there was a sudden burst of tears onto her pretty face.

Alex gently took her into his arms and held her as tightly as he dared. "I'm so sorry, Honey. Can you ever forgive me?"

Tillie nodded as she hung onto her husband and cried.

"I love you, Tillie," he said as he touched her soft hair and caught the wonderful scent of her favorite perfume.

"I love you, too, Alex."

He brushed some of her tears away with his hand and gave her a tender kiss on her lips. Inwardly, he sighed with relief. At least his marriage was one thing he would never have to worry about.

*****

After finishing an investigation for a London bank, Marquette and Tara returned to their home just outside of Washington, D.C. An invitation to Alex and Tillie's house for Christmas was in their stack of mail. According to Angel's letter, they had invited the entire family to celebrate Christmas in the Black Hills. Marquette called Tillie to accept the invitation and learned that everyone, with the exception of James Martin and his son, Sam, had accepted. James and Sam were to host a children's benefit at the Minnehaha Country Club that Christmas, and could not miss it.

"But she did not seem herself," Marquette said to Tara after his telephone conversation with his sister.

"What do you mean?" Tara asked as she set their dinner on the table.

Marquette shook his head as he held out Tara's chair. "I do not know. She was evasive and said she could not talk."

Tara took her seat. "Perhaps she was busy with the children?"

Marquette shook his head as he seated himself across from his wife. "Something has gone awry, Tara, my love. I feel it within my spirit."

Tara looked away from her husband, pretending to study the meal on her plate...*Father, please help....*

*****

Bobby and Ginger's baby was born in early December. Ginger attempted to reach Tillie by phone, but there was never an answer. After two weeks, Ginger placed a call to Rosa.

"Well, hello, Ginger!" Rosa exclaimed. "Congratulations! We received your announcement. Did you get our gift for the babe?"

"Yes," Ginger answered. "Thank you...but I'm really calling about Tillie. I haven't been able to reach her. Is something wrong?"

"Everything is wonderful in the Black Hills!" Rosa lied with a smile in her voice. "We are going out there to celebrate Christmas!"

The truth was that Rosa and Guiseppi hadn't heard from Tillie in the weeks since receiving the invitation, and only Marquette had been able to reach her by telephone.

"You know she has been dreadfully busy since the election," Rosa went on. "She and Alex are very popular now."

"Okay, then," Ginger answered. "I guess I'll just keep trying to get a hold of her. Will you tell her to give me a call?"

"I certainly will," Rosa agreed, *just as soon as I get a hold of her myself.*

*****

Noah followed Shondra back to Alex's office. He hadn't had business with Alex since the beginning of December. Sometimes he saw Alex and Tillie in church, but Melinda was adamant about keeping Noah away from them.

"I think I saw Alex more when he lived in Sioux Falls," Noah joked.

Shondra forced a smile at Noah's attempted humor, but inside she was worried. Alex had been gone far more than he needed to be, while his deputy sat around and did *nothing*. Even though he'd promised Tillie he'd be around more after Thanksgiving, he allowed his schedule to remain packed. He stayed in a hotel in Pierre most nights, even when he worked in Rapid City during the day. Alex had made what he called "an executive decision" to be away from his family so that he could focus on the continuing file transfer in the attorney general's office.

Shondra knocked on Alex's door and opened it to let Noah in. Alex rose behind his desk to extend his hand in greeting, and Shondra left them alone.

"Hey, Alex," Noah greeted with a smile as he shook Alex's hand. He took a seat in his usual place. "It's good to finally see you again. Where ya been hidin' out?"

"Oh, man," Alex began as he seated himself behind his desk, "I've had so many cases in Hughes County that it's not even funny, and then I've had three in the Supreme Court. I've been in Pierre since shortly after the election."

"We got that house moved off of the lot at Franklin and Mt. Rushmore Road," Noah said. "They finished the hole yesterday. We haven't had any frost yet, you know."

"That's amazing. I can't believe how long the building season in Rapid City is. So, what kind of a time frame can I give Dmitri and his partners for opening?"

"Probably mid-April."

"His partners will be out here in January to sign a lease," Alex said as he reached for his calendar. "What do you have available?"

"I really don't know. Maybe you oughta have Shondra give Melinda a call."

"Okay." Alex nodded, made a note on his calendar, and then looked at Noah. He'd wanted to ask Noah about something since before the election…*I wonder if I can just get him to admit it to me. After all, I am the best attorney in South Dakota. Did he really think I wouldn't figure this thing out?* "Is everything okay, Noah?"

"Sure. Why?"

"You look a little worried or something, and I've noticed that Melinda seems to want to keep you away from me at church. Is there something I should know?"

Noah maintained a straight expression and shook his head. Inside, he was instantly nervous and maybe even a little sick to his stomach. He wasn't exactly sure *why* Melinda was so bent on keeping them apart, but he didn't dare pursue ask her.

Alex's dark eyes bored into Noah as he asked, "How are things going with Melinda?"

"Alex, it's really not going that well, but please don't say anything to anyone."

Alex frowned. *That's not exactly the confession I was looking for…* "I knew something was wrong. You know, Noah, we've been friends for a long time, and I feel terrible about getting you into that whole thing."

Noah scoffed, "It's not *your* fault, Alex." He lowered his voice and continued, "But just between you and me, how much trouble am I gonna be in if I call that wedding off?" He pretended to chuckle. "Since I've got the greatest lawyer in South Dakota, what can you do for me?"

Alex raised his eyebrows and took a quiet breath…*I hope you're not thinking about running off with my wife, because she'll never go for it.* "Well, there are quite a few things to consider at this point; but right off the bat, I can't think of any kind of a claim she'd have against you, except maybe the fact that it would become extremely uncomfortable for her to work there if the two of you were to break it off. She might be able to get some lost wages out of you, but that would be a drop in the bucket. Unless, of course, the two of you have been…" he hesitated, "*Intimate.*"

"No way!" Noah shook his head.

"Well, I didn't think so, but lawyers are regularly put into the position of having to ask the most uncomfortable questions."

"I don't love her," Noah blurted out.

Alex raised one eyebrow…*that's obvious.* "Why are you marrying her?"

"Lots of reasons. She's great with the boys, for one thing." Noah took a deep breath. "Maybe I can warm up to her. You know, we still got about seven months before the actual day, and a lot can happen in seven months. Anyway…" and he changed the subject, "don't you have some leases you want me to pretend to read?"

Alex reached for the file Shondra had left in his office…*so he's going to lie to me about it.* He handed Noah the file and watched his clumsy, calloused fingers flip through the pages…*she'll never even notice you, Noah. You're such an idiot.*

Estelle had the morning paper spread out over the bar and read the political section while she enjoyed a cup of coffee. There were no customers yet, and she had to catch up on the local hero. She had a strange fascination about the man, and Maggie couldn't figure it out. Maggie refilled their cups and peered into the paper over Estelle's shoulder.

"Slam dunked another one," Estelle muttered.

Maggie nodded as she skimmed the article.

"Do you suppose they're still married?" Estelle asked.

Maggie looked curiously at her sister. "What makes you say that?"

Estelle shrugged and pointed to the article. "Says here he was before the Supreme Court three times last week. That's in Pierre, Maggie. Did you know that?"

Maggie scoffed, "Of course I know that."

"He's never in Rapid City," Estelle continued. "So he must not *ever* be with Angel." She snorted and shook her head. "Noah would have been a better husband. I think we should just go ahead and tell Angel about Noah. What do you think?"

Maggie wasn't surprised anymore at her sister's comments. She sighed and reminded her, "Angel knows about Noah, Baby."

Estelle gave Maggie a confused frown. "Well then, why doesn't she leave this guy and come back to Noah?"

Maggie searched for the words to help her dear sister understand. "Church people don't believe in leaving each other — you and Mona have been over this a thousand times."

"But Angel's husband leaves all of the time."

"That's *different*. And it's hard for us to understand, Baby, but Angel can't leave her husband for someone else. And Noah wouldn't want her to do that anyway."

After his meeting with Alex, Noah had to check on a car wash he was putting up on East St. Patrick's Street. It was just a small project, but it was for someone he knew from church. He had just enough time to check on the site and then hurry over to the school. *Maybe, she'll talk to me today.*

As he left the work site, he drove past The Second Time Around, located on the corner of East St. Patrick Street and Elm. He slammed on his brakes when he saw a familiar black Mercedes wagon. He knew only one person in town with a car like that. He turned his truck around and parked in front of the old antique store.

A soft bell sounded when he walked through the door, and the lady at the counter looked up and smiled. "Can I help you find anything?"

Noah smiled and shook his head as he surveyed the antique store, hoping to find her without looking too obvious. He almost laughed at himself. *Too obvious? Okay, what kind of an antique am I looking for? I have to make this look believable.*

He wandered down an aisle filled with glass and spontaneously took an orange tumbler from the shelf. *Yes! Mona's Christmas present!*

Noah turned the corner at the next aisle and saw her, dressed in jeans and a heavy winter jacket. Her black curls fell down around her shoulders, and he sighed with contentment. She was looking through a box filled with old records and, at that moment, appeared to find what she was looking for. He continued toward her until she looked up and gave him a surprised smile.

"Hi, Noah. What are you doing here?"

"Oh," Noah held up the orange glass tumbler and answered, "Mona's Christmas present."

"She collects Floragold?"

Noah hesitantly nodded. *Floragold?* "Yes," he answered, trying to sound sure of himself.

"Ma`ma collects Floragold," Tillie said as she admired the tumbler. "She has for years. It was really popular when they first came to America." She peered at the price tag. "But that's just a little overpriced. You might want to look in a couple of other places first."

"Yeah," Noah said, nodding his head as if he knew *exactly* what she was talking about. "I thought it looked a little high." He looked at the old record in her hand. "What are you doing here?"

Tillie smiled and flipped the old album over. "For Papa, for Christmas. This was his favorite Jim Reeves album. It includes *The Shifting Whispering Sands.*" She looked back into Noah's eyes and added, "He'll really enjoy it."

"Still listening to his old cowboy music?" Noah asked with a smile. They'd talked about it while they danced that day in the little run-down cowboy bar that was now The Sluice.

Tillie shook her head sadly. "You know, Noah, I don't want to talk about the *old days*, or remember how much fun we had. Those days are *over.*" She began to back away, trying to avoid his compelling gaze.

"Sorry. I didn't mean to —"

"It's okay, Noah," she stammered as she backed away. "I have to stop at the store before I pick up the kids, and…and —"

She was unaware of a large trunk behind her, but Noah saw that she was about to stumble.

"Tillie —"

But she was at her panic point and bolted backwards. She tripped on the trunk, losing her balance, and Noah caught her in his arms. He should have let go of her when she had gotten her balance back, but he couldn't — or didn't want to. He drew her closer to himself — close enough to smell her perfume and feel her soft hair against the side of his face.

For a brief moment, Tillie thought about struggling away, but it was so wonderful to be in his arms again that she allowed a few seconds to pass before she pushed on his chest and backed out of his arms. When she looked at him, there were tears in her eyes.

"*Let me go,*" she whispered. "And *please*, don't think about us anymore."

"I'm sorry."

"Stay here until I leave, and don't come to the school early anymore." She tried to gulp her sorrow away, but some of her tears spilled onto her face. "*Please, Noah. This is very hard for me right now.*"

Noah was ashamed of himself. The last thing he ever wanted was to make her cry, and he would have rather died than be responsible for that.

Tillie turned and went to the counter, while Noah waited for her to pay for her album. He didn't move from the spot where she'd left him until he heard the bell go off, signaling her departure. Then he put his glass back on the shelf and left. He got in his pickup and sat there for a while to think about the stupid thing he'd done. *Why can't I control myself?* He shook his head as he remembered that he'd never been able to control himself where she was concerned. He'd only known her a few days before he asked her to marry him, and he would have married her on the spot had she been old enough. Noah shook his head again. *I actually made her cry.* "I'm a stupid oaf."

Tillie couldn't drive away fast enough. She headed for the school, praying that he'd respect her wishes and not show up there right away. *Why can't he just stay away from me? Especially considering our past. Do I have to fight this thing on my own? Can't he help out a little? Isn't it bad enough that the witch he's engaged to is always calling, wanting to talk about their wedding? Does he have any idea the pain I feel every time I see them together? Does he even care, or is he just consumed with his own end of it?*

Tillie found a parking spot and turned off her car. His pickup wasn't anywhere to be seen, and she started to cry again. Being held in Noah's arms for that brief moment was agonizingly joyous for her, and she wished it had never happened. She sobbed uncontrollably for quite some time, thankful that she had arrived early enough to get herself together before the children were released.

She craved the comfort Alex's arms used to give her, but he wasn't available. They were lucky if he bestowed upon them the time it took to drive his family to church, sit through a sermon, and then drive them home again, where he closed himself in his office with his many files. He was gone at least three or four days a week, and sometimes he would even call her from Pierre before she had realized he had left! He always had the same excuse: "I just want to get this stuff out of the way so that we can enjoy Christmas."

Christmas was approaching, and there was no sign that Alex planned to take any time off at all. Tillie regretted inviting her family to town for the holiday, wishing instead that she could go to her parents' home. She wanted out of town, and she wanted out fast. Whatever she felt for Noah was spiraling out of control, and her only solution was to run. She wanted her *old* life back, the one where she believed Noah to be a drunken blackguard and Alex to be the only knight that could satisfy her every dream. She wanted to be back in the safe, small house where Alex came home to her every night. Where he took her into his arms and told her that he loved her, over and over again, trampling the memory of Noah she'd hidden in her heart. But it was impossible to go back, and only God knew when Alex would come home.

*****

A few days later, Tillie was home alone in her studio upstairs. She had created a fantastic portrait of Rosa and Delia walking through the Black Hills National Forest. She cringed when her telephone rang. It was only a few days before Christmas, and she thought maybe she should answer it in case it was one of her family members. On the other hand, she didn't want to talk to any of them, because there would be questions concerning Alex's whereabouts, and that would be uncomfortable. *It could be Melinda, calling with her semi-weekly torture treatment.*

Tillie's eyes narrowed. *It's time to give that horrible woman a piece of my mind!* She grabbed for the telephone.

"Hello!"

"Tillie?" a familiar voice asked.

"Yes," Tillie replied, changing her tone to one of politeness.

"This is Noah. Please don't hang up. I have to tell you something."

Tillie snorted. *The man is completely out of control.* "What do *you* want?"

Noah sounded down when he answered. "I just wanted you to know that I've got an idea. My housekeeper, Vera, will be taking care of the boys' rides to school, so you don't have to worry about that anymore...and..." he paused, "she can bring Jake over to play with A.J. and pick him up later, so you don't have to find a million excuses why they can't get together anymore. They're really great little buddies, and they shouldn't have to suffer because of me."

Tillie was relieved and surprised, remaining quiet as she pondered the solution.

"Tillie? Are you still there?"

"Yes. Thank you."

"Tillie, I'm really sorry about the other day. I never meant to hurt you."

"It's okay."

"It's *not* okay, but I *can* and *should* stay out of your way. I had no right —"

"It's okay," Tillie gently interrupted. "I really appreciate what you've done. Thank you."

"You're welcome." He took a soft breath. "I gotta go. Take care of yourself."

"You too," she replied, as the tears left her eyes and the line went dead. There. It was over again.

Chapter 14
Christmas Eve, 1986

Alex burst happily through the garage door and set his suitcase on the floor. Tillie was at the stove, and she looked at him with a scowl.

"Well, I see you finally made it home," she remarked dryly.

Alex's happy expression melted into a confused frown. "What are you all bent about now?"

She turned back to her cooking. "My family's been here since yesterday. They're in the family room with the kids."

"What are *they* doing here?"

"Humph! It was *your* idea to invite them, remember? After skipping out on Kate's Thanksgiving."

"Did they say anything?"

Tillie rolled her eyes. "No, but I'm sure they're wondering. I didn't tell them I haven't seen you since December 1st, or that you haven't even bothered to call in *over a week*."

"Are they all staying here or what?"

"Papa, Ma'ma, Marquette, and Tara. Everyone else got a room at the Howard Johnson's."

Alex nodded...*wow, she's really ticked off*...He put his hand softly on her shoulder, but she shrugged away.

"Knock it off, Alex," she warned.

"What now?" he questioned.

"We're not about to make up." She said through gritted teeth. "You can't fly through the door like the hero you're *not* and expect everything to be fine."

Alex sighed. "What's your problem now, Tillie?"

"*My* problem? I'll tell you what *my* problem is. I lost my husband about nine weeks ago." She narrowed her eyes. "And you *promised* this wouldn't happen again."

"Listen, Tillie, you knew I'd be busy —"

"Shut up, Alex," she muttered as she turned back to her cooking. "I saw Robert over at Albertson's the other day."

At her words, the hair on Alex's neck prickled...*did Robert tell her?*

As if she'd read his mind, she replied, "Oh, yeah, he told me all about his two-week vacation, because, hey, there's nothing for your deputy to do at the AG's office anyway, beings you're so gracious to handle *everything* on your own."

"Tillie —"

"Don't even bother, Alex —"

Tillie's words were interrupted when her brother, Petrice, came into the kitchen.

138

"Well, hello, Alex," he greeted, smiling warmly and extending his hand to his brother-in-law. "I did not realize you were home."

"I just got here," Alex replied with an artificial smile.

"Alex, it is so good to see you!" exclaimed Vincenzo from the doorway of the kitchen. "When did you arrive?"

"Just now." Alex tried to smile.

Vincenzo extended his hand to Alex. "Merry Christmas."

"Merry Christmas, Vincenzo."

"Why do we not help you with your bag," Petrice offered, and he stooped to collect Alex's suitcase.

"Thanks, guys," Alex replied, thankful to be off of the hot seat with his wife as his brothers-in-law hurried him from the kitchen.

Tillie shook her head and went back to her cooking…*it's a miracle he even made it home.*

"Angel, can I help with something?" Tara asked.

Tillie didn't even look up at Tara and shook her head in response. She'd deliberately saved her cooking for that day so that she wouldn't have to spend time with her family.

Tara nervously cleared her throat. "Angel, you have been dreadfully quiet since our arrival yesterday. Please talk to me."

Tillie shrugged. "What's to talk about, Tara?"

"Obviously things are not going well for you and Alex right now. Perhaps we should talk about that."

Tillie plastered an artificial smile on her face and looked at Tara. "Everything's great, Tara. Please don't worry."

Tillie had resolved to make a perfect Christmas out of the situation. She'd set her formal dining room table with her wedding china and crystal and created a work of art with evergreens and berries for the centerpiece.

"Your decorations are beautiful, Angel," Kate said as they seated themselves for dinner.

"Thanks, Kate." Tillie smiled her way as Alex pretended to lovingly seat his wife.

It didn't go unnoticed that there was something amiss between the host and hostess this Christmas Eve. Tillie hadn't so much as given Alex a peck on the cheek when he arrived, nor were there any loving glances between the two of them. The cold silence around the table was deafening.

"Your trees are gorgeous," Elaine suddenly offered. She'd noticed that Tillie had decorated two — one for the sunroom, and one for the formal living room.

"Thanks, Ellie."

Alex seated himself at the head of the table but was uncomfortable to say the least. The Casellis were obviously displeased with him.

Guiseppi beamed, feasting his eyes on the pasta bowls Angel had filled with ravioli. "This looks delicious, my Angel! Old Doria's recipe?"

"Of course, Papa." Tillie's hard face seemed to soften a little for her father.

"And tomorrow she will roast us a turkey!" Rosa exclaimed, looking to the grandchildren for some exuberance.

They cheered for their grandmother, and Rosa tittered, "And if everyone is very good, we shall receive cannoli for dessert!" The children cheered again.

Silence again engulfed the table until Marquette cleared his throat. He narrowed his eyes in Alex's direction and asked, "So, how is the attorney general's office?"

Alex nearly choked...*so, the skinny little guinea wants to get into it right here*. "Things are going well, Marquette. Thank you for asking."

Tillie shot Marquette a glare...*please, not here.*

Guiseppi was sitting next to Marquette and gave him a kick beneath the table.

"I saw your picture in the paper!" Guiseppi said with enthusiasm. "The murder trial up at Ft. Sisseton was a blowout."

Alex nodded. "We had a very strong case."

"And how is your deputy, Robert, coming along?" Marquette frowned at his father and whispered, "Please do not kick me again, Papa."

Tillie rolled her eyes...*this oughta be good.*

Guiseppi clamped his jaws shut and waited for the fireworks to begin.

Alex was stunned by Marquette's question. Awkward silence again engulfed the table.

"Not too well, then?" Marquette goaded.

Alex took a breath. "He's not coming along as well as I had hoped."

"Ellie and I have an announcement!" Petrice interjected.

All eyes were upon him, and if they'd all known the truth, Ellie didn't have a clue as to what the "announcement" was all about. However, she was prepared to go along with whatever he said. Anything was better than watching Marquette and Alex square off for Christmas Eve dinner.

"Please speak, my brother," Vincenzo encouraged.

"We have decided to take our children to *Italia* in January," he said. Michael and Gabriella gasped with surprise, but Ellie maintained her elegant quiet, as if she'd known all along.

She nodded with a smile, "Yes, we thought it was time the kids saw where the Casellis came from."

"Oh, that is just wonderful!" Vincenzo replied. "And Marquette has kept our old place so well-cared for."

"Oh, yes," Rosa agreed quickly. "When Guiseppi and I were there for our fiftieth, we were so impressed with how much it still looks like home."

"We own all of the land from your old place and up to the Andreotti property line now," Tara added, gently laying her hand on her husband's knee beneath the table. "We have secured all building rights and easements to assure that it remains as it was meant to be."

Marquette shoved a giant ravioli into his mouth. *Unfortunately*, his family was going to keep him from getting into it with Alex tonight.

After the disconcerting Christmas Eve dinner, Vincenzo and Petrice collected their families and headed for their hotel. Guiseppi and Rosa hid out in one of the guest rooms upstairs.

Alex and Tillie put their children to bed, and once they were in the hallway alone together, he confronted his wife.

"I can't believe you told Marquette about Robert!" he whispered.

"I didn't tell him *anything*," Tillie snapped. "He must have just guessed."

"Oh, baloney! You've been gossiping about me behind my back."

"No way, Alex," Tillie denied. "I don't do things like that. I might be really, really mad at you, but I'd never gossip about you with my family."

Alex frowned. "Why on earth are you mad at me? You agreed to this."

"I never agreed to live apart. The kids never see you. You stay more nights in Pierre than you stay here in our home."

Alex sighed. "Well I guess you're just going to have to get used to it because I'm really busy right now."

"I don't like it. I don't think it's good for our family."

Alex took a deep breath and closed his eyes with frustration. "Tillie —" He stopped himself and opened his eyes. "I have to make a couple of phone calls. Can we talk about this later?"

Tillie's mouth fell open. "On Christmas Eve?"

"Yes, on Christmas Eve. Most people have to *work* for a living." And with that he stormed into his office and closed the door.

Tillie shook her head and closed herself in their bedroom.

Marquette's anger had reached its limit by the time he and Tara found their way to their guest room.

"He is at it again," he whispered. "I have never seen a man become so crazy that he forgets about the love of a good wife and children. Is he possessed by Satan himself?"

Tara sighed and shook her head. "Things do not seem to be favorable at all between the two of them. Angel does not look well."

"She looks nearly *sick*. What is *wrong* with her? You do not suppose that Alex has done something she is fearful of telling to us, do you?"

"Oh, no, Marquette." Tara shook her head. "I do not believe Alex would do something like what you are thinking. I think it is just loneliness. There have been a great many changes in Angel's life these past few months."

Marquette agreed somewhat, but how could Angel go from being perfectly happy in a marriage to a man she absolutely adored to being miserable and unable to even look at him?

Rosa sat in their bed watching Guiseppi pace.

"She is depressed," he whispered. "I cannot bear to see this dreadful melancholy in my own daughter."

Rosa nodded, for she had seen it too.

"She does not seem to enjoy her life at all," Guiseppi went on. "I cannot think of a time when I have seen her eyes so filled with sadness. Not even after Noah did she ever grieve this way."

"Alex must be spending a considerable amount of time away from here."

Guiseppi took a deep breath and stopped his pacing to look at Rosa. "I imagine he has given his entire heart and soul to his work."

"Does he not have people to help him?"

Guiseppi shrugged. "Apparently Robert is not working out."

"Are there not others?"

Guiseppi shrugged again. "I guess not, my Rosa."

Tillie crept out of her room. As she came down the hall in her stocking feet, she noticed the light was still on under the door in Alex's office and she could hear the soft drum of his voice. *He's still on the phone?* She shook her head and frowned. *He has absolutely no intention of talking to me tonight, or he would have finished up by now. What's wrong with him? Can't he just shut it off for a few days so we can get our relationship back on track? After all, it is Christmas Eve.*

She made her way to the sun room downstairs and snuggled into the soft love seat. She wrapped herself up in a warm afghan and allowed her mind to wander. *How different things would have been had I married Noah.* She laid her head back on the cushions and closed her eyes as she remembered that weekend she spent with him so many years ago. She'd been trying to forget it forever, but tonight she allowed herself the wistful memory. His eyes, his smile, his voice. Everything about him felt so wonderfully right. When he held her again the other day, she wanted him to sweep her off her feet and carry her away.

If only I could go back...I'd march into Maggie's and tell that woman to take her hands off of him! I should have given him the chance to explain, instead of betraying him the way that I did.

She smiled as she recalled his dancing blue eyes and the expression he still had for her. *Noah still loves me, and it's plain to see every time he looks at me.*

She sighed as the tears began to fall. *How different things would be had I married Noah...I'd be in his arms right now, instead of alone on this love seat....*

Tara had heard Tillie's soft footsteps go by, and she crept through the dark house, trying to find where her sister-in-law had gone. After just a few moments, she found the bundled silhouette in the dark sun room.

"Angel," Tara whispered as she came into the sun room.

Tillie jumped with a little start, and then she saw that it was Tara.

"Can I sit with you for a moment?" Tara asked.

"Sure," Tillie answered. She unwrapped herself and offered Tara some cover beneath the afghan.

"Where is Alex?" Tara asked.

"He's on the phone, believe it or not."

"*On Christmas Eve?*"

"Alex has to *work* for a living," Tillie answered, and Tara heard the tears in her sister-in-law's voice.

Tara took Tillie into her arms and held her close. "Please, Angel, tell me what is wrong?"

"I *can't*," she cried.

Alone in the hotel parking lot, Vincenzo puffed on his pipe while he paced beneath the falling Christmas snow. *How much longer before Marquette attacks?* Vincenzo shuddered. *And to think they are sleeping in the same house this night....*

Christmas vacation, so far, hadn't been going well. Vincenzo had gone to see Noah the day before, only to wish him a Merry Christmas and see how he was doing. Melinda had been exceptionally rude and had even gone so far as to make a smart remark about Vincenzo's "broken English." Vincenzo snorted and shook his head. *My broken English? What is she talking about? I speak far better English than even Melinda.*

"Hmmm," Vincenzo mused aloud. "Now why would Melinda want to alienate Noah from his friend?" His thoughts progressed from there, and he revisited his suspicions from a month ago. *Is there even the most remote of chances that our Angel is Noah's Angel?*

Vincenzo shook his head and laughed at himself. *Why am I always doing this? Of course she is not the same Angel. If she were, Noah would have told us by now. But he hasn't so much as mentioned her for the better part of this year.*

Vincenzo sighed and tried to push his thoughts away. *I am just looking for an excuse to get her out of the marriage. Even if she is the same Angel, she is bound by vows and would never dream of breaking them.*

Chapter 15

Everyone returned to Alex and Tillie's house on Christmas Day to open their gifts. While there were gifts in abundance for everyone, the Casellis couldn't help but notice that there wasn't a single gift from Alex to his wife under the tree. Angel tried very hard to hide her disappointment, but it was obvious to everyone.

After they'd endured a tense Christmas feast, Alex left for the rest of the day to do research at the Law Library, returning home well after bedtime. In his absence, Tillie's family tried to talk to her about how things were going, but she insisted everything was fine and that the situation was only temporary.

Marquette lay awake all night, his anger boiling as he tried to think of a way to rescue his sister from the man he'd hated since before her birth. How their father had been so fooled into giving her hand in marriage to an unfaithful blackguard was beyond him. Certainly, this horrible scenario was not God's plan for Angel's life! How could it be?

I will find a way out for you, my Angel, he silently promised himself in the darkness. *I cannot allow you to live in this hell any longer....*

*****

He was dressed in a black suit with a matching hat when he appeared before Lori's desk the morning after Christmas. He wasn't his usual charming self, but he smiled at the gracious lady. "I need to see my brother-in-law," he requested as he took off his hat.

"He's in his office," Lori answered, sensing Marquette's agitated demeanor. "He has a meeting with Noah Hansen in about five minutes, but you can go back and see him before Noah gets here."

"Thank you."

Shondra was just exiting her office and smiled as she met Marquette outside of Alex's closed door. "What are you doing down here?"

Marquette sighed with a frown. "Before I go in there, perhaps you would like to tell me a thing or two about why Alex does not share his workload with the deputy attorney general."

Shondra's eyes opened wide with panic, for she was all too familiar with the bad feelings between Marquette and Alex. "Marquette," she whispered, pulling him away from the door, "what are you going to do?"

"Just visit with the old blackguard for a few minutes. And why did you not answer my question?"

Shondra shook her head. "I'm dealing with this the best I can —"

"But he does not give any work to his deputy, does he?" Marquette interrupted with a scowl.

Shondra clamped her lips together and shook her head.

"That is all that I needed to know," Marquette said, and he reached for Alex's office door.

As Shondra watched him go inside and close the door, she remembered the last time this happened. *But James and Sam had been there to pull them off of each other before anything too drastic happened.* She shivered...*I'd better just wait here for a few minutes...maybe I should just call the cops now and get it over with....*

Alex looked up with surprise when Marquette walked into his office. He stood behind his desk, while Marquette positioned himself on the other side of the office.

That deranged guinea is here to pick a fight, Alex thought. He frowned and asked, "What do you want, Marquette?" *I'm not afraid of you, and I never have been.*

"My sister is not herself."

Alex rolled his eyes and shook his head. "There's nothing wrong with Tillie. She's a little unreasonable, but everything else seems to be fine."

"There is a dreadful sorrow behind her smile. I am not surprised in the least that you do not see it."

Alex sighed. "What are you here for, Marquette? Because I'm in a hurry this morning, and I don't have a lot of time for whatever tripe you've come over to peddle."

Marquette attempted to control his temper by locking his jaw and looking at his feet for a few moments. He twirled his hat between his hands and put it on the rack by the door. He finally returned his eyes to Alex; but when he saw his brother-in-law standing behind his desk, looking so proud and stubborn, his hatred for the man was unrestrained.

"You are being a *terrible* husband and father," Marquette growled as he stepped toward Alex.

"Oh, really," Alex retorted. "And you've always been such a *perfect* man yourself. For instance, just a few months ago when you nearly ruined my election. God only knows what you *really* do for a living."

"At least I *love* the gift that God gave me." Marquette shot back.

"I love my wife," Alex defended as he came around from the other side of his desk. "And what gives you the right to insinuate that I don't?"

"You do not even see the sorrow you are causing her!" Marquette yelled. "Any man in love with his wife would not allow her to suffer this way!"

"You know, Marquette, you've always had some kind of a strange obsession with your sister. Maybe you should see a professional about that!"

Marquette grabbed Alex by the lapels of his suit coat and thrust him up against the wall.

Alex was amazed that Marquette would even attempt such a stunt, seeing as how Alex was at least six inches taller and twice as broad as the slightly built Italian. "I can really hurt you, you *stupid skinny guinea*," Alex threatened. "Now let go of me!"

"Me first, Alex!" Marquette shouted as he pulled back his fist and prepared to beat out whatever evil Alex had within him. However, the door suddenly opened and someone's strong arms pulled Marquette away. Shondra stepped quickly into the office and closed the door.

Marquette struggled away from whoever had grabbed him from behind. He thought about taking out his frustrations on *that* person, until he saw that it was Noah.

"What's going on?" Noah asked. He and Shondra had listened by the closed door at the shouting voices. Noah decided it was time to go in when they heard the loud thump against the wall.

"He's a lunatic!" Alex shouted, pointing his index finger at Marquette. "I knew he was nuts the day I first laid eyes on him thirty years ago!"

Marquette attempted to lunge at Alex, but Noah dove between them.

"Marquette, what's wrong?" Noah asked.

"He does not take care of Angel!" Marquette shouted. "He is a worthless, racist man, and I *regret* the day my father gave her to him!"

"Come on, Marquette," Noah coaxed. He put his hand on Marquette's shoulder and tried to look into his eyes. "Maybe we should take a walk."

Marquette dodged Noah's friendly touch and continued to shout, "If she were not the godly woman that she is, I would take her as far from you as I could and *never* allow you to hurt her again!"

"Your sick infatuation with your little sister is out of control!" Alex yelled. "And, frankly, I'm really tired of pretending that it's not there!"

"Alex!" Noah gasped as he attempted to hold back a furious Marquette.

"Well it's the truth! He's *psychotic* when it comes to her!" Alex growled.

Noah tried to usher Marquette toward the door. "Come on, Marquette, let's go have some coffee or something." He gave Marquette a friendly pat on the back, and Marquette finally relented.

He reached for his hat on the rack and turned toward Alex for one final admonishment. "*I hate you.*"

"Like I care whether or not some stupid guinea wants to be my friend," Alex sneered. "I've got more important things to worry about."

Noah was horrified at Alex's racial slur. "Alex?" he said, raising his eyebrows.

Alex only rolled his eyes.

Marquette jerked open the door and Noah followed him.

Noah paused to look at Alex before he left. "Can I come back in a couple of hours or so?"

"Sure," Alex answered. "But be careful. He's always been a nutcase."

Shondra closed the door behind Marquette and Noah and looked at Alex, who was straightening his tie and calmly moving to the chair behind his desk. "What happened?" she asked.

Alex barked, "Who let him in here in the first place?"

"Lori, I suppose."

"Don't *ever* let him back in again. And tell Lori to call the cops if he ever shows up here again."

"Alex, he's your brother-in-law."

"He's a dangerous man," Alex snapped as he took a seat behind his desk.

"He's just worried about his sister, and I can't believe you spoke that way to him."

"Give me a break, Shondra," Alex retorted. "He's tried to attack me before, and you know it."

"Alex, I've known you for almost twenty years, and you're just not yourself these days —"

"Shondra," Alex interrupted with a frustrated sigh, "don't you have *something* to do?"

Shondra clenched her teeth together and left Alex's office. She slammed his door behind her and stomped down the hall. *Alex is going to wreck his life, and I hope it hurts!*

Marquette stormed along with Noah all the way to his pickup. They got in, and Noah started the engine as he wondered what to say. Angel had said there was *some stuff there between him and Alex*, but Noah could never have dreamed it was about the outrageous accusations he'd heard a few minutes ago. Marquette didn't seem to have a *thing* for his sister. Noah was still so shocked at Alex's charge, along with the racial slur, that he couldn't find the words to ask Marquette about it.

Noah pulled out into traffic without a clue as to where he could take Marquette. He couldn't take him over to his own office, because that would provoke Melinda. He headed west on Main and silently prayed for God to guide his steps.

"I left my car behind at the blackguard's office," Marquette mumbled. "Perhaps you can return me there later."

"Maybe I oughta pick it up for you," Noah offered.

Marquette let out a heavy breath. "Please, take me to my sister's house. She will have coffee, and we can visit."

Noah groaned, "I *can't.*"

"Oh, poor Noah." Marquette smiled faintly. "Are you are *still* under her spell?"

Noah nodded. "We're a lot closer to my place anyway. My housekeeper has the day off, and the boys are with Josh. Why don't we go over there?"

"Certainly," Marquette agreed, and the rest of the trip was made in silence.

Marquette sat down at the table in Noah's small kitchen while Noah started a pot of coffee. In a few moments, Noah joined him.

"So, why do you hate Alex so much? In all the years I've known you, you've never said anything about it."

"I just always have," Marquette admitted. He took off his hat and tossed it onto the table. He took a deep breath and rubbed his temples. "For years I have suspected Alex to be somewhat prejudiced against anything other than whiteness, or his *royal* Spanish blood, and I have watched Alex being driven by his ambition...not to mention the cowardly way he avoided the war."

"You mean Vietnam?"

Marquette nodded. "For a number of years he and Andy had planned to go to war together when they were old enough; but, when the time came, Alex secretly registered at Harvard so he would be protected from the draft."

"What about all this stuff he says about you and Tillie? What's he talking about?"

"Humph." Marquette rolled his eyes. "I am not romantically inclined toward my sister, if that is what you are asking, but I do love her very much, *as I love my brothers.* Perhaps I *am* very protective of her, but she brought something into our family that was not there when it was only my brothers and me. My mother prayed for eleven years for a baby girl, and we were given Angel in answer. You cannot imagine the thrill it gave my parents to raise a daughter after having raised three sons — my mother especially." Marquette smiled and continued, "The same spell she has over you, she has had over our family for years. Unfortunately, Alex is immune to that spell, as a blackguard would typically be. Well, you know what happened when the babies were born. He wasn't even there. Noah, we almost lost her that day, and I wanted to die right along with her. Thank God He closed her womb and prevented her from having anymore children with the unfaithful rat."

Noah shook his head. "I can't believe how much he leaves her."

"He is gone frequently then?"

"Hasn't she told you?"

Marquette shook his head. "No. She will say practically nothing, and we have all tried to question her about it. He did not even make it to Reata for Thanksgiving, and we all suspected at that time that things were not going well."

"Well, I know he's been out of town since December first. He's got quite a bit of business in Pierre. The Supreme Court is there, you know. I saw him more when he lived in Sioux Falls."

"So who handles *your* business?"

"He does. He does it all."

Marquette looked curiously at Noah. "Is it a dreadful temptation for you to know that he is away?"

Noah's face flushed as he looked away from Marquette.

"Oh, dear," Marquette murmured.

Noah shook his head and looked back at Marquette. "Please don't think I would do that. It's not like that at all, Marq. There's...it's... well...she and I..." Noah stuttered and tried to swallow. He took a deep breath and began again. "It's just not like that...I won't...."

His stuttering lightened the moment, and Marquette laughed.

"Noah Hansen, why can you not shake this?"

Noah shook his head and accidentally blurted out, "I've never been able to shake her."

"What?" Marquette chuckled. "What did you say, my friend?"

Noah sighed. "If I tell you something, Marquette, can you give me your word, as a man of honor, that you won't share it with anyone else in this whole world? Especially your brothers?"

"I will try."

"I'll be right back." Noah rose slowly from his chair and walked into his office. Marquette heard him open a drawer and rustle through some papers and then his footsteps returning. Noah laid down the old photograph before Marquette and set a small, gray felt box beside it.

"What is this?" Marquette looked curiously at the photo, picked it up and held it closer to his eyes. He suddenly took a breath and looked from the photo to Noah. "Angel?"

Noah nodded.

Marquette's heart pounded as he reached for the felt box, wondering what surprise it held. He lifted the lid to reveal the tiny diamond Noah had bought for her that April in 1975.

"Read the inscription," Noah said.

Marquette pulled the ring from its soft nest and peered at the inner circle of the gold band...*For Angel 4/75.*

"*Our Angel* was the girl?" Marquette gasped in a whisper. He suddenly frowned. "*Why would you allow her to marry Alex?*"

"I didn't. I had no idea she'd married Alex until shortly before they moved here."

Marquette was stunned as he looked from the ring to the old photograph. "But why would she leave *you?*" he whispered as he looked at the reflection of Angel's younger self gazing so adoringly into Noah's eyes.

"It was a mistake, I guess."

"So you have spoken with her about this?"

"Yep, and she had no idea that Alex and I were friends."

"I am so confused," Marquette whispered. "She actually agreed to marry you outside of our father's permission?" Noah nodded, and Marquette continued, "Does Alex know about this?"

"No. She made me promise not to tell anyone, and I know she's really tore up about it. It was an accident, Marquette. It wasn't her fault. She was just too young and I was too stupid —"

"But *why* did she leave?"

"She misunderstood something that happened between me and Carrie, who wasn't even my girlfriend at the time," Noah answered. "I never had the chance to explain until just recently."

Marquette narrowed his eyes. "Did you ever ask her to compromise her honor?"

"No, *never*. It wasn't like that…I mean…of course, I have desire for her, but I've always wanted God's *forever* with her — not just some roll in the hay. Marquette, I still love her, and you can't imagine what it does to me every time I have to see her. Sometimes I look at Alex and can't believe she chose him over me —"

"It was not like that at all," Marquette interrupted. "Alex had been away at Harvard for many years and waited until I went to Norway for three months before he made his move. By the time I returned, the relationship was spiraling out of control and being encouraged by our parents —" Marquette suddenly stopped speaking and snapped his fingers together. "Oh, my! It was *not* the fight with Patty after all! It was *you!* I brought her to Rapid City with me that year. She became extremely ill, so I took her back home to be closer to Ma`ma. I thought it was the flu. Shortly thereafter, she had a terrible argument with our brother, Patty, and became depressed and withdrawn. She stopped painting altogether and eventually changed her planned major. Vincenzo and I blamed Patty — and even went so far as to admonish him for what he had done to her." Marquette paused and bit his lip. "If only I would have known, I would have sought you out, demanded an explanation, and certainly would have prevented any kind of a relationship with Alex."

"If I could have found her, I would have done anything to get her back."

"And I know that you looked because we have spoken of this many times, but now there have been vows and children. I do not know how to help you — or her. Surely she must be grieving."

"Do you think your parents know?"

"Perhaps. Whether or not they are aware of your identity is uncertain. I would have to ask them, and you have requested confidence of me."

"Please, I promised her I would never tell anyone."

"I will honor my word, but allow me to share it with my Tara, for we have no secrets between us," Marquette requested.

"Sure."

Marquette looked back at the photograph and the delicate ring in his hand. He smiled sadly. "And you love her still?"

"More than ever."

"Then why marry Melinda?"

Noah took a deep breath. "I didn't love Carrie, either, when we first married…" He paused and smiled when he saw the stricken look on Marquette's face. "Now, just listen to me, Marq. Carrie got pregnant by this lowlife that worked for her stepfather, and she wanted to have an abortion. She claimed that she loved him but couldn't be with him, and her family was really screwed up…blah, blah, blah…and to make a long story short, I told her to marry me. I mean, why not? It had been about eighteen months since Angel bugged out on me, I could see she wasn't coming back, and I figured Carrie and I might as well get married for this little baby she was carrying…and…" He paused and shrugged. "Of course, once the baby was born, one thing led to another, and pretty soon I had this great life and I totally forgot about Angel. Thought maybe it might work that way with Melinda."

Marquette stared at Noah with utter disbelief and amazement. Noah's explanation of his marriage to Carrie seemed so simple to Noah. The man was even more of a knight than Marquette originally thought, and it only solidified his regrets about Alex. He smiled. "You are a *perfect knight*, my friend, but it will *never* work out that way with Melinda."

"I am not a perfect knight. I actually *tricked* Alex into bringing his family to church that first day just so that I could see her...and don't forget about my little problem with *coveting*."

"Bah! There is a *big* difference between lustful aspirations and merely being in love with someone! The two *do not* go hand in hand. However, you *must* attempt to keep a better guard of your heart and your desires so you do not do something to hurt her. My sister is grieving terribly at this time, and I do not know if it is because of what her husband has done or if she feels a certain measure of guilt for what she did to you. Perhaps it is a little bit of both."

"I'm trying to stay away from her as much as possible," Noah said. "I don't like it, but —"

"But she needs time away from you right now. For if Alex continues his blackguardly behavior, she would surely be tempted by you, and neither of us wants the two of you to travel that dangerous road."

Noah drove Marquette to his car. He watched to make sure he got into it and drove away before he went up to Alex's office. Shondra wasn't around, so Noah went down the hall, knocked on Alex's door, and poked his head inside. Alex was alone at his desk.

"Can I come in?" Noah said with a faint smile.

Alex looked surprised, but he nodded his head. Noah came in, closing the door behind him.

"How's it goin'?" Noah asked as he took a seat in front of Alex's desk.

"Better. Why were you gone so long?"

Noah shrugged. "Just thought I should cool him off a little."

"Man, he's *crazy*." Alex said, but thought to himself, *just like all the rest of the lunatics who came back from Vietnam*...he looked at Noah...*I suppose you'll be the next one to attack me.*

"He's just worried about his little sister." Noah said.

"He's sick about her," Alex grumbled...*just like you...no wonder the two of you seem to have so much in common.*

Noah shook his head. "Now don't say stuff like that, Alex. She's pretty special to all of them, and they're traditional folks. He says she's lonesome."

Alex sighed disgustedly. "Tillie's not lonesome. She's got lots of friends at church, and I know she sees Mrs. Romanov at least once a week. She can do without me for just a couple more weeks. I've just about got this transfer complete."

*****

Alex had called Tillie as soon as Marquette was through with his tirade and Noah had gotten him out of the office. They argued briefly, until Tillie ended the call by hanging up on her husband.

Guiseppi, Rosa, and Tara pretended not to have heard, and a tense silence ensued. The three of them crept through the house as quiet as little mice, wondering what would transpire between Tillie and Marquette once he returned. Tara pretended to have the time of her life in the kitchen with Tillie, making turkey noodle soup, while Rosa played Scrabble, Jr. with A.J. and Laura in the living room.

Guiseppi slipped upstairs and placed a secret call to Vincenzo and Petrice, who, thankfully, were still at the hotel.

"Apparently he and Alex have argued most heinously," Guiseppi whispered into the telephone.

"What would you have us do about it, Papa?" Vincenzo asked.

"Find him, my Vincenzo. Take your brother Patty with you and find Marquette."

"And then what, Papa?"

"Tell him to stay away from this place. Angel is upset. She did not want her family interfering, and now he has."

"We will do our best, Papa," Vincenzo promised.

"Uncle Marq is back!" Laura joyously announced from the living room downstairs.

Guiseppi groaned, "Pray we live through this day, my son, for your brother has returned. I must go." He hung up the phone and headed for the stairs, feeling as if an anvil were upon his chest.

Tillie had heard the announcement as well and was making a beeline for her front door. Guiseppi managed to cross paths with her in the living room and reached for her hand.

"My Angel, please forgive your brother —"

"Papa, were you listening?" she asked with a frown.

Guiseppi shook his head. "*Never.* I just have the strangest feeling that Marquette's passions have overtaken him —"

Tillie's frown deepened into a scowl and she said, "Marquette started spoiling for a fight on Christmas Eve, Papa. Today he went down to Alex's office and deliberately picked a fight with him. Now Alex thinks I've gossiped about him to my family."

The front door swung open. Brother and sister stared silently at one another. Rosa scurried Laura and A.J. out of the room, and Tara hid behind a corner in the kitchen.

Marquette took a deep breath. "I have done something so wrong today. I must ask you for forgiveness."

Guiseppi smiled and attempted to defuse whatever argument Angel may have had in her. "There, see, he is so sorry. Let us forget this dreadful offense."

Tillie was amused by her father's desperate antics, but she hid her mirth behind a frown. "It's okay, Marquette. Alex is going to Pierre this afternoon, so you might as well stay another day or two."

"Well," Guiseppi sighed with relief, "all is well again."

Tillie's hard expression softened as she looked at her father. "Come on, Tara has some *great* turkey noodle soup in the kitchen, and I'm starved."

"Yes, me too!" Guiseppi exclaimed as he took her by the hand. "Now come along! We must enjoy the turkey until the end!"

*****

"What happened this morning?" Tara asked her husband as he crawled into bed with her that night.

He propped himself up on his elbow. "What did Alex say?"

"I do not know, but it was assumed the two of you quarreled. Angel hung up on him."

"She did?" Marquette tittered. "She is certainly getting spunky in her old age." He whispered, "I had quite a visit with Noah this morning."

"You did?" Tara's heart beat like a drum in her ears.

"Wow," Marquette whispered as he lay back on his pillow and looked up at the ceiling. "He gave me permission to tell *only* you, and I do not even know where to begin."

Tara gulped so loudly that Marquette looked at her with surprise. "My Tara, do you know of this secret between Noah and our Angel?"

150

Tara slowly nodded. "Since the babies were born." Sudden tears rolled from her eyes. "I am so sorry, Marquette. Please forgive me. I promised your parents —"

"My parents know of this?"

"They were afraid to tell you. Angel made them promise not to tell her brothers when she returned from Rapid City. She has always been so embarrassed by her sin."

Marquette frowned. "They knew about Noah before they gave her into this insidious marriage?"

Tara nodded, and more tears fell. She was so relieved to finally be able to share the secret with her husband; but there was *more*, and it began to tumble from her trembling lips. "Rosa began praying for a little boy in 1960. He was the young brother of a minister and Rosa heard about him through Frances Martin's brother. Remember Uncle Mac?" She paused and Marquette nodded, so she continued, "The little boy's name was Noah —"

"So it was no *accident* that they met."

"No, and your father has condemned his decision to give her to Alex for years, but he did not realize what a wonderful man Noah was until *after* Alex and Angel were married. Angel came home with blackguardly stories of a drunk who she never wanted to see again. Papa chose to protect her and never told her of their prayers for Noah. You cannot imagine what he has gone through over the years, watching Alex and Noah become friends and having to hold his breath every time you and Vincenzo talk about the girl who broke Noah's heart."

"And you kept this from *me?*"

"I did not know what else to do. Please forgive me, Marquette, but I am afraid of what you will do with the information now that Noah has given it to you."

Marquette took her in his arms with a heavy sigh. "Oh, my Tara, I forgive you. You did what you felt was best at the time; and knowing what a fool I can be when it comes to Angel, I do not blame you. And as far as doing anything with the information, well, that is out of my hands as well. There are vows and children to remember, and Angel will *never* divorce, nor would she ever remarry should Alex divorce her, so it is unlikely she and Noah can ever be together."

"I am so sad for them," Tara cried.

Marquette sighed with regret and held his crying wife, sorry that it had been his treacherous passions that had forced her to carry such a heavy burden for so long. "I love you, my Tara," he whispered as he kissed the top of her head tenderly. "Do not feel one drop of guilt for this secret, for the responsibility of that rests completely upon my own shoulders."

PART II

REDEMPTION

Chapter 16
March, 1987

Alex poured his whole life into his position, and everyone in the church noticed his absence. But while many of the parishioners gossiped about the situation, Mrs. Romanov found a Christian reference book entitled *How to Fix Your Marriage*, and she brought it to Tillie one afternoon. Mrs. Romanov's English still wasn't very good, but she understood the words "fix" and "marriage," and she knew that Tillie's Russian would help her to understand the rest.

Tillie was touched by the sweet gift Mrs. Romanov offered on her front step that day and invited her in for tea. They sat in the kitchen together, going through two pots of tea while Tillie translated in Russian the information in the book. The general idea advised the wife to be faithful and loyal to her husband and be supportive, especially in matters of the husband's livelihood.

"This cannot hurt to try," Mrs. Romanov pointed out, speaking in her first language. That was her favorite part of getting together with Tillie. She never had to worry about having to speak English. "There must be some way to bring him back."

Tillie nodded. "I agree you with you, Mrs. Romanov...but —" Tillie paused and sighed deeply, turning her eyes away.

"Child?" Mrs. Romanov reached for Tillie's chin and coaxed her to turn back. "What is this that I see in your eyes?"

"There are things you don't know, and that I am ashamed to talk about."

Mrs. Romanov raised an eyebrow. "Is it of a sinful nature?"

"It isn't yet."

Mrs. Romanov nodded and exhaled. "Noah Hansen perhaps?"

Tillie's mouth fell open and Mrs. Romanov chuckled.

"How could I not notice. Are you in sin with him?"

Tillie shook her head. "Not yet, and I try not to think about him..." She hesitated as her eyes filled with tears. "Can I tell you something in confidence?"

Mrs. Romanov nodded, and Tillie's heart gave way. She told everything that had happened between her and Noah in 1975. She told her how surprised she was when they first met at the church and that she'd decided to keep it from Alex until just recently.

"I want to tell Alex, but I don't know how," Tillie cried. "It's gotten so far out of control that I don't know what to do."

Mrs. Romanov nodded. "Well, telling Alex at this point cannot hurt anything, but *do not* expect the information to keep him at home. Alex is fighting his own demons right now, and he may not be willing to understand the severity of yours. Your responsibility is to your own sin now, Tillie —"

"What sin?" she interrupted with a confused expression.

"Oh, Tillie," Mrs. Romanov tittered, "you may not have committed adultery with Noah, but you *covet* him nonetheless."

Tillie swallowed hard and nodded her head.

"Thou shalt not covet — our tenth commandment. As a woman, I *do* understand," Mrs. Romanov went on. "I believe we were created specifically for the marriage relationship. Remember, God gave Eve to Adam so he would not be alone — our Lord said that it was not good for a man to be alone. Then, when the marriage relationship *becomes* lonely, it is very difficult for a woman. When we are not allowed to fulfill that marriage relationship — and Alex is not allowing you fulfillment — I think we look for another way to satisfy our created purpose. But Tillie, you must resist Satan's temptation to be unfaithful...whether or not you commit the act of adultery, you could still become unfaithful in your heart. Do not have lustful thoughts, and do not wish that Noah belonged to you. Serve to God what is Alex's share while Alex is away, and I believe you will be rewarded for your obedience." She smiled into Tillie's eyes and reached across the table to take both of her hands into her own. "Will you pray with me?"

Tillie bowed her head and began to cry. "Father, forgive me."

*****

Out of the blue Alex called and announced that he'd be home for his birthday, and Tillie thanked God for the opportunity. She prepared Alex's favorite meal, and A.J. and Laura stayed with the Romanovs for the evening. She set the table with her wedding china and crystal and was wearing Alex's favorite pink dress. She hadn't seen her husband in three weeks and had talked with him over the telephone only twice in that time. Intimacy hadn't existed between them since before Thanksgiving. But Mrs. Romanov convinced Tillie that all they needed was some time together to talk about things, including Noah, and that all would be right once again.

Tillie looked at herself in front of the full length mirror in their bedroom.

"Not bad for someone who's darn near thirty," she complimented herself, and the telephone rang. She reached for the phone beside their bed.

"Hello."

"Hey, Tillie, it's me," Alex said.

"Hi."

"Hey, I thought I'd better let you know that I won't be making it back to Rapid today."

Tillie swallowed away her tears of disappointment...*be supportive*, she reminded herself. "Why not?"

"We've had something come up and I'll need to spend the rest of the week in Pierre."

Her heart dropped into her stomach. "But you promised A.J. you'd be here by Friday for his Little League sign-up."

She heard him sigh into the phone. "I don't know why you keep doing this to me, Tillie."

"Doing what?"

"This constant guilt trip. I can't take it anymore."

"What guilt trip?"

"Listen, Tillie," he retorted, "you've gotten everything you've ever wanted, and now it's my turn. I want to explore my possibilities in politics."

"So what are you saying, Alex? You don't want to come home anymore?"

"I think it's okay for me to be away for awhile until I get my career off the ground. I stayed at home for more than five years with you and the kids, and now I'm behind the competition."

Tillie was stunned. "I don't know what to say," she whispered.

"Well, for starters, you could say, 'Way to go, Alex,' or congratulate me every now and then instead of setting up the kids to send me your guilt cards."

That one hurt. Poor little Laura had fretted around with her homemade pictures and cards, asking about when her Daddy would be back, and finally insisted that Tillie put them in the mail to his office in Pierre.

"I didn't set her up, Alex," Tillie said as the tears began to burn. "The kids really miss you a lot —"

"Oh, whatever, Tillie," Alex barked. "They don't even notice that I'm gone. They're just little kids." He took a deep breath and continued, "Listen, I've gotten myself an apartment in Pierre —"

"You what?"

"You heard me. It's too hard to drive back and forth all of the time and I can't stand the motels. And I *need* to be here."

"Alex, I don't like that idea. I don't think it's good for a husband and wife to live apart like this."

He sighed disgustedly. "I knew you probably wouldn't like it, but that's the way it's going to be. It's only temporary. I'll probably move back to Rapid before summer."

Tillie shook her head and, without even saying good-bye, hung up the phone. She looked at herself in the mirror and wondered what had happened between the two of them. Alex didn't even sound like himself.

*****

Robert Taylor was Alex's deputy attorney general. He loved the solitaire game on his secretary's computer, and whenever she went to lunch, that's where Robert could be found.

"Have you beaten it yet?" Shondra asked with a sly smile.

"Several times," he answered, concentrating on the screen.

Shondra pulled a chair from another empty cubicle in beside Robert and sat down. Just about everyone in the office was at lunch, and now was a good time to talk.

Robert looked surprised. "What?"

"Turn that thing off," she whispered.

Robert shrugged and switched off the program. "What's going on?"

"I heard you're resigning."

Robert slowly nodded. "Well, I *was* going to resign, but after talking to Alex this morning, I think I'll stay on just a couple more months."

Shondra nodded. Alex had announced that he would be throwing his hat into the ring for the United States Senate seat available that fall, and he'd assured a very excited Conservative Party forum that he would easily beat the Liberal nominee. Of course, once Alex became the senator — and everyone, including the Liberal nominee, knew that he would — Robert could then take over his position as attorney general.

"Well, if he doesn't straighten out this mess he's got going with his wife, I'm quitting my job," Shondra snapped.

Robert's eyes were wide with surprise. "He told me she doesn't mind his being away at all."

Shondra rolled her eyes. "He's a liar. Tillie and the kids are really missing him right now. Marquette was up here last week looking for him, *again* —"

"Thank goodness they didn't connect."

Shondra leaned closer to Robert and whispered, "And now he's gotten an apartment in Pierre." She shook her head and snorted, "Seriously, Robert, I think I'm going to quit my job."

"But you've been with the Martins for twenty years."

"I don't care. I can't work for someone like that."

Robert thoughtfully frowned and rubbed his chin. "Well, if you're quitting your job, maybe you'd consider being my deputy?"

Shondra forced a tense smile. "Thought you'd never ask."

*****

Marquette and Tara had stopped over in Rapid City for a short visit to check on Tillie and her children, and they were startled at the change in Angel's appearance. Where there had always been a sparkle in her pretty black eyes, there was now only grief and sorrow. She was no longer planning special projects and making her house just so. But what alarmed them the most was the fact that the door to her studio was closed.

"Could we not have just a peek at any new work?" Marquette said with a gentle smile, hoping to draw his sister's interest back to her painting.

Tillie feigned a happy expression. "I've just been too busy to start any projects, Marq."

Marquette didn't have a chance to respond because A.J. and Laura dashed into the room, excited to see their aunt and uncle.

"My teeny little sweetie people!" Marquette exclaimed as he bent over to greet them.

"Hi, you two!" Tara greeted them with kisses. "What have you been up to?"

"Baseball!" A.J. announced, and then his little black brows knit into a frown. "Have you seen Daddy?"

Tillie was embarrassed.

Marquette tried to hide his surprise and answered, "I have not. Why do you ask?"

"He hasn't been home for a long, long time," A.J. spilled, and Tillie held her breath. She had no intention of telling her family that Alex had gotten himself an apartment in Pierre.

"Well he comes to town when he can," she tried to explain with somewhat of a smile. "But he's pretty busy. It will be better by summer."

Tara and Marquette looked at Tillie with sincere pity in their eyes...*poor Angel is only fooling herself.*

*****

Mrs. Nixon watched Noah from her place by the door, as she had for the past several months. She followed his gaze to Tillie Martin, who was with a small group of ladies not far from where he stood. Tillie happened to look up, caught him watching, and smiled politely. Noah blushed and looked the other way. Mrs. Nixon shook her head. Whatever was going on between the two of them was getting worse.

"Did you see that?" Mrs. Warren whispered into her ear.

Mrs. Nixon nodded. Other parishioners had noticed as well, setting off an undercurrent of hot gossip.

Melinda was furious, for she'd seen the whole encounter. Marching across the lobby to Noah's side, she grabbed his hand and began to lead him into the church. *I'm supposed to marry you in less than three months, and you're still a fool for Tillie Martin!*

"Did I tell you that I've finished with the living room?" she said with a smile as they walked into the sanctuary.

"Ah, no," Noah stammered, wondering if she'd seen his little exchange with Tillie.

Melinda pretended another open smile. "Oh, Noah, it's just so beautiful. You're really going to love it."

I'll bet, he thought. The house he was building for Melinda in Quartz Canyon was nearly completed, and Melinda planned to move in at the end of May. She had already filled it with incredible pieces of furniture and art, sparing no expense to turn the house into quite a showplace. Noah was certain it was suitable for photography by *Better Homes & Gardens*. He wondered how his boys would manage in the palace she'd designed for herself, as they were accustomed to simple split-foyer living. Their greatest efforts consisted of taking their shoes off at the door and making sure the dirty underwear found its way downstairs. Vera told Noah that she would not be able to keep the *monstrosity* clean and that her duties would have to focus on simply caring for his boys while he was away. Melinda replied with, "Well, that's fine…we should probably find someone younger anyway." Of course, that remark hadn't set well with Vera, and she complained to Noah that she wouldn't be able to get along with Melinda once they were married. Her employ would end at that time.

"I thought maybe we should have an open house once it's finished," Melinda went on. "I've already talked to Copper Creek to cater."

Noah nodded as he paused by the pew and waited for Melinda to slide in ahead of him. He sat down next to her just as Tillie walked by. His eyes followed her all the way to her seat, and Melinda couldn't help but notice the soft smile on his lips.

I have got to get that woman out of this church! If Alex was aware of Noah and Tillie's past, he would definitely put an end to this.

*****

A.J.'s fear of his father not being able to join them for his much-anticipated baseball season became reality.

"I just don't wanna play without Daddy there," A.J. whined from the backseat as Tillie drove him over to the first practice at the Timberline Little League Complex.

"But Nonna and Grandpa will be coming, and so will your uncles," Tillie encouraged. "Besides, Daddy will be home by summer, and he'll be around to watch your games."

A.J. was hopeful, but he'd been made promises before.

It was mid-April and unusually warm in the Black Hills, bringing back the most wonderful memories for Tillie. The heat of the day had drawn the smell of pine out of the trees…*What I wouldn't give to see Noah pull into the parking lot on his Harley-Davidson and ask if I wanted a ride…and I'd go…*.

Laura stayed with Heidi Romanov that afternoon, so Tillie was at the practice alone with A.J. She found a seat on the bleachers, while A.J. joined the crowd of children and a few men by the dugout. There was a familiar man with a clipboard, checking in the little ball players, and Tillie smiled. Noah. He wore a blue baseball cap that read "COACH" just above the bill. When he checked in A.J., he looked up, found Tillie, and waved. She smiled and waved in return. Noah handed his clipboard to the man next to him, said a few words, and trotted in Tillie's direction. She held her breath…*Noah, I'm more sorry than you can ever know…*.

"Hey, Tillie." He sat down next to her on the bleachers, looking into her eyes.

"Hi, Noah." He openly adored her, and it was the most reassuring feeling in the world. She remembered when Alex used to look at her that way. *Please help me, Lord Jesus.*

"I would have called, and I hope this doesn't make you uncomfortable, but I just got the roster this afternoon. I didn't know A.J. and Jake were gonna be on the same team, and that's the truth."

"It's okay. Don't worry about it."

156

"It's really good to see you here," Noah blurted out.

Tillie only smiled, and he lost himself in her sparkling expression. They were so close at this point that he was tempted to kiss her. Just once. *Would anybody notice?* His heart pounded in his ears, and he felt his face flush.

"I better get back," he finally said with a smile. "Will I see you later?"

Tillie only smiled and nodded, and Noah left his place beside her to rejoin his team.

As she watched him walk away, she began to pray, *Father forgive me — I want him so bad....*

*****

Harv saw Melinda preparing copies of a lengthy document in the conference room. She'd laid out many stacks and was being meticulous about their collation. He stepped into the conference room, closing the door behind him.

"Hi, Miss Melinda."

She had been so intent on her project she startled at his voice and jumped, dropping a small stack of papers to the floor. She frowned when she saw it was Harv.

"Look what you've done!" she scolded as she stooped to pick up her papers.

Harv stooped to help, but she slapped his hands away. "Don't touch anything!"

Harv jumped to his feet and took a step back.

"What do you want?" she ranted.

Harv swallowed. "I just saw that you were working really hard today, and I thought maybe I could buy you some lunch."

Melinda looked at him with an incredulous expression. *You must be mentally challenged.* "Why on earth would I want to go to lunch with you?"

"Listen, Miss Melinda, you might as well give me a try. Noah's sorta hung up on Mrs. Martin —"

"What are you talking about?"

Harv rolled his eyes. "Come on, you know I understand you and your ambitions. We could have a real good life together."

Melinda's frown deepened. "Get out of here, Harv, and if you ask me out again, I'm going to sue you for harassment."

Harv sighed and nodded his head, and with that he left her alone.

Unbeknownst to Noah and Alex, the Joker had drafted and signed a proposal of astronomical proportions. Melinda had intercepted the proposal and held it for a few days until she'd finally concocted a most complicated plan to finally expose the torrid affair in the church. She'd finally found a way to rid herself of Tillie Martin, once and for all.

Melinda frantically dialed the number she'd fooled a young intern into giving her. *That stupid Alex Martin is so hard to get a hold of these days.* She'd taken great pains in researching his schedule for the next few days; and, while even his own wife was not aware of where he would be, Melinda had all the information she needed. If this didn't work, she'd move on to Plan B, and that was to quit her job and sue Noah for everything she could get.

"Office of the attorney general."

"Alex Martin, please," Melinda requested.

"Who's calling?"

"Hansen Development in Rapid City, South Dakota. And we have an emergency." Alex wouldn't *dare* refuse a call from his biggest client, especially for an emergency. Even more than the prestige, Melinda suspected his drive was attached to money as well.

"One moment, please."

Melinda waited only seconds before Alex came on the line.

"Noah?" he asked.

"It's Melinda," she said with a cat-like smile.

"What's up, Melinda?" he asked in a friendly tone, which was unusual for Alex these days. Every lawyer in South Dakota was avoiding him, or so the papers had said. Nobody wanted to go up against the murderous attorney general.

"I've got a signed proposal from the Joker," Melinda began. "It's *big*, Alex. Even bigger than what you guys wanted in the first place. Are you interested?"

"You know I am. Everyone wants a deal with Scott McDarren."

"Well," Melinda began, taking a breath and glancing at the notes in front of her. Her words had to be perfect. "When are you going to be around?" She knew *exactly* where Alex would be. He was scheduled to try a case in Belle Fourche, which was just fifty-five minutes north of Rapid City. He'd be less than an hour's drive away.

"I'll be in Belle until Wednesday afternoon," Alex answered. "I guess I could drive down to Rapid and take a look at it. I should probably check in with Tillie and the kids anyway."

"Hey, I've got an idea." Melinda started shaking and broke into a sweat. "Why don't you just pop into the church when you're done at Belle? We're having a potluck at church on Wednesday night, and I can have the proposal with me. It would save you having to go to the office, and you could have some time with your family."

"Great. I'll see you on Wednesday."

Melinda nodded and hung up the phone. She swallowed hard and tried to stop shaking. *Unless you're a blind idiot, my problems will be over by Wednesday.*

She told no one that she'd received the signed proposal from the Joker, though she was sure to leave a copy on Noah's desk for his review. She had quite a hearty laugh about it, too, because Noah's desk was a mess. He'd never see it before Wednesday.

*****

Melinda saw Alex come into the fellowship hall in the church basement, and she ducked out of sight. She hurried to Noah with the proposal and pulled him aside.

"Hey," she said sweetly, "I promised I'd give this to Tillie, but I've gotta run. Can you do it for me?"

"Sure." Noah smiled as he took the proposal out of her hands. *What a stroke of luck!* He was so grateful for the opportunity to talk to Tillie that he missed the change in Melinda's behavior.

"Thanks." Melinda smiled sweetly and pointed to where Tillie visited with another lady. "She's right over there. I'll see ya later." With that, Melinda rushed off, and Noah sighed with relief.

"Well, if this isn't the most convenient thing," he said to himself as he walked over to Tillie, unaware of the trap Melinda had set.

By the time he reached Tillie, the lady she'd been visiting with had moved on, and Tillie was by herself. Their eyes met, and they smiled at one another. Noah handed Tillie the proposal.

"Hi. Melinda said I was supposed to give this to you."

Tillie glanced at the papers with a confused smile. "Thanks. What is it?"

Noah shrugged, "Don't know. What's it say?" He took a few steps closer, standing beside her, almost touching. He was tempted to put his hand on her waist, but something told him not to. He looked over the papers in her pretty hands and enjoyed her familiar fragrance.

"It's from somebody named McDarren...don't you guys call him the Joker or something?" She smiled into Noah's eyes. "Why would Melinda give me this?"

From across the basement, Alex watched the entire scene between Tillie and Noah. He noticed how close they stood and how adoringly Noah looked into her eyes. He felt sick as he watched the two of them together. It was all he could do to make his long legs carry himself to where they were.

Alex stood before them for a few seconds, close enough to hear them talking, and they hadn't been able to turn their eyes away from one another long enough to notice he was there.

"Hi," he interrupted, and they both jumped apart with guilty expressions.

"Hi, Alex." Tillie smiled at her husband. "What are you doing here?"

"Hi, Alex," Noah said. "I didn't know you were in town."

Obviously. Alex frowned at his wife and glared at Noah. "I was up in Belle and drove down to get a proposal from Melinda." *She wouldn't dare, especially not with a loser like you.*

Noah's heart almost stopped as he figured out what Melinda had done. No wonder she'd given him something to give Tillie. *It had all been a big setup*, and now they were into it up to their ears.

Tillie was graceful at that point, and she looked down at the proposal as she handed it to Alex. "I was wondering what this was. Melinda told Noah to give it to me, but he's never seen it before."

Alex looked confused as he took the proposal from Tillie and gave it a quick glance. He looked at Noah and asked, "You didn't know about this?"

Noah shook his head. "That's the first I've seen of it. I would have called you if I'd known we had gotten something like that from the Joker."

Alex looked back at the proposal. "Melinda called me a couple of days ago and told me to meet her here so I could pick it up."

Tillie frowned and snapped, "So, you'd drive all the way to Rapid City to pick up some proposal but not to see your wife and kids?" She stomped her foot and marched away.

Noah thought, *Thanks, Alex...everything was going along really great until you showed up.*

Alex sighed, shook his head, and looked at Noah. "She's always mad at me anymore. I don't know what to do."

"Why don't you try spending some time with her," Noah blurted out.

Alex frowned. *I suppose you think you could make her happy.*

Noah shook his head and said, "Man, Alex, you're outa control. *I* don't even see you anymore —"

"You didn't even know that we had received this proposal." *And I don't have the time for whatever garbage is going on between the two of you.*

Noah raised one eyebrow. "I don't know how that proposal got in without me knowing about it. I'm there *every day*."

"Well maybe you should worry about checking in with your fiancée, before you get too worried about my wife," Alex snapped.

Noah swallowed and sighed. "I'd better go. Call me when you got time, and I'll see if I can track down a copy of that thing." Noah abruptly turned from Alex and went to find his children.

Alex stood alone for a few moments and pretended to read the proposal. *That was the strangest thing. Neither one of them knew what it was that Melinda had given to Noah...to give to Tillie.* That sick feeling in his stomach returned, and he headed for the door. Something didn't feel right.

Noah asked Mona and Joshua to watch the boys for just a few minutes while he went to talk to Melinda. He told them it was important business but that he'd be back before it was time to put them to bed.

By the time Noah reached Melinda's house in Robbinsdale, his temper had sufficiently stewed out of control. *Why did she pull this stunt? I take her out constantly, buy her stuff for that stupid house, and I've already paid for the honeymoon trip to Hawaii. That woman gets everything she wants! Then she turns around and pulls a horrible trick like this. I have half a mind to call off the wedding.*

Melinda's kitchen light was on, so Noah knew she was home when he pulled into the driveway. He marched loudly up the back steps, banged on the door, and heard Merry begin to bark from inside. It took too long for Melinda to get to the door, so Noah tried the knob. It was open, and he stormed inside. Merry stopped barking the instant she saw him and wagged her tail. He bent over and gave the dog a pat, and that's when Melinda appeared.

"Well, well," Noah snarled as he stood up. He shook his head and narrowed his eyes. "Why on earth did you do something like *that*?"

"What are you talking about?"

"Slipping that proposal to me to give to Tillie," Noah retorted. "And you know good and well what I'm talking about. Now why did you do that?"

Melinda took a breath and frowned. "Because I wanted Alex to know what a little *tramp* he's married to."

If Melinda had been a man, Noah would have beaten her to a pulp. "I can't believe you said that."

"I can't believe you can't let it die! Don't you think it's time the two of you grew up and got over it?!!"

"All right, who told *you*?"

"Nobody told me. I found that stupid photograph in your desk."

Noah swallowed as hard as he could in an effort to keep his temper under control. "Listen, Melinda, the engagement, the wedding, this whole nightmare with you is *over!* You can have that ugly ring and the house, and even the trip to Hawaii, but I *refuse* to marry you."

"Oh, come on, Noah," Melinda pleaded, shaken by his threat to end it. She never dreamed he would get so upset with her about the whole thing. "You really don't mean that."

"Yes, I do. You're not a very nice person, and I don't want to ruin what I have left of the rest of my life."

Melinda glared at Noah and put her hands on her hips. "I hope you don't think you're ever going to be with Angel —"

"No!" Noah shouted. "I don't think that! I know I don't have a *chance* to be with her! There! Does that make you happy?! I tried to forget about her with you! Do you think that makes me feel very good about myself?!"

Melinda stood very still and said nothing. "Noah," she finally said with quiet sweetness, "maybe we can start over now. We've got a better chance now that she won't be coming around so much —"

"What? Why *won't* she be coming around?"

"Alex certainly won't allow it, not after what he saw tonight."

Noah rolled his eyes and shook his head. "Melinda, Alex doesn't care about stuff like *that*. He couldn't give a *rip* about what happens to his family." He glared hatefully at her. "Guess what, it didn't work."

Melinda took several quick breaths and flew into a rage. She picked up a nearby vase of flowers and hurled it through the air at Noah. He dodged it in time, and the vase smashed against the wall behind him. Melinda screamed in frustration, pulled a framed photo from the wall, and threw it as hard as she could. Noah wasn't quick enough to dodge that one, and the corner of it caught him on the eyebrow as he attempted to lunge for the door. He had just managed to get out through the back door when he heard something else shatter against the other side. Wow. He had *never* made a woman that mad before, not even in his drinking days.

Blood had gushed down his face, into his eye, and all over his shirt by the time he made it to his pickup. He prayed she didn't try to shoot him from the window. He started the truck and peeled out of the driveway. He turned on his dome light and leaned over for a look in the rearview mirror. He cringed when he saw the exposed bone beneath his brow and grumbled, "Boy, she's really mean." He turned off the light and headed for the emergency room.

When Alex arrived at his home in Carriage Hills, all of the lights were off, except for the one in his bedroom. The kids were probably in bed, and this would be a good time to talk to Tillie. Hopefully she wouldn't nag him about being away so much and they could have a decent time together for once. He let himself in through the garage and made his way to their upstairs suite. He opened the door and found her sitting up in bed, reading a book. He closed the door and gave her a faint smile.

"So, you decided to stay here tonight," she said.

She's already mad. He took off his suit jacket and loosened his tie as he took a seat on the edge of the bed next to her.

"Why do you even come here?" she asked.

Alex looked at his pretty wife and saw the horrible sadness pulling on her face. She had dark circles under her eyes, and her mouth was turned down instead of the perpetual smile he'd gotten used to over the years. She looked older somehow.

"Tillie, are you feeling all right?"

"I'm feeling fine, Alex. Why?"

Alex reached for one of her hands, "You don't look so good."

The sincerity in his voice and the warmth of his hand set off a river of tears she couldn't stop. Alex was surprised at her intense sadness, and he impulsively gathered her into his arms, held her close, and listened to her sob against him. "What's the matter, Honey?" he whispered.

"I miss you," she whispered. "I miss the life we used to have, and there are so many things that I need to talk to you about." She wanted to tell him about Noah, but something stopped her.

Alex sat very still as he held his crying wife. He missed *some* of the life they used to have, but it was only temporarily on hold. *Very soon now I'll have everything in order, and we'll have plenty of time together. Why can't she just let me do this? Doesn't she realize that this is what I've worked so hard for? All those years at Harvard, working my butt off, and out-graduating even my own father, are finally paying off. I'm the best attorney general South Dakota has ever had, and I'm unbeatable.*

"What do you want from me?" he asked.

"I told you, I want you to come home. I don't want you living in Pierre, away from me. Do you have any idea how hard it is to raise two little kids by yourself?" *Why doesn't he ask me about Noah? Didn't he notice?*

"I'll be home before summer. Robert will be able to take over quite a bit by that time. He's just not quite ready yet."

"Summer is only a few weeks away," Tillie sadly pointed out. "If Robert's not ready by now, he's never going to be."

"He'll be ready."

"Alex, do you even want to be married to me anymore?"

"Tillie!" Alex gasped in a whisper. "Of course I want to be married to you. I love you."

"But you don't want to *be* with me. How can a marriage survive this?"

"It's only temporary," Alex answered. "You're just letting it get to you. Lots of the men who work at the capitol have wives that live in other towns, and they don't seem to mind."

Tillie gave up then, like she had gotten used to doing. The truth was that Alex wouldn't care about the circumstances with Noah. Mrs. Romanov was right. Knowing about Noah wouldn't keep Alex at home, and it was no use to argue with him. He was going to do this for himself, no matter the cost.

*****

Alex called Noah at his house early the next morning and asked him if they could meet about the McDarren proposal. Noah agreed and went to Alex's office for the meeting, thankful not to have to face Melinda in case she showed up for work.

Shondra's eyes opened wide with surprise when she saw Noah's swollen and bruised forehead and several stitches in his brow.

"What happened to you?" she asked.

"Oh, me and Melinda broke up last night," Noah answered with a simple expression.

Shondra almost laughed. "Are you joking with me, Noah?"

"Does it *look* like I'm joking?"

Shondra swallowed another laugh. "Well, I'm really sorry about that. The break-up I mean," she lied. Inside, she was ecstatic that Noah had finally gotten rid of the woman.

"Well, I'm not," Noah confessed. "She was driving me crazy."

Shondra giggled as she let him into Alex's office, where Alex stood with surprise behind his desk. Shondra giggled again and left the two of them alone.

"What happened to you?" Alex asked.

"Me and Melinda broke up last night," Noah said, and as he smiled he winced. It really hurt when he smiled.

"Did she hit you?"

"Sort of," Noah answered. "She threw a picture frame at me, and I didn't get out of the way in time."

Alex pressed his lips together as tightly as he could so that he wouldn't smile. *It's not a funny situation, but that's what you get for leering at someone else's wife.* "Well, I'm sorry to hear about it." He reached for the McDarren proposal. "But this is gonna make you feel a whole lot better."

A very flashy Marquette Caselli strolled into the downtown office of Hansen Development, LLC. He'd dropped Tara off with Angel so they could spend some time together and then found his way over to Noah's office for a surprise visit. Noah's ruthless ex-fiancée was at her desk with a giant box, putting everything into it that wasn't nailed down. The rest of Noah's staff watched from their desks, occasionally glancing her way but pretending not to.

Marquette approached her with a charming smile, removed his hat, and greeted, "Good morning, Miss Melinda, how are you this day?"

Melinda glared at him and growled, "You know, I really *hate* your whole entire family."

Marquette's eyes opened wide with surprise. "That was uncalled for."

Melinda rolled her eyes and continued her packing. "Listen, I know all about your little sister and Noah and how they can't get over each other, but *she'll be sorry*."

"Can I see Noah?"

"Don't know where he is. Maybe you should try Angel's house. They're probably over there getting it on."

Marquette was astonished at the way the woman spoke. As he replaced his hat and began to back away, he said, "You have a foul mouth, young lady."

Melinda stopped packing and looked at him. "Listen, pal, your sister wrecked my life. If anyone's foul, it's *her*, so why don't you stop yammering at me and go over there and tell those two how pleased you are that they're finally together. You know, I always wondered what a guy like you would want with someone like Noah."

Marquette was without words for the woman. He had just left Angel's house, and Noah was nowhere to be seen. Marquette heard the doors behind him open, and he turned to see a very beat-up-looking Noah stroll into the office.

"Noah!" he quietly exclaimed as he observed his injured forehead.

Noah gave Marquette a small wave and then he looked at Melinda as he began to cross the office. He passed Marquette and stood in front of her desk. "I see you showed up today."

Melinda looked over the damage she'd done the previous night. "I see you didn't just man it together with a staple gun. Went for the professional stitch job. Do I still get the ring and the house?"

"Alex is getting the paperwork ready." Noah looked at the box she was filling. "Are you quitting?"

"Yes, so I'm going to want my last paycheck *immediately*."

Noah was so relieved, but thought it best not to sigh in front of her. Instead, he nodded and lowered his voice, "Listen, Melinda, I'm really sorry about everything. Please forgive me."

Melinda looked into his eyes and saw the sincerity in his apology...*must have found some of that Christian repentance his brother is always peddling.* She'd never loved him, but it still could have worked.

"Whatever, Noah," she muttered. "Just order my check."

Noah nodded, looked at Marquette, and went toward his own office. "Come on, Marq."

Marquette fell in behind Noah, removed his hat once again, and they went into his office. Noah motioned for Marquette to take a seat as he picked up the phone and dialed.

"Yeah, this is Noah. Can you put Harv on?" There was a moment's pause before Noah began again. "Yeah, Harv, it's Noah. Hey, Melinda's gonna quit her job today, so will you get a check up here as soon as possible? Yep, she's still here, but she won't be for much longer...go ahead and give her six months. She's gonna have some huge utility bills this summer. Thanks, Harv." Noah hung up the phone and looked at Marquette.

Marquette frowned curiously. "What happened to you, my friend?"

Noah rolled his eyes and gingerly touched a place close to his injury, "Oh, me and Melinda had a fight last night. I called off the wedding."

Marquette swallowed his laugh. "What did she do to you?"

"She threw a bunch of stuff at me."

Marquette had to swallow again, and he shook his head. "My Tara has never thrown anything at me."

"Well, Tara's a normal person. Anyway, it's finally over. She's gonna keep the house and the ring, and I'm gonna keep my sanity." Noah shook his head. "I'm so disgusted with myself, Marq, I could just scream." He took a deep breath. "Melinda set me up at the church last night, and Alex caught us."

"Oh, my. How did that go?"

"Didn't seem to bother Alex, but Melinda totally flipped out...and I was really cruel to her."

Marquette frowned. "Is that why you asked for forgiveness?"

Noah nodded. "And now she's quitting her job, and we just landed a huge deal with this goof from Texas. I'm gonna have to replace her right away."

"You have a substantial staff," Marquette remarked hopefully. "Cannot anyone else do Melinda's job?"

"My foreman, Ben Simmons, will take over her position. He's been with me for years."

Marquette looked into Noah's anxious expression. "Is there something you need to tell me, Noah?"

Noah swallowed and nodded. "Marquette, I'm in some huge sin, and I don't know how to get out of it."

Marquette gasped softly, "Not with my sister, I hope."

"No. She behaves herself. *It's me*. It's *always been me*. I am coveting her so much, you wouldn't believe it. I want her in my home, with me and the boys. I want her kids, and I want her entire family. I want to come home to *her* after work."

"Do you have lustful thoughts of her?"

Noah shook his head adamantly. "I wouldn't do that to Angel."

"Very well, then," Marquette sighed with relief. "We should deal with your sin this moment, before it goes any farther." He reached across Noah's desk for one of his hands. "Please pray with me, Noah."

Noah bowed his head. "Father, forgive me."

Chapter 17

Tillie sat on her stone patio, enjoying the early June sunshine as she listened to her children play in the creek. The water was still very cold, but they couldn't resist, and even enticed their grandfather into taking off his shoes and socks to wade around with them.

Guiseppi and Rosa had come for Tillie's birthday. Rosa had prepared Tillie's favorite raspberry lemonade, and a capon slowly roasted in the oven. Every now and then the smell of the cooking meat wafted onto the patio.

Tillie closed her eyes and inhaled deeply as she lost herself in memories of her childhood. *Everything was so easy back then.* She took a sip of the lemonade and smiled at her mother. "It's perfect, Ma`ma. Just like you."

"You have always been such a gracious daughter, my Angel," Rosa replied as she took a seat near Tillie.

Tillie sighed as she looked into the distant Hills. "Thirty years old today. Wow. What happened to the year, Ma`ma?" It seemed like only last week Alex had led her romantically down the beach in Clearwater, Florida. Now he was nowhere to be found and hadn't even called to wish her a happy birthday.

Rosa swallowed away her tears of pity. "Please believe me, Angel, you are in our prayers every day, all day long."

"Thanks, Ma`ma." She sighed heavily. "In a couple of weeks, we'll celebrate our tenth wedding anniversary. If I had only known then what I know now."

"But perhaps, without Alex, you would not have had the babies," Rosa offered.

Tillie snorted and rolled her eyes. "*Anyone* could have fathered those babies, Ma`ma."

Rosa was shocked by her daughter's reply. "You mean Noah?"

Tillie sadly nodded and looked into her mother's eyes. "I wish I could go back."

"We are to never look back, only forward. Press on toward your goal, my Angel, and that is heavenward."

"I know, Ma`ma, and I'm sorry. Sometimes it's *really hard.*"

"I know, my dear." She looked curiously at her daughter and asked, "How often do you see Noah?"

"About twice a week and always at church. He's coaching A.J.'s baseball team, but he keeps his distance." Tillie hesitated. "You know, Ma`ma, he's everything a father should be. He'd do *anything* for his kids. I'm sorry for all that I did to him, and I'm sorry that we didn't get the chance to have children...I'm even sorrier about the father I chose for A.J. and Laura." She sighed and shook her head. "Of course, now I'll never have children with anyone ever again."

Rosa shook her head. She didn't understood why God had closed Tillie's womb, but she was certain His reasons were perfect.

"My Angel, are you coveting Noah?"

Tillie sighed and looked away from her mother. "I want him pretty bad, Ma`ma...if that's what you're asking."

*****

A messenger from the local travel agency delivered a large envelope to Shondra and told her it had been ordered by Alex.

"I'll make sure he gets it," she promised.

When the messenger had left the office, Shondra frowned and opened the envelope. *Now* where's he going?" She pulled out two airline tickets, and her frowned deepened. One was for Alex and the other for Tillie, dated for their anniversary, and the destination was Paris...*where they honeymooned.*

Shondra smiled and took a deep breath as she set down the envelope. *Thank you, God, for hearing my prayer and softening his heart.*

When Alex arrived at the office she handed him the tickets. "I'm really pleased that you did this. It's gonna be really good for you guys."

Alex smiled. "I'm glad you approve, and I need to ask you for a favor today."

"Sure."

"Today is Tillie's birthday," Alex said. "And I've got a huge meeting with Noah and McDarren up in Spearfish. Could you bring her up to The Sluice at about six o'clock? We should be done by then, and she and I can have some dinner together. I'll surprise her with the tickets, and then I'll bring her home."

"Sure." Shondra was flabbergasted by his sudden interest in his wife. "But what about the kids?"

"Her parents are there. I'm sure they'll watch them," Alex answered. "Just tell her that we're having dinner for her birthday, but don't tell her about the tickets. I want it to be a surprise."

"You bet," Shondra agreed with a smile.

*****

Noah walked to the bar and took a seat. Maggie was waiting on a customer at the other end, but she finished quickly and came to Noah. She noticed that his injury was healing nicely and that the stitches had been removed. A flat, purple scar above his eyebrow, which would probably fade with time, was all that remained.

"You're looking good today," she greeted in her gruff way. "Have you heard from the little battle-ax?"

Noah laughed. "No, and I don't plan to. I signed the house over to her, and she's as happy as a lark. Besides, I heard she might be having a fling with Scott McDarren. One of the secretaries at my office said she saw them having dinner together at The Pirate's Table."

"No foolin'?"

"And I've got a huge meeting with him and Alex up in Spearfish in a couple of hours, so I'll try and get some information out of him."

"I saw the write-up in the paper about McDarren's new project. Wow, that's gonna be something else."

"It's my biggest one yet," Noah said proudly. "Super-deluxe hotel, with two restaurants and a shopping mall, all rolled into one. I'll be really busy for quite a while."

"And how are things with Angel?"

"Same as ever," Noah sighed.

"Is her husband ever home? Because I see him in the paper *constantly*, and he's *always* in a different town."

"I don't think he's ever home, and I don't know why I was ever even friends with the man. I can't *believe* how he treats his wife. Doesn't he know how lucky he is to have someone like her? If she was mine, Maggie, things would be a whole lot different."

Maggie nodded. *Too bad Noah doesn't believe in divorce.*

*****

Tillie was shocked when Shondra showed up and announced that she was taking her to meet with her husband for dinner. She considered flat out refusing the invitation, but then thought perhaps Alex *might* be starting to come around. Maybe this initiative was his way of breaking the ice.

I don't want to go to The Sluice, she thought as she changed into Alex's favorite pink dress...*Noah took me there.* She sighed with regret. *What I wouldn't give to go back...*she pulled her curly hair into an elegant French twist. *Why am I even bothering with this sham? Alex probably won't show anyway.* She put on her heart-shaped diamond pendant, the matching earrings, and the diamond bracelet. She touched the backs of her ears with Chanel No. 5, and looked at herself in her bedroom mirror. *Dear Jesus, are You providing us with an opportunity to really communicate, or will he let me down again?*

Guiseppi and Rosa prayed as they watched their daughter leave with Alex's assistant.

"He does not deserve her," Guiseppi whispered.

Rosa shook her head. "But perhaps this can create a fresh beginning for them."

*****

The Sluice hadn't changed much since the day she'd been there with Noah twelve years ago. It was still small, dimly lit, and decorated with heavy Western motif. The old wooden tables had been replaced with new wooden tables, and a few booths had been added around the perimeter. Cattle horns and Old West paintings hung here and there, and the old wooden dance floor was still up front. The Cowboy Band readied themselves for a performance, and Tillie smiled. *Wonder if they're the same old guys we listened to.*

"Can I help you?" the hostess asked.

"Yes," Tillie replied. "I was supposed to meet my husband here at six o'clock."

"Did he have a reservation?"

"Martin."

"Follow me."

Tillie followed her to a romantic, but empty, table for two by the dance floor, where a bouquet of white roses waited. Tillie seated herself and looked at the roses. *He remembered. Oh happy day.* She sighed. *Maybe there's a chance we can have a really great time tonight and start putting things back together.*

Alex and Noah were just finishing their meeting with Scott McDarren. They showed him the plans and went over particulars on the building site. McDarren was interested in more than just this one project, and he'd asked Noah and Alex about the area around Deadwood. A late afternoon storm had started moving in, and thunder rumbled in the distance.

"I'd sure like to drive up there and take a look around for a spell," McDarren drawled in his heavy Texan accent. A cigar grossly dangled from the side of his mouth as he chewed the other end. "Do you suppose one of you boys might like to show me the area?"

Noah hid his grimace behind a smile. "I promised my boys I'd take 'em to a movie tonight, but I can bring you up tomorrow."

"I gotta get back to Texas tomorrow," McDarren drawled. He winked at Noah. "I'm a takin' your Miss Melinda to see my ranch."

Noah faked a smile.

Alex frowned. "Just a minute, I gotta talk to Mr. Hansen for a second." He waved Noah aside and spoke low enough so McDarren couldn't hear. "Listen, I'm supposed to meet Tillie at The Sluice for her birthday."

"It's her birthday today?"

"Yeah," Alex continued as he drew the envelope from his inside breast pocket, "and she's probably already there. I had Shondra bring her up so I wouldn't have to drive all the way back to Rapid. Could you just pick her up on your way back to Rapid? Give her this envelope and tell her I'll be home in a couple of hours."

Noah stared at Alex in disbelief. *He's actually going to blow off his wife's birthday to drive McDarren around Deadwood?*

"I don't think that's such a good idea," Noah replied, shaking his head. "It's her birthday and she never gets to see you."

"She'll be fine when she sees what's in the envelope." Alex gave Noah a pat on the shoulder. "Thanks, Noah." With that, he turned toward McDarren and said, "I'm gonna take you up to Deadwood."

Noah watched the two of them start for Alex's black Mercedes and he shook his head. *What a genuine loser.*

By the time Noah reached The Sluice, the storm was above him. It painfully reminded him of the last time he'd been here with Tillie. They'd barely had time to park his bike before the storm hit. He sighed and hurried from his truck. *I wish I didn't have to do this here.*

"Can I help you, sir?" the hostess asked.

"I'm looking for someone. A dark-haired lady. Sitting by herself."

"The Martin reservation?"

"Yes."

"Follow me."

The hostess led Noah to where Tillie waited by herself, dressed in his favorite color, quietly drumming her pretty fingers on the table to the beat of the soft cowboy music. Her curly hair was up, showing off the delicate shape of her jaw line and neck. *Wow, he actually chose that stinking, wrinkled-up, old Texan over this?*

He took a seat beside her, and she looked at him with astonishment.

"Noah, what are you doing here?" Her focus narrowed, and she looked at the purple mark on his brow. "What happened to your eyebrow?"

"Oh, me and Melinda broke up, and she kicked my butt a little," Noah joked with a smile, and Tillie laughed. Then her eyes got big and round again, as if she might panic.

"Noah, you have to go! Alex is going to be here in a few seconds."

Noah looked into her eyes, unable to come up with the words he knew would disappoint her. His not saying anything told her all she needed to know.

She sighed with disgust. "He's not coming, is he?"

"He got tied up," Noah tried to excuse in a gentle tone. "He said to give you this," and Noah handed her the envelope.

Tillie opened the envelope and pulled out the two airline tickets. "Hmmm. They're for Paris on our anniversary."

168

"Didn't you guys go to Paris on your honeymoon?"

Tillie looked at him with surprise, put the tickets back into their envelope, and set it down on the table. "You knew about that?"

"Of course I knew. I used to be Alex's best friend. I probably knew everything about you, except who you really were."

"Really."

Noah reached for her hand, and to his surprise, she didn't try to get away. He felt the warmth and softness inside of his palm, and he smiled into her eyes. "I know *everything* about you. I know that you love white roses and brand new puppies. Your favorite story is *The Sound of Music*, and you get up before the sun. You make the best ravioli on the planet, and your brothers adore you. You wear Chanel No. 5..." Noah deeply inhaled, "and it still smells *great* on you. And sometimes when I look at you, it's like yesterday all over again — I *wish* it was yesterday and we could have another chance."

Tillie looked back into his sincere blue eyes, feeling the gentleness of his calloused hand over hers, wanting to live in this moment forever.

Noah saw the sadness in her expression. Her black eyes rarely sparkled anymore, except when she would allow him a small smile, and it made his heart ache for her. Noah would have never allowed the light to go out in her eyes.

The thunder was suddenly loud above them, and Tillie jumped with surprise, clutched his hand, and then laughed at herself.

"It's getting ready to storm," he said. "We should probably be getting you home anyway, because I could do something *really stupid* at any moment now."

Tillie hesitantly released her hands from Noah's and rose from her chair.

Noah got to his feet as well but put his hand on her shoulder and smiled into her eyes. "Wait a second. Would you dance with me? Just once, you know, just for your birthday?" Tillie nodded, and Noah smiled again. "Okay, wait right here. I'm gonna see if they know your favorite song...'cause I know *that* too."

He went over to the trio, spoke for a few moments, got nods all around, and hurried back to offer her his hand.

In a matter of seconds, the mandolin played the first notes of Tillie's beloved *Annie Laurie*.

"Oh," she breathed as tears filled her eyes. "You remembered."

"The last song we danced to." He smiled as he waited for her to take his hand.

She thought for a moment and then placed her hand into his. They went to the dance floor, and she nestled into his arms.

He drew her hand to the side of his face, and she felt the scruffy stubble of his whiskers on her skin. "You still have the prettiest hands I've ever seen," he whispered as he held her as close as he dared.

"You said that before," Tillie whispered, and as she took a breath she smelled the wonderful fragrance of *Old Spice* and dust. A few tears rolled onto her cheeks, but she smiled into Noah's eyes and continued to follow his steps.

"Don't cry," he whispered as he dried the tears with one of his rough thumbs. "It's all gonna be okay. I just know it will." Noah took a deep breath and hoped his emotions didn't allow his temptations to run away with him. "I'll tell you one thing, if there was no Alex, I'd have you married to me so fast, you'd wonder what happened."

"Really? You'd still marry me after what I did?"

"You were just a kid," he lovingly excused. "And I pushed you too fast too soon. Please don't blame yourself for what happened. We should have taken it slower. And I was older. I should have known better."

"I'm glad you didn't, or we wouldn't have had what we had, and I would have been spending my thirtieth birthday alone."

The music stopped and Noah looked into her eyes. He wanted more than anything to kiss her, but she was still another man's wife, and even *he* couldn't take it that far. He hesitantly released her from his arms. "We gotta get you home. It would look awfully strange if we didn't get you back before Alex got there."

He took her by the hand, led her back to the table, and they collected her envelope and roses. They drove back to Rapid City in complete silence, except for the thunder and rain pounding the top of the pickup.

The storm had cleared by the time they reached her house, and the sun was setting as they pulled into the driveway. Guiseppi was on the front porch, and he frowned curiously at them.

"I'll bet he wonders what's going on," Noah said.

"Don't worry, I'll explain everything." She looked into Noah's eyes, "Thanks for a *great* birthday."

"You're welcome," he said with a smile, and then he noticed Guiseppi had started to walk toward them.

"I gotta go," she said as she quickly opened her door and started to get out. "But I'll see ya around."

"Okay."

Tillie closed the pickup door and met her father in the drive. "Hi, Papa," she said as she heard Noah's pickup pull away.

"Hello, Angel," he said with a frown. "Why were you with Noah?"

"Alex stood me up." She laughed and shook her head. "And he actually sent Noah to get me."

Guiseppi raised one eyebrow as his mouth fell open in surprise, and Tillie laughed again. She reached for her father's chin, gave it a gentle push as she pretended to close his surprised expression, and he smiled at her.

"Well," he took a deep breath, put one arm around Tillie, and began to escort her to the house. "How did everything go?"

"Pretty good." Tillie smiled at her father. "Noah was *never* a blackguard, Papa, and he still isn't."

"I know, my Angel."

*****

Guiseppi paced around the guest room while Rosa watched him from the bed.

"I am completely torn," he said. "I do believe the child is in love with Noah, and furthermore, my Rosa, I am almost pleased for the small delight in her life. Pray that God does not strike me while I sleep tonight."

Rosa was surprised at her husband's honesty.

Guiseppi sighed and sat down on the side of the bed. "I cannot bear up under this, my Rosa, and I do not know how Angel can either. I have regretted my decision to keep them apart for years, and now God makes it plain what His intentions were." He shook his head in disgust. "And then Mr. Wonderful shows up with plane tickets to Paris. What is *that* all about?"

"I suppose he realizes that he must do something. Surely, he must see the changes in his wife."

Guiseppi shrugged. "He actually *sent* Noah to her. Can you believe how they are tested?"

"What I cannot believe is how strong the two of them have been for the last months. Can you imagine their temptation?"

Guiseppi nodded. "But Noah is a knight, my Rosa. If he were any other man, he would have given into his *flesh* by now, and our Angel would have already fallen."

*****

Tillie felt that it was her obligation, as a Christian woman, to do what she could to mend her marriage, and that included going on the anniversary trip to Paris. She'd made vows to God and had no desire to break them. She prayed for help with her feelings about Alex and the things he'd done.

In an effort to rekindle old memories, she took out their wedding photos and different keepsakes from their first trip to Paris. She told the twins all kinds of stories about how surprised their mommy was when Daddy spoke French in front of her for the first time, and how many wonderful places he'd taken her to see while they were in France.

Guiseppi and Rosa prayed as they watched the plans Tillie made — and asked God for a miracle.

*****

It was soon the day before the planned trip. Tillie and Alex had spoken of it, but only in passing, because Alex's schedule was so demanding. He hadn't been in Rapid City at all until that Wednesday, the night before they were to leave.

Before he came home that night, Alex picked up a magnificent diamond anniversary band he'd ordered from O'Berg's. He stopped at Villa Flowers and picked up a dozen long-stemmed pink roses and headed for home. When he came through the back door, Rosa was cooking at the stove.

She smiled at him and his roses. "Well, Alex, how thoughtful."

But Alex had no pleasant expression for Rosa. He frowned and asked, "Where's Tillie?"

Rosa sensed his tense demeanor. She swallowed and hesitantly smiled again. "She is up in your room. I think she is finishing some packing."

"How 'bout the kids?"

"They are in that creek again with their grandfather." Rosa pretended to laugh. "I cannot keep them out of it."

Alex forced a smile as he went up the winding steps. The door to their room was open, and he saw the suitcases spread out on the bed. Tillie looked up and smiled at him. "I'm just about ready. Did you bring your luggage?"

Alex strode toward her with his gift and placed the box into her hand. "Here, Honey. Happy anniversary."

Tillie's heart fluttered as she opened the lid to reveal the incredible diamond band inside — *Diamonds? Oh, no!*

"Oh, dear," she whispered. She stumbled to the edge of the bed to sit down and looked up into his eyes. "We're not going, are we?"

"Honey, I'm really sorry," Alex said as he knelt down in front of her, still holding his pink roses. "I have to go to Pierre tonight, and I won't be done until Friday. I've already switched our tickets."

"Oh, just forget it," Tillie whispered, and the tears covered her face. She shook her head and cried, "Just forget the whole thing. You don't care about me or our marriage or our children. The only thing you care about it is being the most awesome attorney general that you can be."

"Tillie, that's not true," Alex said with a frown.

"Oh, it's true all right," she said disgustedly as she got to her feet. She walked to the other side of the room.

Alex stood and saw an expression in her eyes that had never been there before.

"Listen, Alex," she said as she looked at the diamond band. She frowned and suddenly snapped the lid shut and threw it at him. "Get out of here, and don't expect me and the kids to be here *if* you come back on Friday, because we'll be long gone."

"And exactly where are you going with my children?"

"We're going to Italy for the summer. Marquette told me we could stay all summer, or the rest of our lives if we want."

"My kids are *not* going to spend their summer with that lunatic."

"Like you can stop me."

"Oh, I can stop you from taking my children out of the country," Alex argued.

"Just give it a try," Tillie taunted. "You think you're such hot stuff being a state's attorney general. Well, just wait until you try to take on a United States' Senator. Do you really think you can get away with *that!* I've got a few tricks up my sleeve, too, you know! And I'm sure I can out maneuver *you!*"

"This is nuts. I can't believe you. Why can't you just wait a couple of days. Do you have any idea how *unreasonable* you sound?"

Tillie shook her head in disbelief. "*I'm being unreasonable?* Get out, Alex."

Alex clenched his jaw. "Fine." With that, he stormed out of their room, down the steps, and through the kitchen. He threw his roses into the sink on his way by.

"Alex?" Rosa said as he passed her in the kitchen.

"You shouldn't have spoiled her — now I can't do anything with her!" Alex admonished as he left through the garage door, slamming it loudly behind him.

Rosa turned off the stove and trotted up the steps as quickly as her short legs could carry her. Tillie was talking on the telephone.

"Friday?" Tillie asked, and there was a brief pause. "Of course, I have their passports in order." Another pause, and she looked at her confused mother. "That'll be great. Thanks, Marq. I gotta go. Ma`ma is waiting to talk to me. I love you, too." She hung up the phone and looked at her mother.

"Marquette?" Rosa asked, and Tillie nodded. Rosa took a deep breath. "What happened, my Angel?"

"What do you think, Ma`ma?" Tillie said as she sat down on the bed. "Alex put the trip off until Friday, but you know he'll never go through with it, so me and the kids are going to Italy. And I'm leaving for good. I'll be safe with Marquette and Tara. I can't fight this thing with Noah anymore. I've gotta get outa here."

"Oh, Angel." Rosa took a seat beside her daughter and put a loving arm around her. "I am so sorry."

Tillie rested her head against her mother's shoulder. "Marquette and Tara are finishing their last hearing before the Tower Commission tomorrow, and then they'll fly out of Washington and help me and the kids get to Italy. I'm gonna try to get tickets for a Friday departure. I gotta get outa here before I do something really stupid."

"What if Alex *does* return on Friday?"

"He won't, Ma`ma," Tillie began to cry. "He doesn't even live here anymore. He has his own apartment in Pierre."

Rosa gasped, "Why Angel?"

"He says it's more convenient and that he doesn't like the hotels."

"What can I do for you, Angel?"

Tillie sighed and shook her head. "Nothing. But you and Papa could come to church with me and the kids tonight. I want to see Noah, tell him good-bye and where I'm going. Do you think that would be okay?"

Rosa shrugged. "Let us ask Papa."

Guiseppi's answer was, "A little prayer would do us all some good, and saying good-bye to Noah will not hurt anyone." They got into Tillie's Mercedes and drove over to the church on South Canyon Road. The parking lot was already full, and Tillie had to park along the curb in the street.

A.J. and Laura found their dearest little friends, Jake and Ty Hansen and Heidi Romanov, and went to the children's prayer service together.

Tillie felt terrible when she saw the delighted children together. They'd soon miss an entire summer...*because I can't trust myself.* But she *had* to get away from Noah.

Tillie had made it nearly to the sanctuary when she realized she'd forgotten her Bible in the car. "I'll be right back," she assured her parents. "Go ahead and get seated. This will only take me a few seconds."

Guiseppi and Rosa continued inside, while Tillie hurried across the street and to her car. At about that time, Joshua and Noah stepped outside to visit and strolled into the parking lot. Tillie had retrieved her Bible and was just turning away from her car when she saw Noah. She smiled and waved.

Noah smiled and waved in return as Tillie began to cross the street. She looked only at him and didn't see the oncoming car, but Noah saw it and tried to call out to her.

"Angel! Wait!"

Tillie turned her head just in time to see the car coming right at her. She couldn't get out of the way, and it struck her. The impact sent her body over the hood, and she slammed into a nearby tree. She landed in the grass along the side of the street. Joshua ran into the church to call an ambulance and find her parents.

Noah sprinted to the place where she lay. The driver of the car knelt beside a motionless Tillie. She lay on her back with her eyes closed.

"I'm so sorry," the driver said. "I didn't see her."

"Angel." Noah took one of her hands into his own, afraid to even touch her. He felt her hand close around his, and her eyes opened. Her forehead and the left side of her face were badly scraped, already bruised and starting to swell.

"Noah? Is that you?"

"It's me, Angel."

"Oh, there you are."

Noah could see that it was very hard for her to breathe.

"Just be still," he whispered.

"It hurts...this is bad."

Noah swallowed as he watched blood trickle from her nose. "Just be still. I think you're gonna have to go to the hospital."

"The babies," Tillie whispered as she looked into his eyes, fighting the overwhelming urge to fall asleep. "Take care of my babies, Noah. Alex lives in Pierre now, and he won't want them."

Noah spoke sweetly, "Angel, don't talk like that. You'll take care of your own babies, just like you always do." He saw the blood seeping from behind her head and into the grass, and he started to shake.

Footsteps quickly approached, and he looked up to see that Mona was there, breathing heavily from her run across the parking lot.

"Josh called an ambulance," she breathed. "And he's finding her parents."

"You're gonna be all right," Noah assured with a tender smile as he looked into Tillie's eyes.

Tillie tried to nod, but she couldn't feel anything except for Noah's hand, and she smiled into his eyes. "I'm so sorry I screwed everything up for us —"

"Please, Angel, just be still. You're gonna be okay. Josh has an ambulance coming."

"I'm sorry for my sins," Tillie whispered. "I'm sorry, Jesus... forgive me." She gave him another faint smile and whispered, "Noah, do whatever you can for my babies."

"Angel," Noah whispered as he watched her eyes close. He raised his voice as he said, "Angel?" There was no response from Tillie, and he shouted, "Angel!" Tillie only lay motionless, and the clasp she'd had on his hand loosened.

Noah shook his head and began to cry as he held her hand as tightly as he could. He put the side of his face against hers. "I love you, Angel. I've always loved you, and I'm never gonna stop."

Mona hesitantly reached for the pulse point on Tillie's neck. She swallowed hard and whispered, "Her heart's still beating, Noah."

Noah heard Mona's whisper, but he could only nod as he wept over his beloved Angel.

As if watching someone else's bad dream, Noah was vaguely aware of the commotion taking place around him and Angel. At some point Josh, Guiseppi and Rosa were there because Guiseppi dropped to his knees beside Tillie. He covered her face with kisses and wept, "Angel!" But no response came from Tillie. Noah heard Rosa tell Guiseppi to call their sons and he wondered why.

Sirens were getting louder, and Noah wondered how much time had passed. He looked at Guiseppi and found the old man looking at him. "I'm sorry, Mr. Caselli...please forgive me."

Guiseppi's black eyes overflowed with tears as he put one of his old hands on Noah's face. "Listen to me, Noah Hansen, *you* did nothing wrong. The omission was mine and mine alone —"

Several firefighters were suddenly upon them, equipment in hand.

"We need some room," one of them said as he took a position directly over Tillie, but Noah didn't move. He was aware that EMT's were working around him and that they were having some kind of a discussion, but it was all so foggy—as if the bad dream was getting worse and worse.

"Sir, how old is she?" the EMT asked brusquely.

"Thirty," Noah heard Guiseppi answer

Noah heard the screech of tires on pavement and more men with more equipment surrounded them.

"Give us just a little room, sir," a firefighter said, placing his hand gently on Noah's shoulder as he attempted to coax him away from Tillie.

"I can't," he whispered.

"Please, sir," the firefighter said gently, putting both hands on Noah's shoulders. "We have to take her now...before it gets any worse."

Noah let go of her hand and got to his feet. EMT's put Tillie onto a flat board before they placed her on a gurney and loaded her into the ambulance. Before the last paramedic got into the ambulance he said, "We have room for one rider."

Noah felt someone shove him from behind.

"Take him," Guiseppi said.

Noah looked at Guiseppi with confusion.

"Go!" Guiseppi demanded. "Joshua will bring Rosa and me."

Noah got into the back of the ambulance, the doors closed, and they screamed away.

Guiseppi looked at Joshua. "I will call my Vincenzo from the church."

Once inside the church, Joshua had a friend show Guiseppi where the office was located, while he and Rosa went to look for Mona and the children. Guiseppi's shaky fingers had to dial Vincenzo's number several times before he finally got it right and made the connection. He was overwhelmed with relief when his son was the one who answered the phone.

"Vincenzo," Guiseppi sobbed into the phone in their first language, "*Oh, il mio Vincenzo.*"

"What is it, Papa?"

"It is Angel," Guiseppi cried. "She has been hurt very bad, and you must call your brothers and find a way to get them to Rapid City. It is *very bad*, my Vincenzo."

"Papa," Vincenzo gasped into the phone, "what happened?"

"She was hit by a car. Oh, Vincenzo, I do not see how she can make it this time."

"Okay, Papa, I will call my brothers. Is Alex there?"

"No. He is somewhere on the road between here and Pierre. I do not know how we will find him."

"I will call Sam," Vincenzo said. "Perhaps he will know how to find Alex."

Joshua and Rosa came down the steps as Guiseppi stepped into the foyer of the church.

"Mona's gonna take the children over to our place," Joshua said as he hurried them out of the church and into the parking lot. "We told them we'd call just as soon as we can."

"They cried, Guiseppi," Rosa said, taking ahold of Guiseppi's hand. "And Laura wants her daddy."

"That wretched blackguard," Guiseppi cursed as Joshua led them to his car.

Chapter 18

As Joshua hurried Guiseppi and Rosa through the emergency entrance at Rapid City Regional Hospital, Noah and a nurse were exiting the triage area.

"What is happening?" Guiseppi asked, looking frantically to Noah for an explanation.

"They're taking her into surgery," Noah answered, but from the expression on his face, Guiseppi could see that things were still very bad.

"I'm taking you to a different waiting room," the nurse explained as she coaxed them all to follow her. "This way you'll be close enough so the doctors can send someone out to visit you during the surgery. She'll be in for a little while."

She led them through several corridors, more swinging doors, and finally to a small waiting room with a window and a phone.

Noah could think of nothing else but the ambulance ride. Angel had gone into shock and stopped breathing. They'd intubated her, but she arrested and her heart was started again with the electric paddles. After that her eyes opened, but were without expression. The paramedic had commented that her pupils were *not* reactive to light. She didn't acknowledge Noah's soft cries as he whispered her name and told her that he loved her.

"A doctor will be down to visit with you just as soon as they know where they're at," the nurse said. "Have you notified her family?"

"Yes," Guiseppi answered as he slumped into a chair beside his Rosa and put his arms around her.

"Do you need me to call your clergyman?"

"I'm Mrs. Martin's pastor," Joshua answered.

The nurse nodded. "If you need anything, there's a nurse's station just down the hall and to the left, but don't leave this room for very long."

They all nodded, and the nurse left them alone.

Joshua took a seat by Guiseppi and Rosa. "Do you want to pray?"

Noah began breathing hard as he tried to swallow away tears. He shoved his hands into the pockets of his jeans and began to back toward the door. "I don't wanna pray, Josh," and his voice caught on a sob. "I'm gonna go for a walk."

Joshua stood and reached for Noah's shoulder. "Come on, Noah. You can do this for Angel."

"I *can't*."

"You have to," Joshua insisted.

"Please, Noah," Guiseppi pleaded into Noah's eyes. "It is all that we can do for her. *Please help us.*" He held his arms out to Noah.

Noah couldn't fight the compulsion he had at that moment, and he dropped to his knees before Guiseppi and Rosa. Their arms went around him. Joshua knelt beside him, and soon Noah felt the arms of his brother, and he began to pray.

Vincenzo called Petrice first, and the two of them decided the fastest way to reach Angel would be to have Petrice and Marquette fly directly from Washington to Sioux Falls, aboard Petrice's plane. They would meet Vincenzo and Kate there and fly to Rapid City. Petrice estimated they could be in Rapid City before midnight.

Vincenzo then called Sam and told him about the accident, and Angel's critical condition. He explained that they did not know how to reach Alex, or even where to look for him. Sam told Vincenzo he would take on the responsibility of finding Alex.

The first call Sam placed was to Shondra's home phone.

"Shondra, this is Sam Martin, and I've got a dreadful problem."

"What's the matter, Sam?"

"Tillie was hit by a car about an hour ago, and nobody can find Alex."

"Oh, Sam," Shondra softly gasped into the phone, "I know he left for Pierre about three hours ago by car, so you should try his apartment."

"His *what?*" Sam asked, thinking that he'd misunderstood.

"His apartment?" Shondra repeated. "In Pierre. Didn't you know about that?"

"No," Sam stormed. He clenched his teeth and growled, "Why does he have an *apartment?*"

"Because he's turned into the biggest blackguard on the face of the earth," Shondra retorted. "Who are the twins with?"

"The pastor's wife."

"Listen, Sam," Shondra went on, "I resigned my position today. I refuse to work for a liar. He called off their anniversary trip to Paris—even lied to Tillie and told her that he'd rescheduled it. I just hate him, Sam."

Sam sounded like he had growled into the phone again, and he said, "Give me the number to his apartment. I hope I don't kill him when I see him."

Shondra put Sam on hold for a moment and returned with the number. "I'm going over to the hospital," she said. "I know Guiseppi and Rosa are probably there, but they don't know anybody else in town."

Sam sighed heavily into the phone. "And I'll try to track down Alex."

"I'll find a way to call you from the hospital so you can let us know what's happening with that."

After they hung up, Shondra grabbed her purse and headed for the hospital. She shook her head in disgust as she started the car and began backing out of her driveway. It had only been a few weeks since she had wondered how God would get Alex's attention.

The four of them had been waiting for over an hour when Shondra arrived. Guiseppi and Rosa looked like two tiny gnomes as they sipped coffee from Styrofoam cups, holding each other's hands. Joshua was beside them, reading from his Bible, and Noah was by the window. He turned around when he heard Shondra come in, and the look on his face broke her heart.

Shondra went first to Guiseppi and Rosa, and they put their tender arms around her.

"Sam called me," she said as she looked into their grieving expressions.

"Thank you for coming to us, Shondra," Rosa said. "You are such a wonderful lady."

Shondra went to Noah and put her arms around the forlorn-looking creature. "What's happening?" she whispered.

"We don't know yet. They said they'd send somebody down with a report, but we ain't seen anybody yet."

A short young doctor with a full black beard, dressed in blue scrubs, appeared at just that moment and silence fell upon them. "Is this the Tillie Martin family?"

"Yes," Guiseppi said as he got to his feet. "What news do you have of my Angel?"

"I'm Dr. Peterson," he said as he extended his hand to Guiseppi. "I'll be the one giving you updates on her progress. She's still in surgery, but we wanted to let you know how things are going." He took a breath. "She has several different injuries. There was a lot of internal bleeding. There are several broken ribs, which caused a puncture in her left lung and also on the lower lobe of her liver. Her skull was fractured, and there might be some damage to several sinus cavities...and there might be some brain damage. We don't know yet."

"Will she make it?" Guiseppi asked, so quietly they could barely hear him.

The doctor hesitated. "We don't know."

Guiseppi felt the floor buckle beneath his feet and the room began to spin. Noah saw the little man struggle to keep his balance and rushed to his side, grabbing Guiseppi's arm and helping him back into the chair beside Rosa.

"I'm sorry," Dr. Peterson said, "but you should know that there just happened to be a surgeon's convention in town, and we've called in the best people in the business for Senator Caselli's sister."

Rosa's black eyes brightened. "How did you know?"

Dr. Peterson shrugged. "I don't know who knew. Somebody on the trauma team recognized her, I think, and had our emergency department make the calls." They all sat in silence until Dr. Peterson finally said, "Well, I'm going back in, but I'll be out as soon as we know some more." He turned and hurried down the hall.

"I'm gonna call Mona," Joshua said. "See how everything is going with the kids."

Sam dialed the number Shondra had given him and was astounded when Alex picked up the phone.

"You jerk!" Sam yelled into the phone.

"Who is this?" Alex asked.

"It's your brother!" Sam barked. "And don't you *dare* hang up on me. You're wife is almost dead, and you've gotta get back to Rapid City."

"What are you talking about?" Alex retorted.

"She was hit by a car at about seven o'clock," Sam stormed. "And it doesn't look good."

"Hit by a car? Where?"

"I don't know *where!*" Sam yelled. "But why weren't you there?! Why aren't you *ever* there?! I can't believe you got your own apartment!"

"Where are you, Sam?" Alex asked.

"I'm in Sioux Falls. Patty's picking us up!" Sam shouted. "So, *chances are*, the way you operate, I'll be in Rapid City before you!" With that, Sam slammed down the phone so hard Becky-Lynn thought it might break.

"Calm down, Sam," she said as she put her hand on Sam's shoulder. "Do you want me to call your parents?"

"No," Sam groaned and shook his head. "Dad is eighty-eight years old. He'll have a heart attack if I go to him with this."

Becky-Lynn sighed and began to pace around their living room. "Well, you'd better get going, but I'm gonna stay here and wait for you to call. That way, somebody can be here for your parents, you know, if something happens."

Petrice and Marquette, along with their wives and Petrice's children, were about half-way to Sioux Falls, South Dakota. Marquette had finally been able to get the on-board telephone to connect with Rapid City Regional Hospital. His call was transferred to the telephone in the waiting room. He was surprised when Guiseppi was the one who picked up the phone.

"How is she, Papa?"

"We have gotten one report." Guiseppi began to cry. "It is not going well for Angel. But there are some special surgeons in town this day, so she is getting very good care. How long before you arrive, my son?"

"Patty says we are about ninety minutes out of Sioux Falls. It will be under an hour from there."

"Have everyone pray, my Marquette," Guiseppi pleaded, and he saw Dr. Peterson in the doorway again. "I must go. Call me when you reach Sioux Falls." He quickly hung up and looked to the young doctor.

"There's a pretty bad head injury," the doctor said with a serious expression. "There may be some trauma to the spine, but we couldn't tell because of the swelling in her back tissue." The doctor took a breath and continued, "They should be finished in about an hour or so. They've stopped the internal bleeding, and that's good. But we won't know if she can breathe on her own until they're done."

The silence in the room was deafening, and after a long moment, Dr. Peterson left them alone again.

Mona tried to entertain all of the children with her wonderful Southern stories, but it was difficult for A.J. and Laura to keep their minds off of their mother. All they'd been told was that she was hurt and had to go to the hospital. However, they were only six and half years old, and the stress of being in a different environment, without either one of their parents, wore on their little nerves.

"Did Daddy call?" Laura asked as she snuggled into Mona on the sofa.

"No," Mona answered as she put her arm around the tiny girl.

"He never calls us anymore." Laura sighed and shook her curly head.

"Can we call Mommy?" A.J. asked.

"No, we can't," Mona answered gently. "She's busy with the doctor."

"How about Dad or Uncle Josh?" Ty suggested. "Could they talk to us?"

"Maybe." Mona thoughtfully considered the request and began to nod. Joshua *had* given her the number directly into the waiting room, and he told her to use it if she needed to.

Mona made the connection with the waiting room, and the twins were able to speak with their grandparents. Guiseppi and Rosa took turns speaking with the children, reassuring them that the doctors were taking good care of their mommy and that they didn't need to worry one bit. Guiseppi promised he would call again as soon as he could. After he hung up the phone, he sighed and turned to his wife.

"Rosa, my love, do you have your small Bible with you?"

Rosa looked away from Guiseppi and nodded.

"Well, can I please see it?" he questioned.

"No. Please, do not ask again."

"Yes, my Rosa," Guiseppi insisted as he took her hand into his. "I want to tell them."

Rosa reached for her purse and pulled out her old Bible, the one Tillie had carried with her the day she married Alex. She handed it to Guiseppi, who knew exactly where to turn, and he pulled an old photograph from between the pages.

"I believe you were the one who took this photo, Joshua," Guiseppi said as he handed it to him. "At least that is what we were told. Do you remember?"

Joshua frowned at the old photo, and then smiled with recognition. "Yes, I remember." He looked at Noah and showed him the photo. "Remember this? It was the day you came home with the old Harley and made me take your picture." Joshua looked at Guiseppi with surprise. "Where did you get this?"

Guiseppi smiled and handed another photo to Joshua, this one being the photo Estelle had taken of Noah and Tillie together in the bar. "I do not know who took this photo, but it was taken with *my very own camera* — the one I saved from the war — and my Angel developed it herself when she returned from Rapid City that year."

Noah and Joshua gazed into the old photographs, and Shondra's curiosity made her come closer to have a look for herself.

"MacKenzie Dale is the brother of Alex's mother, Frances Martin," Guiseppi explained. "She gave Rosa the photo of Noah and his motorcycle. Rosa had found photographs in Angel's room and suspected the young man to be Noah. She asked Frances for the photograph for verification, but told no one of her discovery except for me."

Joshua and Noah looked at Guiseppi with curiosity, but he only smiled back at them. He looked down into the old words of the Bible. "This is the last gift that Rosa's mother ever gave to her, and it is very old, but Rosa has marked in the margin *"Venti uno Dicembre, Noah,"* the date of December 21, 1960, and the name "Noah." And that is the date she first heard of you, Noah — a small boy, struggling with the loss of his parents and the authority of his older brother." Guiseppi looked back to the old words. He read them first in Italian, paused to look at Joshua and Noah again, and translated, "The words say, 'And this I pray, that your charity may more and more abound in knowledge and all discernment, so that you may approve the better things, that you may be upright and without offense unto the day of Christ, filled with the fruit of justice, through Jesus Christ, to the glory and praise of God.' "

Joshua and Noah shared the same dumbfounded expression.

Noah stumbled backwards and slumped into a chair. "That's my birthday... December twenty-first is my birthday."

"It was no accident you met our Angel," Rosa said with a small but sad smile. "For your life changed forever on that day."

Shondra's mouth fell open as she waited for further explanation.

Joshua stammered, "Noah hasn't had a drink since the day he met Angel."

"You knew about me?" Noah whispered with a confused expression.

"Oh, yes, we knew," Guiseppi admitted. "And I thought about seeking you out — or even sending my Marquette to pummel you — but Angel begged us to let it go. She was very concerned with her sin in the matter and did not want anyone to know what she had done." He swallowed and smiled faintly as he remembered. "She even considered going to Italia to live with Marquette and Tara."

"It wasn't her fault at all," Noah explained as he shook his head. "It's my responsibility. I should have known better —"

Guiseppi held up his hand. "Noah, Angel had been married nearly three years before I found out how wrong we had been about you." His voice caught on an unexpected sob, which he had to swallow away before he could continue. "Rosa and I allowed the thing with Alex to happen because he seemed to heal her heart after she had returned —"

"But she *loved you,* Noah," Rosa interjected, breaking as the tears streamed down her face. "She wept for you, and my heart ached for the child."

"When you brought Alex to the hospital, now nearly seven years ago," Guiseppi continued, "I knew then that I had moved out of God's will by making a decision that my heart has always regretted. I should have sought you out, no matter what the discomfort to my Angel…but…I could not bear another tear from her eyes, and I was afraid to risk her precious heart one more time. So I kept your identity hidden deep inside of my deceitful heart, while Alex charmed her pain away."

Guiseppi shook his head and looked at Noah. "And when you became such close friends with Marquette and Vincenzo, my heart was overwhelmed with grief. My Marquette does not befriend *just anyone*…I am so very sorry. God intended *you* to be Angel's husband, and He shows me again what a fool I have been. It is *you*, Noah Hansen, who comforts and prays with us, instead of the wretched blackguard I gave her to. Please forgive me, Noah. I have made such a mess." Guiseppi broke then. He hung his head and wept and wept.

Alex wasn't able to get a charter out of Pierre, so he headed for Rapid City by car. The drive was nearly three hours, so he estimated he'd arrive shortly after midnight. It took him nearly an hour to make all of the necessary arrangements to leave Pierre and put the hearings for the following day into the charge of Robert. Alex was more than a little miffed about that. *If Sam exaggerated this just to get me home, I'm going to be really mad. Obviously Tillie isn't "almost dead." She must have felt good enough to give him the number to my apartment.*

He stewed as he drove along, remembering his argument with Shondra from earlier that afternoon. *The old spinster actually gave me her resignation. Now I'll have to find another assistant. All because I cancelled my anniversary trip? What's her problem anyway? And what business is it of hers? Tillie must have set her up to that. Why is that woman so uncooperative? Why can't she just submit like other Christian wives and go along with the plan of supporting her husband? Doesn't she want to see me succeed? Or is she so wrapped up in herself she doesn't even stop to think about me anymore?*

Alex shook his head disgustedly. *Now she has me driving down the interstate while a near half-wit handles those hearings at the capitol tomorrow. I have half a mind to turn around and ignore this whole stunt.*

At eleven thirty, Dr. Peterson appeared in the doorway of the waiting room. He hadn't come back within the hour he'd estimated, and everyone was worried. They looked hopefully at the fatigued doctor and waited for him to speak.

Dr. Peterson took a breath and exhaled slowly. He hated these conversations. "She's out of surgery now," he said. "They're taking her to an intensive care unit." He knelt down in front of Guiseppi and Rosa. "It didn't go as well as we would have liked. And before I take you up to see her, I want you to prepare yourselves. She's on a respirator, and she's fairly catatonic right now —"

"What is that?" Guiseppi questioned, but Noah knew exactly what the doctor was talking about because he had seen it on the way to the hospital.

The doctor took a breath as he tried to find the perfect words to explain to such a worried father. "She appears to be awake, but she's not."

Rosa reached for Guiseppi's hand. "What caused this?"

"We think the blow to her head —"

"But she was talking to me right afterward," Noah interrupted.

The doctor nodded and looked at Noah. "But there's been swelling and bruising now, and that's actually what causes the damage." He paused and looked back to Guiseppi and Rosa. "We had to shave her head, so her appearance is going to be very different when you see her."

"Please take us to her now," Guiseppi requested.

Dr. Peterson nodded and got to his feet.

Dr. Peterson couldn't have prepared them for what they saw when they were shown into Tillie's room. Through the glass walls of the intensive care room, they saw Tillie, flat on her back, staring at the ceiling. There was a tube taped to the side of her mouth, while a rhythmic machine hummed next to her bed. Her head was completely wrapped in gauze; not one of her glorious curls had been saved. Her forehead and the left side of her face were swollen more than when Noah had left her in the care of the surgery team, and both of her eyes were black. A nurse sat beside her to take her blood pressure and listen to her heartbeat.

"Angel," Guiseppi whispered, falling to his knees at the end of her bed and bowing his head. Rosa dropped beside him, and they started praying in their first language.

Noah felt as if someone had hit him so hard he couldn't breathe. He slowly made his way to the side of the bed, where one of her pretty hands rested on the sheets. He took it gently into his own, noticing that the other one was bound with gauze and an IV.

"Angel," he whispered as he looked into her vacant expression, "Can you hear me, Angel?" He started to cry. "Forgive me, Angel...forgive me, Father."

Shondra lost her breath and began to fall until someone steadied her by taking hold of her arm. It was Dr. Peterson, and he led her back into the hallway. Joshua's reaction wasn't much different, except that he was able to keep his balance. He followed them to a place just outside of Tillie's room.

"Are you okay?" Dr. Peterson asked Shondra.

Shondra nodded and whispered, "How long will she be like this?"

"We don't know exactly what's going on," Dr. Peterson answered as he looked into the traumatized expressions of Joshua and Shondra. "Her pupils are not reactive to light, which tells us there's some brain damage. To what extent it's hard to say until there are more tests, and we'll be doing EEG's as often as we can."

"What are EEG's for?" Joshua questioned as he rubbed one of his shaking hands along his forehead.

"We'll measure for brain wave activity."

"How about the rest of her injuries?" Shondra asked quietly.

"Well," Dr. Peterson began as he took a breath and scratched his head. "She's got quite a few broken bones in her left leg, and the knee joint was especially damaged. Maybe a back injury. We thought the spine may have been affected, but now the surgeon is thinking the symptoms are all due to the head injury. It's hard to tell at first. When the swelling goes down, we'll be able to make a better assessment."

They heard footsteps in the hallway behind them, and Joshua and Shondra turned to see Alex strolling toward them with a frown on his face.

"Hi, Shondra. What are you doing here?" he demanded.

"Hi, Alex," Joshua said, attempting to stay calm as he suddenly realized that Noah had to get out of their fast. Unfortunately they'd all gotten so caught up in the emotionally devastating confession of Guiseppi, as well as Angel's probably fatal injuries, that they'd ignored the reality of Angel and Noah's *real and current* relationship — and that was that she was still a married woman.

"Where's my wife?" Alex asked brusquely. "Admittance sent me up here."

"Who are you?" Dr. Peterson asked as he glanced through the glass walls at the man holding Tillie's hand and then back at Alex...*isn't this guy that new attorney general that's bragging of taking on the United States Senate seat?* And then he suddenly remembered...*Senator Caselli's sister is married to the AG....*

Alex rolled his eyes and sneered, "I'm your attorney general, Alex Martin. Now where's my wife?"

"She's in there," Dr. Peterson pointed toward Tillie's room, where Noah stood holding her hand.

Shondra's heart nearly beat out of her chest. This was going to get out of control very soon now.

Alex's frown deepened, and he took a step forward but was held back by Joshua. "Just wait a second, Alex. You should really talk to the doctor first."

Alex scowled. "I can talk to the doctor later." He broke free of Joshua's grasp and charged into the room.

Noah heard the footsteps behind him and turned around to see Alex's angry face just inside the doorway. He set Tillie's hand on the bed, and his face twisted with rage.

"*You*," Noah growled. It only took him two steps to cross the small room, and he grabbed Alex by the knot in his tie. He backed him out into the hall where he slammed him hard up against the wall. Several nurses saw the commotion and ran into Tillie's room.

The move took Alex by surprise, and he instinctively punched Noah in the stomach. Noah winced but held onto the knot. With all he'd been through that night, it was going to take more than just a punch to bring him down.

"What's wrong with you!" Alex exclaimed as he attempted to break free of Noah's grasp, but Noah slammed him hard again, nearly knocking the wind out of Alex.

"I'll tell you what's wrong with me!" Noah shouted. "We've been waiting for you for hours! *Where have you been?! She's dying —*" His voice broke in a sob, and he cried, "*She's dying,* Alex, because you didn't take care of your blessing! We have to take care of our blessings or they get taken away!"

By this time Joshua was behind Noah and tried to pull him off of Alex. Dr. Peterson attempted to move between the two men, but Noah couldn't be budged. He looked into Alex's eyes and growled through his sobs, "If I could have, Alex, I would have stolen her away from you, and I would have never let you ruin her life!"

"Come on, Noah," Joshua coaxed. "Come on, let's go for a minute."

"No!" Noah cried. "I can't lose her again!"

Dr. Peterson managed to push himself between Alex and Noah, and Joshua was able to coax Noah's hand from the knot in Alex's tie, releasing Alex from his clutch. Joshua was then able to pull Noah back a few steps.

Alex staggered away from the wall and straightened his tie as he looked to Shondra for an explanation. "What's going on here?"

Shondra shook her head as she looked at her former boss. "We've had a long night, Alex."

"I'm Dr. Peterson," the doctor introduced. "And we should really discuss the condition of your wife."

Alex nodded and followed Dr. Peterson into Tillie's room. He took up the post beside her bed and reached for her hand as Dr. Peterson began to speak.

Noah watched from the hallway and shook his head. "He never deserved her. She should have been *mine*."

"I know." Joshua took his brother into his arms.

"I hate him, Josh."

"No, Noah, you've never hated Alex."

Shondra shook her head as she watched a very stricken Alex listen to the news Dr. Peterson gave him, while Guiseppi and Rosa continued to pray at the end of the bed — they hadn't missed a beat.

Alex held his head in his hands, and Shondra felt a pang of compassion for him. She wondered if he could hear God's voice calling out to him. If Tillie and their children ever needed him before, they were certainly going to need him now.

When Dr. Peterson had finished speaking, he patted Alex on the shoulder and walked out of the room.

"All of us are on call tonight," he said. "This is a top-notch unit. We'll see if she gets through the rest of the night, and then we'll take a look at the situation in the morning."

Shondra nodded and watched Dr. Peterson walk to the nurse's station a few steps away.

Joshua looked at Shondra and asked, "Hey, would you take my brother for a cup of coffee or something?"

"No, Josh," Noah protested. He stood stubbornly still, looking through the glass wall into Tillie's room.

"Please, Noah. I have to talk to Alex for a couple of minutes, and then we're gonna have to check in with Mona and see how the kids are."

Shondra put her arm around Noah's waist and smiled up into his eyes. "Come on, Bruiser. If we're gonna be up all night, we need to get some coffee."

Noah nodded reluctantly and started down the hall with Shondra.

Joshua watched the two of them walk down the hall and out of sight. He sighed and went into Tillie's room, being careful not to disturb her parents. They hadn't stopped praying, even for Noah and Alex. Joshua pulled an empty chair from the corner up next to Alex and took a seat. Alex turned his grieved expression to Joshua and looked into his eyes.

"I guess your brother thinks this is somehow my fault," he said, and then he looked back at Tillie and shook his head. He felt Joshua put a friendly hand on his shoulder, and he continued, "I suspected he had feelings for her. He hasn't managed to hide it very well."

Joshua took a deep breath. "Did you know they met several years ago? *Before* you started to date her?"

Alex looked at Joshua with a puzzled expression. "When would she have had the time to meet anyone? I've known Tillie since the day she was born. *I'm* the only date she's ever had."

"In 1975 she came out to Rapid City for an art show, and they happened to meet up over at that little bar that my dad used to own —"

"The one he gave to Maggie West?"

Joshua nodded. "You know the stories, Alex. Noah was a rebel who spent *all* of his free time drinking and driving around on that horrible motorcycle until suddenly, in 1975, he straightens himself around. Nobody could figure out what had happened. About eight months after she left, Noah finally told me about her. Apparently they spent the whole weekend together, and he had asked her to marry him. She accepted and promised to return in a couple of weeks, but the meeting never materialized."

"Why didn't they tell me about this when I was dating her?" Alex asked in disbelief.

"I think she was a little bit afraid of Noah at first. She led him to believe that her name was 'Angel,' and so Noah didn't realize that Tillie Caselli and 'Angel' were the same girl."

"He must have realized it at some point," Alex replied with a frown.

"Shortly before you moved here, when he saw her painting in your office in Sioux Falls."

"And he kept it to himself?" Alex questioned.

Joshua nodded. "Even Tillie didn't know until that first day you guys came to the church."

Alex's eyes opened with sudden realization. "You mean Tillie's the girl who left him at the altar? The one he built —" he hesitated and took a surprised breath, "*Angel's Place!*"

"She's the one."

"Why didn't they get married?"

"She misunderstood something," Joshua answered, "and decided to end it without an explanation."

Alex nodded as he remembered the patience required of him during their courtship. He had always blamed her lousy prom date. "Are they having an affair?" he asked.

"Are you kidding me?" Joshua frowned at Alex and shook his head. "Mister, I don't know your wife very well, but I know her better than *that*. And my brother would certainly *never* do something like that."

"And how would *you* know?" Alex frowned. "They've kept all of this from *me* for the last twelve years."

"I told you, they weren't aware of one another for many years."

"Whatever." Alex shook his head and looked back at Tillie, so lifeless and so unaware of what was happening around her. He couldn't even ask her for an explanation.

Joshua sighed as he got to his feet, looked down at Alex, and said, "Please forgive my brother – - forgive all of us. I let this get out of hand here tonight."

He paused at the end of the bed where he knelt beside Guiseppi and Rosa. He prayed for Tillie and begged for God's intervention. He rose to his feet and left the room, only to find Tillie's brothers, along with Sam Martin, making their way down the hallway. Joshua stopped them before they reached Tillie's window.

"Pastor Hansen," Petrice said. "Is our sister here?"

Joshua nodded. "But I need to talk to you guys before you go back there. Where are your wives?"

"They went to Angel's house," Vincenzo answered. "We thought the cousins should be together."

"The twins are actually at my house," Joshua said. "But I'll call Mona and see if they're up. They're pretty upset about things and would probably do better with their relatives."

Marquette placed his hand on Joshua's arm and looked into his eyes. "How is she, Pastor?"

Joshua was exhausted, and the situation hit too close to home. The realization that Noah's beloved Angel was dying made it difficult for him to maintain the "reassuring Pastor look" he'd mastered over the years. On top of that, he wondered how long it would be before a family member, other than Alex, realized that Noah shouldn't be there.

Joshua's lower lip quivered as he looked into their anxious expressions. "She's hurt pretty bad."

Marquette began to stagger, much the same as Joshua had seen his father do, but Vincenzo grabbed him hard and held him steady.

"None of this, Marquette!" he scolded. He looked at Joshua. "What is wrong?"

"She has a head injury," Joshua answered. "And when you see her, it's going to look like she's awake, but she's actually unconscious. She's on a respirator, so there will be a tube giving her air through her mouth...and..." He hesitated and swallowed hard. "There's some swelling and bruising on her face that changes her appearance, and she doesn't have any hair because of the surgery they had to perform. She's going to look very different."

"Where are our parents?" Petrice whispered.

"They're praying in there right now," Joshua answered. "Alex is in there too, and that's a pretty hot situation because my brother is here. And I don't know if any of you know about Tillie and Noah's past, but that's all out now, and Alex is pretty upset about it."

"Oh, it *was* Angel," Vincenzo whispered. "I *knew* it."

Marquette looked at Vincenzo and frowned. "How did you know? I did not breathe a word to you."

"I am not without a brain," Vincenzo retorted. "I figured it out for myself."

"What are the two of you speaking of?" Petrice questioned with a frown.

Sam was confused but remained quiet as he hoped for an explanation.

"We will tell you later," Vincenzo said.

"Where is Noah?" Marquette asked.

"Shondra took him downstairs for awhile," Joshua answered. "He wants to rip Alex apart."

"Well, Alex has really been a schmuck," Sam grumbled. "Dad and I haven't been able to get along with him in months. And I don't know if any of you know, but he's taken his own apartment in Pierre."

"He what!" Marquette gasped in a whisper. His eyes narrowed, and he frowned at Sam. He took a sudden step forward and clenched his fists but was caught in the tight grasp of his brothers, one on each side.

Sam nodded. "Shondra just told me tonight. Apparently he's been living in Pierre for quite a while."

"Now, listen, Mr. Caselli," Joshua said as he looked at an enraged Marquette. "This is a hospital intensive care unit, and we're all gonna get thrown out of here if there's one more fight. So don't go off on him in there." He sighed heavily. "And my brother hasn't behaved so well these past months — Alex has the right to be upset with him and Angel right now."

Vincenzo frowned and shook Marquette. "Angel needs us to be strong, Marquette. Can you, for once in your life, overcome this rage within you for Alex? If only for Angel's sake?"

Marquette took a deep breath and nodded. "Let us see our sister now."

Joshua turned and led them to the glass walls, where a very disfigured Tillie lay, staring up at the ceiling without expression.

Marquette staggered into the room and slumped beside his parents. Petrice and Vincenzo followed. They encircled each other with their arms, crying and speaking to one another in Italian. Joshua stood speechless at the door, while Sam took the empty chair next to Alex. Sam put his hand on his brother's shoulder, and Alex looked at him and shook his head.

Joshua walked away to find a phone. It was time to call Mona.

Chapter 19

Mona must have been beside the phone because she answered it on its first ring.

"How are things going?" she asked.

"It's bad, Mona," and at last Joshua's tears gave way. "Remember when Swede Roberts' daughter was in that car accident?"

"Yes."

"That's what this looks like. She just lays there and looks up at the ceiling. I don't think the doctors expect her to make it through the night."

"Oh, please no," Mona whispered. "Did Alex make it?"

"Oh, the big jerk is here all right," Joshua grumbled. "And I think he's mad that his life got disturbed or something. His brother is here, and Tillie's brothers are here too. There were quite a few fireworks between him and Noah, and I told him about their past. He's pretty ticked off about that, and he'd like to think they're having an affair."

"Understandable," Mona replied. " 'Cause you know, Josh, whether or not it happened in his body or his mind, Noah has committed adultery with Angel." She took a deep breath. "How's Noah doin'?"

"He's pretty broke up about things. I sent him to get some coffee with Shondra...remember the lady who works for Alex?"

"I remember her."

"And I don't think Guiseppi likes his son-in-law very much, which could turn into a *major* issue up here — but, we can talk more about that later. Will you call over to Angel's house? Her brothers' wives are over there looking for the kids. Maybe you oughta just run 'em over there, maybe stay the night, and send the ladies to the hospital. This looks like it's really gonna go bad tonight, and these guys are gonna need their wives with them."

"Sure, Josh," Mona agreed. "I'll take 'em over there right now."

"Thanks, Mona," Joshua said, and then he quietly added, "I love you, Mona."

"I love you, too, Joshua."

Noah and Shondra returned to the Intensive Care Unit as a team of technicians and two doctors pushed more equipment into Tillie's room. Noah and Shondra waited just outside the doorway as the technicians explained that everyone would have to leave for a few minutes while they performed an EEG and that they could come back in as soon as it was finished. After everyone obediently filed out, the technicians drew the curtains on the glass wall and closed the door.

Alex and Noah deliberately looked away from each another when Alex came out of the room, but Marquette threw his arms around Noah. Guiseppi and Rosa went into a quiet corner by themselves, and Sam and Alex walked down the hall a short distance way.

"I cannot believe that *she* was the one," Vincenzo whispered, still astonished at the story Marquette and Noah were quickly spilling out. "I knew in my heart that it was Angel."

Petrice didn't seem as impressed with the story and he frowned at Noah. "I saw your eyes following her at the twins' birthday celebration. Have you been coveting her?"

Marquette stepped between Noah and his brother. He looked down at Petrice and shook his index finger beneath his nose. "Whatever were Noah's sins of the past, he has repented of them. I have personally witnessed this."

Petrice shoved Marquette. "Permit me to question him myself."

Noah grabbed Marquette's shoulder. "It's okay, Marq." Noah looked at Petrice. "Senator, I'm sorry…Yes, I've coveted your sister."

"I prayed with him myself," Marquette growled

"Petrice," Vincenzo said as he put his hand on his older brother's shoulder, "Noah is an honest and good man. Marquette and I have come to know him very well over these past seven years, and we have loved him as a brother. He confided in us many years ago about the loss of his *Angel*, and *none of us* ever put two and two together until just recently —"

"But should he be here with us?" Petrice interrupted.

"We cannot very well cast him away from us at this point," Vincenzo argued. "Noah is more to us than just an acquaintance."

"And he means even more to our parents," Marquette barked. "They have prayed for Noah for many years…before he even laid eyes upon our Angel."

Petrice sighed and looked at Noah. "And what do you feel for Angel this day?"

Noah swallowed away a sudden lump in his throat, and tears fell from his eyes. "I'm in big trouble," he whispered.

Petrice nodded with understanding, and then he looked at his brothers and Joshua, then back at Noah. He spoke with authority, but gentleness, "You gave your heart to my sister — even when you knew she was married to your friend?"

Noah nodded.

Petrice slowly shook his head, as if deeply grieved. "I am torn in the matter of whether or not to allow you to stay with us —"

Marquette interrupted his brother with a growl, "Do not attempt to admonish us, Petrice!"

Petrice snapped his fingers and frowned at his younger brother, as he would have a disobedient child. He clenched his teeth in an effort to control his temper as he spoke, "As much as I see the compassion that you all have for one another, and I truly believe that it is genuine, it does not change the fact that our beloved Angel is in an adulterous relationship with Noah!"

Vincenzo frowned and slapped his older brother on the side of the head. "*Adulterous* is a very strong term, Petrice," he said. "Are you certain that is the word you want to use?"

"Guys," Noah interrupted, "I don't think Angel is in this relationship with me. It's been all very one-sided." He looked at his brother. "Josh can vouch for that. I've shared everything with him."

Joshua nodded.

Petrice took a deep breath. "Well, then we must pray together."

While the Casellis visited and prayed with Noah and Joshua, Alex muttered out the story to Sam a short distance away.

"Apparently they had some kind of a whirlwind romance back when she was seventeen, and they've probably never been able to forget each other." Alex snorted and shook his head. "And I'm stuck not even being able to ask her about it."

"Wow." Sam swallowed hard and shook his head. "She never said anything about it?"

"No," Alex answered with a frown. "Never said a word about being in love with my *best* friend." He shot them all a dirty look. "He's in, and I'm out. They prefer the home wrecker over the faithful husband. Who'd have ever guessed *that* one?"

Sam swallowed again and bit his lower lip. "I don't think that's entirely right, Alex —"

"Listen, Sam, I'm not around so much anymore. Who knows what they've been up to. You should have seen them at church a couple of months ago. They were all over each other. Noah can't keep his face from turning bright red every time he looks at her."

"I just can't imagine Tillie doing something like that. She's such a great gal."

"She's not that great anymore, Sam," Alex complained. "She's changed *a lot*. She nags me constantly about not being home enough, and we argue all of the time."

"Did you argue about your anniversary?"

Alex narrowed his eyes. "How did you know about that?"

"Shondra told me."

Alex snorted again. "That old spinster doesn't know how to keep her nose out of everyone else's business."

Sam grabbed Alex by the arm, gave him a hard shake, and scowled into his eyes, "That *old spinster* worked for me and Dad for just about twenty years but couldn't take a full year with you!"

Alex jerked his arm out of Sam's grasp and glared at his brother. "Knock it off, Sam!"

"You're acting like an idiot," Sam quietly stormed, trying to keep their argument between just the two of them. "I can't believe how *selfish* you are. Your loving, beautiful wife is dying, and you're more worried about whether or not she's having an affair? Tillie would *never* do that to you. But, *you*, on the other hand, have completely forsaken your wife and children for your career. You even got an apartment *away from them*."

"I've been a faithful husband. I've never so much as *looked* at another woman, let alone what they've pulled."

"They haven't pulled anything," Sam shot back. "Stop being so *unreasonable*. Don't you even care?"

"Of course I care, it's just different now, that's all."

"You're mad because your life got interrupted," Sam coldly accused. "All you can think about is how Robert might screw things up. I can't believe you're the same man who promised that girl for better or for worse."

"Well she promised me the same thing, and look at what she's done. Waited until I was busy with something else so she and Noah could start up again."

Sam shook his head. "I refuse to believe it."

"Well don't believe it then!" Alex shouted. He shoved Sam out of the way and stormed down the hall and out of sight.

Everyone looked up at the commotion and saw Alex leave.

Sam walked to where Tillie's brothers were with Noah and Joshua.

"Tell me the truth," Sam said as he looked into Noah's eyes. "Are you having an affair with my brother's wife?"

Noah nodded. He swallowed hard and began, "Not physically...but my heart fully belongs to Angel —"

"Noah is a man of honor," Marquette interrupted in defense. "And my sister would never be party to such an offense."

"Why didn't anybody tell Alex?" Sam asked.

"She really hated me when she found out," Noah answered. "And she didn't want Alex to know because she was afraid it would hurt the relationship that he and I had."

"When *did* she find out, Noah?" Vincenzo asked.

"Not until the first day they attended church," Noah admitted. "I found out a few months before, and I invited them to hear Josh preach." He paused to swallow his emotions. He was really tired, and the stress of having to lose Angel again was wearing on him. A few tears escaped as he said, "I missed her so much. I just wanted to see her again...if something happens to her, I just don't know what I'm gonna do."

Sam had to fight to control his own emotions. Noah was obviously more concerned with Tillie's well-being than even her own husband, and it cut Sam to his core. He wondered who would fight for the marriage — because he certainly wanted to end it right now, and the offended party was his own brother.

The door to Tillie's room opened, and the technicians and two doctors exited with their equipment. A tall man with gray hair and bifocals, along with a shorter man with dark features and a beard, walked to where the group stood.

"Tillie Martin's family?" the taller man asked. Guiseppi and Rosa immediately rejoined the group for some news on their daughter. "I'm Dr. Mills," the tall man introduced. "This is the surgeon, Dr. Parsons, who performed some of the surgery on Mrs. Martin." He looked around the group and frowned, "Which one of you is her husband?"

"He's not here right now," Sam answered.

"We are her parents," Guiseppi piped up. "What can you tell us?"

"We performed another EEG," Dr. Parsons said, "and it was inconclusive."

"So you know *nothing*," Guiseppi huffed.

"We will repeat the test in a few hours," Dr. Parsons offered. "Her vitals are stable now, and I would have to encourage you that that is a very good sign."

"But what kind of damage will be left by this?" Guiseppi asked, and his eyes again spilled tears he could not hold back. "That person in there does not even *look* like my daughter."

"At this point, we don't know," Dr. Parsons answered. "All patients recover differently. If she regains consciousness within twenty-four hours, we could have a better diagnosis for her." He took a breath. "We're on call tonight, so if anything happens, we can be back up here quickly. There are two other surgeons who worked on her midsection, and they're having a nap downstairs. They'll be up to check on her in about an hour or so. Do any of you have any questions?"

No one responded.

Dr. Mills took a breath. "There are lots of theories out there about catatonic patients, and one thing we've noticed is that they recall certain things that happened in their room. They remember family members talking to them, encouraging them, etcetera. Sometimes they hear us, and sometimes they don't. So even though she can't communicate with you, you might want to talk to her. Tell her that her kids are fine. Tell her about your day. Things like that."

Rosa's face lit up with hope, and she gave Guiseppi's hand a hard squeeze.

"We'll be up again in the morning," Dr. Mills said, and he and Dr. Parsons began to back away. "We'll see how she's doing then."

Rosa pulled Guiseppi into the room with her, and everyone followed. She went to her daughter's side, took hold of her hand and placed a delicate kiss upon Tillie's cheek. "Hello, my Angel," Rosa smiled, as tears ran down her cheeks.

Alex charged through his back door, surprised to see his sister, Kate, sipping coffee at the kitchen table.

"What are *you* doing here?" he frowned.

Kate got to her feet and lovingly put her arms around him. "How's she doing? Mona should be here any minute now with the kids."

Alex pushed her away and frowned at her. "Who else is here?"

"Ellie and Tara, and our kids," Kate answered with a confused expression. "Alex, how's Tillie?"

"Bad," Alex answered. "She's completely catatonic, and they don't know why." With that, he stormed through the kitchen, up the stairs, turned into Tillie's studio, and closed the door.

Kate sighed and slumped into a chair. She wanted to ask Alex some more questions, but his demeanor frightened her...*what if...?*

Tara and Ellie came down the stairs and into the kitchen. "Did we hear Alex?" Ellie asked.

Kate answered with a nod. "And he's really stressed out. Must not be going good up there."

"Then why did he leave her?" Tara asked.

Kate shook her head. "He wouldn't talk to me, and I was afraid to ask."

Tara put a gentle hand on Kate's arm. "Let me try."

Kate nodded, "Go ahead. He's in her studio. I'll come up in a few minutes."

In Tillie's studio, Alex had pulled several boxes from out of the closet and emptied their contents onto the floor. Evidence had to exist that corroborated his theory, and this would be the place she'd hide it from him.

As he tore angrily through her old books and memories, something caught his eye, and his glance was drawn to the ledge by the window. All by itself sat the tattered, old red book of poems. He dropped the papers in his hands and took the old book from the ledge. The pages automatically opened at her favorite, *Annie Laurie*, and then he saw the photograph. He held his breath as he saw her in Noah's arms, looking lovingly up into his eyes. Alex thought his heart might stop. He turned the photograph over and read the faded ink: *Me and Noah, Roubaix Lake, April, 1975.*

Alex tucked the photo between the pages and closed the book. *How could they do this to me?* He shook his head. *There's probably even more recent evidence. I just need to find it. Joshua said they met in that old bar. What was the name of that place?* He looked at his watch. It was nearly two o'clock in the morning, and there was no one at the office to pull the file. He'd have to find it himself.

Tara knocked on the studio door, but Alex didn't answer. She opened the door to peek inside and saw Alex near the window with the familiar red book of poems in his hand. Her heart skipped a beat. *He knows.* She let herself into the room and closed the door behind her.

Alex looked up from the book and frowned at Tara. "Did you know about this?"

Tara was extremely tired, and the stress of the situation was unbearable. Before they'd received the call to come to Rapid City, she and Marquette had spent three grueling ten-hour days in a row testifying before the Tower Commission. She tried to hold Alex's dark stare, but the intensity was too much for her, and her tears betrayed her as they rolled down her cheeks. She tried to wipe them away, but it was too late. Alex saw them.

She stepped closer to him as she looked into his eyes. "Yes, Alex, I knew, but it is not what you are thinking."

"Who else knows, Tara?"

Tara shook her head, unable to make words come from her mouth.

"How did Pastor Hansen find out?" he demanded.

"I imagine he must have told him. Alex, she did not think she would ever see him again —" Her words were cut off by unexpected sobs.

"Does your husband know?" Alex questioned.

Tara nodded.

Alex shook his head and frowned. "Did you know *before* I married her?"

"Yes, but we did not learn that Noah was your friend until after the babies."

"But you knew about Noah *before* we were married?" he questioned.

Tara hesitantly nodded her head, and a sob caught in her throat again.

"Jeez, pull yourself together, Tara. You thought it was just fine to keep your little secret up until now. Try not to get too broke up over the fact that it's finally leaked out." He slipped the small book of poems into the inside pocket of his suit jacket and started for the door.

"Alex!" Tara reached for him as he went by and caught hold of his arm.

"Let go of me, Tara," he demanded.

"Please, Alex, let me explain," she begged.

Alex angrily snatched his arm away from her and opened the studio door "The time to explain was years ago." He stepped through the door, slammed it shut from the other side, and stomped down the steps and into the kitchen.

"Where are you going?" Kate asked with a frown.

"Who cares?" Alex stormed past her, heading for the back door.

"Please spend some time with your kids, Alex. They're on their way."

He rested his hand on the doorknob and looked at his sister, "Well, big sis, they're gonna just have to wait because I've got something I have to do."

"Alex, don't you *dare* leave this house," Kate scolded.

Alex laughed. "What are you gonna do, Kate? Spank me?" He left through the back door, slamming it shut behind him.

Sam called Kate so they could figure out how they were going to tell their parents about the situation with Tillie. Alex had been gone for quite some time, and everyone was getting concerned about his absence. Possibly the ladies had heard from him or, better yet, maybe he was with the twins.

"Oh, he was here," Kate said. "He stormed out about an hour ago."

"Are the kids there?" Sam asked.

"They are now," Kate answered. "Ellie and Tara are helping everybody into bed. The twins were really excited to see their cousins, and I think that's going to help them a lot. As soon as we get everyone settled in, we'll come over to the hospital. Mona says she's gonna stay here. She's such a nice lady." She hesitated. "How's Tillie?"

"Oh, Kate," Sam whispered into the phone as he felt a lump in his throat. "She's bad. It's the most horrible thing I've ever seen. I can't believe Alex would leave her like this. It doesn't even *look* like Tillie. Her skull looks all smashed-in and her face is swollen beyond belief. She just lays there and stares at the ceiling, but she's unconscious."

Kate swallowed hard, then whispered, "What's the doctor say?"

"They don't know."

"How are Rosa and Guiseppi holding up?"

"Pretty good," Sam answered. "They talk to her a lot, but she can't respond, so it's pretty sad. Marquette's in bad shape, but his brothers are being fairly strong."

"Is she gonna make it?"

"I don't think they know," Sam whispered. "And we're going to have to let Dad and Mom know what's happening, because it's probably gonna hit the morning paper or there will be something on the news during the day. There's already been some news people in the hall just outside of this unit. Believe it or not, they want to interview Patty. Shondra's been trying to manage the press, but I don't know if she's in good shape herself — *emotionally* that is. She's been here all night."

"Brother," Kate moaned. "You're gonna have to send Becky-Lynn over to talk to Mom and Dad, but tell her not to say anything about Alex." She took a breath. "Tara told us about Noah."

Sam let out a heavy sigh. "That's a bad deal. I've questioned Noah. I don't think there's anything going on, though he admits to being very taken with Tillie —" He was interrupted at that moment when he heard Rosa scream, and several nurses sprinted for Tillie's room. "I have to go. Something's wrong. I'll call you right back." With that he hung up the phone and ran into Tillie's room.

"She is choking!" Rosa screamed, while Guiseppi tried to pull her out of the way of the nurses. Tillie's brothers and Noah huddled together by a window and watched with stricken horror, while Joshua and Shondra stood still in the doorway.

"She's *not* choking!" a nurse said in a calm shout. She looked at one of the two nurses beside her. "Call Dr. Peterson." One nurse ran from the room, while another put her hand into Tillie's hand. "Come on, you," she commanded. She looked at Tillie's closing eyes, "*Come on.*" The nurse gasped with a smile. "She's fighting the respirator. She's trying to breathe on her own."

"Is this good?" Guiseppi asked with wide-open eyes.

"It can be," the nurse answered.

"Her eyes are closed," the other nurse commented.

"She squeezed my hand," the first nurse whispered with a smile. "And her eyes moved."

An unfamiliar doctor pushed his way into the room.

"She's coming around," the nurse frantically informed.

"Give her morphine," the doctor instructed calmly. He reached for Tillie's eyelids and suddenly barked, "Hurry it up!" He held open one eyelid and turned on the light above the bed. "Her pupils reacted. Did anybody call Peterson?"

"Yes," the first nurse answered, while the other administered the morphine.

There was a very loud choking noise, and everyone in Tillie's room gasped.

"We have to get that thing out of there," the doctor said.

The nurses began to usher everyone out of the room.

"Why can I not stay?" Rosa asked.

"Because the tube might have to go back in," one nurse explained as she hurried everyone out the door. "It's not something you'll want to see."

"I cannot imagine things could look any worse," Guiseppi grumbled as they left the room and huddled with their sons in the hallway.

"Dr. Peterson is on his way up," the nurse said from the doorway as she escorted the last of them out. She pulled the curtains shut and closed the door.

"This could be good," Guiseppi encouraged.

"Papa," Marquette cried, flinging his long arms around his father and mother. "She will be fine. I just *know* it."

Noah staggered into the wall and leaned up against it. He took several deep breaths, and Joshua put his hand on Noah's shoulder with a smile.

"This might be okay," he smiled into Noah's eyes.

Dr. Peterson ran up the hall, into Tillie's room and closed the door.

"Come along, everyone," Rosa said with authority. "We will pray for our Angel." Everyone obediently dropped to their knees near Rosa and Guiseppi, and they began to pray.

Alex went to his office downtown and looked for his uncle's files on the Hansen family, where he was certain he'd find the name of the bar Noah's father used to own. Unfortunately, the file was old and, according to the notes in his office's filing system, it had been stored away in the basement of the building several years ago.

Well, Alex thought, as he headed for the basement of the bank *that's just fine because I've got all night to find it.*

While they were still on their knees, Tara, Ellie, and Kate arrived. The ladies were alarmed to find everyone kneeling outside of Tillie's closed door. The Casellis and Noah got to their feet, and the men greeted their wives with sighs of relief.

"What's happening?" Kate asked.

"They are attempting to remove the respirator," Vincenzo answered with a small smile. "She may be waking up, but we do not know yet."

"They tell us nothing," Guiseppi grumbled.

"I gave birth to that child," Rosa complained, "and they do not even offer me the dignity of being with her —"

Tillie's door opened, and Dr. Peterson looked at Rosa.

"Ma`ma, I presume?" he smiled.

Rosa's heart skipped a beat, and she nodded her head.

"She's asking for you," Dr. Peterson reached for Rosa's hand.

Everyone inched toward the door, but Dr. Peterson cautioned with a smile, "Just a couple at a time so we don't get her too excited. She's in a lot of pain."

They all reluctantly backed off as they watched Guiseppi and Rosa go into Tillie's room, and the door was closed again.

Noah thought he might faint, but he smiled and breathed a sigh of relief. Tillie's brothers laughed out loud and slapped everyone's backs.

"Our Angel lives!" Marquette proclaimed, too loudly for an intensive care unit.

"Settle down, Marquette," Petrice laughed.

Sam smiled and shook his head. *It's really too bad that Alex isn't here.*

"Angel," Rosa whispered as she came to her side and took her hand. She sighed with relief when she felt the pressure of Tillie's hand close.

"Ma`ma," Tillie rasped as she tried to look at her mother, but she could only open her tired eyes about halfway. A nurse was still close beside Tillie as she checked her blood pressure and listened to Tillie's heart with a stethoscope.

The doctor that had rushed in earlier examined a tube beneath the sheets. "There's still quite a bit of drainage from that lung," he commented, and the nurse nodded.

"Can she see me?" Rosa asked. "Because her eyes cannot seem to open."

"Yes," Dr. Peterson answered. "That's from the morphine."

"Blood pressure steady at ninety over sixty-five," the nurse beside her informed.

"It hurts, Ma`ma," Tillie rasped.

"I know, my Angel." Rosa softly touched Tillie's cheek and smiled at her.

"The babies," Tillie began.

"They are with Pastor Hansen's wife and all of their cousins," Rosa answered with a smile. "They were so excited to see everyone come to visit."

"I didn't make anything to eat," Tillie said, and Rosa saw her daughter try to frown.

Rosa chuckled and kissed Tillie's cheek. "That is alright, little one. I will take care of it, or someone else will."

Guiseppi looked into Tillie's drugged expression and smiled. "Can you see me, Angel?"

"I see you, Papa."

"Let's ask her some questions," Dr. Peterson said. "Ask her the babies' names and how old they are."

"A.J. and Laura," Tillie answered. "And they are both six and a half."

"Twins?" Dr. Peterson asked.

"Yes," Tillie answered, and her eyes completely closed. "I'm tired I guess, but I'm thirsty." She tried to open her eyes again. "Noah?"

"He is here, my Angel," Rosa smiled.

"Don't tell Alex I'm here," Tillie whispered.

"Why not?" Rosa asked.

"I'm going to Italy. I have to leave by Friday."

Dr. Peterson appeared to be alarmed. "Is this making any sense?"

Guiseppi nodded. "She had planned on staying with her brother for the summer. He has a residence in *Italia*."

Dr. Peterson looked relieved. "Mrs. Martin, what's your brother's name?"

"I have three brothers. Petrice, Vincenzo, and Marquette."

"And who were you going to Italy with?"

"Marquette," Tillie answered with a soft smile. "He lives on the lake in a pink castle."

Guiseppi laughed quietly and nodded his head at the doctor.

Dr. Peterson whispered to Guiseppi, "She's asked for Noah a couple of times now. Is it okay?"

"Get him," Guiseppi ordered. Sam probably wouldn't like it, and neither would her brothers, but he really didn't care. Alex had left her in her most dire hour of need, and Noah had stayed. If she wanted to see Noah, Guiseppi certainly wasn't going to refuse her at this point.

Dr. Peterson went to the door and opened it to find everyone still waiting outside. He knew exactly who Noah was — the man who hadn't left her since her arrival. "Noah, she asked for you."

Noah's face lit up, and he stepped into the room with the doctor. He found his way to Tillie's side.

"Angel," he said with a smile of relief, and tears fell from his eyes. Rosa let go of Tillie's hand and moved out of the way, and Noah took her place.

Tillie's smaller hand closed around Noah's, and she whispered with a soft smile, "I let this whole thing go too far...you'll have to leave before Alex gets here...please forgive me, Noah."

"I do," he breathed. "And forgive me, Angel. I'm so sorry. It's all my fault."

"It's okay, Noah. I could have been a whole lot stronger — *should have* been stronger...now look at me. I was dragged away and enticed...which was exactly the reason I wanted to stay away from you." Tillie smiled. Her eyes closed again and she said no more.

"It's the morphine," Dr. Peterson assured as he checked the vital signs on the screen next to her.

"Heart rate is excellent," the nurse observed. "Respirations are coming at regular intervals. A little rattle there."

"But it's draining really well," the other doctor stated, and he looked at Guiseppi and Rosa as they stood behind Noah. "By the way, I'm Dr. Rossiter. I did the surgery on her lung."

Guiseppi looked bewildered, for he had met so many doctors in that long night that he could hardly keep track of them all. "How many of you were there?"

"Quite a few," Dr. Rossiter answered. "She had a number of different injuries. The little gal was lucky the convention was in town. Dr. Parsons is from Denver."

"Blessed," Guiseppi corrected the physician. "And what of her prognosis now that she is awake?"

Dr. Rossiter shook his head. "We'll just have to see. She's young and in good shape. If there's no infection, she'll heal quickly." He paused and looked at the nurse beside him, "Make sure you get a note in the chart that Dr. Berke be called immediately in the morning. We need to get that leg looked at and set." The nurse nodded and bustled from the room.

"Dr. Mills and Dr. Parsons will probably be up in a few minutes," Dr. Peterson said. "I had a nurse call them both."

Rosa looked hopefully at Dr. Peterson. "But my Angel will live, will she not?"

Dr. Peterson smiled at the sweet, old lady and nodded his head. "I think she'll make it."

Guiseppi and Rosa wrapped their arms around each other and began to weep.

"God is a mighty God," Guiseppi sobbed as he held his Rosa close.

Chapter 20

Maggie and Estelle arrived at their little bar on the north side of town before eight o'clock.

"Wonder if it'll get hot today, Maggie May," Estelle said as Maggie turned her keys in the front door.

"Hard to tell." Maggie opened the door for Estelle.

"Gotta start the coffee." Estelle flicked the light switch by the door and headed for the coffee machine on the counter.

Maggie heard tires screeching into the parking lot behind her, and she turned to see a black Mercedes bounce to a stop.

"Who in the world...?" She squinted for a better look, and her stomach turned when she recognized the attorney general. "Good grief." She hustled to the counter, wishing she'd had time to lock the door. "It's Angel's husband. We gotta get rid of that painting."

Before Maggie could reach the painting, Alex stormed into the building.

"Good morning, ladies," he greeted with a scowl. He caught sight of the painting, and the furrow between his black brows deepened. "I've already found what I came for." He took several long strides across the bar, coming to a stop in front of the portrait.

"What do you want?" Maggie tried to put herself between the painting and Alex. She was a big lady, but no match for a man Alex's size.

"How about you tell me how long Noah's been fooling around with my wife?"

"He's *never* fooled around with Angel," Maggie denied, wishing she'd gone for her trusty Remington beneath the counter.

Estelle hurried to the painting to put herself between Alex and her beloved possession. "You just go on and get outa here!" she scolded as she pointed her finger at Alex. "You been a *terrible* husband, and you ain't took care of her! Now *get out!*"

"Oh?" Alex raised a brow and clenched his teeth. "Is *that* what he told you?"

"Listen, mister," Maggie began, trying to keep her voice calm. "Noah hasn't said anything about you —"

"Nobody tells me nothin'!" Estelle snapped. "I make my own mind up about things, and you're a bad man!"

Alex reached over Estelle to pluck the yellowed photograph from its place in the corner of the frame, and he turned for the door.

"No!" Estelle screamed in anguish as she lunged for the huge man, but Maggie stopped her. He was acting far too strange to push, and she decided to just let him have the thing if he really wanted it. She'd seen his kind before, and she didn't want Estelle getting hurt.

"That's *mine!*" Estelle yelled from the safe confines of her sister's arms. "She was ours *first!*"

Her words stopped Alex in his tracks. He turned around and pointed the photo at them with a yell, "She's *mine! She's always been mine!*" He turned and stormed out of the building, started his car, and screeched out of the parking lot.

Estelle cried as Maggie held her. She laid her head against Maggie's shoulder and sobbed, "She was *ours first*, Maggie."

"I know, Baby," Maggie comforted as she patted Estelle's back. "I know."

By eight-thirty that morning, Dr. Parsons and Dr. Mills had finished with their second visit to Tillie's room since she'd regained consciousness. They'd asked her question after question about her life, what year it was, who was president, and when her birthday was. She'd responded to everything accurately and then fell asleep.

"And she seems to recognize *most* everyone," Dr. Mills said as he visited with Tillie's brothers in the hallway just outside of her room. While everyone else had gone to breakfast, they'd stayed behind, along with Noah, and promised to come to the cafeteria if something should go wrong. "But she becomes extremely agitated when we talk about Alex…and that's her husband?"

The three of them nodded as they glanced through the glass at Noah. He stood beside the bed, holding Tillie's hand, watching her sleep. And though Tillie had asked him to leave, her parents were reluctant to enforce the request. When she'd so quickly fallen asleep, and didn't realize that Noah had stayed beside her, Guiseppi and Rosa kept the request to themselves, hoping the doctors didn't repeat it to anyone.

"Who's *that* guy then?" Dr. Parsons questioned.

"Just an old friend of the family," Vincenzo answered.

"Well," Dr. Parsons said with a yawn as he scratched his head, "We're ordering some more tests, and then we'll be up to see her again this afternoon." He hesitated then continued with a frown, "I overheard some of their first conversation — and I don't know what's going on and it's none of my business — but she told him he had to leave *before* Alex shows up. If Alex shows up and it upsets her, make him leave, too. She's in a considerable amount of pain right now and will be for quite awhile. She's *my* patient. Her *condition* is *my* business, and she's still critical. I don't want her upset."

Tillie's brothers nodded.

"Do you guys have any questions for us?" Dr. Mills asked.

They shook their heads in response, and the two doctors nodded and walked away.

"She has asked him to leave her," Petrice said so quietly his brothers almost didn't hear him. "Why did our parents not share that with us? Certainly they must have heard her say it."

"I am afraid that we are all going to make some very bad decisions this day. Our hearts are so fond of Noah — and we are at odds with Angel's husband," Vincenzo said as he watched Noah.

Marquette yawned and rubbed the back of his head. "Let us allow Noah this time with Angel and not make a fuss. I think the episode was harder on him than even on the three of us, and you must realize that Alex did not even care."

Petrice glared at Marquette. "Speaking of *bad* decisions."

Marquette scowled and was about to respond when they noticed that the nurses had asked Noah to leave once again. They watched Noah reluctantly place Angel's hand back onto the covers and leave the room. The curtains were closed, the door was shut, and Noah rejoined her brothers.

"They're checking the drainage from her lung again," he said.

Marquette gave Noah a friendly pat on the back. "And how are you, my friend?"

"Fine. But I suppose I'm gonna have to leave pretty soon. She told me to get out of here before Alex comes — so I probably shouldn't be here."

Petrice put his hand on Noah's shoulder. "How about some breakfast first?"

"Well, I feel things are safe enough to get ourselves some coffee and perhaps an egg or two," Marquette said. He yawned again and smiled mischievously. "What do you say we give those nice reporters in the hallway a few delicious nuggets on the *Iran-Contra* investigation on our way to the cafeteria? When the administration asks us about our lack of discretion, we can feign exhaustion."

Petrice chuckled. "Excellent idea." And they started down the hallway together.

As they reached the end of the hallway, nearing their turn, a very angry Alex stormed toward them. Without warning, he smashed his fist into Noah's face. The blow sent Noah nearly off his feet, and he staggered backwards.

"Why did you sleep with my wife?" Alex screamed at the top of his lungs. His voice echoed through the hallway of the hospital.

Noah had been up for more than twenty-four hours, and the last twelve had been spent wondering whether or not Angel would live or die. Alex's unexpected punch did little to improve his mood. He quickly regained his balance and hauled back with a devastating blow of his own directly into Alex's face, knocking him flat on his back. Noah lunged for the knot in Alex's tie. He held him down and looked into his eyes. It wouldn't take long to knock Alex out. He did nothing but sit around all day, and Noah was confident of his own strength.

"She wouldn't do that to you, you *idiot!*" Noah yelled into Alex's face. "And if you cared about her at all, you would *know* that about her!"

Noah pulled back for another punch, but someone caught him from behind, and he was suddenly pulled off of Alex. Sam was there, and he helped Alex up from the floor and then held him. It had been Vincenzo and Marquette who pulled Noah off, and it was taking both of them to restrain him.

"Then what's this?" Alex shouted. He breathed hard and threw the photo he'd taken from Maggie and Estelle just a few minutes ago. The photo fluttered to the floor, and Petrice picked it up.

He looked into the younger version of Noah placing a delicate kiss upon Angel's cheek. "This photograph is *very* old, Alex. In fact, it has even yellowed." Petrice turned the photo over to see if there was any writing, but there wasn't. He held it out and asked, "When was this taken, Noah?"

"1975," Noah said, "the weekend she came out for the art show." All Noah could think of was how devastated Estelle must be. He looked at Petrice. "That photo belongs to very good friend of mine. We have to get it back to her right away."

Petrice took a breath and carefully tucked the photo into the pocket of Noah's shirt.

Sam held his brother firmly while Alex tried to catch his breath. Vincenzo and Marquette continued to hold Noah. He was breathing hard and occasionally tried to struggle away from them.

Marquette considered letting him go. He had no love for Alex, and Alex *deserved* this beating and more. Had it not been for the love of his Lord, Marquette would have encouraged Noah to *kill* Alex on the spot.

Petrice turned toward Alex and spoke as calmly as he could. "You have much bigger worries than this, Alex. Your Angel is doing a little better, but she is hurt very badly and requires your love and attention." He paused and looked into Alex's hard expression. "You do still love her, do you not?"

"Of course I love her," Alex answered disgustedly. "But how would you feel if this were *your* wife?"

"I would give her the chance to explain," Petrice answered.

"Alex, you are being quite unreasonable," Vincenzo added with a frown. "For we all know this situation, and it is none of the things you have concocted."

"Why didn't she tell me?" Alex raged.

"Because she *loves* you," Noah answered, and his heart broke at the words. "She didn't want to screw up our friendship because she knew how much it meant to you."

"That's the most pathetic thing I've ever heard," Alex dismissed.

"You *idiot!*" Marquette suddenly shouted, and Petrice was so alarmed at the possibility of both he and Noah attacking Alex that he stepped quickly to Marquette's side and attempted to grab hold of his arm. "You do not believe it," Marquette continued to shout, "because you could never make such an unselfish choice for her!"

Police officers suddenly arrived and approached the agitated group of men in the hall.

Petrice was the first to notice that several photographers were only a short distance away. He sighed with remorse and scowled at Alex. "Look at what you have caused."

"Okay, boys," an officer began, and his eyes fell on Petrice with surprise. "Senator Caselli?"

"In the flesh," Petrice wryly admitted.

"What's going on here?"

"It is a disagreement," Petrice explained, deciding to use his influence as the Senator to somehow keep Alex and Noah from getting arrested. "We have been here with my sister since early last evening and have had no sleep. Our tempers flared and words were spoken, but we have ironed out our differences."

"Your sister is ill?"

"She was injured in an accident," Petrice answered. "She was near death for quite some time. Certainly you can understand how a group of men, who so unfortunately allowed their wives to leave them alone during this time, could make such a mistake." Petrice took a breath and pointed at Alex. "Your own attorney general is so deeply grieved, because it is his wife that is my sister."

The officer looked at Alex and noticed his swelling, black eye. "I'm very sorry to hear that, sir."

Alex only nodded.

The officer looked at Noah, who had a similar bruise. He frowned and looked from Noah to Alex and then back at Noah. "Do either one of you want to press charges?"

Both of the men surprised everyone by answering, "No."

"Well," the officer said as he took a deep breath, "keep yourselves under control. This is a hospital, and we're right downstairs. I'll arrest both of you if there's another incident."

All of them nodded, and the officers walked away. They pushed through the small crowd of reporters now approaching Petrice and Marquette.

"Senator," a young reporter said as he came closer with a microphone, "can you give us any kind of a report on your sister?"

"I wouldn't do that if I were you," Sam warned him.

"No questions today, my friends," Petrice said, and he waved them away. He turned everyone around so their backs were facing the reporters.

"Can we let go of you now?" Vincenzo asked, and Noah nodded. Sam released Alex as well but stayed close beside him.

"You can't be here," Alex frowned at Noah. "I don't want her to see you anymore."

The expression on Noah's face was one of great sadness and regret, but he swallowed hard and began to nod his head.

Petrice shook his head. "Noah may at least wait with us in the waiting room. She has already asked him to leave —"

"I'm her husband!" Alex interrupted through clenched teeth. "What I say goes!"

Petrice snarled, "Away from your wife is where you chose to be this night — this night that we all stayed beside her and prayed, while you attempted to find ridiculous evidence in order to incriminate her for something she could never possibly even consider." He took a breath and stared hard into the eyes of his brother-in-law. "It sickens me to think that you believe yourself so glorious and without sin that you can march in here and begin to give orders where Angel is concerned, for we all know that you have chosen to take a residence separate from your beautiful wife and the children she nearly died giving to you —"

Alex attempted to open his mouth and interrupt with some kind of a reply, but Petrice was quick to hold up his hand.

"Do not attempt to admonish me in this matter, Alex. You made this decision many months ago when you separated from your wife and neglected your God-given duties as a husband and father. Now my sister lies in a bed, still barely hanging to life, and I will not allow your ridiculous request to be fully honored. Furthermore —" and he looked at Noah as he shook his index finger, "if you choose to honor this request, you will be a friend of mine no more, and I will curse the very ground you walk upon. Your comfort and well-being are unimportant, and if it is inappropriate for you to be near me and my brothers and my parents, when it gives us comfort, then that is a consequence you will have to face on your own. This situation we find ourselves in comes from the decisions of two foolish men. The two of you made this mess with your own selfish actions, and the two of you will see it through to the end." Petrice looked from Noah to Alex. "That is, if you are truly *repentant* men of God."

Noah nodded his head in embarrassed submission and looked at his feet. Petrice was right, and he knew it. If only he had kept his eyes to himself, or told Alex immediately the day he'd realized. There were so many things he could have done differently, but he had chosen the things that served *himself* the best.

"You make it sound like she bears no responsibility whatsoever," Alex muttered with an angry frown.

Petrice's frown deepened and he snapped his fingers at Alex as he had Marquette earlier. "She repented the *moment* she awakened!" he admonished. "And as far as I am concerned, these consequences she is suffering are enough!"

"You always spoiled her," Alex accused with an angry scowl. "From the time she was a little kid, and now she's a grown woman —"

"Shut up!" Petrice barked, and he looked at Sam. "Take him from this place and do not bring him back until he has sought the face of God for his many sins." Petrice's face was so hard at that moment and his eyes filled with so much anger that Sam didn't dare argue.

"Come on, Alex," he said as he tried to lead his brother away. "Let's go talk." Alex's face remained hard, but he stepped back. He finally turned around and they both walked away.

Petrice let out a heavy breath and looked at his two brothers and Noah. "Thankfully our wives did not witness that episode."

"Tara would have complimented my restraint," Marquette said with a grin.

"I'm so sorry," Noah said as he stared at the floor and shook his head. "This is all my fault. I've wrecked their marriage."

"There will be no martyrdom on this day," Petrice grumbled and snapped his fingers at Noah. "You did not *wreck* their marriage. You may have contributed; however, it all began with me and my endorsement of Alex last spring."

"And on top of that," Vincenzo added, "Alex is the one who moved out and away from his wife and children. Certainly you cannot bear responsibility in that matter. Whether he knew of your and Angel's secret should not matter. Living with his wife is where he belonged, not gallivanting around the state of South Dakota."

"Alex has fallen very far from the will of God," Marquette said with a sigh. "And as much as I *detest* his very being, we must *all* pray for him. My heart is heavy for the condition of his soul."

"I think you should go home and talk to the kids, and then I think you should come back up to the hospital," Sam suggested. He and Alex were alone in the parking lot. "If you could be there beside Tillie when she wakes up you could tell her that you love her and promise to be there for her. You heard Patty. He's not going to allow Noah to be with her. You need to be there for her, Alex."

Alex rolled his eyes. "Sam, you know I don't have time for this nonsense."

"Nonsense?!" Sam frowned. "You're unbelievable, Alex."

"*I'm* unbelievable?" Alex snorted. "Give me a break, Sam. You heard the *dignified* senator; he's siding with Noah on this. I'm not about to sit around that hospital and watch my wife's adulterous partner hover over her."

"That's not what he was saying, and Noah won't attempt to compete with you for Tillie's attention. He truly wants what's right."

"Listen, Sam, I have to get back to Pierre. Robert will ruin the hearings this afternoon if I'm not there."

"Back to Pierre?" Sam was astounded. "What about the kids? Aren't you going to talk to them?"

Alex huffed. "That's not my problem. If Tillie's family wants to support her adulterous decisions, then they can worry about the kids too. I don't have time for this *stunt*."

"Stunt?"

Alex nodded with a frown. "You *know* she stepped in front of that car on purpose to get attention. And like the idiot she is, she miscalculated how bad her injuries might be."

Sam's mouth fell open, and he stared his brother. "I can't believe you're my brother," he whispered.

Alex shook his head and cursed. "And I can't believe you're mine." With that he stormed away from Sam.

Sam shook his head and went back inside.

Kate and her sisters-in-law had returned from breakfast, and Sam quietly pulled his sister aside.

"Listen, we've got a big problem with Alex," he whispered.

Kate nodded. "I heard about the fight."

"It's worse than that," Sam groaned. "He says he's going back to Pierre."

"Are you kidding me?"

Sam heaved a sigh. "He's so focused on being the attorney general; I don't think he can *make* room for Tillie amongst his other concerns."

"What about the kids?"

"He says they are her family's problem now."

Kate swallowed and took a soft breath. "I guess we'll just have to play it by ear then. I talked to Mona a couple of minutes ago, and she's taking the whole clan out for pizza and then over to a Post 22 game later this afternoon. I think the girls and I should join them. That way the kids won't feel so out of the loop if there are some adult relatives around. I'm a little worried about Guiseppi and Rosa. They really need to get some rest."

"I'll talk to the boys and see if they can get Guiseppi and Rosa to go over to Tillie's and take a nap or something. Then I'll call Becky-Lynn and tell her to go over to Dad and Mom's place, and I'll make the call."

"That's a good idea," Kate agreed.

They walked back to Tillie's room, where Dr. Peterson was talking to her brothers just outside the door.

"Her reflexes have not returned," Dr. Peterson said. "But let's give her a few days and see what happens."

"How about her head?" Vincenzo asked.

"Dr. Parsons says that he is quite impressed with the way the swelling is subsiding," Dr. Peterson answered. "The injury seems to be recovering at a phenomenal rate."

"Will there be other complications from that injury?" Petrice asked.

Dr. Peterson nodded. "There is always a certain amount of rehab required with a head injury. She'll probably have a hard time with her balance and maybe some hand and eye coordination, and that will be complicated by the injuries sustained in her leg and knee. But she's recovering well so far, so I'm not going to sit down and worry about it. In fact, I've *never* seen a patient begin recovery this quickly. She's already sipping water, and that usually doesn't happen for a couple of days, let alone a few hours."

Marquette smiled, "The grace of God. He chose to heal His child in this way."

Dr. Peterson looked curiously at Marquette. "Well, we'll just keep looking after her. I'm leaving her in critical condition for awhile, and that means she'll remain in ICU for at least another couple of days. By the way, has anyone heard from her husband? She wants to see her kids, but I think we should wait on that." Everyone was strangely quiet, and the doctor repeated with a frown, "I think we should make her wait just a few more days. I'd like to get the swelling on her face down before we let the kids come in. What do you think?"

"I will speak with my sister," Petrice offered. "She will understand. It is just that her children are so very special to her."

"She's seems like a really sweet lady," Dr. Peterson said with a smile.

"She is the best," Marquette said.

Dr. Peterson took a breath. "Well, if you guys don't have any further questions for me, I'm going to get something to eat. Don't be alarmed if a bunch of doctors and technicians are in and out of there today. She still needs a lot of specialized care with her punctured lung, and so there will be respiratory therapists and other people coming and going."

"Thanks, Doc." Vincenzo smiled and stretched out his hand. "You have been most gracious to deal with."

"Why, thank you." Dr. Peterson smiled at Vincenzo, and he glanced at all of them. "You guys need to get some rest."

They all laughed, and the doctor turned and left.

Noah and Joshua came up the hall. They stopped where Sam and Kate and Tillie's brothers waited

"You just missed the doctor," Marquette said with a smile, "and he had a *very good* report."

Joshua nodded and looked at Tillie's brothers, then glanced at her parents, who were still in the room with her. "Would you guys mind if I left for just a little while and went over to see my wife?"

"Of course not," Petrice replied. "And perhaps you should get yourself a nap."

"And maybe you should talk Rosa and Guiseppi into going with you," Sam added. "They've been up all night long."

"I agree," Vincenzo nodded.

Petrice looked into the room and saw that Angel had awakened. "I will tell them you are waiting, Pastor, and hopefully they will be out shortly." He took a deep breath and walked into his sister's room.

Guiseppi was sleeping in the chair beside the bed, but Rosa was standing by Tillie.

Petrice looked into his sister's swollen black eyes. "Hello, my Angel."

"Hi, Patty," she whispered.

Petrice looked at his mother. "Ma`ma, Pastor Hansen wishes to go and visit his wife for a little while, and he has agreed to take you and Papa with him so that you may rest. Would you be willing to do that?"

"I do not know." Rosa hesitated and shook her head. "I do not want to leave her."

"I will stay here," Petrice offered. "Vincenzo and Marquette will also be here. I think you should do this."

Guiseppi heard the voices in the room and came out of his sleep. He got to his feet and stood beside Petrice. "Is everything okay?"

"I'm fine," Tillie whispered.

"Patty thinks we should go and sleep," Rosa said with a yawn.

Guiseppi looked at his daughter. "I do not know. What if something should happen?"

"Please, go check on my babies," Tillie begged.

Guiseppi swallowed. "I am sure they are perfectly fine with Mrs. Hansen and their cousins."

"Please, Papa."

"All right, Angel." Guiseppi leaned over Tillie to softly kiss the one place on her face that wasn't swollen and bruised. "We will go, but we shall return soon."

"Thank you."

Guiseppi took Rosa by the hand and led his hesitating wife from the room, while Petrice took Tillie's hand into his own and looked into her eyes.

"Maybe they can bring the kids back." Tillie's speech slurred from the medication.

"My Angel, I cannot permit those babies to see you until you are feeling just a little bit better. You have some marks upon your face that may frighten them."

Tillie attempted a frown and slurred, "Are you in charge or something?"

Petrice chuckled. "In a manner of speaking. I have decided to step in and make decisions regarding you — as you must be well aware you are fairly incapacitated at this time. It would be difficult for anyone to deny my authority, especially seeing as how your husband has set up a separate residence in another town. As well, I am extremely influential —"

"Whatever, Patty," she interrupted. "I know Alex was here. The doctor told me."

"Do you want to see him?"

"I don't know. He's really mad at me."

"What for, Angel?"

"The anniversary trip…he cancelled it, and I yelled at him."

Petrice nodded. "When did all of this start with him?"

"When everyone left. Right after the election."

"Why did you not tell us of his apartment?"

"I didn't want everyone to get mad at him."

"But we could have talked with him, perhaps changed his mind."

"Well, go talk to him then," Tillie slurred.

"I have. He does not listen very well."

"Nope." Tillie's eyes closed.

Before Alex returned to Pierre, he appointed a young associate as his new assistant and told him to collect the Hansen Development files. He instructed the young lawyer to have a letter hand delivered to Mr. Hansen that day at the ICU waiting room at Rapid City Regional Hospital.

"'Dear Mr. Hansen '," Sam read aloud, "Due to the extreme conflict of interest that has developed in our relationship, it is my express desire to quit representation in any and all matters pertaining to your business. Please have your new attorney retrieve your files, forthwith, from the office of Martin, Martin & Dale, A.P.C.L., no later than tomorrow.

"'Pending investigation, your adulterous relationship with my wife may or may not produce a substantial lawsuit in accordance with South Dakota Codified Laws'…wow," Sam sighed.

Tillie's brothers were all in the room with her, visiting while she slept. The ICU had quieted down considerably since the rest of the family had departed, and the staff was relieved to have their facility back under control.

"I called my assistant a few minutes ago," Noah said. "He and I are gonna go over there tomorrow, pick up everything, and take the stuff over to Dennis Marx's office. He's close to my office downtown. Do you know him?"

Sam nodded. "Great guy. Used to be the secretary of labor for the state. Really smart, I think. You'll be okay."

"McDarren's not gonna like it at all."

"Well, tough," Sam mumbled. "He's already signed off on the project, and if he doesn't go through with it, I'll sue him for ya."

Noah smiled and chuckled, "He married Melinda last weekend — in Vegas."

"No fooling?" Sam raised an eyebrow.

"Yep. She bagged one of the richest guys in America. I can't believe she's over me already."

Sam laughed as he rubbed the whisker stubble on his chin. "I gotta be honest with you, Noah, I don't think she ever really *liked* you to begin with. That whole deal was a long shot."

"Yeah, well, win some, lose some."

A bulky old black woman with a silver-streaked beehive and a terrible frown trudged toward them. She was wearing a white apron over her clothing, and clutched an enormous black purse with a tarnished clasp.

Noah smiled. "Maggie May. How'd you know I was up here?"

"Good grief, Noah," Maggie grumbled. "It's all over the news. I figured you'd be here."

"Maggie," Noah turned toward Sam, "this is Sam Martin. Sam this is my friend, Maggie West. She used to work for my father. Josh gave her the old bar and grill."

Sam extended his hand. "Nice to meet you, Ms. West. Still running that old place?"

"Like a top," Maggie quipped, and she looked at Noah. "How's Angel?"

From where he and Sam were waiting, Noah could look into Tillie's room where her brothers stood together near her bed. "She's doing better than they thought she would, but she's got a long way to go."

Maggie looked at the crumpled figure in the bed and fought back tears. *Tough stuff happens to people everyday...it is what it is.* She swallowed hard and barked at Noah, "Listen, your buddy was over and raised Cain with Stellie this mornin'. He took her picture."

Noah remembered the photo in his shirt pocket and handed it to Maggie. "Here ya go. Sorry about that, Maggie. Is Stellie okay?"

Maggie shook her head. "She cried all day. I couldn't get her to do a thing, but," and Maggie held up the photo, "she'll be okay when she gets *this* back. I'm glad you had it."

"Me too." Noah smiled.

"Well, gotta go," Maggie abruptly announced, tucking the photo into her purse. "Call me if you guys need anything, ya know, like a sandwich or somethin'. I'll run somethin' over to ya." She turned and trudged back down the hallway and out of sight.

"Thanks, Maggie!" Noah smiled as he watched his oldest friend head out of sight. He grinned at Sam. "She's not as mean as she'd like me to think she is."

Chapter 21

After ten days, Tillie was moved out of the ICU and into a regular room at the hospital. By then the bruises and swelling on her face and the darkness beneath her eyes had started to subside. Dr. Parsons was comfortable with removing the dressing from her head, leaving only a small bandage at the base of her skull where the injury was.

Tillie stared into the mirror Rosa held, thankful that no other family members were there. The nurse had propped her into a slightly elevated position in her bed, which was all she could stand. If they propped her up much farther, she became dizzy.

"Oh dear," she breathed, "I'm growing whiskers."

"*What?*" Rosa asked with astonishment, leaning closer to Tillie's face for a better look.

"On my *head*, Ma`ma," Tillie whispered.

Rosa swallowed so hard it sounded like a gulp, and Tillie looked at her mother. Rosa smiled sweetly and reached into the pile of scarves at the end of the bed.

"It will turn into hair soon enough, Angel. How about this one?" She held up a bright blue scarf with a wide yellow ribbon winding through it.

"Nice," Tillie said, turning her eyes back to the mirror. She attempted to reach for her head, but her arm lumbered and swung without purpose.

Rosa reached for Tillie's hand and set it back into her lap.

Tillie sighed, "It *still* won't work."

The forewarned complications from her head injury had become a reality. Her hand and eye coordination was nonexistent. She couldn't even feed herself.

"It has not even been two weeks since your accident," Rosa comforted. "This will take some time." She quickly draped the scarf over Tillie's head and tied a glamorous bow with hanging sashes.

"Tuck it behind my ears," Tillie suggested.

Rosa nodded and tucked the scarf behind Tillie's ears.

Tillie gave a half smile. "There. Now all I need is a golden earring and a crystal ball."

Rosa snorted a spontaneous laugh, and Tillie looked at her mother.

"I am sorry, Angel, but you are just so very funny at times."

Tillie's sense of humor had returned and that comforted her family during the next round of crises. As visitors began to come to the hospital, she recognized very few people from her church and occasionally forgot the name of one of her nieces or nephews. She had no idea who Joshua was, and she couldn't remember Mrs. Romanov, though she easily filled in her broken English with Russian. The people she consistently remembered were her parents, her children, and her brothers. And though her family was certain she remembered Alex, she never asked about him. They never mentioned him, and they didn't tell her that Noah was spending a considerable amount of time in the waiting room.

One afternoon when Tillie was alone, Petrice went into her room and closed the door. She was just waking up from a nap, but smiled sweetly at him from her bed.

"Hello my Angel," he smiled. "Do you have a moment for me?

"I have lots of moments for you, Patty."

Petrice sat down on the edge of the bed and took one of her hands into his own. He softly kissed it and looked into her eyes. "I must speak with you about something of a very serious nature."

Tillie's heart pounded — *now what?* "Am I okay?" she stammered.

Petrice nodded with a chuckle. "Yes, you are fine. I want to talk to you about Alex — do you remember him?"

Tillie swallowed hard and nodded.

Petrice frowned quizzically. "Then why do you not ask about him?"

Tillie took a soft breath and hesitantly replied, "None of you have mentioned him since I've been here. I know that he was here initially, because the doctors told me he was here. I just figured he had to get back to work..." she paused and smiled, "You know things with his job should be a lot better in a few months."

Petrice didn't know if he should be angry or horrified with her reply. He sighed heavily and asked, "Do you know how long you have been here now?"

Tillie looked nervous, but she replied with a scoff and a smile, "I've only been here three weeks, Patty."

Petrice nodded. "Three weeks is an awfully long time for a husband to be away from his wife — especially when she's in your condition."

So they've noticed, she thought as she looked at her brother, trying to dream up an excuse, or at least a joke, that would get Alex off the hook.

"My Angel," Petrice continued, "Noah has been in the waiting room for the better part of these past three weeks."

Tillie's eyes opened wide with surprise as she whispered, "I told him to *leave*."

"Yes, he told us. But I told him he could stay in the waiting room and provide comfort for our parents and brothers — as you know, Marquette and Vincenzo are quite attached to him."

Tillie rolled her eyes and shook her head. Tears began to well up and suddenly they dropped to her face. "I'm in big trouble, Patty."

Petrice nodded. "I know what happened — we *all* know what happened."

Tillie shook her head again as the tears flowed. "I don't know what to say, Patty. I'm so very sorry."

"I know, Angel. I'm not here to admonish you...I just wanted to visit with you about a few things." He sighed and began, "We have not received so much as a phone call from Alex, nor have your children."

Tillie couldn't hide her shame. She shook her head and looked away from Petrice.

Petrice continued, "But Noah is such a marked part of our lives at this time. For instance, he has been taking your children to the baseball practices with his sons and they have become quite close. Your little ones thrive when they are with Noah's sons. He is sincerely concerned about their welfare at this time — as he is about yours, and he has asked us if he could see you again. Papa has asked me to have this visit with you." He took a deep breath. "It appears to the rest of us that your husband is not coming back —"

208

"He'll be back, Patty," she interrupted, but she didn't even believe herself.

Petrice raised his eyebrows. "Please allow Noah a few visits. He suffers most grievously, my Angel."

"But what about my marriage, Patty?" she asked with a bewildered expression.

"I think your marriage has run its course," Petrice answered honestly. "And you would do well to stop protecting that blackguard you're married to."

"We don't believe in divorce," she argued.

"I am not advocating a divorce, Angel, but it is quite obvious that Alex is not coming home. I think it is time to be honest with yourself and move on. You have a wonderful friendship with Noah, and that is all that it can ever be —"

"But it's better than nothing," she said with a groan.

Petrice nodded. "Yes, my Angel, it is better than nothing."

While Noah would have liked to have been beside Tillie twenty-four hours a day, the needs of his own children and his business demanded he spread his time between them all. His visits settled into a pattern of early morning hours, where he came to the hospital shortly before sunup and waited for her to awaken. Without fail, Noah was in the chair beside her bed when she opened her eyes.

"Hey," he said with a smile as he got out of his chair and leaned over the railing of her bed. "You slept in a little this morning."

"Guess I partied too much last night," she joked. "So what's up?"

"I got those pictures developed." He pulled a small stack of photographs from his shirt pocket. "It's the boys in their new Little League uniforms. Wow, they're doing really great this year."

Tillie looked at the photos he slowly flipped before her. She suddenly frowned. "Wait a minute…is that Laura in the outfield?"

Noah turned the photo around and looked at it. "Yep, that's Laura, and Heidi Romanov is with her. Sometimes they play a little outfield, you know, just for the fun of it." He chuckled. "That little Heidi can really run, and Laura's got an arm that just won't quit…like her brother."

Tillie sighed. "I'm missing so much."

Noah's heart broke at her words, but he plastered a huge a smile on his face and said, "Hey I forgot to tell you something."

"What's that?"

"Remember Melinda?"

Tillie rolled her eyes. "How could I possibly forget *her?*"

"She ran off and married the Joker."

Tillie laughed out loud, and Noah's heart sang. That was the first time she'd laughed since her accident.

"I never liked that woman," Tillie said as she giggled.

"Me neither."

The nurse bustled in with Tillie's breakfast and set it on the bedside table. Tillie's smile faded as she looked into Noah's eyes, and he knew what that meant. She was very self-conscious about not being able to feed herself and didn't want anyone in the room during that time.

"Hey, I gotta go," he quickly volunteered. "But I'll see ya this afternoon. The kids want to come up again. Jake's got some new jokes for you…is that okay?"

"Yes," she answered, her smile slowly returning.

"I'll bring the paper if you want me to."

"Can you remember the political section this time?"

"No problem," he promised. He backed out of the room. "Bye, Angel."

"Bye, Noah."

When he was out of sight, the nurse smiled and shook her head. "That man gets better looking every time I see him."

Tillie sighed. *Poor guy...he shouldn't be wasting his time on me.*

*****

Three weeks turned into six, and Alex did not so much as call the hospital or anyone at his house. Tillie's family was wishing he would stay away forever.

The heavy cast that stretched from her left hip all the way to her toes was originally blamed for Tillie's inability to balance. When physical therapists attempted to get her into a vertical position, she became sick to her stomach and her vision blurred. They set her quickly into a chair, where she regained her vision and the nausea dissipated.

Dr. Parsons was alarmed to say the least, as she had presented with such a dramatic recovery so quickly after the accident. He performed several tests and consulted a specialist Senator Caselli recommended from Johns Hopkins University. His name was Dr. Joseph Welsh, and he made a trip to Rapid City in order to more appropriately diagnose Tillie's condition.

Dr. Welsh studied all of the x-rays, CT scans, MRI's, and EEG's. He spent nearly three hours with Tillie, asking question after question, writing down her answers, and then asking random questions to compare with her original answers. Within two days, he called for a meeting with her family.

In an office at the hospital, an x-ray of Tillie's skull was backlit before her brothers and parents.

"Her skull was fractured at this point," Dr. Welsh said as he pointed to the back side of the x-ray with his ballpoint pen. He looked at her family, prepared to continue with his technical explanation, but something made him stop. "You want to know when she will be better."

They nodded.

"Rehabilitation from brain injuries varies from patient to patient. The damage to her brain is not as severe as some cases that I've seen, but I *am* concerned about her recovery. During my interview with her, I discovered that she is going through some marital troubles, though she would not specify what they were. That alone will complicate whatever depression she experiences, because *all* head trauma patients go through some kind of depression. It cannot be avoided. She hesitates to even attempt movement of her arms or hands, and the only way her coordinated movement can possibly return is through strict rehabilitation. Now, whether or not her coordination will ever completely return, I cannot say. Every patient is different."

Dr. Welsh took a deep breath and continued, "It should interest you to know that her ability to communicate in Russian has remained completely intact. I speak fluent Russian, and I was able to prompt a lengthy conversation in that language. That encourages my diagnosis further, because not only does it reflect the obvious fact that a substantial portion of her long-term memory is still there, but it tells me that she is willing to try. She just needs a little encouragement." He paused and looked at her quiet family.

"When will she be able to leave this place?" Guiseppi asked.

"Probably not for a little while yet. Dr. Parsons, Dr. Mills, and I have concluded that she should at least be able to feed herself before we let her go home, and even then she'll have to have rehabilitation and nursing care on a *daily* basis for a number of months. She cannot simply be left alone to fend for herself and care for her small children. Whatever problems she is experiencing with her husband should be dealt with and resolved *immediately* so her rehabilitation can be the most successful."

"I can be with my daughter," Rosa volunteered.

"And that's fine," the doctor responded. "But she will also need the skills of a health-care professional for quite some time. Your daughter is not mobile on her own, nor will she be for an undetermined amount of time." He frowned. "Now why won't anyone talk about this marital situation? Are they separated or getting divorced or what?"

Petrice quietly cleared his throat. "We do not know exactly what to expect from her husband. We have not communicated with him since the accident, and we do not know when he will be around."

"What was their status *before* the accident?" Dr. Welsh was clearly becoming impatient.

"We are not entirely sure," Guiseppi answered. "My daughter is a fine Christian woman, and she would not gossip about her husband behind his back. We found out only recently that he had taken a separate residence in another town."

Dr. Welsh raised one brow. "And you're not *entirely* sure?" He shook his head. "I don't worry that much about the improprieties of gossip and I'm not a Christian, but a separate residence in another town is a fairly obvious sign that things weren't that great between them." He took a deep breath, as if he needed it to calm himself down. "How long have they been married?"

"Ten years," Rosa answered.

"And how were those years?" Dr. Welsh asked.

"Most of them were wonderful," Vincenzo replied. "It was only these past eight months, after his election, that things went downhill for them."

Dr. Welsh nodded. "We're ordering some pretty intense rehab for her, and I don't know how long you folks can stay, but I would recommend doing so for as long as reasonably possible. Family encouragement can be the best thing, especially with her husband out of the picture."

"My wife and I can stay until September," Petrice volunteered. "As you know, the senate is on summer break at this time."

"My wife and I work for ourselves," Marquette added. "We will be able to stay indefinitely."

"That's great." Dr. Welsh nodded as he stood from his chair, which prompted all of them to stand.

"Thank you, Doctor," Guiseppi said, extending his hand and giving the doctor's a firm shake. "We appreciate your help."

"It has been my pleasure."

With that, the meeting was finished. The Casellis made their way back to Tillie's room, where she was working with her physical therapist. Noah had arrived shortly before they were to see Dr. Welsh, and had promised to stay until they returned.

As the Casellis walked toward Tillie's room, they saw the tall, dark man whom they had gotten used to having around. Ben Simmons was Noah's new assistant. He brought papers to Noah at the hospital, delivered things all over town, and juggled Noah's complicated schedule to perfection so he could have a few minutes here and there with Tillie. Noah handed him his usual rolled-up bundle of papers, complete with rubber band, and Ben graciously accepted the jumble.

"And what about that inspection over on West Main?" Ben asked. "I can hit it on my way up to Spearfish if you want to stay in Rapid this morning."

"I would really appreciate it," Noah said as he watched the Casellis approach him. He lowered his voice. "They've been to talk to the doctor, and I really want to find out how that went."

"I understand," Ben replied with a nod. "I will be seeing you tomorrow then?"

"I'll be in around 7:15 or so," Noah answered.

Ben smiled as he started to walk away, giving the Casellis a friendly wave on his way by.

"How did physical therapy go?" Rosa asked. She peeked into the room and noticed that her daughter was fast asleep.

"She's really tired today," Noah answered. "They tried to get her up again, and it was a disaster." He didn't tell them that she'd cried about the ridiculous things that her arms and legs did on their own. It broke Noah's heart to see what had happened to her.

"What did the doc say?" he asked.

"Just that she will have a lot of rehab," Marquette answered. "And that it will take a long time."

"But when will she be better?" Noah asked.

Vincenzo sighed and looked at the floor. "He does not know *if* she will get better."

Noah was afraid of that, but he swallowed his own emotions to make some kind of a show of encouragement for her family. "Well, we know she'll get better. It's just a matter of time."

Guiseppi smiled at Noah and patted his shoulder. "Thank you, Noah."

"Oh, she is awake," Rosa said, bustling into Tillie's room. The rest of them followed.

She wore a bright purple scarf today, one that Rosa had carefully tied over her head before they left to see the doctor. She was bundled under several blankets after complaining that she was cold, and all they could see of her were her face and neck.

Noah thought she'd become even more beautiful since her accident, but, then again, maybe it was just the fancy scarves Rosa had provided.

"Would you like to sit up, little one," Rosa asked as she stood by the bed and bent over Tillie.

"Please."

Rosa slowly raised the mechanical bed until it was in a semi-sitting position, allowing Tillie to see all of them. She looked at Petrice. "Did you ask your secretary about those special publications?"

"Better yet," Petrice answered as he walked toward her. "The secretary of defense is having his own report copied and sent overnight. You will have *his* version of the truth even before the rest of America."

Tillie smiled with interest. "That'll be cool." She looked at her quiet family and asked, "What did Dr. Welsh say?"

"Oh, nothing much." Guiseppi walked to her side and reached under the covers for one of her hands. "Just that you will have to put your nose to the grindstone and work very hard."

"I can do that." Her eyes became wide with surprise. "Alex?"

Everyone turned around and saw Alex, bigger than life, in the doorway of her room. He wore his typical disappointed frown and a black suit and tie.

"Hi, Tillie," he greeted.

"What are *you* doing here?" Marquette growled, taking a step in Alex's direction.

Vincenzo quickly put his hand on Marquette's arm and whispered, "Do not upset her…remember, it causes confusion."

Alex took a breath. "I need to talk to you."

Noah's anger burned. It was all he could do not to attack the man where he stood. *What gives him the right, after all this time?*

"Hey," Alex said as he looked around at everyone, "could I please talk to *my* wife? *Alone.*"

"She is not to be upset at all," Petrice said as he took a step toward Alex.

"It's okay," Tillie said. "I won't get upset."

They all stood very still, until Guiseppi nodded his head. He kissed his daughter's cheek and gave her hand a soft squeeze. "We will be right outside." He looked at Alex. "Only for a few minutes."

Alex didn't acknowledge what Guiseppi had said. He only stood very still and waited for all of them to file past, until he and Tillie were alone. He let out a deep breath, pulled the red, tattered book of poems out of his inside breast pocket, and approached her bedside. When she didn't reach for it, he laid it beside her left hand.

Tillie glanced at the book, but she didn't reach for it because she didn't want him to know she couldn't. She knew what he'd found in the old book.

"Where did you find this?" she asked.

"In your studio, the night of your accident. Why didn't you tell me?"

Tillie looked into his handsome eyes and her heart ached for him. They had loved each other so intensely for so many years, and now he was like a stranger that stood before her.

"You and Noah were such good friends for so long. I just didn't want to screw things up for you," she answered.

"How long did you know that Noah was my friend?"

"Not until that first day at church."

"Were you happy to see him again?"

"No," Tillie answered honestly. "Alex, why are you here?"

Alex looked thoughtful and asked his last question. "Do you love him?"

"Alex?" Tears began to burn within her eyes. "If only you could come back home, maybe we could work things out and be a family again. You're the one I promised God forever with…you're the father of our children —"

"Just answer the question, Tillie." He grilled her as he would have anyone on the witness stand. "Do you love him?"

Tillie's tears gave way as she cried, "Alex, please forgive me. I am so very sorry for everything. I was wrong to keep it a secret for so many years. I should have told you when we started dating — at the very least when I realized that Noah was your friend. This is all my fault and I take full responsibility." She swallowed and looked into his eyes as the tears ran down her cheeks.

"Humph." He shook his head disgustedly and started backing toward the door.

"No, please don't go, Alex," she pleaded. "I *know* we can work this out."

Alex shook his head again, looked into the hallway, and then back at Tillie. "I'm going over to see the kids for a few minutes."

An unfamiliar man, dressed in blue jeans and a plaid shirt, entered the room and walked to Tillie's bedside.

"Matilde Rosa Martin?" he asked.

"That's me," Tillie answered, feeling terror creep into her heart…*what has he done?!*

"I'm the county constable," he said as he placed two envelopes beside her hand on the bed. "You've been duly served."

"What?" Tillie asked with a confused expression.

The constable turned and left the room.

Alex looked at Tillie. "You've got thirty days to answer those complaints, and my best advice would be to get a good lawyer." He left the room and stepped into the hallway where the county constable waited for him.

"And that's Noah Hansen," Alex said as he pointed in Noah's direction.

Sensing that something had gone wrong, Guiseppi and Rosa rushed into Tillie's room.

The constable handed Noah an envelope and said, "You've been duly served," and he and Alex walked away together.

Noah tore open the envelope, while Tillie's brothers watched in quiet confusion.

"It's a summons and complaint," Noah said with astonishment. "He's *suing* me."

"*For what?*" Petrice grabbed the complaint and scanned the words. He gasped. "Oh, goodness. 'Alienation of affection and loss of consortium, pain, and suffering'." Not only was Alex suing Tillie for divorce, but he had filed a separate lawsuit against Tillie and Noah for damages sustained to himself due to their "adultery."

Noah ran after Alex and caught up to him at the end of the hallway.

"Alex," he called.

Alex turned around and faced him.

"What are you doing?" Noah asked.

"You can read, can't you?"

"Of course I can read," Noah said with a dumbfounded expression. "But why are you doing this? You guys don't believe in divorce. That's not what she wants."

"I guess the two of you should have considered the consequences. I'm completely within my rights, as a Christian man, to divorce my unfaithful wife."

"It's not like that at all —"

"Please." Alex put up his hand in protest. "I'm not an idiot."

"Yes, you are," Noah retorted. "She needs you to come back home and work this out so she can get better again. Don't you want her to get better?"

"She looks like she's coming out of it," Alex said.

"She can't walk," Noah said, and there was suddenly a lump of emotion in his throat. "She can't even feed herself, Alex."

"I guess that's *your* responsibility now, Noah, or don't you want her anymore — now that she's broken."

Alex's cruel words cut Noah to the quick. He wanted her more than ever, broken or not. He shook his head, turned, and walked away. It was impossible to believe they'd ever been friends, or even worse, that Alex had the ugly heart to deal his suffering wife such a devastating blow.

Tillie's brothers were in her room, and Noah made his way in there to be near her. Petrice had opened both of the envelopes, finding a complaint for divorce and a copy of the same complaint that was served on Noah.

"I didn't do that," Tillie cried as she rested limply in Marquette's arms. She looked at Noah as he entered the room and demanded, "Tell them, Noah. Tell them we didn't do that."

"We know, Angel," Marquette wept with her. "We know all about it."

"Why is he doing this?" she cried.

"Because he is lost in his sin," Marquette wept as he kissed the top of her scarved head.

*****

Kate was surprised when she saw Alex's black Mercedes roll into the driveway. Her husband hadn't had the chance to call, so neither she nor her sisters-in-law had heard about Alex's stop at the hospital.

"Look what the cat dragged in," she said to Tara, who was folding a load of laundry on the couch.

Tara looked out the front window and squinted. "What is *he* doing here?"

Kate shook her head. "Where's the kids? I want to find out what he's doing before I let them see him.

"They are in the back with Jake and Ty."

Kate sighed. "Too late." She watched A.J. and Laura rush to their father. She shook her head and went outside.

"Daddy! Daddy!" the twins squealed at once, "Where have you been?!"

Kate walked to the driveway and watched Alex kneel down to "embrace" his children. Her stomach turned, and for a moment she thought she might be sick. *This isn't real...what's he doing here?*

"I've been working very hard," he said to them.

"Mommy's really sick," Laura said. "Have you seen her?"

Alex nodded. "But Mommy's been *really bad* —"

"Alex!" Kate gasped. "What are you doing?"

Alex stood up and scowled at his sister, "Giving them a little of the truth —"

"Mommy's been bad?" A.J. questioned.

Kate reached for the twins' hands and pulled them away from Alex. "You get out of here, Alex, and don't you *ever* come back." She looked down at the twins and said, "Your mommy has *not* been bad."

Alex jerked Kate's hands away from his children, and she abruptly slapped his face. Alex flinched and let go of their hands. Kate quickly grabbed them up again and headed for the steps.

"No, Auntie Kate," A.J. pleaded. "Let us see Daddy."

"No!" Kate scolded as she hustled them to the house. The twins started to cry, and Kate shook her head.

"Kate, what do you think you're doing?" Alex snarled as he started for her.

The front door burst open and Tara and Ellie, along with his very tall and well-built nephew, Angelo, stepped onto the porch.

"Get out of here, Alex!" Tara shoved him away from the children.

"You can't stop me from seeing my children!" he stormed.

"We *can!*" Tara shouted. She scowled into Alex's eyes, "Now leave this place and do not *ever* return, or we shall teach you a lesson you will not soon forget!"

Kate pushed the twins into the house and turned to face her brother. "I *hope* you don't want this to get physical, Alex," she warned, "because there are four of us and only one of you."

Alex frowned. "So that's what this has come to? You'd attack me in order to defend and protect what their mother has done?"

"She hasn't done anything wrong, Alex," Ellie said. "You have to get this out of your head. You're making a big mistake."

Alex shook his head. "I don't believe you people." He shook his head again. "I guess we'll just have to see what the court has to say about this."

"Don't bet on having too many friends left out there, Alex," Ellie spouted. "You've alienated every colleague you've ever had."

"Whatever," Alex muttered as he turned to go. "We'll see." And he stormed away.

The ladies and Angelo watched him get into his car and screech out of the driveway. They breathed a sigh of relief.

*****

Noah's new attorney, Dennis Marx, was partnered with a woman named Jacqueline Holliday Patterson. She was touted to be the best family law attorney in

South Dakota. She had never lost a divorce or custody battle, and Mr. Marx referred both Tillie and Noah to her. She was eager to take on the pompous attorney general and make mush out of his allegations, until she met with Tillie.

Ms. Patterson was a very tall and beautiful woman, with blond hair and extraordinary green eyes. She wore a smile and laughed easily, which made Tillie more comfortable during the interview. Ms. Patterson was thrilled to meet Senator Caselli, even though she was a staunch member of the Liberal Party.

Ms. Patterson was taken aback when she came to the hospital that day, finding the young lady propped up in her bed, wearing a white turban, and unable to move her arms. Even in her experience, she had not seen such cruelty dealt during divorce proceedings, and it was all she could do to maintain her composure. It was unbelievable that he'd actually served her in her hospital bed. He'd pay *dearly* for this, and Jacqueline would make sure of that.

Before the meeting began, Tillie demanded that everyone leave the two of them alone. Her family and Noah left the room and closed the door behind them.

"Now," Jacqueline said as she glanced at her notes, "he says he'll let you keep the house, but he wants half of his equity in it. He wants all of the wedding pictures, and he wants the kids six months out of the year. He's doing that so it will diminish your child support, but I'll get you an enormous amount of alimony. Then, he goes on to say that you've never been gainfully employed —"

"What does that mean?"

"It means you've never had a job."

"Oh." Tillie nodded.

"He has also dispatched a letter to me," Jacqueline continued, "requesting that you change your surname back to 'Caselli'. He stated in that letter that he will not be paying your household bills anymore, such as utilities, groceries, etcetera. Those bills will be forwarded to your home address instead of to his accountant's office." Jacqueline stopped there and took a deep breath. "He can't possibly be awarded any of this. No judge in his right mind would allow any of this. He must be trying to start a fight."

"It's okay," Tillie said with a sigh. "Just give him whatever he wants."

Jacqueline hesitated and looked at Tillie. "How will you *pay* for half of the equity in your home? And what about your utilities and groceries?"

"I have an inheritance from my Uncle Angelo," Tillie answered. "I've *never* touched it. My brother Marquette has managed it for years, and he says I'm loaded."

"Does Alex know about it?"

"He should. He's known me since the day I was born."

"He doesn't mention it," Jacqueline observed as she quickly paged through the complaint again.

"Maybe he forgot about it," Tillie said. She took a deep breath, "Ms. Patterson —"

"Call me Jacq. Everybody calls me Jacq."

"Jacq," Tillie continued with a faint smile, "this is what I want you to do. Give him everything that he wants."

"But he's a wealthy man. You could stand to gain quite a bit if you fought this thing. You could collect alimony instead of having to spend your inheritance."

"I don't want to fight him." Tillie's eyes glistened with tears.

"But why not? His accusations are *preposterous*! And once this goes before that conservative ol' boy, Judge Taggert, he'll clean his clock. Nobody does this to their wife of ten years when she's down and out in a hospital bed."

Tillie smiled, but her tears rolled out onto her face. "I remember when things were *really great* with Alex, and I remember when he loved me."

Jacqueline was without words. She was rarely moved to emotion, even during a divorce, but *this divorce* was suddenly different. She sat quietly for a few minutes, and then she asked in a very soft and cautious voice, "Do you *want* this divorce?"

"No," Tillie cried. "I just want him to come home and be with me and the kids."

Jacqueline nodded and swallowed hard. "What about this Noah character?"

More tears rolled from her eyes. "You know, Jacq, Noah's become my best friend. But..." She paused to take a deep breath. "I have prayed and prayed, and I *can't* be with Noah."

"But he's crazy about you, and once you're divorced —"

"Once I'm divorced, I can never marry again. Alex didn't leave me for another woman...and in my neck of the woods remarriage at this point becomes adultery."

Jacqueline gasped. "Oh, Tillie, people remarry every day."

"I know. But that's not for me, and it's not for Noah either. I made vows to a holy God, and a simple divorce can't change that. I don't believe that way. I've already sinned enough the way it is. I don't need to go looking for more."

Jacqueline thought she might fall off of her chair. She took a deep breath and steadied herself before she asked the next question. "Do you *love* Alex?"

Tillie slowly nodded her head, causing more tears to fall. "We had a lot of good years — *great* years, in fact. It was just this last year — after the election — that things went to pieces on us. I know that if he'd get down off his high horse and come home we could work this out."

"I see," Jacqueline nodded with a sigh. "Well, what do you want me to do?"

"Give him *everything* he wants. Then ask him how much to settle the other lawsuit. Ask Marquette how much I've got in my inheritance, but don't tell him what I'm planning. He's got a little bit of a temper, and he'll never understand."

Jacqueline sighed and reluctantly agreed. The professional, driven part of her wanted to walk away, with her perfect win record intact, and tell Tillie to have someone else take the case. However, there was a strange part inside of her that couldn't find the words to refuse Tillie. Jacqueline's win record would soon be marred with her first deliberate settlement, and she was going to just let it happen.

Chapter 22

Alex rounded the corner on his way to his office in the capitol. He glanced down at his watch for a second and bumped into someone.

"Excuse me." He didn't even look at the person he'd jarred but attempted to continue on his way. To his surprise, someone with a grip of steel grabbed his arm and wheeled him around. He was staring into the angry eyes of his older brother.

Alex frowned and jerked his arm from Sam's grasp. "What are you doing here?"

Sam shoved Alex and scowled into his eyes. "Kate called."

Alex let some breath out. "So, what do you want, Sam?"

"You're actually going to divorce her? After all she's been through?"

"Well I'm not staying married to the little tramp —"

Sam slapped Alex's face.

Alex stood still and looked at his brother. "Listen, Sam, I don't want to get into it with you here. And if you don't walk away right now I'll call security and have you arrested. Do you understand me?"

Sam nodded. "Yeah, I understand. And I hope you go straight to hell for what you're doing."

Alex shook his head and walked away. *They're all wrong about this. Why can't they see the truth?*

*****

Tillie was hooked on an afternoon soap opera — the really good one that came on just after lunch. Her brothers and Papa hated it and always left at that time. But Rosa thought it was somewhat interesting, and she and Tillie watched the program together every day.

"That Erica is really a devil," Rosa commented when the program went to commercial.

Tillie sighed. "Hopefully she'll get Christopher back...even though that Fredrick guy fathered the baby."

"Well, it was only an accident," Rosa excused.

Tillie giggled. "How does someone *accidentally* get into a predicament like that?"

Rosa shrugged. "Apparently it happens all of the time."

Tillie nodded and looked at her mother. "Ma`ma, I need to ask you for a favor."

"Anything, Angel."

"Alex wants our wedding photos back."

"He what?"

Tillie nodded. "They're in a white, lacey album on the top shelf of the closet in my studio. Will you please send them to him?"

Rosa's mouth hung open in surprise.

"It's okay, Ma`ma. He must want them for a reason, so I'd better send them to him. Maybe he'll look at them and remember the good ol' days."

Rosa sat up straight. "But I don't want him to remember *the good ol' days*. I want him to forget about you and the twins so that...so that...."

"So that Noah and I can start over?"

Rosa guiltily nodded her head. "Please do not tell your Papa on me." She couldn't help the change in her beliefs. She'd watched Noah look adoringly on Tillie for weeks now — when her own husband hadn't even been able to find the time for a phone call.

"Ma`ma, you know that's not how you raised me. I can't just start over with Noah now. He'd never go for it anyway."

"But he *loves* you, my Angel."

Tillie's eyes glistened with tears. "But it would be all screwed up, and he knows that. I have children with Alex. The kids belong with *him*, not Noah."

Rosa sat very still, contemplating her daughter's words. She finally whispered, "I will do what you ask."

"Thank you, Ma`ma."

*****

"Listen, I know how you're feeling, but *please* consider Angel's feelings in this matter." Jacqueline attempted to calm Noah down as he stormed around her office.

"I don't want to offer to settle! I want to sue him to kingdom come!" Noah growled. "I can't believe she just wants to settle this!"

"I'd love to beat the daylights out of him in front of the court, and I *know* I could," Jacqueline said as she narrowed her eyes, "but Angel is really struggling with this. She doesn't believe in divorce, Noah."

Noah threw his arms into the air and shouted, "I *know that!* Why do you think he served her with the papers in the first place?!"

Jacqueline looked confused.

"So that she *couldn't* marry me!" he said as he thumped his hand against his chest. "He wanted to make sure she *can't* marry me if something happens to him! She was raised a whole lot differently than the rest of the world, and he knows that!"

Jacqueline raised one eyebrow as she remembered Tillie's words...*remarriage at this point becomes adultery.* "Now I really hate him," she murmured.

Noah nodded. "He's been a jerk to her for ten years —"

"But she said only these last few months, after the election, were bad. Is there more?"

"Back when she had the twins, he was going through one of these political episodes, except he wasn't so important. He didn't even make it home for their birth, and she nearly died." Noah shook his head and threw his arms into the air again. "But I guess she was so young *she didn't even notice!*"

Jacqueline smiled at the handsome man who'd charged around her office for the last thirty minutes. "You've been hanging out with those Italians way too much. You're starting to act like one."

Noah rolled his eyes and looked away.

Jacqueline sighed. "Listen, Noah, I can't imagine what you're going through. She's a lovely lady, and she deserves so much more. But the two of you believe what you believe, and no lawsuit will ever change that."

Noah swallowed and looked at Jacqueline. "Are you a Christian, Jacq?"

She shook her head. "And I don't understand the way you people think, *but* what I do understand is that those of you who are the *real deal* love and respect your God's ways and each other very much. I don't believe that you really want this fight with Alex either. You're just very hurt and angry right now."

Noah let out a deep breath. "Okay. Offer to settle."

*****

Alex received the wedding photos from Rosa, Jacqueline's answers to his complaints, and the offers of settlement. *Why are they doing this? They've hired themselves the best family lawyer in the state of South Dakota. This has got to be her first settlement.*

The truth was Alex had already planned his appeal to the Supreme Court, because he knew once it got in front of Judge Taggert, he'd lose his shirt and *have* to appeal. He had just filed the lawsuits to hurt them as much as they had hurt him, and he had planned a long, drawn-out punishment. Of course now they were submitting to whatever he wanted, and it perplexed him to no end.

It was odd, too, that his father hadn't shown up or called to give him grief about what he'd done, and that befuddled him as well. Even Kate hadn't so much as called to scream, nor had he heard from his mother. *They've probably all thrown in with the adulterers, and this is just an elaborate trick to get me out of the picture and have Tillie and Noah married as soon as possible. Apparently she doesn't care about the adultery after all...I suspected that she probably didn't.*

Alex decided to think on their offers, and he put them in a neat stack on the corner of his desk in Pierre. *I'll let them wonder for a while.*

*****

"How is Angel's rehab coming along?" Ben asked Noah one day late in July. They were going over equipment orders and materials on a job site in the small town of Hermosa.

"The same," Noah answered. "And this lawsuit with her husband is really bringing her down. She doesn't even try anymore."

Ben took a deep breath. "You know, Noah, my stepmother took a terrible fall down the stairs some years ago. She was hurt far worse than Angel. In fact, she is still in a wheelchair. But she had the same problems with coordination like what you describe with Angel, and my sister brought her a puppy."

"A puppy?"

Ben nodded. "My sister read somewhere that animals can sometimes help during rehab. Her retriever just had puppies. Perhaps you should take her one. See if it helps."

Noah looked thoughtful for a moment. "Well, it certainly couldn't hurt, and my boys really miss Melinda's dog. I suppose I could get a puppy. I'd have to ask her family and her doctor first. When can I pick it up?"

Ben nervously swallowed. "Oh, I can bring them in, and you can choose one. My sister is very shy."

"Okay," Noah agreed, not noticing the slight change in Ben's demeanor. "I'll talk to Angel's parents this afternoon and see what they say. They'll probably have to check with the doc first."

Guiseppi and Rosa were willing to try anything. Tillie's condition had deteriorated as she spiraled into a deep depression and lost weight. She didn't smile at Noah anymore and was uninterested in the report the secretary of defense had written especially for her review. She didn't ask to see her children as much as she had, and she slept a lot of her days away. Her doctors were considering moving her to a rehabilitation center — a nursing home.

Guiseppi called Dr. Mills and asked if Tillie could be taken outside for a short time, securely fastened in a wheelchair. He told him of Noah's idea to bring all of her nieces and nephews, her own children, and his, along with a box of puppies. Dr. Mills agreed with reluctance and placed conditions on the plan. The trip to the outdoors would be closely monitored by a nurse, and should Tillie display any signs of confusion, she would be immediately taken back to her room. They could take her no farther than the green lawn just outside of the hospital and would have to cooperate with the nurse if he or she felt that Tillie needed to be returned to her room.

Guiseppi agreed and relayed the message to Noah, who called Ben and told him to pick up the puppies and meet him at the hospital. Tillie's brothers collected all of the children and their wives and prayed. Their Angel was wasting away before their very eyes, and perhaps Ben Simmons' idea would somehow bring her back.

Rosa was concerned about how comfortable Tillie would be in the flimsy hospital gown when they took her outside, so she had Tara drive her to the Rushmore Mall, where she found a soft, pink jogging suit. On their way out of the mall, Tara spied a matching scarf. They purchased it, along with a lightweight t-shirt, in case the weather became warm.

Tillie hesitated when her mother woke her later that afternoon, presented her with the new clothing, and told her they had a surprise waiting for her. A nurse helped her dress and an orderly was called to lift her into the wheelchair, where she was securely fastened at the waist and around her legs. Her hands rested limply in her lap.

"There is nothing on my feet," Tillie observed as she saw her bare toes poking out in front of them. "And I haven't had the chance to paint my toes. I look *stupid.*"

"You do not look stupid," Tara admonished with a smile. "You look like an elegant, pink gypsy."

"Humph." Tillie watched them push her closer and closer to the doors. "Where are we going?"

"I told you," Rosa replied, "we are going outside."

"Why?"

"To see if it improves your mood."

"My mood is improved," Tillie argued. "I feel fine. I want to go back."

The nurse pushing the wheelchair slowed down and paused just short of reaching the doors. He looked at Rosa and Tara.

"Please," Rosa begged, putting her hand on his arm. "Let us at least give it a try."

"Please, Angel," Tara pleaded as she knelt before the wheelchair and looked into Tillie's eyes. "Your children are already there waiting for you, and they haven't seen you in so long. All of our nieces and nephews and your brothers...and *Noah* has a special surprise for you."

Tillie looked back at Tara. "Noah has a surprise for me?"

Tara smiled excitedly. "He is *so* anxious to see you this day, Angel."

Tillie seemed to think it over and bit her lip. "Well, okay. But just for a minute."

Rosa and Tara sighed with relief, and the nurse continued on his journey. They opened the doors, and he pushed her through.

Tillie squinted in the sunlight as the nurse pushed her chair along the sidewalk, feeling the wonderful heat of the day soak into her bare toes. She laid her head back, closed her eyes, and inhaled deeply, surprised at how good the sun felt on her face. The song of birds filled the air, and Tillie heard the wind blowing through nearby trees. She hadn't heard those sounds in so long she had forgotten about them.

"Here we are," Rosa announced.

Tillie opened her eyes as the wheelchair came to a stop at the edge of the grass. She saw everyone waiting just a short distance into the lawn. They sat quietly on blankets spread out on the grass. She recognized all of her brothers and their wives, her nieces and nephews, her parents, and her own children. Noah and his boys were seated beside a stranger with a big, brown box. When they all smiled and waved at her, Tillie had the compulsion to wave back, but she knew she couldn't. So she just smiled at them.

"Can I go over there?" Tillie asked.

"It'll be a little bumpy," the nurse answered. "Are you up for it?"

"Yes," Tillie answered with a deep breath.

"Okay, here we go." The nurse carefully pushed her through the grass.

A.J. and Laura got to their feet, and Guiseppi whispered, "Remember not to surprise her or rush at her." They nodded, and everyone else stayed seated on the blankets and greeted her with smiles and waves.

"Hi, Mommy," the twins said in unison, and then they giggled at each other. Tillie smiled, too, as she looked from one to the other.

"Hi, guys. What are you doing today?"

"Mr. Hansen has a surprise," A.J. said excitedly.

Laura clapped her little hands together and giggled, "I can't wait for you to see them."

Tillie looked at the box and the stranger near Noah, and she couldn't help but wonder what was happening. She was uncertain whether or not she was supposed to know the stranger as well, and had simply forgotten him.

The wheelchair came to a stop at the edge of the blankets, and Tillie thought she heard the soft whine of new puppies.

"Hi, Angel," Noah said as he slowly got to his feet and went to where she had come to a stop. He knelt in front of her and smiled into her eyes, "Your new scarf looks *great*."

"Thanks." She smiled in return at his dancing expression, feeling unusual joy in her heart. *My best friend in all the world...what would I do without you?*

"I got something for you to look at," he said with a grin, and Tillie heard everyone around them chuckle. Her eyes went to the box and the stranger beside it.

"Do I know him?" she whispered.

Noah shook his head. "No. He's a friend of mine. He's got Melinda's old job."

"Oh, Melinda." Tillie smiled and wrinkled her nose. She looked at her brother, Petrice, who was seated beside her. His expression was anxious, and she wondered why.

"Can I sit by Patty?"

"You *are* sitting beside me, Angel."

"No, I want to sit on the ground with everyone else."

They looked to the nurse behind her, and he slowly began to shake his head. "I don't know. Doc didn't say she could do that."

"Please," Tillie begged.

"I will hang onto her," Petrice offered.

The nurse took a deep breath, seemed to think it over, and answered, "Okay. Tell you what, I'll lift her out, but her back has to be braced by something." He looked at Petrice. "You'll have to hold her against yourself so she doesn't get sick."

Petrice nodded. Noah and the twins moved out of the way while the nurse unbuckled the restraints. He bent over to scoop her into his arms. "Are you sure about this?"

"Yes."

The nurse lifted her out of the chair and eased her into Petrice's arms, being sure that her back was braced up against his chest. "Put both of your arms around her," he instructed as he tucked Tillie's left arm under Petrice's. "That one's the worst. Don't let go of it." Then the nurse sat down beside Petrice and looked at Tillie. "You doing okay?"

"Yes."

"Are you sick?"

"No," she answered, and the crowd around her sighed with relief.

Noah went to the box, followed closely by Laura and A.J., and Tillie was *certain* she heard the whine of new puppies. Her nieces and nephews and Noah's sons seemed hardly able to contain their delight. Laura giggled almost out of control as she took a seat as close to her mother as she could. Tillie smiled at her daughter as a surge of anticipation overcame her.

Noah laughed as he sat the box down beside Tillie and drew out a cream-colored puppy. The puppy squealed and whined for all that it was worth, and Tillie saw his tiny tail wag frantically behind him. She gasped, "He's so cute!"

Noah placed him on the ground, while several little hands reached for him. Then he liberated another one. Tillie gasped again. It felt strangely secure to have all of these people suddenly crowded around her, and she thought perhaps they would let her go home after this.

"How many do you have?" she asked.

"Eight," Noah answered as he continued to set the staggering puppies on the ground as close to her as he dared. "Ben's sister has a golden retriever. They're her puppies."

"Oh," Tillie replied, smiling as she looked at the precious, stumbling little puppies. "How old are they?"

"Six weeks," Noah answered, "and just about ready to find families. I think me and my boys are gonna take one."

The puppies attempted to make their way around, while children and adults carefully reached out for a touch. The puppies tumbled over each other and the scene before her was so comical that she laughed. She wanted to touch one but knew that her arm would go flying, and she did not want to frighten her children. They were having so much fun with the puppies; her erratic movements would certainly spoil the moment.

As if he had read her thoughts, Noah picked up a puppy and held him close enough to Tillie so that she could look into his little, shiny eyes, and she smiled. The puppy cried and cried and licked Tillie's face. She laughed out loud.

"Oh, you're just the cutest little thing!" she giggled.

The little guy wiggled unexpectedly and Noah dropped him. He landed right in Tillie's lap. She laughed again and impulsively reached for the puppy.

Noah and Petrice held their breath, wondering what would happen as they watched Tillie's right arm lumber toward the puppy in her lap. Her pretty hand clumsily came to rest on top of the puppy's head, and her fingers awkwardly tried to move in a petting motion.

"Help me, Noah," she whispered.

Noah reached for her hand and steadied it on top of the puppy's small body, while he wriggled and squirmed beneath it. Tillie laughed again as she felt the warmth of Noah's calloused, but loving hand on top of her own and the soft sensation of the puppy's velvety fur in her palm.

"He won't hold still," she laughed. She looked for a moment at Noah and then back at the squirming bundle in her lap. Petrice smiled as he held his sister and gave her a soft kiss on top of her pink scarf.

Noah tried to fight his tears of thankfulness. She was actually making an effort, and he praised God. He looked at Ben, who was smiling with satisfaction.

"Thanks, Ben," he said as the tears fell from his eyes.

"No problem."

Tillie looked at Noah and saw his tears, and she smiled into his eyes. "Don't cry. It's gonna be okay. You said so yourself."

Noah swallowed and nodded. "It's gonna be okay."

*****

James Martin had just read all of the grisly details of the attorney general's pending divorce in the Friday edition of the *Sioux Falls Argus Leader*. He was outraged. First of all, at what his youngest son had done and, secondly, because his elder son had kept it from him. The article was quite comprehensive and included the callous way in which the attorney general served his wife with two separate actions while she lay immobile in her hospital bed. It also went on to state that Mrs. Martin could not walk or feed herself and that Senator Caselli had recently announced he was considering resigning his Senate seat. James frowned and shook his head, tucked the paper under his arm, and shuffled into Sam's office, standing before his desk.

"Hi, Dad," Sam said as he glanced at his father and back down at the file before him.

James rolled up the paper and smacked Sam on the side of the head with it. "Why didn't you tell me the *rest of the story?*"

Sam looked up in stunned surprise, and James threw the paper on his desk.

Sam looked at the paper and was shocked to see that Alex and Tillie's pending divorce had actually made the front page. He looked guiltily at his father. "I'm sorry, Dad. We thought he'd snap out of it and never go through with it. We didn't want to upset you and Mom."

"Upset me?" James shouted. "Of course I'm gonna be upset, but that's no reason to keep me in the dark —" James suddenly grabbed his chest and reeled backwards.

Sam jumped to his feet and caught his father before he fell to the floor. "Somebody call an ambulance!" he yelled into the hall.

"Keep me alive until he gets here," James demanded in a horse whisper. "I have to talk to him."

224

Chapter 23

Alex was in the governor's office when the call came in. Upon hearing that his father had suffered a massive heart attack, the governor put Alex on his own private charter. He arrived at Sioux Valley Hospital in Sioux Falls in less than an hour.

Vincenzo, Kate, and their two children were whisked to Sioux Falls aboard Petrice's jet. No one told Tillie that Alex's father had taken ill, because they were afraid it would upset her — and her physical therapy had *finally* started to come along. Vincenzo's family had left with Petrice, and they decided to wait to see how James was before they gave her the news.

Sam and Becky-Lynn were in the ICU waiting room with Vincenzo, Kate, Alyssa, and Angelo when Alex arrived. All of them gave him a cold stare.

"How's Dad?" he asked.

"He's in tough shape, Alex," Sam answered with a scowl, and he shoved Alex. "He was reading all about your divorce on the front page of the *Argus* when he had a heart attack. Hope you're finally happy."

"What are you talking about?"

Kate flew into her brother's face and cried, "You *idiot!* We tried to keep it from Dad and Mom, but somebody leaked the story to the paper!"

Alex sighed tiredly at his sister's ranting and rolled his eyes. "Where's Mom?"

"She's with Dad," Sam answered. "And he said he wanted to see you as soon as you got here. Come on, AG, I'll show you where they've got him."

Alex followed Sam to their father's room. He saw his mother from the doorway, holding his father's hand. She looked up at Alex with sorrow in her eyes. He hadn't seen his mother since the day of the election last November, and he was surprised at the marked change in her expression when she looked at him. He hesitated in the doorway until Sam gave him a push, and he stumbled inside. James eyes turned toward the commotion, and one arm reached out for Alex.

"Come here, son."

The last time Alex saw his father, they'd argued profusely about Alex's abandonment of his family. Alex had become extremely angry and asked his father to leave, and there had been no words between them since.

Alex went to his father's side, took hold of the hand he offered, and looked into his eyes. James' face was a strange gray color, and his black eyes were only half open. A tube beneath his nose gave him oxygen, and his lower lip trembled as he spoke to his son.

"What are you doing, Alex?" Tears rolled out of James' eyes. In his entire life, Alex had never seen his father cry.

"It's just over between Tillie and me," Alex answered. "Dad, she has someone else now."

"There's never been anyone else for Tillie," James retorted feebly. "You're the one who left home. I know all about it now, Alex. The apartment in Pierre, how you ditched her on your anniversary. I know *everything*. You're the one who messed this up, son, and now it's time to take responsibility and put it back together."

"I just *can't*." Alex's eyes filled with tears as he looked at his father.

"Why not?"

"She loves him."

"She loves *you*, Alex. I watched her promise God that she would love you forever, and you know about those Caselli promises, Alex. They mean what they say." James took a ragged breath. "Whatever led you to believe that she was having an affair with Noah Hansen?"

"I walked in on Tillie and Noah at the church, and they were standing *so close* together."

"And you *still* stayed away? You actually suspected something was going on and you *still stayed away?*"

Alex shook his head and looked at the floor. "I actually sent him to pick her up once, when I decided to do a deal with McDarren. It was her birthday and I was supposed to have dinner with her. I knew she was alone at the restaurant, but I sent him anyway."

James laughed weakly. "Do you know what that tells me, Alex?"

"No, sir."

"That tells me that you *never* thought anything was going on in the first place, and that you trusted your wife enough to know she would never do anything so horrible to you. The only reason you're pushing for a divorce is because you're too big of a chicken to go back and tell her you made a mistake by staying away. You know what the Casellis believe about divorce, so by doing *that* to her, you want to make sure she's *never* able to be with Noah. How close am I, Alex?"

Alex looked at his father and tears of shame fell from his black eyes as he confessed, "I just loved the work so much. I can't begin to tell you what it feels like to walk into a courtroom and know that nobody in there, including the judge, knows as much as you do about the law at hand."

"Brother," James muttered, "you fell into Satan's oldest trap...A man's pride shall bring him low: but honor shall uphold the humble in spirit."

Alex recognized the Proverb that his grandfather had quoted for years, and the truth of it suddenly rang loudly in his ears. His pride had destroyed his marriage, the relationships within his family, and his dearest friendship. With the details of what he had done on the front page of every South Dakota newspaper, it would soon destroy his reputation as well.

"I'm sorry, Dad," Alex wept, "I don't know what happened —"

"Oh, malarkey," James interrupted with a soft scowl. "You know darn good and well what happened. You chose *yourself* over Tillie and the kids. That was your *first* sin, but you made it worse by trying to concoct a story in your mind to justify staying away and not having to face the reality of what you'd done. Remember when she had the babies, Alex? She almost *died* giving us those babies, and you weren't there. She was so loving and forgiving, like it didn't even happen. It amazes me still how she picked up and went on with your marriage, like you had merely forgotten to pay the water bill or some other trifle. She must really love you."

Alex's tears flowed uncontrollably. He remembered feeling guilty over missing the birth of his children, but even that offense didn't compare with the weight that he was feeling on his shoulders now.

226

James took a labored breath and confronted his son. "Alex, I've watched you *pretend* our Christianity for years. Sure, you knew the Scriptures better than anyone else, and you followed the rules better than anyone else, but it didn't make you one of us — and it didn't make you one of the Lord's. It's your rotten fruit that gives you away."

Alex sobbed as he realized the dark reality of his inner character. He fell to his knees beside James' bed. "I'm so sorry, Dad," he cried as he held onto his father's hand and bowed his head in shame.

"Make it better, Alex."

"How?"

"You take your sins and lay them at the foot of the cross and ask Jesus to forgive you."

"He *can't* forgive me for this. I'm going to hell."

James sputtered a small laugh. "Jesus died for you, Alex. He took beatings and nails for you. Do you think your sin is bigger than any of ours? Certainly our Savior will forgive you for this." He squeezed his hardest on Alex's hand. "Come on, son, I want to see you in heaven some day. Don't let me go thinking I raised a blackguard."

Alex sobbed and nodded his head. Then he bowed to pray with his father.

Vincenzo and Kate were just on their way into James' room when Frances stopped them in the doorway.

"Not now," she whispered.

Vincenzo and Kate looked into James' room and saw Alex kneeling by the bed, praying with his father.

"Today my son was finally saved," Frances wept.

*****

Tillie was standing in the rehab unit of Rapid City Regional Hospital, while Noah and their children cheered her along. Her left arm was tightly bound to the side of her body so it wouldn't throw her off balance. She attempted to hobble along by using her right arm to support the three-footed cane in front of her. Her steps were crooked because her left toes turned in at a right angle. Physical therapists on either side promised to catch her if she fell. She had been up for a full five minutes and hadn't experienced the dizziness or queasiness that usually came with this activity.

Dr. Mills happened to walk in during the episode and smiled with surprise. Tillie had been in his care for ten weeks, and the nurses had reported that her mood had significantly lifted since the day with the puppies. She looked forward to every evening — after supper or after a baseball game — when Noah brought their children and his boys' new puppy, Vanilla, to the hospital for a short visit. When regular rehab sessions were scheduled after the lunch hour, Noah made sure their children were there to support her.

The coordination in her right arm had improved to the point that she could feed herself. It was sloppy and shaky, but it emboldened her to try other movements. The nurses credited her dramatic improvement to Vanilla and the loving kindness of Noah and the children.

Tillie was still very thin, and her muscles had atrophied a great deal. However, Dr. Mills was encouraged by her stamina. She worked very hard, and he didn't think it would be much longer before she started making even further strides in her recovery.

He stopped just short of where Tillie paused. She breathed heavily and leaned on her cane, but she raised her head to look at him with a smile.

"My goodness," he said. "They told me you were down here."

Tillie took several deep breaths, and one of the therapists pushed her wheelchair underneath her and helped her to sit down.

"When can I go home?" she asked excitedly.

Noah and their children held their breath. It was a question she asked every day.

"Well," Dr. Mills took a deep breath and knelt down in front of her. "What do you think, Tillie? Can I trust you to work *hard* when you go home? How do I know you won't slip back into depression and forget about working on all of these things."

"I promise," Tillie replied with a smile, and her pretty black eyes sparkled. "I'll work as hard as I can. Papa and Ma`ma will stay with me, and Marquette and Tara will be there to help tote me around. I *promise* not miss any of my appointments."

"Hmmm," Dr. Mills mused. "Well, actually, Dr. Parsons and I have already written your discharge."

Tillie softly squealed, and Noah and their children clapped and rushed to where she sat. A.J. and Laura threw their arms around their mother to cover her face with kisses, and Tillie laughed. "When?"

"I called your parents, and they're on their way," Dr. Mills answered. "We're sure gonna miss ya up here."

Guiseppi and Rosa rolled her into the home she'd left on that fateful night last June. Noah had built a ramp to the front door for her wheelchair, and another one off the sunroom so that she could get outside if she wanted.

Tillie was so happy to be home she couldn't stop smiling, but she noticed Vincenzo and Kate's absence. She wondered where their children were. Marquette and Tara were there, as were Ellie and her children, but Petrice was missing as well.

"Where is everybody?" she asked as they wheeled her into the sunroom where Ellie had her favorite raspberry lemonade. She saw the pink liquid on the table and gasped. "Oh, who made the lemonade?"

"I did," Ellie answered, bending over Tillie and kissing the top of her head. "And we are so happy to see you, Angel."

Guiseppi sighed. "We must visit, my Angel." He placed a straw into a tall glass and held it before her.

"Thanks, Papa." She took a sip and looked into her father's troubled eyes. "What's the matter, Papa?"

"It is a very difficult thing that we must tell you, but it cannot be helped. My Angel...Alex has lost his father this day."

"James?"

Guiseppi nodded.

"What happened, Papa?"

"He was eighty-eight, my Angel, and he was very sick for these past few weeks. They will bury him on Monday, and Petrice will come for Marquette and Ma`ma and I, so that we may attend the funeral. We must pay our last respects to the man who brought us to America, my Angel. Ellie and Tara will stay with you, and we will be back that same afternoon."

"Oh, poor Alex..." Tillie's eyes filled with tears. "He must feel so terrible." She looked at Marquette. "Just think, Marquette...what if something happened to Papa? Imagine how sad we would be."

Marquette wore a peculiar expression. "He must feel dreadful, Angel."

"What does that mean, Mommy?" A.J. chirped, and Tillie turned her head to see that her son was next to her. His sister was next to him, but she didn't seem too worried about what was transpiring.

"It means that Granddad Martin has gone to Heaven," Tillie explained.

"To be with Jesus?" A.J. attempted to clarify.

Tillie nodded and smiled at her children. "He was a very good man, and he loved Jesus very much."

"And did he ask Jesus to forgive his sins?" Laura questioned.

"Oh, yes, many years ago," Tillie answered. "Jesus has been preparing a place in heaven for Granddad Martin for many years."

*****

Pastor Andy Engleson officiated the funeral for the father of his childhood friend. His own parents stood with Frances Martin, and Guiseppi, Rosa, and their children stood just behind them. No one comforted Alex or even reached out to say they were sorry. He was on his own, and that made Andy's heart ache for his oldest friend.

Andy had read the story in the headlines of the *Argus Leader*, and was astounded. Obviously Alex had changed a great deal in the year he'd been away from Sioux Falls. He'd changed so much that even his own family did not want him. In addition, it appeared he'd severed his ties with the Casellis as well, and Andy could hardly believe that. The Casellis were the most caring and forgiving people in the world, and they had loved Alex from the moment they met him.

In the fellowship hall just across the street from Christ The King, the Ladies' Altar Society put on a reception for the family and friends of James Martin, Jr., which was held shortly after the interment. Everyone in Sioux Falls had seen the article about the attorney general's divorce and additional lawsuits, and very few people approached Alex to offer their condolences. He suffered alone, without even his own mother to help him through it. His sister and brother didn't so much as look at him.

Petrice, Vincenzo, and Marquette stood together at the reception, and they noticed that Alex was alone at the back of the hall, sipping a cup of coffee. "The poor devil," Vincenzo muttered. "How *alone* he must feel."

"It is a hell of his own making," Marquette snapped. "And I actually have to talk to him now." His brothers looked surprised, and Marquette sighed. "Angel has given me a letter to give to him." He rolled his eyes and shook his head. "She actually feels sorry for the blackguard."

Petrice nodded. "She is a good girl."

Alex watched Marquette with suspicion when he saw him approach. He supposed there would be a vicious altercation in a matter of moments.

"Hello, Alex," Marquette greeted with coldness. "I am very sorry for the loss of your father."

"Thank you, Marquette."

Marquette pulled the envelope from his inside breast pocket and handed it to Alex. "This is a note from Angel. It was written by me, but they are *her* words."

Alex took the envelope from Marquette's hand. "How is she?"

"She came home last Friday. There are still some problems that she has to work out. She still cannot write, and her left arm is completely useless. She can take a few steps with the cane, and Dr. Mills is very hopeful."

Alex sadly nodded. "How are the kids?"

"Fine," Marquette answered. "They will be missing their cousins when school begins again, but they will still have Noah's boys around to keep them company."

Alex looked like someone had hit him hard in the stomach, and he took a deep breath. "He's *still* coming around then?"

Marquette frowned. "What do you expect, Alex? He is in love with her. You have been gone for three months. None of us expect you to come back at this point, and Angel is attempting to go on with her life in the best way she can. He loves her children, and he brings a sweetness to her life that helps her cope. He has a devotion I have only seen between my own parents."

Alex was shocked at Marquette's words, trying to understand why a man would settle for less than everything. Why would Noah *simply settle* for a crippled friend, when he could have a young, vibrant wife?

"And something else you should know," Marquette added, "My Ma`ma has prayed for Noah since 1960, when your very own Uncle Mac told her about the suffering little boy who'd lost his parents. It was no accident the two of them met."

"Then why did Guiseppi allow me to marry her?"

"Because he believed you when you promised to love her for the rest of your life. He thought you were telling the truth when you promised to love her through everything, no matter what the trials." Marquette's eyes filled with tears. "Papa *loved* you, Alex, and he trusted you with his most treasured gift."

"I'm sorry, Marquette."

Marquette swallowed very hard and forced his tears away. "It is too late for that, Alex. What you have done to my sister and her children is truly unbelievable. I sincerely regret the day Papa gave her to you." With those final words, he turned and walked away.

Alex looked down at the letter, afraid to open it and read whatever words of anger and hurt might be written inside. She had only wanted him to come home, and he'd fought her every step of the way so he could make a name for himself. Well, he had made a name for himself, and it wasn't a very good one.

He tore open the envelope, pulled out the familiar pink stationary, and began to read Marquette's handwriting.

"Dear Alex, I am very sorry about the death of your father and regret that I cannot be there to pay my respects. He was a most kind and generous man, and he will be sadly missed.

"Rest assured, your father has gone Home to our Lord, and I rejoice for him. He was a fine man, and you should be proud of the life he led.

"Also know, Alex, that your father was very proud of you. While I know he did not say it to you nearly enough, it was there in his heart and in the reflection of his eyes when he looked at you. He wanted you with him always — that I am most sure of — and it was very hard for him to share you with the rest of the world. It was not that he disapproved of your political endeavors; it was just his own fears of having to watch you grow away from him. He loved you, Alex, only as a father could love a son, and he missed you when you went away.

"Take care of yourself, Alex, and try to mend whatever you can between you and your mother so she can grieve this loss with all of her children, for she will need all of her children around her, holding her up and helping her through this time. Please do not deny her the comfort that only a child can bring.

"I realize this letter is probably not the time or the place, but I do not know when we will ever have the opportunity to see one another again. Please forgive me. I should not have kept Noah's identity a secret. I should have told you about him from the beginning of our courtship, and especially when I learned of your friendship with him. I am more grieved about these omissions than you could ever know.

"Please understand, Alex, I harbor no ill will toward you, and I will pray for your grieved heart to soon mend."

Alex's tears were flowing by the time he reached the end, and especially when he saw that Tillie had attempted to sign her own name at the bottom of the page. The letters were scratched out like a sloppy child had written them, without balance or measure, and his heart broke with what he had done to her. She had wanted nothing more than for him to come home and resume their marriage and the family life she loved.

In his soul, Alex *knew* that there was nothing going on with Noah. His father was right. He'd concocted that story within himself so he could justify staying away and working on his career. It was easier to believe that Tillie was fooling around with Noah than to have to admit to his own selfish and unrestrained passion for his work.

"Alex." Andy rested a friendly hand on Alex's shoulder.

"Hi, Andy." Alex looked into the eyes of his childhood friend.

Andy saw his tears and put his arms around Alex. No one else would do it, and Andy couldn't help but feel pity for Alex.

"I'm so sorry," Alex cried as he hung onto his friend. "Andy, I've really done a horrible thing."

"I know. Are you ready to talk about it?"

*****

Vincenzo called Tillie from Reata, and told her that he and Kate had decided to remain there as school would start very soon. He also said that Kate wanted to be closer to her mother during this time but that he would visit as soon as he could. Tillie understood and did not attempt to change his mind. She'd had them for the entire summer, and it was time they return to their own lives.

Petrice and Ellie made a similar announcement once Petrice returned to Rapid City with their parents and Marquette. However, Marquette and Tara committed themselves to stay indefinitely, as did Guiseppi and Rosa. They felt they were in positions that allowed them to remain to be of whatever help they could be to Angel. She still had a long road of rehabilitation before her, and they reasoned it would go easier for her to have some of her family with her during that time.

Tara and Rosa took care of Tillie's personal needs, such as helping her in the bathroom, bathing, and getting dressed. The stairs were always a concern, as Tillie refused to have a chairlift installed. She thought it would make her children worry. Instead, Marquette carried her downstairs every morning and back up again in the evenings when it was time for bed.

Tara took over the duties of housework, while Rosa maintained the cooking and the grocery shopping. Marquette paid the bills, and Guiseppi volunteered to maintain the yard around the house.

"I do not know how she did it all herself," Tara exclaimed one day after school had begun and everyone else had left them. She was on a step-stool, dusting the chandelier above the dining room table, while Rosa folded a load of clothes. Guiseppi and Marquette worked on the lawn together, and Noah had stopped by with Vanilla. They were in the backyard, where Noah had set Tillie in a lawn chair, and given her a ball to throw for the excited puppy.

Rosa laughed. "She was a little pistol, that is for certain."

She glanced out of the sunroom doors in time to see Tillie attempt to throw the ball. Her movements were clumsy and haphazard, and Noah had to hold her left arm still so she didn't jar herself out of the chair. Her hair had grown in a great deal by now, and short, thick ringlets covered her entire head like a fresh permanent. She still liked to wear the flashy scarves, but not completely covering her head as they once had. The late summer weather was still warm in the Black Hills, and Tillie was wearing a pair of bright blue shorts and a white T-shirt. Rosa could see the horrible, purple scar where they had repaired her left knee joint. It reminded Rosa of the other scars on Tillie's abdomen and mid-section. She had been quite taken aback the first time she helped Tillie change her clothes. The girl had been sliced to pieces.

Tara saw Rosa watching Tillie and got down off her stool to put a gentle arm over Rosa's shoulders. "She is doing so much better, Ma`ma." At that moment Tillie threw the ball again, and Vanilla scampered after it. Tara laughed. "See how far she threw it?"

Rosa wiped away some tears. "It is very hard to see her like this, knowing all that she was before."

"She is still all of those things." Tara smiled for Rosa's sake. "This is just a brief pause."

"And what of this thing with Noah?" Rosa whispered. "What will ever become of them now?"

Tara sighed and watched Noah smile into Tillie's eyes. "He *loves* her, Ma`ma, and she loves him. Them not being able to marry matters not. They will still share a loyal friendship that lasts into old age."

"Perhaps we should not have allowed him to risk his heart this way."

"Noah does not consider it a risk. I think he feels it his duty to do whatever he can —"

The garage door opened at that moment, and a very distressed Guiseppi stepped into the kitchen, followed by Marquette and...*Alex?* Rosa and Tara stared at the threesome, and their mouths fell open in surprise.

When Rosa had recovered her surprise she charged toward Alex, shaking her fist at him. "You must go! She is having a very good day, and I will *not* have it spoiled with one of your tantrums!"

Guiseppi reached for Rosa, took her into his arms, and held her close. "Rosa, my love, he only wants to ask her for forgiveness. Perhaps we could allow only that."

"Forgiveness!" Rosa gasped as she shot Alex a glare. "You would actually *expect forgiveness?!* After all that you have done?!"

"Rosa," Alex began, "I am so sorry. *Please*, believe me."

"No!" Rosa shouted. She shook her head back and forth and pointed her index finger at Alex. "You have proven yourself to be a blackguard and by yourself have chosen to end whatever relation we had with you! *You must go!*"

"Please, my Rosa," Guiseppi begged. "He should be allowed to at least ask for forgiveness."

"What if he upsets her?!" Rosa shouted. "She startles so easily, and things still confuse her." Tears dropped from her eyes. "You have not been here for her, and you do not know how she still suffers!"

Alex took a deep breath as he tried to find whatever words it would take to allow just this one last visit. He looked away from Rosa, and his eyes happened to glance through the kitchen window, where he saw Tillie and Noah in the backyard. Noah had put the puppy into her lap and tried to guide her convulsive left arm into a position over the little dog. The puppy suddenly licked her face, and Alex saw Tillie laugh and smile into Noah's eyes. His heart ached with a pain he'd never experienced in his life. Noah didn't care that she was *broken*, as Alex had so cruelly accused him of weeks ago. He truly loved her and just wanted her to *get better*.

Guiseppi saw Alex watching them, and he quietly commanded, "Leave me with my son-in-law for a few minutes. There are things I must tell him."

Rosa shook her head in protest, but Marquette reached for his mother and led her gently into the other room.

232

"Do not allow him to upset her," Rosa frantically insisted over her shoulder as she walked away with Marquette and Tara.

When they were alone together, Alex sighed and said, "Marquette told me that Rosa has prayed for Noah for nearly thirty years."

"My Rosa is a faithful woman."

"Does Tillie know about that?"

"No," Guiseppi answered. "I have been afraid to confuse her."

"Maybe you *should* have told her," Alex said as he watched Noah and Tillie from the kitchen window. "Maybe her life wouldn't be this big of a mess if she had married Noah instead of me."

"Most certainly not," Guiseppi agreed with a frown. "One thing I know for certain: the omission I made released a precious gift intended for someone else into your own arms, and I have watched you squander it *shamelessly*."

"I am so sorry, Guiseppi."

Guiseppi shook his head disgustedly. "You have broken every promise you ever made to me. You broke all of your promises to Angel, and worse yet, you broke your promise to God. I am trying to forgive you, Alex, and it makes me sick to know that my Angel has already released your responsibility. Even in her most desperate situation, she lives in more freedom than her ma`ma and I."

"Please allow me to ask her for forgiveness," Alex pleaded.

Guiseppi looked at the floor. He closed his eyes as he called upon the Lord's direction and felt his head begin to nod. He looked up at Alex. "I suppose, but you must not startle her or squabble with her at all. I will release my Marquette to *pound* you, Alex, if you make her cry."

"I won't," Alex promised.

With a heavy sigh, Guiseppi led Alex to the doors in the sunroom, where he stepped out onto the patio. Alex stepped out with him, and Tillie and Noah looked up with surprise.

"Alex," she said with a small smile, "what are you doing here?"

Noah said nothing at all. He just stayed beside Tillie.

"I was just wondering if we could talk," Alex said.

"That's what Jacq's for," Noah growled.

"Angel," Guiseppi began as he knelt before her chair and looked into her confused eyes, "I think you should listen to what he has to say." He paused and looked at Noah. "Please, Noah, do not be angry."

Noah clenched his teeth and scowled, "Don't be angry?"

"Please, Noah," Guiseppi whispered, "I promise to explain."

Noah shook his head as he reached for the weight to hold Tillie's left arm still, carefully placed it around her wrist, and laid her hand on her lap.

"Come, Noah." Guiseppi gently placed his hand on Noah's shoulder. "Let us leave them for a short time."

"I don't agree with this," Noah protested.

"Please, Noah." Guiseppi begged.

Noah swallowed hard and looked into Tillie's eyes. "You gonna be okay?"

Tillie nodded and smiled into his eyes.

Noah stood and leaned close enough to Alex to whisper a threat. "If you upset her, I'll make you sorry."

"I won't," Alex said.

Noah took Vanilla out of her lap, and he and Guiseppi left them alone. They stepped into the sunroom and closed the door, and Alex went to where Tillie sat. He knelt down on the ground in front of her, looked up at her, and faintly smiled. "Your hair is looking really good."

"Thanks." She smiled as she looked back at him, seeing an expression there she'd never seen before. "I'm really sorry about your dad."

Alex nodded. "Thank you for your note. I shared it with Mom and Sam and Kate."

"How are they?"

Alex shrugged. "Sad, but we'll be okay. It's just going to take some time, I guess."

Tillie looked curiously at her soon-to-be ex-husband. "Why are you here, Alex?"

Alex swallowed hard and put his hand gently on her knee. "I came to ask you for your forgiveness, Tillie. I'm so sorry for the things that I've done, and what's really important to me now is that you know how much I love you and that I never thought for one moment that you had an affair with Noah."

Tillie's mouth fell open in astonishment as she struggled to find the words to respond. She finally shook her head and whispered, "Then why...?"

"Because I wanted to do the attorney general's job better than anyone had ever done it, and I *did*. But it took more of me than what God wanted me to spare. The only way I could silence His voice was to bury myself in what *I* wanted."

"Didn't you want me and the kids anymore?"

"I don't know how to explain this so that you'll understand, but I really thought I could get a bunch of hard cases under my belt, and then the senate would just be an easy step after that. Everyone in the state would already know my name, and a campaign for the senate would be a cinch. That's how it started. As time went by, and I won more and more cases, I couldn't just walk away from it. When I would walk into a courtroom, it would be full of reporters and cameras, and the judge would even cringe because he knew I would slaughter my opponent."

Tillie listened to his unbelievable confession, and she slowly nodded her head. The confusion in her eyes was gone when she whispered, "Pride."

"Pride," he repeated. "And it destroyed us, and I'm sorrier than you can ever know."

Tillie bit her lip with a soft frown. "Alex, I don't know what to say. I guess you should know that the kids ask about you a lot. Maybe you should come by and see them sometimes. I haven't told them about the...." She couldn't even say the word.

"Tillie, I filed a motion to dismiss this morning."

"What's that?"

"It dismisses the action against you for divorce," Alex answered. "It also dismissed the action against you and Noah together. That way..." He paused and let out a breath, and Tillie saw tears in his eyes as he swallowed and began again. "That way, if something should ever happen to me, you'll be able to remarry." He looked into her surprised eyes and offered her a small smile. "I resigned my position as the South Dakota attorney general yesterday. The press will have it tomorrow, but I wanted to let you know before it hit the papers. I found an apartment just a little way from here, so I can see the kids more often and try to be a better father."

Tillie stared at him, completely bewildered, and she asked the only question she could think of. "Who will be the attorney general now?"

"Robert. And he's asked Shondra to be his deputy."

Tillie's eyes sparkled and she smiled. "I'll bet she's *really* excited."

Alex nodded.

"And what are *you* going to do now?"

"I'm going to go back to my office downtown. See if I have any clients left." Alex took a deep breath. "Maybe I'll ask my wife if she'll spend some time with me. Maybe she'll let me try and work this out with her."

Tillie clumsily reached for his hand. "She will. Just ask her."

Alex noticed that she was still wearing the mother's ring he'd given her last fall, and it barely hung on her slender fingers. He glanced at her left hand, lying motionless in her lap, and saw that she still wore her wedding ring. Tears fell from his eyes.

"Please, Tillie, please forgive me and let me come home. I love you so much, and I'll try so hard to put this back together and make it right for you and the kids."

Tillie slowly nodded and smiled as tears fell from her eyes. "Okay."

Tillie asked Alex to leave for a short time but to return as soon as A.J. and Laura were home from school. She needed some time alone with her family and Noah to explain.

She sat very close to her father on the love seat in the sun room, and Guiseppi wouldn't stop shaking his head. Rosa wept in a chair not far from them, unable to say anything at all.

"No, Angel." Guiseppi was quiet, but adamant. "Do not do it. It will be *nothing* but trouble. It is good that he is not divorcing you, but let us see if he can make good on his promise to spend more time with his children first. You can always begin to work things out later —"

"But, Papa, he's the father of my children, and it would make them so happy to have him back again," she interrupted.

"Oh, my dear Angel," Guiseppi sighed and shook his head. "Do not bring him back so that he can leave you all again. What good would that do their little hearts? They are finally adjusting to being without him."

"Papa, tell me where God says that I shouldn't do this. Give me one verse, and I will listen."

Guiseppi pressed his lips together and frowned at his daughter.

"It's your heart, Papa," Tillie sweetly confronted, "not your head you're thinking with. Sometimes our hearts can be deceitful and desperately wicked. Your heart deceives you where this decision concerns me. You have *always* made decisions from your heart concerning me. God wants me to at least try with Alex. He has asked me for forgiveness, and Jesus says Himself, in His own words, that we must not deny forgiveness to a brother. Even if he comes before me seven times in a day, I must forgive him."

"Jesus never intended for His words to be so abused," Guiseppi muttered disgustedly. "Alex asked you for forgiveness once before, and you granted it, and he has now returned to his sin."

"If Alex comes home and has not changed, then I will ask him to leave. But he must be given the chance."

Marquette shook his head and let out a heavy sigh. "Angel, perhaps, you are not thinking clearly. Alex has proven himself to be irrational. After all, you have not even begun to finish your rehabilitation. Certainly you are only confused, and you should wait until you have further mended before taking on the repair of your marriage."

Tillie frowned at her brother. "I'm *not* confused, Marq. I know *exactly* what I'm doing."

"She knows what she's doing, Marquette," Noah said suddenly, and everyone turned their heads in surprise. They were so intent on talking Tillie out of reconciling with Alex, that they'd forgotten he was there. Noah sighed and walked to where Tillie sat beside her father on the love seat. "Can I sit here, Mr. Caselli?"

Guiseppi left the place beside his daughter and took a seat close beside his grieving wife. Noah sat down beside Tillie and smiled sadly into her eyes. His heart pounded, and he could already feel his tears burning. He took her right hand into his own, gave it a tender pat, and sadly smiled again. "You know, Angel, when Alex comes back, I won't be able to see you anymore. You do understand that, don't you?"

Tillie looked into his wonderful, blue eyes and nodded. A wave of tears streamed down her face.

"Oh, this is *nonsense!*" Rosa sobbed from her place in the corner, and Guiseppi put his arms around his wife.

"No," Noah said as he gently touched the tears on Tillie's cheeks with a rough finger. "This is *not* nonsense. This is what Angel believes God wants for her life. Right?"

Tillie slowly nodded her head again, unable to speak through her tears.

Noah smiled faintly at Tillie's family as he continued, "When we were all in the hospital, wondering what would happen, I asked Petrice how you came up with the nickname 'Angel,' and he told me that it happened when Angel was a newborn. Mr. Caselli said that she had the beauty of something from heaven, yet the determination of a warrior." He looked down into Tillie's eyes and said, "He recognized your strength right away."

"Because angels know one another," Guiseppi whispered.

"I cannot bear up under this," Tara cried, and Marquette put his arm around his wife. "How can you exchange Noah for this lying blackguard? He will only hurt you again."

"Just promise me this," Noah whispered through his tears, "that none of you will leave her until she is completely well again." He looked at Marquette and commanded, "Promise me, Marquette, no matter how uncomfortable Alex makes you, you will not leave her until she's better. *Please.*"

Marquette could only nod through his tears, unable to speak through the sadness within him. Tara sobbed against his chest.

"There's no one more determined than a righteous woman," Noah said with a sad smile. "Just ask my brother. Angel *has* to do this, whether we like it or not. This is what Angel believes to be right, and God will bless her and her family for this." He tipped her chin to look into her eyes. "It's gonna be okay. I just know it. It's gonna be okay."

*****

It snowed in the Black Hills in late September that year, and Noah's crews hustled to cover freshly poured cement.

"This is ridiculous," Noah muttered to Ben as they stretched plastic sheeting over a basement floor.

"I cannot believe it," Ben grumbled as he fought the unruly plastic in the cold, wet snow. "There was not a forecast for this."

"Anything to make my life *more* miserable." Noah pulled the corner of the plastic tight and hammered it down. "There," he said as he stepped back to look at the floor. "That oughta hold it."

Ben happened to glance over Noah's shoulder as a black Mercedes pulled onto the building site. He touched Noah's shoulder and pointed. "Look at that."

Noah followed Ben's glance and his mouth fell open with surprise. *What on earth is he doing here?* Marquette had said that Alex had moved in the day he came to see Angel. *What does he possibly have to hassle me about now? Lecherous, old blackguard.*

Ben watched Noah's glance turn into a hateful glare, and he gripped Noah's shoulder. "What are you thinking, my friend?"

"How many times I can break the bones in his legs before the cops get here."

Ben took a breath as he watched Alex trudge through the wet snow and mud in a dressy, black trench coat. He was a huge man, but Ben doubted he could best Noah in a test of strength. Ben had watched Noah work alongside men fifteen years younger than him, and he possessed unusual strength and endurance.

"Remember your children," Ben reminded. "He is not worth going to jail for."

"Hi, Noah," Alex said with a smile.

"What do you want?" Noah growled.

"You haven't returned any of my messages, and we need to talk." Alex smiled politely at Ben. "Do you mind?"

"Yes, he minds," Noah barked.

Ben took a breath. "Listen, boss, there is fresh coffee in the trailer. Perhaps some time out of this wet snow would do you some good."

"I don't want any coffee." Noah looked at Ben and ordered, "You go and get yourself some coffee, and I'll take care of this guy out here."

"Sure, boss," Ben replied. He gripped Noah's shoulder again and reminded, "Do not forget your boys, Noah."

"I won't," Noah growled. Ben released his grip and hurried away from Noah. "Now what could you possibly want?" Noah demanded.

"I want to apologize," Alex offered. "I'm sorry for all that I've done to you, and I'd like to try to make amends for the kids' sakes. They shouldn't be kept apart because of our differences."

"Are you serious? You actually care about that now?"

"I've made some mistakes —"

"*Mistakes?!*" Noah thundered. He clamped his lips together and fought the tears he'd managed to bury over the last month. He lowered his voice and growled, "You left her when she needed you most, and you didn't come back until you were sure she was gonna get better."

"And I'm sorry, Noah."

Noah couldn't hide his disgust and he said, "Do you have any idea how much I *hate* you?"

Alex took a breath. "Please, Noah, my kids are asking about your boys. I can hardly keep them apart much longer. A.J.'s been asking me to lead his Boy Scout troop, and I know it's because he thinks he'll get to see Jake there."

Noah let out a disgusted breath. "I s'pose. I'll just have to suck it up and be a man about the whole thing and pretend that you're *Mr. Wonderful* and we all love you so that you can make things work with your kids." He shook his head. "I've never met anyone quite like you, Alex."

Alex stood silent as he looked into Noah's angry eyes. "I'm truly sorry, Noah, but you know, all of this could have been avoided the day you saw her painting in my office."

Noah rolled his eyes. "Like *that* would have kept you at home. Whatever, Alex. I know. I'm the bad guy here. I sinned the most and the worst when I coveted your wife."

"I totally forgive you, Noah." Alex pulled a square felt box out of the pocket of his trench coat. "Here."

"What's this?"

"It's a watch," Alex said. Noah groaned and rolled his eyes again as he opened the lid of the box. It was a really nice watch, artfully decorated with Black Hills Gold.

"It's an original," Alex said. "I thought you might like it."

"It's great.   Thanks." Noah frowned.   *Marquette said you slipped Angel some more diamonds, but all I get is a watch...so I can watch the time go by....*

"Let's just try to put the past behind us," Alex offered with a smile.   "We've both made mistakes, but we have children to consider —"

"I can't pretend to be *just friends* with your wife."

"I know," Alex admitted.   "And I promise, you'll never have to see her again."

To be continued...

A SPECIAL MESSAGE FOR THE READER

"Alex, I've watched you *pretend* our Christianity for years. Sure, you knew the Scriptures better than anyone else, and you followed the rules better than anyone else, but it didn't make you one of us — and it didn't make you one of the Lord's. It's your rotten fruit that gives you away."

Wow. Harsh words from a dying father — but at least old James Martin had the guts to say them to his perishing son.

Alex knew the Scriptures and followed the rules of the Church. He even "repented" once, shortly after his children were born. But Alex continued living a life of schemes, manipulation, and lies. Paul warned of what the Church commonly refers to as false conversions (**Pretenders)** when he wrote: *"Those who live according to the sinful nature have their minds set on what that nature desires; but those who live in accordance with the Spirit have their minds set on what the Spirit desires."* Romans 8:5 **NIV** Alex's father saw clearly that his son was living *"according to the sinful nature."* He'd dealt *treacherously with the wife of his youth,* (See Malachi Chapter 2 **NKJV**) and was unrepentant when confronted. Alex was a blackguard of the worst kind — he pretended to be a Christian.

Though Alex was a young vibrant man, excelling in everything he set his mind to, he was in worse shape than his dying father. James Martin would soon leave this earth, but have a home in heaven with his Savior, Jesus Christ. Had Alex left the earth before asking forgiveness from Jesus Christ, he would have received his just reward — a place in hell with the father of lies.

Shortly after Alex bowed his head and sincerely asked forgiveness, the Spirit's nature took over and led him back to the wife and family he'd deserted. Had Tillie not had her mind *set on what the Spirit desires,* she would have sent Alex away and married Noah without a thought.

Beloved, no matter what we've done in this world, whether adultery or **pretending**, it's never too late to ask Jesus to forgive our sins. *"Believe in the Lord Jesus and you will be saved."* Acts 16:31 **NIV** Honest and sincere repentance will lead you to pick up His Word and study His ways. The Spirit will take care of the rest, and you will be assured a home in heaven.

For future release date information, check out
www.PretenderBook.com

SPECIAL SNEAK-PEEK PREVIEW

BOOK IV
THE GIFT

He started down the familiar hall, stopping to look out the window at the end facing west. He smiled as he gazed into the hills she'd loved...*that paned glass was for her...*

The door to the master suite was open, and Noah peeked inside, drawn into the room he'd planned to share with her. Floor to ceiling windows faced the west in this room as well, but the smaller room, just adjacent, had windows facing the east...*so she wouldn't miss the sunrise if she was with the baby...*

He smiled as he walked through the room, passing the bathroom with the old-fashioned claw-foot tub he thought she'd enjoy, and then stepped into what was supposed to have been the nursery. While Vivian had put furniture in the main room this room was strangely empty, and Noah frowned. *Well, Vivian's always been eccentric.*

He walked slowly back through the room, noticing that there wasn't a speck of dust on the light fixtures, or even a cobweb in the corner. Vivian's employees took excellent care of the place and Noah was pleased. She had allowed no one to smoke in the house, so it smelled only of the pine trees surrounding it.

Noah sighed with a melancholy smile as he left the room and started back down the hall. He laughed at himself as he descended the stairs and headed for the kitchen. *It's far too soon to be making these plans.*

Noah found Vivian perched in some Victorian furniture in the studio just off the kitchen. She gazed out the paned window facing the west while she sipped at her coffee with a most thoughtful expression.

"I found the problem," Noah said as he took a seat across from her. "There's a shutter that's come loose on the dormer. I'll have to pick up a hinge, but I can have it fixed by tomorrow."

"Very good." Vivian shifted her thoughtful gaze from the Hills to Noah, and she frowned. "Ya know, Hansen, I always wondered why you built this place."

Noah gave Vivian a mysterious smile and said, "It was just a little experiment."

Vivian raised one of her black-penciled eyebrows. "A *little* experiment?"

"Well..." Noah sighed as he looked out the window...*this was supposed to have been Angel's studio....*

"I noticed the wood work had been done by hand," Vivian grumbled. "And after about ten years at the place, I realized that you must have intended this house for something other than a bed and breakfast." She frowned. "Why didn't you ever live here, Hansen?"

Noah shrugged. "Guess I just never got around to it, Viv."

"Humph." Vivian set down her cup on the table and reached for Noah's hand. "Help me up, Hansen. It's time for me to go."

Noah got to his feet and helped Vivian out of the chair. They shuffled into the kitchen where Mavis was making a list.

Vivian barked at her manager, "Hansen says it's just a shutter. He'll be up to fix it tomorrow."

Mavis acknowledged with a smile and said, "Thanks, Noah. See ya tomorrow."

Noah nodded and he and Vivian continued into the foyer and out the front door, where Dan waited beside the car.

"I'm gettin' *old*, Hansen," Vivian said as he helped her manage the steps on the porch. "I don't know how much longer I'll be able to lease this place from you."

"Whenever you're ready to leave it, you just let me know," Noah said as he opened her car door.

Vivian looked at Noah with surprise and paused before she got into the car. "Would you be willing to let me out of my lease, without all of those penalties that Martin wrote in?" she asked.

Noah nodded his head and smiled at Vivian as he answered, "However you want to do it, Viv. You just let me know."

Vivian narrowed her eyes with mirth and cackled out a scratchy laugh. "You want the old place back for yourself, don'tcha Hansen...."